A smooth-looking woman in ~~...~~
brushed against him...

"Aren't you Arch Holden, the new pianist at Henri's?" Her throaty voice had a charming French accent.

He nodded, perhaps a bit more eagerly than he had intended. He knew he had met her somewhere but couldn't immediately place her. So fragile a bit of mystery made her seem all that more attractive to him and he realized, all at once, that he was starved for attention.

In her dark eyes, there was now a bold and commanding look—the look of a huntress. "Just to refresh your memory, I'm Catherine Vaillant." She gave him a long, calculating glance. "How long will you be in Paris?"

"About six months or so."

"Six months can be a long time for an America[n] in Paris now... perhaps even dangerous. But," she added, "you don't look particularly help-less..."

John Hohenberg

the Parisian Girl

AVON
PUBLISHERS OF BARD, CAMELOT, DISCUS AND FLARE BOOKS

AVON BOOKS
A division of
The Hearst Corporation
1790 Broadway
New York, New York 10019

Copyright © 1986 by John Hohenberg
Published by arrangement with the author
Library of Congress Catalog Card Number: 85-90792
ISBN: 0-380-89615-X

First Avon Printing, March 1986

AVON TRADEMARK REG. U. S. PAT. OFF. AND IN
OTHER COUNTRIES, MARCA REGISTRADA, HECHO EN
U. S. A.

Printed in the U. S. A.

K–R 10 9 8 7 6 5 4 3 2 1

the Parisian Girl

Chapter One

"You an American?"

"Yeah."

"What're you doin' here?"

"Looking around."

"Tryin' to find a girl?"

"Wouldn't mind."

"You're in the right place, Mac."

The speakers had met each other in the middle of a crowd of costumed party-goers on their way to the Four Arts Ball, the annual Parisian festival of youth. Both were in raincoats and bareheaded—one small, dumpy and baldish; the other tall, broad-shouldered and presentable, with a mop of curly light hair.

The baldish one, who had been asking the questions, now introduced himself:

"Guy Saffron, reporter for the *Paris Press*, our great daily in the English language."

The other replied, "Arch Holden. I play the piano at Henri's Bar, Place St. Michel, just around the corner."

"Thought Charley Fourier had that job," Saffron said with journalistic directness, immediately suspicious.

"Charley's my pal," was the response. "He's in Nashville, working with a country-western outfit. Brought me on for this job. Just got here a week ago tonight."

"Like it?"

"Don't know. Can't find any girls."

Saffron laughed. "You must be blind." He tugged at the younger man's arm. "Come along, fella. You're gonna see some eye-openers."

1

They struggled through the mob toward an ancient stone palace. It was an imposing pile, complete with portico and terraced stone steps situated on the left bank of the River Seine, and it combined faded grandeur with a certain cheerful decadence.

Saffron told his young companion, while they were inching their way toward the entrance, that a prime minister of France had once installed one of his mistresses there and lavished the riches of the Republic on her until the ungrateful wretch left him for a young poet.

"What prime minister?" Holden asked with the suspicion of a new arrival for Parisian lies.

Saffron grandly waved one hand. "Does it matter? There have been so many prime ministers with so many mistresses. And..." He paused with a reproachful upraised finger. "Who would want to inquire too closely into the love life of a poet in the city of Francois Villon?"

Holden grinned his appreciation. "Just so nobody inquires into my love life."

"What you did before you got to Paris doesn't count," Saffron said. "Have you ever seen a palace as crazy as that one?" He pointed dramatically to the building before them.

The place was aglow with youth, alive with music and laughter. Despite the misty rain, people in various stages of undress were still spilling out of cabs and private cars on the fringes of the crowd.

It was a noisy but friendly carnival where every stranger became a bosom friend in two minutes. True to Parisian tradition, nobody tried very hard to channel the crowd or to regulate traffic around it.

The police indulgently surveyed the raffish scene. Behind them two police vans were parked discreetly on a side street, but nobody was being arrested. The gendarmes, known as "flics," had on riot gear.

"The flics don't bother us," Saffron explained. "They just haul off a drunk now and then when he gets noisy."

"I don't get noisy," Holden said.

Every once in a while, for no particular reason, the crowd would cheer. Then, there would be a great surge forward. A few people would get bowled over, but they soon bounced back. Strangers were offering each other drinks, kissing each other. And every driver of a motor vehicle considered it his sacred duty to honk furiously, grind gears and shower insults on anybody who would listen.

The result was predictable. There was utter chaos. It made everybody happy.

"What you got on under that raincoat?" Saffron demanded at one point when their progress seemed hopelessly stalled.

Holden opened the raincoat to display a swimmer's outfit— tight white trunks over his slim hips. "Think it's all right to go in bare-chested?"

Saffron considered the matter carefully. "Well, I don't know," he began with an air of judicial calm, "but if you get the bum's rush, what'll they do to me?"

He opened his raincoat to display a hairy, potbellied nude body including bowed shoulders and knock-knees. "Some costume, huh?"

"Will they let you in?" Holden asked, mildly amused.

Saffron held up a longish blue ticket in front of his companion. "Hell, this is Paris. My ticket is all I need. Got yours?"

Holden produced one from the inner pocket of his raincoat. "Got it from the boss tonight. He let me off early. "

"Henri's a good guy," Saffron said. "Runs a nice little joint, and he's got a coupla really hot B-girls, too. How come you didn't get next to them?"

"I'm not much on B-girls," Holden said.

"Gawdamighty," Saffron murmured, "you're too high-toned. Musta gone to Harvard."

"Nope. Best I could do was Curtis, the music school in Philadelphia."

"Ah, Philadelphia!" Saffron exclaimed, as if that explained everything. "When they go to bed in Philadelphia, they sleep."

Holden disregarded him. "Seems to be raining more," he observed.

"We're getting there," his companion said. "You wet?"

"Not too bad."

All about them, however, were clusters of damp and disheveled revelers who were not so fortunate. Here and there, Holden saw a few patroness-dowagers who had come fully dressed and swathed in furs that were now getting soggy.

The younger women, in far less substantial and more revealing costumes, did better. Some even had towels, which they used occasionally to dry themselves off. As for the men —those eternally hopeful males ranging from 18 to 80—most of them were shivering in the shreds and patches they wore on their lumpy bodies.

Once inside the palace with the obliging Saffron, Holden felt more comfortable. They mingled with the throng, which generated so much warmth they were immediately able to dispose of their raincoats at the checkroom.

Holden felt just a bit abashed about his bare-chested swimmer's costume, but Saffron wasn't in the least concerned about his nudity.

By common consent, they joined the ragged lines of human traffic that led directly to the grand ballroom. In front of them, two semi-nude girls glanced admiringly at Holden and chattered in French. Then one pointed at Saffron and made a laughing remark to her friend.

"What're they saying?" Holden wanted to know.

Saffron translated. "They think grandpa"—and he pointed to himself—"should have a flannel nightgown." He retorted to the seeming insult with a smooth flow of French that brought shrieks of laughter from the girls.

"What did you say?" Holden inquired.

"Just that I brought you along to handle the both of them, and I thought you could do it."

Holden shrugged. "Thanks," he said. "I appreciate that."

At 25, with a bare torso, slim hips and sturdy legs, Holden looked like a Notre Dame fullback. Having one of the relatively few decently developed male bodies in the place and an attractive American look about him—a big grin, frank brown eyes and a curly damp mass of taffy-colored hair—he soon found that too many hands were being laid on him. Male as well as female.

In self-protection, he maneuvered himself beside a wall. Saffron objected, "Tryin' to get away from me, Mac?"

"No, but I'm not into perpendicular lovemaking."

"Y' don't know what you're missing," Saffron said. Then,

4

as a little black-haired nude squeezed in between him and Holden, he exclaimed, "Hey, what have we here?"

The little nude, however, wasn't interested in him. She ran her hands playfully over Holden's chest and asked him something in French. When he looked inquiringly at his companion, Saffron translated. "She says she wants you to dance with her."

Holden was not impressed with the offer. "Thank her, please."

The little nude wasn't to be brushed off so lightly, however. "I spik Eengleesh," she replied, trying to be obliging.

Holden attempted a polite shake of his head, but it didn't work. The little nude's hands were straying below his waist. Evidently trying to distract her, Saffron pointed to Holden and, adopting a dolorous expression, said something in French. But the girl was unimpressed.

"I told her," Saffron translated, "that you were mutilated in the war."

"What war?"

"What does it matter? You were mutilated, see?"

"And what did she say?"

"She said, *'Merde.'*"

"What does that mean?"

"The American equivalent would be 'Bullshit.'"

Holden sighed. "What do I do with her?"

"Your problem, brother." With a broad smile, Saffron moved away. "You wanted a girl and you got one. I'll see you around."

Holden meditatively surveyed the little nude and wondered how to cope with her. He put a strong hand about each of her wrists. "Quit it," he said.

In English, she asked, "You do not like me?"

"You are very nice."

"I make love," she offered; and added, to be sure there was no misunderstanding, "Money, money."

"How much money?" He was curious, but not particularly interested.

"I make you good price, twenty-five dollaire."

"No."

"Too much?"

"No."

"My name is Francine, I am very good," she assured him.

"I'm sure you are."

"What is your name?"

Reluctantly, he replied, "Arch Holden."

"Make love with you, Arch?"

He sighed at her persistence and shook his head.

She faced him with a mischievous smile on her street-gamin face. "You make a mistake, Arch. I will be good for you."

"Sorry."

"You have a girl here?" she demanded.

"I'm damned if I know," he replied.

She laughed at him. "You are not sure of anything, Arch."

"You are so right."

"Then I dance with you like this." And she rubbed against him and tried to free her hands.

He held her firmly. "Wrong guy, Francine."

By this time, they had reached the ballroom entrance where a French rock bank was blasting away. With a wrench, she freed both hands and suggested, "Maybe twenty dollaire?"

"No, Francine."

She was regretful.

With another laugh, she ran one hand playfully down his body and turned aside. He watched her as she drifted away in the crowd with a mocking wave of one small hand. He saw her approach and embrace an elderly French gentleman with a beard and pince-nez who seemed delighted with her attentions.

Holden was looking for something different. As he explained to Saffron, who met him again inside the ballroom, "Francine's not my type. There's got to be something better here."

Saffron gave him a sardonic look. "You wise guys from Philadelphia give me a pain in the ass."

"Because I won't pay twenty bucks to be laid in Paris?"

"No, because you guys come over here expecting to meet Marie Antoinette in orchid pajamas or Madame Pompadour in black net panties. And they're very dead."

Holden nodded toward the dance floor. "Lots of live ones out there."

"If you're trying to pick up a classy French dame, you'll have to look very hard for one here, Mac."

"Name's Arch Holden," the younger man repeated.

"I know, Mac. All I'm saying is that you'd better pick a girl and hang onto her, because these kids get bored pretty fast. What they're looking for is action, not philosophy."

"You think I'm too picky, don't you?"

Saffron turned away, muttering, "Oh, balls." He edged onto the dance floor, evidently looking for a disengaged girl.

What he said was true enough: the pairings on the dance floor, and somewhat later in what were called private rooms upstairs, seemed to be matters of the moment. As Holden watched the shifting scene on the ballroom floor, he noticed girls changing partners, leaving older men for younger ones. And the men were not hesitating to pick up more attractive girls than the ones with whom they'd arrived.

It was that kind of a party.

Above the rasp of many voices in the ballroom, the sound of the French rock band was deafening. They called themselves "Les Huitres Joyeux" (the Jolly Oysters). If they did not play well, Holden concluded, at least they played loudly.

The beat was ragged. So was the mood. It was enough, despite the disorderly human mass on the ballroom floor, to set the dancers whirling, gesturing with sexual overtones and stomping furiously. Here and there, a few of the youngest were tossing themselves into break-dancing, the latest craze to be imported from America. And since this involved a certain amount of risk to life and limb among participants and by-standers alike, the breakers—"les demi-Americains," or small Americans, as they were called—were given plenty of room for their operations.

To add to the air of popular celebration, people began offering Holden everything from wine to brandy. Had he accepted every drink, he would have wound up in an alcoholic stupor—but he had enough self-discipline to avoid that calamity.

Still, he couldn't help being involved in other encounters. Once, a girl in black bra and panties suddenly decided that she was an adagio dancer and screamed at Holden in French to catch her. He turned just in time to see her sailing toward him,

7

arms and legs flailing. With a desperate lunge, he caught her just as she was about to crash into the floor, headfirst.

The girl regained her footing and her dignity. Seeing at once how uninterested Holden was, she said coolly, "Pardon, M'sieu'."

"Okay, babe," he replied.

A somewhat more appreciative Frenchman at once slid his arm around the girl's black-bordered waist and walked off with her.

Having been a saloon pianist who had roamed the United States, Holden was scarcely surprised by what was going on about him. He'd been around swingers, male and female, for most of his working years. However, as he kept looking over the field for a partner, he had to admit that the French *did* generate their own special excitement.

It didn't make much difference to him if some of the young men made up their faces, wore an earring and walked with an exaggerated feminine style. Nor was he shocked when a leggy woman brushed past him in sweater and pants with a mannish haircut and a feminine adaptation of a male swagger. He did feel vaguely repelled, however, by the cynical young men on the dance floor who were working over giggling, outlandishly costumed matrons old enough to be their grandmothers.

Despite that, the people on the dance floor fascinated Holden. Where else could one find a girl clad in a tiger's skin, cracking the whip over a young man who was crouched on all fours? Or a dignified graybeard dressed as the god Pan, including the horns, who pranced about two long-haired girls in floating, diaphanous white gowns?

This was hedonism at the fullest—people crazed to experience pleasure for pleasure's sake. The fate of the Republic was not at stake when a statuesque woman in her thirties appeared tipsily on the dance floor wearing nothing but a burnished brass helmet and waving the French flag. Nor when a bewhiskered man strode around in a fancy musketeer's costume, complete to plumed hat, and suddenly took it into his head to undress in public.

Holden understood that, and yet he remained somewhat detached from the gaiety and the folly and even the drinking until, inexplicably, he caught the dominant mood of excitement. He told himself sternly that he was no mere kid of 16 or 17 to be thrilled by the sight of totally uninhibited nude girls. He tried to turn his attention to the more ribald costumes, but his gaze kept straying back to this girl and that. Now, insensibly, he wanted them to come to him, to brush up against him.

For a while, nothing much happened to him—and that too was tantalizing. He was even just a bit envious of Saffron, who had finally attracted a partner, a gaunt woman in a red chemise with long black hair and thick eyeglasses. As for the little nude, Francine, she had now abandoned the elderly French gentleman and tentatively started in Holden's direction. But before he could claim her, she flung herself into the arms of a muscular athletic youth in a black sweater.

Overseeing all these proceedings was the leader of The Jolly Oysters, a grinning sliver of a man with a sweeping black mustache. He kept fingering his singer, a scantily dressed blonde in red who crooned into a microphone but couldn't be heard clearly above the crowd noises. It didn't matter. The top Oyster and his canary seemed happy together even though the dancers paid little attention to them.

While Holden was wondering what he should do next, a smooth-looking woman in furs brushed against him, looked back, smiled archly and turned. She had the air of someone on the make even when she was merely being polite. In a throaty voice with a charming French accent, she asked, "Aren't you Arch Holden, the new pianist at Henri's?"

He nodded, perhaps a bit more eagerly than he had intended. He knew he had met her somewhere, but couldn't immediately place her. So fragile a bit of mystery made her seem all the more attractive to him; and he realized, all at once, that he was starved for attention.

She returned slowly, gracefully, and stood beside him looking at him with that small, tantalizing smile. She was what the French call, in their gracious way, a woman of a certain age— a little too old to be called a girl and yet very far from matronly; poised, enormously self-assured, even provocative.

Holden couldn't help being attracted to this mystery—an enormously attractive woman who seemed to be amused because she was able to tease him. She was beautifully dressed

9

and wore a becoming scent. In her long blue gown and her short mink jacket, she would have been more in place at a fashionable party than in this rough catchall of a crumbling palace.

Seeing her long and calculating look as he fumbled for a clue to her identity, Holden felt as tongue-tied as a boy at his first big dance. It scarcely required someone as obviously experienced as this beguiling newcomer to see that he was vulnerable. She smiled encouragingly to ease his evident embarrassment.

"I don't blame you for not remembering me," she said. "You saw me only once, and then it was just for a few minutes."

In her dark eyes, there was now a bold and commanding look—the look of a huntress. Holden flushed uncomfortably. And then he remembered where they had met, and he smacked the palms of his hands together for sheer relief. "I know you now! You're Charley Fourier's girl, aren't you?"

"I *was.*" She emphasized that, and kept looking at him, catching his eyes, holding them with her intense gaze. "Just to refresh your memory, I'm Catherine Vaillant."

He wanted to keep the conversation going. There was a magnetic presence here, and he felt as if he wanted to stay close to her, to catch the faint scent of her exotic perfume. "When did you give up on Charley Fourier?" he asked.

She laughed lightly. "I didn't give up on him. *He* left Paris for America, remember?"

"And you didn't want to go with him?"

She sent him another one of those long, calculating looks. "He never asked me."

She seemed to turn away from him slightly, but he didn't want her to leave him. He clung tenaciously to the small strand of acquaintance that they shared. "And howisit with Charley now?"

She turned back languidly. "Haven't heard from him."

He was encouraged. "And you?"

Again she gave him that big look, a come-on if there ever was one. "I'm a contract translator at the American embassy, as Charley may have told you, but I'm not working at it tonight." With a teasing smile, she held out a small white beaded bag. "When you see me carrying *this,*" and she dangled the bag in front of him, "it means I *may*," and she emphasized the last word, "be at liberty."

"And when you're translating?" He pursued the subject.

"Oh, then I use my big shoulder bag with all my translating stuff. Then, I'm very official."

"But tonight you're unofficial?" he asked in a bantering way.

"Semi-official," she replied. "They're using me as a guide for a visiting VIP—Senator Jerzy Pazlawski of Illinois, just back from a trip to Poland."

He decided he had nothing to lose by pursuing the subject. "Don't see him around right now."

"He's over there," and she nodded toward a corner, "with some of the young embassy crowd."

"How about ditching him?"

She rested one hand lightly on his arm and smiled. "I don't think I'd like to ditch a member of the Senate Foreign Relations Committee. Not if I want to hold my job." As if in afterthought, she added, "Maybe another time. You'll be here awhile, won't you?"

"Sure," he said. "Until Charley gets back."

She let him light her cigarette, looking up at him as she did so. "You piano players are all alike." She breathed out a thin stream of smoke, making an inviting mouth and then laughing at him. "A different girl for every playing date."

It was a challenge, of course, but he responded to it. He wanted to impress this altogether charming woman. "That's Charley, not me," he protested lightly. Although he knew he was being put on by Catherine Vaillant, he rather enjoyed it. Whatever her ultimate purpose might be, he wanted to play along with her.

She was quite open now about teasing him. "Why are *you* so different from all the rest of the piano players around here?"

He put it on the line. "Try me."

She demurred, but she wasn't offensive about it. "For tonight, I'm engaged," she reminded him.

He decided to give it back to her. "So the senator's at the top of your list right now?"

She waved her cigarette lazily, as if to show him that he couldn't get a rise out of him with an insinuating remark. "Now,

now, you're not going to make a *femme fatale* out of me. Not, anyway, with a senator who has a wife and eight children back in Chicago. You piano players ought to get wise to yourselves."

"Oh, we're not so bad," Holden protested in the same vein. "After all, Charley Fourier played at Henri's for more than two years, and he told me you were his only girl, said he even wanted to marry you."

"We played with the idea, but neither of us was really serious," she said indulgently, but there was a compelling intensity in her gaze. "Besides, after two unsuccessful marriages, I was not going to be tied to a piano player who's here today, gone tomorrow."

Charley Fourier had actually given him a quite different story—that Vaillant was a terribly private person who kept all her affairs strictly to herself. "What the hell," Charley had said. "What do I do with a woman who won't tell me where she's going nights, or who she's with or why? She'd drive a guy crazy, that one, so I told her finally that marriage would be a mistake and I was nuts even to have thought of it." However, Holden kept all that to himself because his pitch was for something quite different and he thought Catherine Vaillant might be available sooner or later. Preferably sooner.

So he said with a reassuring air, "Y'know, Catherine, I'll be here for six months, maybe more, filling in for Charley. Maybe you'll have some time for me."

Her smile was enigmatic. "You'll find six months is a long time for an American to be in Paris nowadays."

He couldn't divine her meaning. "You mean that I'm just another stranger; that I don't belong?"

"You don't look particularly helpless," she commented, then stubbed out her cigarette in a nearby ashtray. "Sorry, here comes my date, so take care of yourself. And if you feel like it," she said as she turned away from him with a lingering look, "call me. Henri will know where to find me."

He watched her as a ponderous elderly man in a tight blue suit joined her and led her to the dance floor. The last he saw of her, she had transfixed her partner with that demanding gaze of hers. The senator too was vulnerable, Holden noted in a bemused way. He was holding her closely as they were engulfed by the swaying, disorderly crowd.

12

Holden bit his lip. Catherine Vaillant had made a strong impression on him. In Saffron's terms, she was a classy French dame. But was she really just another embassy translator? A mere tour guide for visiting VIPs, as she claimed? Or something else? Holden didn't know, but he couldn't help wondering.

Just then, through a small opening in the dancing mass, he saw her smiling at him over the senator's brawny shoulder. She waved one hand toward him in a kind of taunting gesture, then slid it easily about the senator's neck.

Holden sighed, then went looking for a drink. He felt he needed it.

Holden maneuvered through the throng of merrymakers, avoided the playful little nude, Francine, and headed for a bar in the balcony. But it was difficult.

People bound for the balcony were surging up a milky white marble staircase, but loving couples had plumped down on the steps and partly blocked the way. Nor would they move when indignant passersby reproached them, even shoved them. Kissing a partly or completely undressed girl that night was serious business.

So Holden found the going very slow. Other people around him were trying various techniques, some reminiscent of goal-line plays in football. One little man, dressed in a red devil's costume complete with horns and a tail, rammed into the crowd and was shoved back. Another, this one in a numbered T-shirt and tattered running trunks, slammed right through the center of the stairway lovers and sprawled on his face.

Everybody nearby cheered at that, then fell on the defenseless fellow and pummeled him for his offensive ways.

The most sensible people gave up, sat at one side of the stairway and casually embraced whoever was nearby, male or female, it didn't seem to matter which.

Holden caught other glimpses of Catherine Vaillant and her senator now and then, but he had to watch the dance floor intently to do it. Huntress though she was, she really was tied up for the evening.

He turned his attention to the balcony above the dance floor. When the ever-shifting mass of unclad and partly clad bodies

13

before him parted momentarily, he saw that some ingenious soul had provided an alternative route upstairs.

It was a giant ladder, mottled with old paint in myriad hues, that rested tipsily on a well-worn green rug at the edge of the dance floor and leaned against the balcony, which was slightly set back. The traffic on the ladder was continuous, primarily because no one wanted to stay in the same spot for very long.

On occasion, the human stream on the ladder halted awkwardly when someone on the way down or up exchanged pleasantries with an attractive stranger. Once, while Holden was watching, there was a violent argument over precedence between two Frenchmen, one in a lion skin and the other in a purple silk jockstrap.

Both were aggressive. Both started pushing. Also shoving. Then, the lion skin wrestled the jockstrap off the ladder and dropped him with a wild punch. However, to demonstrate that it was all part of a game that night, the lion skin hoisted the jockstrap to his feet, embraced him, and kissed him on both cheeks. The crowd cheered.

The crazier the encounter, Holden noticed, the more interesting it was to the viewers below. After a while, he saw a girl, on her way down the ladder, blocked by a large man wearing only a pair of socks who was on his way up. They clung to the ladder, talking amiably awhile; then, having made a decision, the girl beckoned, the man nodded vigorously and they both disappeared toward the private rooms in the balcony.

"Toujours l'amour," someone yelled from down below. The crowd applauded uproariously.

These chance encounters he witnessed gave Holden a sense of loneliness. Although he was surrounded by celebrating young people, he was keenly aware that nobody was paying any attention to him. He was the eternal stranger in a foreign land, as Catherine Vaillant had suggested. He felt walled off from his own generation.

Finally, it dawned on him that what he was waiting for that night was a sign, however vague, that he belonged. He was in the midst of a carnival of youth that should have caught him up in delightful chaos. The scene about him was the very essence of back-alley ballet. The massed bodies on the dance floor were bumping, whirling, prancing. And all the while the

14

musicians were pumping away at a monotonous rock tune in front of their grinning leader.

Yet Holden waited. He told himself that he was being too choosy. Why wouldn't any girl do? The little nude, maybe? She was out there still, being tossed around by the athlete in the black crewneck sweater. Some of the others, with half a scarf coyly covering one breast? What difference did it make? Why not grab one, just anyone? But when he took a step toward an agreeable girl, he just couldn't do it. So he stood there in line before the ladder, waiting. For what, he didn't know.

Not too long afterward, he heard a shout behind him. "Hey, Mac!"

He turned and saw Saffron, still nude and beginning to sweat, standing a few feet away. "Howisit?" he yelled back.

"C'mon over, I wantcha to meet some people."

"Girls?"

"Girls, boys, old, young, what does it matter?" Saffron gestured vigorously. "C'mon, y'hear?"

Holden obeyed. But when he saw a small, nicely dressed family group standing a short distance away and guessed he was being asked to meet them, he hesitated. Almost certainly, they were American tourists. With almost equal certainty, he thought he'd seen them at Henri's. Already he'd developed a profound distaste for American tourists who hung over his shoulder while he was playing and offered to buy him a small beer.

Saffron yanked at his arm. "This guy wants to meet you."

"Forget it, I'm no tour guide."

"Look, Mac, he's important, he's a composer. I've known him since I was a kid reporter on the New Haven *Register*. Can't tell. Maybe he might do you some good."

Holden wasn't feeling very gracious, but he followed Saffron, since American composers, from Roger Sessions to Richard Rodgers, were comparatively rare in Paris.

There were four in the family group—the composer, his wife and their two grown children. The woman, who was small and blond, with a pert, birdlike expression on her pretty face, wore a short, slightly yellowed ermine jacket over a floor-length gown of vivid green. The man, somewhat older and larger, with a strong, rugged face and a mass of wavy gray hair, was in a blue velvet dinner jacket with matching pants, ruffled light blue shirt and dark blue bow tie.

The daughter, the younger image of her mother, wore a wide-skirted pink dancing dress and was taking small, nervous dance steps out of evident boredom. Her brother, a genial young blond giant in a striped blue sweater and jeans, was anything but bored. As Holden approached, he saw the young man dart out on the dance floor, grab a partner from someone else and start swinging and jigging and bumping along with her.

As Saffron and Holden joined the group, the older man said, "Here he is, folks, your piano player at Henri's." And to Holden. "Take a bow, Mac."

"Name's Arch Holden," he introduced himself to the group.

The girl seemed mildly interested and the mother smiled in a friendly way. The man exclaimed, "It's good to know you! Liked the way you played the other night." As they shook hands, the man went on, "We're the Learys of New Haven. My wife, Amy. My daughter, Vivian. My son, Gareth, is out there somewhere." He made a vague gesture toward the dance floor, and continued with a smile, "I'm Pat Leary. Teach music at Yale."

"Hope you were treated right at Henri's," Holden said.

"It was just perfect," Amy Leary replied. "It always is. You see," she explained, and there was a sparkle in her eyes, "Henri was best man at our wedding."

Saffron took up from there. "You'll see 'em tomorrow night at Henri's, Mac. There's to be a midnight supper for Gribov."

"Gribov?" Holden was hazy. He'd been looking at the girl, Vivian, and now they exchanged sympathetic smiles.

"*Nikolai* Gribov," she prompted, as if that would identify him sufficiently.

Pat Leary was more explicit. "The Russian baritone, he's singing at the Paris Opera."

Holden said in apology, "I'm strictly a pop music man. I'm afraid I don't know him."

"I thought *everybody* had heard of Nikolai," Amy Leary said. "There was such excitement when he defected from the Bolshoi Opera four years ago."

"My wife has a special interest in Gribov." Pat Leary chuckled. "I suspect she helped talk him into defecting."

Amy Leary smiled. "Nikolai had his own reasons."

"You'll like Gribov," Pat Leary predicted.

Holden sidestepped further discussion of the Russian. "Staying here long?" he asked Leary.

"For as long as Jean Dessaix of the Paris Conservatory is satisfied to stay at our house in New Haven," Leary said. "We exchanged the house for his apartment on the Rue Soufflot for this vacation."

"There's a story in this," Saffron explained. "It's been twenty-five years since Professor and Mrs. Leary met in Paris, so actually they're celebrating an anniversary of sorts."

"Wish you hadn't put it in the *Paris Press,* though," Pat Leary said. "Calls too much attention to just a little family party."

"After the Met's put on three of your operas, you aren't exactly a nonperson," Saffron replied. "You're news."

"Pat's even thought of doing an opera about Dr. Zhivago with Nikolai Gribov as the star," Amy Leary said, then put one hand over her mouth when she saw her husband was annoyed. "Shouldn't I have said that?"

"It was just an idea I had some time ago, but nothing came of it," he explained to Holden.

"Yeah, I wrote about it four years ago," Saffron said. "You were talking about it at the time Gribov defected, remember?"

Pat Leary smiled gently. "It isn't such a bad idea, y'know. I doubt if any Russian composer will ever do an opera based on the Zhivago story, and it's a shame not to use the material."

During this exchange, Holden kept trying to catch Vivian Leary's eye, but she was watching the dancers now with a wistful air. Her father distracted him. "Are you here for the first time, Mr. Holden?"

"Yes, but it'll only be for six months or so."

"Oh, for six months in Paris!" Amy Leary exclaimed. "Whenever we come here, we can only stay a short while. And this time, with the children..." She spoke with a marked British accent. "Do you know," and she faced Holden, her face aglow, "that Pat and I met right here at the Four Arts Ball just about twenty-five years ago? We've talked about it so often that we wanted the children to see it."

Vivian seemed to want to head off further reminiscence. "We know the story, Mother."

Her father paid no attention to her. He announced, with the air of a man making an important disclosure, "When I met Amy here for the first time, she didn't have a stitch on."

"Just like me," Saffron said.

"Well, not exactly," Leary added, "but you have the general idea."

"Why do you insist on telling everybody about it?" Vivian asked plaintively.

"It's a fact. Made her very interesting."

"For one thing, I weighed about thirty pounds less than I do now," Amy Leary said.

Vivian tried to distract attention from the family revelation by pointing to the dancing mass before them. "Hey, look what Gareth has dredged up."

The largest, youngest and huskiest of the Learys was stomping with Francine, the little nude who had accosted Holden earlier in the evening. His sister applauded ironically. "Bravo, Gareth!"

The young man grinned, waved, grabbed his partner around the waist and slung her about in a circle. Once Francine's high-heeled slippers were back on the dance floor, her moves were both inelegant and explicit. Gareth stood off a foot or two so he could watch; he applauded every suggestive gesture. But Francine, of course, needed no encouragement.

"Did you do that, Mother?" Vivian asked slyly.

Amy Leary wasn't in the least embarrassed. "The girl Gareth is with is very crude, my dear. She may go over big with students in the Latin Quarter, but she's too vulgar for Broadway."

"Nothing is too vulgar for Broadway," her husband said.

"But why, Mother, did you come to the Four Arts Ball without wearing anything?" Vivian asked with a mischievous air.

"I was pretty high," Amy Leary said, "and it was a long time ago. I was twenty-nine, captain of the Leo Brandon Dancers, and we'd just come back to Paris after a successful tour of Eastern Europe and Russia. So we were celebrating. In fact," and she smiled reminiscently, "Leo Brandon was so pleased

18

with us that he flew over from London to join the party and he brought me this little souvenir." She fingered the slightly yellowed ermine wrap.

"Instead of going nude," Vivian commented, "I'd have worn the ermine."

Her father chuckled. "And I'd have run from you. I was only a poor student then. I liked your mother exactly as she was."

"Bare-ass?" Saffron suggested inelegantly.

"That's one way of putting it, I suppose," Leary said.

Vivian tried to cover everybody's embarrassment—everybody, that is, except the unrepentant Saffron who seemed very superior about his own nudity. "Let's say you were a sex object, Mother."

Her mother replied, "I don't see anything wrong with being a sex object. Most men think very well of sex objects. Don't they, dear?" She gazed at her husband with bland innocence.

"My dear," he said, "you've just set back the women's-lib movement by twenty years."

Holden, feeling very much like a bystander during the family banter, decided it was time to interrupt. "I'd like to dance." And to Vivian, abruptly, "How about it?"

Vivian was polite but not enthusiastic. She let herself be led to the dance floor as if she were about to be confronted with a particularly disagreeable plate of yogurt.

Almost as soon as Holden put his arms about Vivian, he knew it was a mistake. She wasn't interested in dancing with him. Once or twice, she did cut loose; but for the most part, they took slow, mechanical steps, facing each other and going through the motions.

After a while, he asked, "You don't like touch dancing, do you?"

"It doesn't matter."

"Or maybe you just don't want to dance?"

"I like dancing." But she glanced about her in distaste. "These *people!*" she exclaimed. "Who *are* they? Where do they come from?"

"Almost everywhere." He was painfully polite, but he began to have second thoughts about Vivian Leary. "A lot of them are or were students. Some of the older ones are artists. There may be a few models, but I'd guess there are more street girls. I haven't been here long enough to know."

"Crummy crowd," she murmured.

He didn't say anything. But he reflected that she had seemed at first glance to be everything he was longing for—an attractive, vital, youthful partner. And yet, as they moved sedately about the dance floor, her evident distaste for her surroundings repelled him. He did try, nevertheless, to be agreeable. He couldn't help noticing she was very bright—and very young.

"Where are you going to school?" he asked.

"I have my degree in economics from Radcliffe," she said crisply, "and I'm going back in the fall for my master's."

"Headed for Wall Street?" he suggested with a small smile.

"Or Park Avenue." She was quite serious.

"How old are you?"

"Twenty-one, which is old enough to know what I want."

"You're lucky," he said. "I'm four years older, never got out of college, and I haven't the faintest idea of where I'm going or why."

She gave him a thin smile, as if to show that that was about what she'd expected of him. "Musicians are so different, aren't they?"

"What do you mean?"

"Only that, at the top, the best ones make scads of money and have people falling all over them. But all the rest are so very impractical."

"And poor?" he asked whimsically, being convinced by this time that she graded people by their economic position.

"Yes, poor," she agreed. "If it hadn't been for my mother, my father would have been just another trumpet player in the New York Philharmonic. As it is, she's made something of him."

"Didn't he have a little bit to do with that?"

"Yes, he had the talent. But my mother had to push him to turn it into something of value."

The band ended its set just then and signaled a break. The dancers straggled from the floor. And Holden led Vivian back to her parents.

He said to her, "Thanks. Enjoyed it."

She nodded politely.

Her mother pretended not to notice her daughter's coolness. "I thought you danced very well together."

"Nice of you to say so, but Vivian deserves a better partner," Holden said. "I haven't danced in quite a while."

Pat Leary said, "Vivian's an expert like her mother."

Upon which Saffron commented, "Well, *I'd* better not try dancing with her."

She gave him a meaningful look, as much as to say, "Good Lord! I'd never dance with you." What she did say was, "I've never tried nude dancing."

"Maybe you'd surprise yourself and have fun," Saffron said, moving off into the crowd.

Holden decided to follow him. "I'll be moving along too," the pianist said to the Learys. "Nice to have met you."

"We'll be looking for you at the Gribov dinner tomorrow night," Amy Leary said.

As Holden turned away, he said to Pat Leary, "Happy anniversary."

He lost Saffron in the crowd, for the time being, and retired to the edge of the dance floor some distance away from the Learys. For a few moments, he thought of leaving the Four Arts Ball and going back to his small apartment in the Rue Bonaparte. But on reconsideration, he decided to stick it out awhile longer.

He feared more than ever that he was out of touch with this joyful Parisian rite of spring. His mood was glum. Looking around at the diverse throng, he felt more isolated than ever.

Catherine Vaillant came up behind him just then and play-fully ran an experimental hand across his shoulders, around his neck and across his head, brushing his hair downward on his forehead. He was about to snap out a rough protest, then caught the scent of Catherine's perfume. Swinging about, he almost bumped into her.

His downcast mood changed at once. "Hey, how we doin'?"

"Doing just fine," she replied. "But what's wrong with you? I saw you out there with a beautiful young girl. Where is she?"

"Too young," he said coolly, and believed it.

21

"But so very pretty," she insisted, and he knew she was putting him on again but he didn't mind.

"Not my type," he amplified. Then, hopefully, "Have you ditched the senator?"

"You don't give up easily, do you?" She gave him that big look. Then, before he could respond, she went on. "No, the senator's tired and I'm taking him back to the Crillon, and then I'm going home myself. Long day tomorrow for both of us. He's talking early to the Franco-American Society and I'm translating."

He held her by both hands. "C'mon back. We'll have fun."

"Well, maybe. I'll think about it." She patted his cheek.

He felt enormously taken with her at that moment, and watched her with regret as she retreated toward the senator. The older man had collected his raincoat, rain hat and umbrella from the checkroom and was glancing about with an evident air of impatience at the ballroom entrance. As she joined him he snatched at her arm and hustled her away without ceremony.

Arch turned resolutely and faced the ladder that led to the balcony with its clinging human embellishments. The Jolly Oysters were rocking along and the French canary was singing once again into a microphone, but nobody could hear her above the uproar.

Holden decided the next attractive girl wasn't going to get away from him so easily.

It was almost 2:00 A.M. A half-dozen members of a human chain had just slithered along the ladder from the balcony. Ahead of Holden, a young man and his girl mounted the rungs and clambered to the top.

Now it was Holden's turn. Behind him, a chorus of voices in French, English and Franglais urged him to move. He glanced back, saw the youthful line snaking away toward the dance floor and waved his hand to show that he was taking off. Then, head down, he began climbing the ladder.

It was a risky business. The ladder wasn't as solid as it looked, and its base was shaky. He realized after mounting a few rungs that there was a ripple of laughter below him. He saw people were looking up, and some were pointing. Some-

22

body called out, *"Prenez garde!"* (Look out!) And there was more laughter.

Wondering if something had gone wrong, he gripped the rickety ladder with both hands. There were a few sardonic cheers. But he kept going slowly, testing each rung before he put his full weight on it.

By this time, he was almost halfway to the balcony. Now the whole crowd began applauding. He could hear people calling advice in French. At least, he presumed it was advice. Thoroughly mystified, Holden looked below once again and saw the same glistening panorama of upturned faces—some happy, others eager, some laughing, others shouting. The whole place seemed to have been caught up in the spirit of the moment. Pandemonium reigned all about him.

"En bas ... down ... down!" people called repeatedly in both languages. But he paid no attention to them.

Then, all at once, he felt a stabbing pain in the hand with which he had gripped the next highest rung of the ladder. The jabbing sensation was so unexpected and so sharp that he yelled.

At almost the same moment, he looked up and saw a handsomely shaped red silken slipper with a four-inch spiked heel crushing the fingers of his right hand. The beauty of the descending legs did not make the pain any easier to bear.

One leg now dangled precariously near his nose, and the red silken heel attached to it brushed against his mouth. A filmy red veil cascaded over his head and almost smothered him.

There was an anguished cry of sympathy from above. The veil was hoisted from his head. The red silk slippers retreated up the ladder and the owner of the pretty legs called down in English, "Oh dear! I hope I haven't hurt you!"

Holden's fingers felt numb where they had been stepped on. And he saw that his hand was bleeding. Yet, when he looked up at the retreating figure in the red veil, his mood swiftly changed.

Above him, a lovely young face stared at him with an expression of mingled anxiety and deep concern. With one hand, the girl thrust back a mass of long blond hair that had tumbled over her face and called, "I'm so sorry. Are you all right?" Without doubt, she was an American.

23

Holden restrained himself. "I'm okay."

"Sure?"

"Just a little cut on the hand." He added with an attempt at gallantry: "It's nothing."

"Oh, let me see." Without warning, the girl resumed her descent, but he remained motionless on the ladder.

The spectators, who had fallen silent momentarily, now took up her cause again. They made loud noises of protest, apparently on the supposition that Holden was refusing to give way to a lady.

She saw he was still looking up at her. When she was directly above him and the veil once more was draping his head, she called out, "Keep your head down and start moving. This veil is all I have on."

The few in the crowd who understood English gave a loud cheer. Somebody yelled, "Take it off!" And there was more applause as a buzz of French spread the news.

Holden, finally realizing the situation, began climbing down cautiously. He noticed that the rock band's drummer was beating his drum in time with the descent and the girl was keeping step. They inched their way downward in ceremonial procession to the time of slow hand-clapping and drumbeat.

When he reached the floor, he had the good sense to hold out his hand to her. She grasped it as she stepped down the last two rungs and stood beside him—a lustrous and handsomely endowed girl with laughing blue eyes and patrician features, a slender body and a magnificent air of mingled self-confidence and style.

"I didn't mean to step on you," she said.

"It's an honor," and he held up his bleeding hand.

Conscious of the people crowding about them, she said, "We're making a scene."

"Then let's get out of here."

They made their way through the crowd and retreated to an alcove off the grand ballroom, where she firmly shut the door on the curious. "Now let me see that hand," she said with a businesslike air. When he held it up again, she gave a little cry. "It's bleeding a lot."

"It'll stop."

24

"Never mind, I'll take care of it." She caught up a section of her trailing red veil and began tearing a strip from it.

"That's not very sanitary," he protested.

"Never you mind. It'll do until we find something better." She began wrapping strips of veil about his hand with a fine show of efficiency.

"Don't tear up too much of that veil," he cautioned. "It's very becoming."

"Really? The men here seem to prefer nudes."

"What about your own man?"

She looked at him gravely. "I don't have one at the moment." She finished with the impromptu bandage, gave his hand a little pat and released it. "All right now?"

"Thanks. I'll buy you a drink."

When they opened the door, they saw the crowd had lost interest and melted away.

Holden stood bemused, looking at the girl. She was casually brushing her hair back from her forehead. "Want to go back to the balcony?" he asked.

She waved one hand toward the dance floor. "Why? There's a perfectly good bar in back of the bandstand."

"Dance?"

"As long as you're not too acrobatic," she said. "I don't like being tossed about."

The ballroom lights went dim just then. A blue-white spotlight touched the clotted mass of dancers. The scene became sentimental.

Holden took the girl in his arms and was surprised at how easily she moved with him. She seemed to be enjoying herself. When the music stopped and the lights went up, they remained arm in arm on the dance floor.

"Like it?" he asked.

"Adore it."

"Want to dance some more?"

"Lots more. Only . . ."

"What?"

"Didn't you say something about buying me a drink?" She smiled at him. "Or are you going to stand me up?"

"Not tonight, anyway."

She tucked her hand inside his arm. Together, they walked

25

from the dance floor to the bar behind the bandstand where he ordered brandies. He saw Pat and Amy Leary dancing sedately past them with eyes only for each other. Gareth, he noticed, was still exercising the little nude with no more emotion than if she'd been a weight in a gymnasium. And at the edge of the dance floor, the statuesque young man in the lion skin was trying his luck with Vivian, who was bored and looked it.

Holden turned to his new girl and found her pensive. "What's the matter?"

With a self-deprecating gesture, she said, "I don't suppose you'll believe it, but I've just picked up a date for the first time in my life."

"And you're feeling guilty?"

"Sort of. My Presbyterian upbringing."

"You can drop me in thirty seconds if you want to."

"I don't want to." She gave him a quizzical look. "Isn't that awful of me?"

"Depends on what you mean by awful."

"I wonder," she murmured. Then, brightly, "Well, whoever you are, let's give it a try, shall we?"

As they picked up their wide-brimmed brandy glasses and faced each other, Saffron popped up behind the girl in the red veil, leered at Holden and made a round O of approval with his right thumb and forefinger. Then he vanished into the crowd.

Holden and the girl took their brandy glasses back to the alcove and settled on a wicker settee. For a few moments, they watched the movement on the dance floor. Then they raised their brandy glasses to each other in a silent toast. Above the glasses, their eyes met in a frank appraisal of each other.

Holden felt comfortable with her. She was not, as he had thought at first, just another giddy kid out for a lark in Paris. Nor was she what she pretended to be—someone out to pick up a guy for a one-night stand. There was a kind of desperation about her, now that they were alone, an air of wanting to be taken out of herself, to be embraced, loved, made to respond. And she seemed so very much alone.

She was mature. Of that there was no doubt. Probably in her mid-twenties, Holden thought. And yet, everything about her fairly cried out for belief, for support, for sympathy. She

26

was very far from being self-assured, calculating, even inviting, as Catherine Vaillant was. And yet, she did not have the fresh-faced innocent beauty of extreme youth, as Vivian Leary did. What this girl needed, Holden decided, was somebody to lean on, somebody to defend her. All at once, he felt enormously protective of her.

"Still feeling guilty about picking me up?" he asked.

A wan smile. "It's wearing off, but slowly." A brief silence, then an outburst: "I don't know what came over me. I've never done anything like this before in my whole life."

He was curious. "Are you married?"

She sparred with him. "Does it make a difference?" He supposed he was imagining things, but he had the feeling that she was afraid of losing him. She affected a careless manner. "It never took." But she couldn't hold her pose of carelessness. Her voice broke slightly. "I'm divorced."

He eyed her curiously, wondering what had happened. "Was it very bad?"

Her mood changed quickly. She lifted her head, forced a smile and tried to turn the conversation away from herself. "Who are you?" she asked in a friendly way.

In a self-depreciating tone, because he didn't want to scare her off, he replied, "I'm nobody much. Just a piano player at Henri's over on the Place St. Michel. Name's Arch Holden."

"I know Henri's." She brightened and clapped her hands, then pointed at him as if she had made a discovery. "Then you must be Charley Fourier's replacement."

"Right!" It pleased him that she could throw off a mood of depression so quickly. He countered with, "And who are you?"

"Nobody you ever heard of," she replied cheerfully, mimicking his tone. "Studied singing at the Juilliard School in New York, and now I'm at the Paris Conservatory. Name's Fay Carroll."

He tried not to seem overeager. Nothing could have persuaded him to abandon this sensitive girl with a deep hurt that was mirrored in her eyes. "Where do you live?" he asked casually because he was afraid she might take offense—and the last thing he wanted to do was to frighten her.

"On the Ile St. Louis." Then, in a mercurial change of mood, she loosed a torrent of words. "Come see me and I'll make

27

dinner for you. And you can play the piano for me. There's a big Steinway in the apartment, a concert grand—" She broke off suddenly, seemingly embarrassed once again by her forwardness. "Oh, I . . . I didn't mean it exactly the way all that sounded. You must forgive me."

He was amused, but tried not to show it. "What for? For inviting a guy over and then telling him he's got to play for his supper?"

She seemed relieved, even managed a little laugh. "I like you," she said. "You're easy to get along with."

With a different kind of girl, he might have made a proposition then and there. But with this one, he didn't dare. He turned the conversation into more conventional channels. "You must have quite an apartment."

"Oh, it's not mine. It belongs to a friend who's in the States right now."

He probed for some answers to the puzzle of attitudes this girl presented. "Close friend?"

With another laugh, she turned his question aside. "None of your business, Arch Holden." Then, as if to reassure him, she lifted her brandy glass toward him. "Here's to us."

He clinked glasses with her and they drank. And now, at what should have been a magical moment for them both, there was an interruption. A throaty, well-remembered voice broke in upon them. "Oh, I'm so sorry . . . I beg your pardon . . ."

He glanced up from his brandy glass in surprise and saw Catherine Vaillant moving away quickly from the open door, looking back over her shoulder at them. Then he lost sight of her in the crowd.

It occurred to him that she had at last ditched the senator and returned to the Four Arts Ball for her own reasons. But before he was able to meditate for more than a few moments on that intriguing notion, Fay Carroll interrupted. "Well, what nerve!"

"Ah, forget it, she just made a mistake." He tried to pass the whole thing off as a mishap.

But Fay was in a cold fury. "Do you know that woman?"

He wasn't prepared for the depth of her emotion. "Just saw her once," he countered. "She was Charley Fourier's girl. Why? You know her?"

28

"Lots of people come to Henri's," she said evasively. "And I couldn't begin to keep up with all of Charley Fourier's girls."

Was it merely his imagination that a quick, even distasteful, look of recognition had passed between Catherine Vaillant and Fay Carroll during that momentary encounter? He couldn't be sure. But Fay was distracted by the incident and he didn't like that. He raised his brandy glass. "Drink up!"

They drained their brandy glasses and set them aside. "Shall we go?" she asked.

"Where?"

"Oh, anywhere," she said carelessly, rising from her chair.

He tried her out tentatively. "My place?"

She patted his bandaged hand, and he saw that she was laughing at him. "Is that a proposition?"

"Take it any way you like," he said.

She met his eyes with a gentle but unwavering gaze. "And what comes after that?"

He guessed that she wasn't ready and answered quite honestly, "I don't know, do you?"

She linked arms with him. "Let's dance, shall we?"

With Fay Carroll in his arms, he felt even more protective of her. All he cared about was that she seemed to be unattached and he liked holding her close to him. As they passed a group of dancers who were moving only their bodies, he leaned over suddenly and kissed her. She only smiled and closed her eyes.

What followed that night became a collection of charming vignettes that gave the images of Fay that flitted in his memory the quality of a lovely dream. Instead of setting his senses tingling in anticipation, she appealed to him in a quite different way. He felt as protective of her as he had of someone else who had been dear to him not so long ago.

In his mind's eye he saw still another image of a beautiful girl with long blond hair. Her blue eyes, so like Fay's, were filled with tears. Try as he might, he couldn't separate her likeness from Fay's, although he made an effort to do so. He kept telling himself that he couldn't live in the past, that he had to look for new life, new experience. He had come here to the Four Arts Ball to try to forget. And he was afraid he never would.

29

That other girl who dominated his imagination was in a hospital, going through the pain and anguish of childbirth. He saw himself at her bedside, holding her hand, looking down into her tearful eyes, murmuring to her over and over again that he loved her.

Then the nurses came and gently persuaded him to leave the room; within minutes, she was wheeled off on a movable cot, looking at him and trying tremulously to smile. The agony of waiting was interminable. The doctor finally came to him, the mask of professional gravity concealing his own emotions, and told him that both she and the baby were dead.

With a convulsive effort, Holden tried to squeeze tragedy from his mind and concentrate on the delightful reality before him in the waning hours before dawn. He wanted to be charmed, beguiled, enticed. He wanted to be led out of himself, to feel new sensations. Instinctively, Fay Carroll caught his mood and played to him unashamedly. It was as if she too wanted to be taken out of herself, to be charmed, beguiled, to be thrust into a new life.

Holden became impatient with the quiet routine of touch dancing. Toward the end of the evening, with an almost brutal disregard for Fay's feelings, he flung her into the violence of crimson and purple disco-dance patterns. At first, she was surprised. Then, realizing that her partner's mood had changed, she suddenly laughed and gave in to him.

It was almost like a free-fall just before the opening of a parachute. From the stylish, well-mannered person she seemed to be, she turned herself into a hoyden, slipping away from him with head thrown back, outflung arms and swaying hips. He caught her, saw the flash of her laughing face as he twirled her away from him and pulled her back, relished the way her tattered red veil whipped about the curves of her pretty body and long, tapering legs.

How long they kept it up, he didn't know. But when the music stopped, they were both breathless, exhausted. And, strangely, Fay Carroll's image had been superimposed over the hospital scene that had been with him for so long and had put him in such torment. It was only a trick of the mind, perhaps, but her face and her personality seemed to have become so

30

entwined with the other girl's that they appeared to merge within him.

He knew he wanted Fay as much as he ever had wanted that other girl. But this time, he cautioned himself, he couldn't fall in love. All he wanted was a quick affair, the quicker the better. He didn't want to get so deeply involved ever again, to see a loved one sicken and waste away and die; to feel that he himself was forever lost, that he didn't belong, that his own life didn't matter. He couldn't go through all that again and survive.

And yet, as he danced with Fay, he already had so many pretty pictures of her in his head. He remembered how dreamily she had reacted when he kissed her on the shadowy ballroom floor, the way she had smiled at him over the wide-lipped brandy glasses, how wildly she had reacted when he began flinging her about. Did she inspire his moods or did she divine them? He wasn't sure. But he guessed that both were true.

When dawn came, she had become so much a part of him that he could think of nothing else. And at the final dance, they clung to each other, embraced each other and abandoned all movement in their excitement over each other. At the last minute, they climbed the paint-mottled ladder once more and kissed each other in the solemn darkness of the balcony.

They stood together at the entrance of the ancient palace, watching the red rim of the sun rise over the dour black scrawl of the rooftops of Montparnasse. All about them, revelers were leaving still another Four Arts Ball. In the soft chill of an April dawn, Holden took off his raincoat and draped it over Fay's shoulders because he saw that she was shivering and clinging to the few remaining shreds of the red veil. The rain had stopped.

"I've had such a lovely time," she said.

The way she said it, he feared all at once that she was signing off, that she would vanish from his life as quickly as she had come smashing into it. He couldn't stand the thought of it. "You're not going to break this up, are you?" he asked coaxingly.

She put her arms around his neck and kissed him. "I thought *you* were going to, you looked so solemn."

He held her tightly. "Let's go somewhere," he said.

"My place!" she exclaimed. "We can have breakfast."

He groaned inwardly. *Good God, breakfast,* he thought, but he didn't want her to leave him and said, "How about my apartment? It's closer."

"My place," she repeated firmly, and took him by the hand. "Let's get a cab."

She pulled him along in the thinning stream of departing revelers, her long hair stirred by the brisk morning breeze, her high-heeled red slippers tapping impatiently down the shallow stone steps. He didn't resist. She was so like that other girl, he thought, always insisting on her own way. The thought was comforting; he had a sense of *déjà vu*.

Cabs were plentiful at the end of the Four Arts Ball. Even the drivers were caught up in the carnival spirit. With an imperious gesture, Fay stopped a creaking old Panhard, almost certainly a relic of World War II, and gave her address on the Ile St. Louis in crisp French. The driver, who was wearing a hat of silver tissue, nodded cheerfully, even got out and opened the door.

With scant ceremony, Holden got her into the back seat and kissed her. But now, strangely, she didn't respond. He asked roughly, "What's the matter with you, Fay?"

"Nothing." But she almost cringed. Then, seemingly with an effort, she lifted her face to be kissed. This time, he thought she responded, but—perhaps he imagined it—the kiss took an effort. Instinctively, he murmured, "Don't be afraid." After the excitement of the night, she seemed to be turning cold. His inner voice was warning, *Don't fall in love.*

But still he felt drawn to her, even though, at the moment, she was hanging back. Certainly, she was a creature of moods. Too many moods, he thought; it crossed his mind that Catherine Vaillant would have known how to handle an affair like this. But, impatiently, he dismissed Catherine from his mind and tried to concentrate on Fay. Maybe, he thought, she might have good cause to be afraid even of a casual encounter. He felt very strongly that he didn't want to lose her. And so he said gently, rashly perhaps, given his past and feelings of caution, "Fay, I feel very much as if I'm falling in love with you."

32

"The passionate rhetoric of a love-crazed youth," she murmured.

He couldn't take that. He crushed her to him and kissed her hungrily. "Now do you believe it?"

"Don't force it, we're not kids," she responded. However, she wasn't unkind. He sensed that *she* was being cautious now, that she also didn't want to be hurt again as she must have been with her divorce.

"But I *want* to love. you," he insisted.

"Of course you do." Now she was trying to soothe him. All at once, she became the protector. She put her arms around him and drew him to her. "But that's not what's really troubling you, is it?"

"I don't want to talk about it," he evaded. "It's too damned personal."

She was comforting, but insistent. "Tell me, darling."

He felt he had to give her some explanation, no details, but enough to satisfy her. "I'm trying to get over something that happened to me a year ago. And it's pretty bad."

"How bad?" He was staring straight ahead, removed from her, and she was desperate to get him back. "You *must* tell me. I want to know."

She was a lot stronger than he had thought. Perhaps he had to tell her in order to purge himself of the pain—and to assure himself he wanted Fay and not a ghost of the past. He was conscious that this deepening of what he had thought would be a casual relationship was something they both instinctively wanted.

She was quiet for the time he needed to sort things through, then softly, insistently, she said, "Tell me. It'll be better for both of us."

It came out baldly. "My wife, Caroline, died in childbirth a year ago."

"Oh."

"The baby died, too."

She didn't say anything.

"Caroline was only twenty-two," he went on, in that dry, pained voice, "and we'd only been married a year."

"Did you love her very much?"

"I guess I'd loved her ever since we'd been neighbor kids

in a little town out on Long Island." He drew in breath in little gasps, as if he were shivering. "It's so damned hard to forget."

"You shouldn't try," she said. "It's a part of your life, isn't it?"

"Yes."

"Then don't try to hide it." She patted his shoulder. "I don't want you to. Not ever."

The ancient taxi took a curve in the Parisian dawn, its wheels squeaking, and Holden turned his head and looked at Fay. "You must think I'm a very strange guy."

"No."

"Then why are you asking me all these things?" He felt bruised because she had forced him to reveal his inner anguish; and now he felt he had become a supplicant for her pity.

"You are a very special person, Arch Holden," she said.

"I like you, too."

"Good!"

"I want you to love me," he went on.

"I'm sure you do." She spoke quietly and calmly, but now she seemed very self-possessed. "Maybe it'll happen to us, maybe it won't, but people who have gone through our experiences don't easily fall in love all over again. Now do they?"

He stifled an impatient reply. "I don't know . . . I just don't know."

"Of course you don't," she agreed. "We only met tonight. Tomorrow, you may never want to see me again."

"That's a chance I'll take," he said.

He was annoyed with himself because Fay had, by her perceptions, dampened the evening that had started so promisingly. He resolved to draw her out in return.

"Why *wouldn't* I want to see you again tomorrow?" he asked lightly.

She wasn't in a mood for confessional, however. "When and if you're really interested," she said, "I'll tell you. But whatever happened to me wasn't anywhere near as serious as what happened to you. A whole family wiped out, and you had to go out anyway and make music in some godawful saloon."

"For a while, I couldn't," he admitted. "I was crazy enough

to think I could be a concert pianist. Even enrolled at the Curtis School in Philadelphia..." His voice trailed off.

"And then?" she prompted.

Reluctantly, he continued. "My savings ran out, the hospital and doctor bills were still unpaid, and this job in Paris came along...so..." He managed a tight smile. "I grabbed it."

"And now you're with me," she said with determination, "and things have got to be better for the both of us."

He squeezed her hand. "They will," he said encouragingly.

Neither had been conscious that the cab had stopped outside an apartment house on the Ile St. Louis facing the gray-green waters of the Seine and the towering Cathedral of Notre Dame on its companion island nearby. But the cabdriver, caught between his need to keep moving and an elderly Parisian's natural reluctance to interrupt lovers, turned with a sympathetic look. *"Alors, madame, m'sieu', nous arrivons."*

Holden, feeling washed out over his confessional, stirred nervously. "What does he want?"

Fay said with a laugh, "He says we're here and he wants to be paid, which isn't unreasonable. I don't have a sou on me in this red fishnet outfit, but"—and she felt in the pocket of his raincoat—"here's your wallet and I hope nobody in the cloakroom took all your francs."

He produced enough to satisfy the driver. "Honest people, Parisians," he commented.

"Wait till you've been here awhile," she said, and led him inside past the big double doors of the apartment house and up the stairs beside the tiny cubicle where the concierge was nodding over a newspaper. Holden followed determinedly. He wanted to show Fay that he wasn't living in the past. He wanted to prove that he could still make love, probably as much for his own good as for hers. And so, halfway up the stairs to her second-floor apartment, he snatched her in his arms and crushed her to him.

For a long time, he stayed with her there, embracing, kissing. She was the first to come to her senses. "We can't stay here forever, Arch. Let's go inside." She turned the key in the front door lock, and once the door was open, she took both his hands, drew him inside and let him embrace her. Yet, he could not seem to give her sufficient assurance, for all his lovemaking, to let herself go.

She did kiss him, but it was in a detached manner. And when she put her arms around him and let him run his hands over her body, he felt no sense of passion in her. It was as if she was experimenting with him, with herself, and he didn't like it.

He swept her up, carried her to her bedroom and ripped off the remaining shreds of her red net costume. She lay on the bed, looking at him, her eyes half closed, then turned on her side as if she didn't want him to see all of her. It didn't matter. She had a supple, languorous figure.

He hastened to undress, and flung open the closet door to dispose of his things. And there he saw an array of men's clothes on hangers and a row of men's shoes arranged on the floor. He whirled and demanded, "Whose clothes are in this closet?"

He stood over her, but she didn't move. Nor did she say anything at first.

It made him furious. "You're living with somebody."

She sighed, shifted to one side of the bed and sat up, pulling the covers over herself in a protective gesture. With an effort she maintained her composure. "When I decided to return to Paris," she said, not looking at him, "I had to have an apartment; and you must know that it's hard to find a decent one in Paris."

"Sure, you said a friend let you live in his apartment," he said bitterly, waving one arm at the clothes in the open closet. "Some friend!"

"Actually," she went on, white-faced but still composed, "this apartment belongs to my psychiatrist, Dr. René Beranger. He was going to the States to do research at the Menninger Clinic." With a catch in her voice, she added, "Dr. Beranger was very kind. He gave me the keys to his Citroën in the garage across the street as well as the keys to his apartment. So I couldn't very well ask him to remove his clothes and shoes." She lowered her voice and managed a wisp of a smile. "Dr. Beranger is very old, Arch. There's no reason to be jealous of him."

An uncomfortable silence smothered them both. He had the

36

grace to look ashamed of himself. She stretched out one arm toward him in a timid gesture of forebearance. "Please, Arch, we've been having such a good time together. Why do we have to spoil it?"

He lashed out at her blindly because he had been put in the wrong and somehow wanted to assert himself. "Psychiatrist!" he almost shouted. "Why in hell did you need a psychiatrist?"

Her lips trembled, but she drew herself taut under the covers and forced herself into a surface appearance of calmness. There wasn't much left of the composure with which she had faced him when he demanded an explanation of Dr. Beranger's clothes.

In a frantic whisper, she pleaded, "It hurts too much to talk about it."

It was his turn to demand, "I want to know. Tell me!"

"All right, then..." Words tumbled from her lips in bursts, and tears welled over on her cheeks. Now and then, there were long, painful pauses during which her teeth clenched, almost as if her jaws had locked. "I told you I didn't want to talk about my divorce, Arch...it was too awful...but if you must know, my husband's family and mine had a very close relationship—and when the break came, only my mother sided with me.... My step-father blamed me, said I hadn't been a good wife, that I was frigid....Frigid! Oh, my God!" She paused and dashed tears from her eyes with the back of her hand. "My husband was in the State Department, always busy, always out nights...I was alone a lot, couldn't take it...and when we were sent to Paris, it became unbearable. Then my friends told me he was going around with another woman, and when I asked him about it, he flew into a rage...called me cold, frigid, impossible...Yes, I needed a psychiatrist...I needed care..." She broke off with a despairing cry. "Oh God, but I don't want to talk anymore about it."

She buried her head in the bedclothes.

Appalled by the scene he had caused, Holden flung himself on the bed beside her. "Fay..."

There were only loud sobs in reply.

"Fay, I'm sorry...I didn't mean to...I didn't know..."

With a wail, she thrust aside the bedclothes and thrust her arms about him. "Don't leave me now, Arch. Please don't. I won't be able to stand it."

He let her draw him beside her and felt her body trembling.

It was a panicky response, very far from what he had expected. But very slowly, even painfully, he began to understand that Fay was going through a crisis. Now the look of hurt in her eyes, the wariness against committing herself that had so annoyed him earlier began to make sense to him. And he saw that she had to convince herself that she was capable of developing a normal sexual relationship.

Still, lying there beside her and feeling her trembling, he couldn't help wondering what would happen to them both if she did indeed prove to be incapable of a normal, loving approach to life.

And then he felt ashamed of himself for even thinking of abandoning this strange but appealing girl at a time when she needed someone to believe in her. She seemed to gather just a little confidence in herself because he still remained beside her after that stormy scene of self-revelation. She was calmer now, and the trembling had stopped.

He took her in his arms. "Are you all right now?"

"I'm fine."

"You almost knocked me for a loop."

"I couldn't help it . . . I'm sorry."

"Are you afraid of me?"

"No," she murmured. The release of her anguish made her bold. But she was timid about sex play, as if she thought that he might be turned off by it. He wasn't. He even encouraged her gently. And then, all at once, she seemed no longer afraid and when she took passionate, even fierce, possession of him, he knew everything would be all right. With rapid movements, he finished undressing and was thrilled when she made room for him in the bed.

"Oh, darling, it's such a lot of fun being with you," she whispered.

And yet he knew that she could not yield to him totally that first time—not after all the self-doubt that her failed marriage had aroused within her. It would take time and care and love and understanding to bring her around. For this was to be the beginning, not the end, and a wild joy surged within him at the thought.

Chapter Two

Paris is one of the few large cities in the world with a cheerful morning face.

Here, one is spared the grim visage of New York heading into the daily struggle for survival, the down-at-the-heels dignity of London, the black-streaked scowls of Tokyo's perennial masquerade, the repulsive death mask of Moscow.

In Paris, the absurdities of life seem a little more bearable. The frailties of humankind, too, are treated with better humor than in most other places. And if this era is not outstanding in the chronicle of world history, it is at least one of civility in Paris.

For in Paris, those who seek haven are not asked whether they are oddball or genius, a free spirit or a clown. The stranger is made to feel welcome. And the only conditions are that he should keep the peace and pay his own way.

So, in these dour times, it is still possible to hear good-natured talk, even laughter, with the rising of the sun over Montparnasse. In the morning, the fishermen still sit placidly beside the Seine. And along its cobbled banks, lovers still stroll arm in arm. Nor do they care what the world thinks if they chance to pause for a kiss or a casual embrace.

As for the workaday citizen of Paris, he still ventures into the street with the self-assured air of a little king. Except for an occasional stray, the buses with the "jump on–jump off" rear platforms are gone. But the modern ones, though they seem more businesslike, still rumble along their routes without too much attention to schedules. And the Metro's gates still slam in the traveler's face just as his train is pulling into the station.

Change comes slowly to Paris, if at all. It remains something more than a city. For its people, it may be a mixed blessing. But for the stranger come to visit, it is at once a symbol of hope, a state of mind and a zestful adventure in living.

To awaken in such a city late on a sunny April morning was a delight for Fay Carroll. She stirred in her bed some hours after returning from the Four Arts Ball when an organ grinder's distant music woke her up. Still drowsy, she pulled the covers over her head.

It didn't work. The odors of bread and cakes just taken from the oven drifted through the open window of Fay's bedroom from the bakery below. As if that weren't annoying enough, there was a brisk clatter of dishes from the cafe next door; soon enough, she detected the enticing smell of fresh-brewed coffee.

She threw back the covers and sat up. The red veil she had worn to the party trailed along the floor. She had nothing on.

The sun had long since mounted above the neighboring rooftops. Now, it sent a slender shaft of gold lancing through her bedroom window. The bells of Notre Dame clanged eleven times. And in seeming harmony, a buzzer in the apartment began droning at measured intervals.

Outside, Fay could hear the clump of footsteps and the scraping of chairs in front of the Cafe St. Louis. The voices, the wails, the shrieks and the laughter of little children at play mingled with all the other morning sounds. And in obbligato, the buzzing continued with maddening timing.

Fay called, "Arch!" No response.

She glanced around the bedroom for some sign that he still was in the apartment—but saw nothing. No swim trunks, not even a white sock or a soft-soled shoe of his costume at the Four Arts Ball. She called again, "Arch!" Only the buzzer responded.

Unable to ignore any longer this orchestration of the commonplace, she bolted from the bed and poked her head into the living room. There she saw his raincoat draped over the grand piano. Well, at least he'd been in the place.

But where was he now? Buzz . . . buzzz . . .

With a groan, she stood at the bedroom window and held

40

a curtain about her bosom as she leaned out. In the narrow, crowded street below, she saw only workaday Parisians and frolicking children. In the distance, the organ grinder stopped long enough to tip his hat to her.

Eventually, she established the source of the buzzing. Taking the precaution of slipping into a yellow silk robe, she ran through the sunny living room to the front door. The buzzer was still sounding, now louder than ever.

With the caution of a seasoned big-city dweller, she called out in French, then in English, "Who is it?"

Mercifully, the buzzing stopped. A familiar voice rumbled, "It's Arch. Open up, will you?"

She called, "What are you doing out there?"

A muffled, "Locked myself out. Open up, will you?"

The ancient French lock resisted her best efforts. Impatiently, Holden called again, "What are you doing? I can't wait much longer." There was a thump at the bottom of the door, as if it had been kicked.

"Don't *do* that!" she exclaimed.

"Well, hurry up."

"I'm trying. But the lock's stuck."

"I'm holding up two big brunches, honey. Get going."

"Be patient."

With a final effort, she turned the key. The door creaked open. He was standing before her, balancing a fully laden tray shoulder-high on his left hand. A white napkin was draped over his right forearm and a white waiter's jacket flapped over his bare torso and swim trunks.

The sight was so grotesque that she burst into laughter. "Where did you get it, darling?"

He walked in, still balancing the tray. "Downstairs at the cafe. Told 'em I was giving you breakfast in bed."

"Then it's well advertised that I kept you last night."

"Not exactly. We didn't get here until after sunup." He managed to turn his head toward her without dropping the tray. "Where do I put this? It's damned heavy."

"On the balcony."

She led the way through the living room and through the sunny entrance to a little balcony overlooking the street. He lowered the tray to a round wooden table, dropped into a

41

straight-backed wooden chair and motioned to her to take the companion chair opposite him. "Let's get started. I'm hungry."

"In a minute." She left the breakfast table, calling over her shoulder, "I'm dressing. Wait for me."

"Brunch's getting cold," he warned, deciding to wait. To pass the time, he took over the piano in the living room and began improvising as he often did to pass the time.

Occasionally, he came up with an agreeable little tune to which, if he felt like it, he'd fit words. And if it pleased him, he'd put the number into his repertoire. He developed a tune now that he liked, repeated it, varied it and then broke off.

Fay called from the bedroom, "What did you play just then?"

"I was just improvising."

"Liked it. How about a lyric?"

Holden didn't mind. He fingered a few chords, broke into the tune he'd just improvised and began singing whatever popped into his head:

"Wake me up in Paris on a sunny, springy day . . ."

As he broke off, she encouraged, "Keep it up."

He called back, "If you want lyrics, write 'em yourself."

She made her entrance just then in a close-fitting beige dress and slippers to match. Together, they whiled away the time picking out Holden's tune and fitting words to it. That occupied them until, quite guiltily, they remembered the breakfast on the balcony. The eggs were stone-cold. "That's what happens when you let a piano player make love to you," Holden said.

With practiced domestic competence, Fay presided over the breakfast table while Holden looked on. Before them were a pot of coffee—somewhat lukewarm after standing so long— a plate of croissants buried under a napkin, mounds of cold scrambled eggs and equally cold strips of bacon.

He tried, but he couldn't stomach the cold breakfast. With the tact of an experienced housewife, she removed the egg plate and the bacon over his protests. "I won't let you have a cold breakfast for your first meal here," she said.

He stopped her. "I can think of something else that would warm me up," he said teasingly.

She froze for an instant. Looking at him, she didn't have much doubt about his intentions. She turned away from him and made her way slowly to the bedroom. He followed, seeing with dismay that she feared he was testing her. She dawdled over undoing the hook at the back of the neckline of her dress. With an appearance of anxiety, she searched his face for a hint of his mood. "You . . . you don't think I'm cold, do you?"

"No," he said gently.

"Or frigid?"

"Good Lord, no!"

She seemed relieved. "I've heard it so often that I had actually begun to believe it."

"Well, don't!" His tone was rough, although he had meant to be reassuring. He added, because he knew she needed to hear it, "You were just great last night."

"And I *do* respond, don't I?" she asked, still faintly anxious.

"You sure do."

"You're not just saying that . . ."

He broke in. "Now stop it, Fay. You're not a psycho. You're a warm, loving, responsive woman, and I want to make love to you—right now."

She said simply, "I want to believe you."

"Then," he suggested, "why not take off your dress?"

This time, she slipped out of her dress and underthings. He smothered her in his arms. For a long time they lay with each other and loved and comforted each other.

The sun was high in the sky when he finally left the Ile St. Louis. He departed only after she had promised to meet him that night at Henri's some time around midnight. For all her insecurities, she was growing on him.

To the relatively few Americans who still called Paris their second home in the 1980's, Henri's was a very special place. Unlike the Dome and the Select on Montparnasse, which had become mere tourists' hangouts, Henri's remained part of an older tradition for Americans in Paris.

Another Henri Durand, the father of the current *patron*, had founded the place in the 1920's as a haven for the moonstruck young American expatriates who had settled on the Left Bank after World War I. Ernest Hemingway had been there, and Scott and Zelda Fitzgerald, Gertrude Stein and Alice B. Toklas and so many others. It was part of a tiny new world then, brave to some, utterly daft to others.

43

Generally, it was circumscribed by the Latin Quarter, dominated by the ancient walls of the Sorbonne; Sylvia Beach's bookshop with its fervent dedication to James Joyce; the zinc-covered Lilas Bar, so favored by Hemingway; the Café des Deux Magots in the Faubourg St. Germain, and the crossroads of Montparnasse where the Raspail and Montparnasse boulevards meet.

It was very far from the postcard Paris of the tourists—the Paris of the Eiffel Tower, the Louvre and the American Express office. But few gave that a thought. For in that happy, far-off time, Americans really did amount to something in France. And most French people viewed the mishaps and crack-ups of young Americans with charity, even indulgence.

With the exception of a few small and little-noticed monuments to the past, Henri's among them, that tiny world has long since crumbled. And the vintage Americans who survived it have, for the most part, concluded that Paris is dead.

Of course it isn't. What *has* died is the special relationship that once existed between Americans and the French. So that neither American intellectuals nor tourists have much attraction today for the sophisticated Parisian. As for the Americans who huddle on their tour buses in the heart of Paris, many of them regard most Frenchmen as thieves, sexual deviates or Communists who charge stiff prices for their wares. The French, as might be expected, reply in kind.

Still, a few places in this latter-day Paris do want to be thought of as friendly to Americans. One, certainly, was Harry's smoky, dingy New York Bar in the Rue Daunou. Another was Henri's, which had tried not to change with the times and fairly well succeeded.

Any American who entered Henri's modest two-story building just off the Boulevard St. Michel was given a generous reception. It also attracted a sprinkling of other foreigners who were still under the influence, however slight, of an era when the United States enjoyed more trust than it does in Western Europe today. In addition, the French survivors of another generation—the fading group that still remembers the liberation of their city by the oncoming French and Americans in 1944—also came to Henri's now and then.

For the French, as for the Americans, Henri's was an exercise in nostalgia.

To the regulars, however, the least nostalgic person in that neat and scrupulously clean establishment was the current *patron*, the son of the founder. In everything he did, he was eminently practical, as was his black-clad ramrod of a wife, Marie, who presided over the cash register. They thought of their place as an incentive to good living. As for Henri himself, he permitted no interference either with his management or with his way of life.

So nobody argued with Henri Durand the younger except his wife. He had never forgotten the lessons of sacrifice and self-denial he had learned with the French Resistance during World War II. And he still, out of wartime habit, listened regularly to the BBC on the short-wave receiver he kept in his bar.

To his customers, Henri was an affable butterball of a man. He was unfailingly dressed in a dark, pin-striped suit, white shirt and dark tie, with slicked-back gray hair, a pencil-thin mustache and a perpetual smile. But to his small staff of waiters and bartenders, his photographer, Stephanie Rivet, and his house girls, Toinette and Josette, he was a sharp-voiced martinet who gave quick, precise orders and expected to be instantly obeyed. He even dominated his temperamental chef.

The only latitude given to anybody at Henri's was allotted to the resident pianist—Charley Fourier for two years, and now his replacement, Arch Holden. To the latter, Henri said on the first night of work, "You are the musician. Play what my customers want, good American music."

By that pronouncement, as Holden well understood, Henri had outlawed all forms of rock and bluegrass, which, in his lexicon of good living, interfered with both the appetite and the digestion. Jazz? Ah, that was different. Henri had been in America with his father as a child in the far-off time when jazz was king. And he still thought of the jazz age as a salutary experience. Whether his customers liked it or not, that too was part of what Henri's pianists gave them.

On the night after the Four Arts Ball, Holden was running through his keyboard routine at Henri's with the tempo of clockwork. He expected the Learys and Henri's special guest, the defecting Russian baritone, Nikolai Gribov. But it was such a nasty night and so late that he had almost given up on Fay Carroll. Peering at the rain beating against the plate-glass windows of Henri's, Holden wondered whether she had completely forgotten him.

Now and then, Holden saw a police car or a bus crawling past the bar in the storm. But the rain-swept sidewalks were deserted. Even Henri's doorman, a giant Tunisian known to all as Shukri, huddled inside the entryway in his yellow rain gear.

The patronage was light that night. Only three regulars contemplated the fate of the universe over drinks at the piano bar. They were Karl Eilers, a muscular German of middle age with a fierce look and a bushy black bartender's mustache; Enzo Pastore, a thin and sad-eyed Italian who tapped his slender fingers on the bar in time with the music; and Marcel Valleau, a delicate-looking French artist with flowing blond hair and an effeminate manner.

The house girls, Toinette and Josette, had long since given up hope of hustling less discriminating customers and were biding their time at a nearby table. As for Stephanie Rivet, the photographer, she prowled among the vacant tables—a shapely figure in a low-cut white blouse and black net tights—with a camera suspended from a strap about her neck. She too had little to do.

Everybody seemed to be waiting for something to happen except Henri, who was listening to the BBC on his radio. It was well past midnight; had it not been for Holden's music, even the regulars might have given up and gone home.

After a while, a taxi crept through the storm and drew up at Henri's. Shukri opened the big oak door for a ghostly figure that braved the wind-driven rain by dashing from the cab to the door. It was Catherine Vaillant, in a dead-white raincoat and soaked white silk kerchief, with an outsize leather bag slung over her shoulder.

Henri left his radio to greet the new arrival, who emerged from her protective garments with the smiling remark, "God, I need a drink." Somebody handed her one. The regulars at

46

the piano bar perked up as she advanced toward them and clambered on a bar stool at the upper end of Holden's keyboard.

"Bon soir, messieurs," she said to the regulars. And to Holden, "Hello, lover."

"Why lover?" he asked, not missing a note.

"Love songs seem to be your routine tonight."

He hadn't been conscious of it. His selections as he played were more or less whatever came to mind. He had a good memory and a good ear, so he dispensed with sheet music as often as he could. He was a little embarrassed that he was revealing his emotions that way. "It's just an accident that I'm playing 'Hello, Young Lovers.'" He shrugged it off.

She tried her drink, but didn't let up on him. "When I came in," she observed, "you were playing, 'Lover, Come Back to Me.'"

"It is so," the sad-eyed Italian agreed. "The whole evening, only a lot of stinking love songs."

To which the Frenchman objected, "It is not so bad, Enzo."

"For the French, love. For the Italians, wine," Enzo said.

"Our friend here was with a beautiful girl at the Four Arts Ball last night," Catherine announced. "He has love on the brain."

"I drink to him!" the German exclaimed, raising his beer glass. "One week in Paris, and already he has a girl."

"But did he go home with her?" the Frenchman asked. "This is a serious question."

"To go home, it is nothing," the Italian objected. "Americans, they talk big, do nothing. Hey, Arch! You sleep with this girl?"

Holden kept playing the piano with the precision of a metronome. "You guys are just jealous."

Catherine finished her drink and called for another. With a judicious attitude, she reminded him, "You have been asked if you slept with her. Yes or no?"

For reply, he swung into an old Ethel Merman number, "They Say That Falling in Love Is Wonderful," and grinned at the howl of disapproval.

"What he say is that they went to bed together," the German concluded. "Arch, she was good in bed? You tell us, yes?"

Holden replied good-humoredly, "Go to hell."

"She must be good," the Italian said. "Look at him." And he pointed to Holden and grinned. "Is all tired out, finished."

The Frenchman asked Catherine with a sly smile, "Was it like that with your Charley Fourier?"

"You mind your own business," Catherine said.

"Catherine has a United States senator," Holden observed. "He is very old and fat."

"Old and fat, maybe, but he could be good in bed," the Italian said.

The German asked Catherine, "Are senators good in bed?"

"Who needs an interpreter in bed?" Her replacement drink arrived and she sampled it. "Anyway, the senator has a wife and eight children in Chicago."

The Italian clapped his hands once. "You see, I told you senators could be good in bed."

"Catherine does not like old men," the Frenchman commented. "Only young ones, big and full of life. Strong! Is it not so, Catherine?"

The German pointed to Holden. "Maybe our friend"—and he nodded to Arch—"should go to bed with Catherine." He laughed as Holden flushed and missed a note. He saw Catherine eyeing him curiously, and tried to be diplomatic. "Catherine is very beautiful, and very desirable," he said diplomatically.

Catherine, unperturbed, sipped her drink. "Nicely said, Arch." She turned to his detractors, "But if the rest of you do not mind, I shall pick my own bedfellow."

Holden exploded with a brilliant series of runs on the keyboard, banged out a few lusty concluding chords and stood up. "That's the set." He beckoned to Catherine. "Time for my break. Let's have something to eat."

She took her drink to a nearby table, and Holden followed her. The regulars at the piano bar relapsed into attitudes of studied boredom. Holden pointed to Catherine's big leather shoulder bag. "I see you're working." For a moment, she was nonplussed, then touched the bag and laughed. "Oh, my translator's bag. Yes, I *was* working. I came here from the embassy. They called me to translate a speech made in the Chamber of Deputies."

After they had ordered supper, he kept watching the door.

48

She noticed, as she seemed to notice everything. "Expecting somebody?"

"The Learys and Gribov, mainly."

"And somebody else, yes?"

He hesitated. Then: "Thought maybe the girl I met last night might show."

"In this weather?" She lit a cigarette. "You piano players expect a lot."

"But she said she might."

"Maybe." She gave him a calculating look. "She *could* be crazy enough to go out in a storm."

"Do you know her?"

"I've seen her around," Catherine responded. "I see a lot of Americans at the embassy."

Holden thought of the moment the night before when the two women had seen each other and seemed to have exchanged a look of recognition. "Her name's Fay Carroll."

"Oh? Is that what she calls herself now?"

Holden took a stab in the dark. "Said she used to be married to somebody in the embassy here. Maybe you know him?"

Catherine was evasive. "These Americans, they come and go." She changed the subject. "Now, that senator I had on tour last night. Do you know he took off for Chicago first thing this morning? Had to get home to the wife and kids and tell them all about Poland. What's so important about Poland?"

"Lots of Poles in Chicago," Holden said. He came back to his theme, Fay Carroll. "But about that girl last night, she's studying voice at the Conservatory."

She was pensive. "You really like her, don't you?"

"Yes."

"Well, be careful."

He laid down fork and knife. "Catherine, are you trying to tell me something?"

"You have a lively imagination."

He refused to be turned off. "Charley Fourier said you seemed to have a sixth sense about people."

She rippled with laughter and crushed out her cigarette. "That's because I could always tell when he was lying. A nice guy, but a terrible liar."

"I thought you two were in love."

"Charley in love?" She laughed again.

"What about you?"

She didn't say anything for a moment. He became conscious once again of that searching, dark-eyed scrutiny he had first undergone at the Four Arts Ball. And he couldn't help wondering what her game actually was. For a mere translator at the American embassy, she dressed far too expensively, seemed to have plenty of money and knew her way around the polyglot foreign community of Paris. What interest could she possibly have in braving a rainstorm to come to Henri's alone?

Holden had to conclude Catherine Vaillant was not exactly what she seemed. But in reality, who was she?

She didn't answer his question. Instead, she leaned back lazily and surveyed him through half-closed eyes. "You know, you're very impressionable and you'd better be careful," she said.

Immediately, he was alert and challenged her. "About Fay Carroll?"

She kept watching him, looking into his eyes, holding his attention. "You ought to know a lot more about that one," she said.

He felt irked at the warning. "What do you know about her?" he asked idly.

Again that big look, a smile—and silence.

He tried again. "What makes you so concerned about me?"

"I don't want you hurt. You're too nice." She reminded him, "I even came back to the Four Arts Ball last night, remember? But you were with her and, well..." She shrugged. "I didn't want to interfere."

She had succeeded in disturbing him. He felt a grudging admiration for the way she had captured and held his attention. He realized that he hadn't looked for Fay Carroll for all of three minutes.

Soon thereafter, Henri went into action. A platoon of waiters set up three tables in a wide U. Next, the tables were decked in the establishment's best snowy white linen and decorated with Henri's own silver tableware and a large bouquet of roses.

During this, Guy Saffron, in picturesque dark green rain gear, stalked in with a loud greeting for the *patron*. "Okay,

50

Henri, here's the kid from Neuilly. Let's get the show on the road."

"*Doucement*, M'sieu' Saffron," was the reproachful reply. "The guests of honor have not yet arrived."

"What, so late?" the reporter glanced at his wristwatch.

"Gribov sang at the opera tonight in *Tosca* and arranged for a box for the *famille* Leary," Henri explained. "It is a long opera, as you know. They could not possibly get here sooner."

Saffron slipped out of his raincoat but kept on his rakish-looking rain hat, which gave him the appearance of a large-headed gnome. "Terrific; gives me time for a drink."

On his way to the piano bar, he paused beside the table where Holden and Catherine Vaillant were finishing their supper. He started in mock surprise, thrust his rain hat back on his head and exclaimed, "Well! What have we here? The Bad News Baby herself!"

Catherine replied with studied insolence, "Saffron, you're drunk. Move along, will you?"

The reporter merely grinned and planted himself firmly by her side. "You still can't keep your mitts off somebody else's guy, can you?"

Holden protested, "We were just having a nice, quiet supper together until you came along, Saffron. How about minding your own business?"

Saffron paid no attention to him, but kept studying Catherine Vaillant, who tried to ignore him. "So what's the game tonight, baby?" the reporter asked. "I find it hard to believe it's just a coincidence that you dropped by in this lousy weather at just about the time that Gribov and the Learys are due."

Catherine murmured to Holden, whose curiosity by now had been piqued. "Pay no attention to him. He's crazy." She concentrated on her supper, but it was evident, beneath her air of indifference, that she was annoyed.

Saffron knew it. He thrust his journalistic needle a bit deeper. "Think you can hook Gribov, baby?"

Catherine flushed. "If you don't stop this nonsense," she said to Saffron in a low, carefully controlled voice, "I'll see that Henri puts you out." That evoked only a leer from the reporter, but she added, "And he'll do it for me, too."

"Okay, baby," he replied airily. Then, to Holden: "Better

watch your wallet with this one, fella. She'll take anything that's not nailed down." He sauntered off with a laugh,

If his purpose had been to call attention to Catherine's presence in the restaurant, he succeeded all too well. Both Henri and Marie could be seen talking together earnestly and glancing in her direction. At the bar, the regulars were buzzing over their drinks as Saffron joined them. And the house girls, Josette and Toinette, were giggling at Catherine's discomfiture.

Even Holden wondered about his charming supper companion, but he didn't have the heart to make her more uncomfortable than she was. Instead, he asked, "If you want me to tell Henri to throw him out, I'll be glad to do it."

"Oh, never mind," she dismissed Saffron carelessly. "He's not worth the bother."

Holden couldn't help asking, "I only met the guy last night at the Four Arts Ball. What's his trouble?"

She made a grimace. "He's always hanging around the embassy, getting some things wrong and picking up other things we don't want printed. You can't believe a word he says, and his paper is just a rag."

"Why is he making such a fuss about Gribov?"

"Like all newspapermen," she replied with quiet deliberation, "Saffron has a lively imagination and a terrible temper. I don't dare think of what he's going to put in the *Paris Press* tomorrow." She glanced up with a distracted air, for she saw the *patron's* wife approaching. "But enough of that," she concluded. "Wonder what Marie wants?"

It was unusual for Marie Durand to leave her post behind the cash register, where she was a formidable presence in black. As everybody who had been to Henri's knew, she never intervened among the customers except for the most urgent reasons.

As she approached, Holden arose out of politeness, but she did no more than nod briefly to him. Her business, it appeared, was entirely with Catherine Vaillant. The two went at each other with bursts of voluble French punctuated by a bit of judicious hand-waving and a continual series of nods and smiles. Finally, Marie ended the conversation with an explosive *"Bon!"* She clapped her hands and gave quick instructions in French to a waiter who hustled off to do her bidding.

Catherine laid her napkin to one side as Holden resumed his seat beside her. "Madame has been very kind," she explained with a nod and a smile toward the retreating Marie. "She noticed that we were almost finished with supper and is seeing to it that Shukri, the doorman, gets a cab for me. It *is* a miserable night."

"But aren't you going to stay for the party?"

She patted his hand gently. "Not tonight. I've a lot of work at the embassy tomorrow and I must get in early." She suggested, "Can I give you a lift in my cab? Charley never had to stay after-hours to play for special parties and I'm sure Henri will let you off."

Holden detected a note of urgency in her voice, and eyed her irresolutely for a few moments. He burned his tongue with too large a mouthful of coffee, swallowed to gain time to compose a graceful refusal. He wasn't about to move from Henri's while there was even the barest chance that Fay Carroll might appear. So he hedged on Catherine's invitation. "Thanks, but I'd better stick at the piano tonight. It's only my first week, and it might not be politic to walk out on Henri. He's a good boss, but Charley warned me never to cross him up."

Catherine's departure obviously had been expedited by Marie Durand. And it had come about, clearly enough, after Saffron had used brutal means to call attention to her presence. Why didn't they want Catherine around? What special business tied together Gribov, the Learys, Henri and Marie? And if there was a connection between Catherine and Gribov, how did that affect everybody else?

Catherine seemed to accept his excuse. She briefly repaired her makeup, got her things together and prepared to leave. She paused briefly beside him once more and presented her cheek to be kissed. "Call me tomorrow for lunch," she said.

She touched his cheek briefly with a negligent hand and swept from the restaurant. Whatever any of the guests may have thought about Catherine Vaillant, she had style. And for that reason, if for no other, Holden had to admire her.

It was difficult for him to believe that she was only an embassy underling, for she invariably gave the impression of being enfolded in luxury. But at whose expense? Gribov's,

53

perhaps? Was that the reason the Durands had induced her to leave so abruptly before the party for the great Russian began?

Holden made his way back to the piano bar and swung into a new John Kander tune, aware that Saffron was watching him curiously from the bass end of the keyboard. For a while, the reporter merely nursed his drink but said nothing. Then, when Holden had finished the number and the three regulars were rolling dice to see who would buy the next round, Saffron asked softly, "How did you get mixed up with those two broads, Holden?"

Holden aimlessly hit a few chords. "Which two?"

"That Vaillant and the one you were with last night."

Holden was quick to catch the implication. "What's wrong with that?"

Saffron emitted a mirthless laugh in a single burst. "Ha!" Then he added with a frown, "Hey guy, you kidding?" But no matter how Holden plied him with questions, he wouldn't say more. Instead, he dipped deeply into his highball.

The sad-faced Italian picked up the theme. "Hey man, why you not go home with Catherine?"

Holden went back to the Kander tune and added embellishments. "I like it here."

"Merde."

"Maybe you want quiet place in Fontainebleau Forest?" The Italian persisted. "I have good place there and I let you have it. No rent." His mournful face softened. "Just want to see you get laid."

"Maybe some other time," Holden said. "But do I have to bring Catherine? Is that the deal?"

"Why? You no like Catherine?"

"Sure, I like her, but why do I have to bring Catherine to the place in Fontainebleau?" Holden asked idly. He didn't mean to encourage the Italian or discourage him, but thought it curious that he was being pushed toward an affair with Catherine Vaillant.

"Maybe you are afraid you can't handle Catherine," the French artist suggested. "She is a lot of woman."

Holden kept quiet with an effort, contenting himself with a virtuoso performance. The Italian laughed. "See? Americans are lousy lovers. She handle *him*, I bet."

54

The Frenchman was more sympathetic. "Catherine, she come here tonight to get you. She wants you. Why you not go?"

The German rumbled, "All you think about is to get laid."

The Italian grinned. "What else is there to think about?"

The four Learys descended on Henri's soon afterward, with the clatter and total confusion of an American family on holiday. Henri led the new arrivals to the specially prepared dinner table.

"Gribov will be here soon, also?" Henri asked.

Pat Leary boomed, "Sooner or later. He was a magnificent Scarpia tonight, and we stayed for all eight of his curtain calls. But I tell you, we had trouble finding a cab with the rain coming down so hard, so he'll probably have trouble, too."

"Ah, but the opera gives him a limousine and a chauffeur," Henri observed. "No trouble."

The *patron* proceeded to make arrangements for the party. Except for two waiters, the chef and the photographer, the rest of the help and the house girls were sent home. Holden, by unspoken agreement, remained at the piano; and the three regulars and Saffron were cautioned that the bar would close after a final drink.

Then, after sending the towering Shukri outside, Henri locked the big front door. "We will be very private," he said to the group about the festive table.

"D'ya know what's going on here?" Saffron murmured to Holden at the piano bar.

"Looks like the boss is having some fun."

"It's something more than that," Saffron said, seeming amused. "Henri's playing games and so is the professor."

"Like what?"

"Just watch and listen."

Pat Leary, attracted by Holden's improvisations, presently walked over to the piano bar, drink in hand. He listened awhile without saying anything. When Holden wound up with a riff, the older man said, "You know, Holden, you have a great deal of talent. Not many pianists could improvise like that."

"Wish I'd had you for a professor at the Curtis School," Holden replied. "They thought all I could do was pop stuff."

"When were you there?" Leary asked.

"Just before I came here. Dropped out when Charley Fourier got me this job."

"More's the pity. If you'd been at Yale, I could have made something out of you."

"Thanks." Holden lifted a glass of beer from the tray of a passing waiter and took a deep draught. He nodded toward Vivian, who was with her mother and was studiously avoiding him. "But I don't impress your daughter."

"You mustn't mind Vivian. She's terribly young."

Holden was feeling let down about Fay Carroll's non-appearance. He eyed Vivian with renewed interest. "She has a mature sense of values," he commented.

"Too damned mature, if you ask me." Pat Leary chuckled. "If she keeps waiting for that rich and famous guy she's looking for, she's going to miss a lot in Paris. She's not at all like her brother," and he indicated Gareth, who seemed to be delighted with the leggy photographer, Stephanie Rivet. "He just takes whatever comes along."

"And you don't mind?"

"I'd rather know what he's doing," was the bluff response, "and not have him carrying on behind my back, getting into all sorts of trouble."

"How old is Gareth?"

"Just nineteen, and he's staggered through his first year at Yale. If they don't toss him out, he'll be lucky. But you can't hold him down."

A sharp rattling of the front door handle cut short his response. Holden moved toward the door. "Somebody's trying to get in and the doorman's gone home."

Leary gave him a pat on the shoulder. "If that's Gribov, just bring him to our table, will you? He's in time for a drink and he'll need it."

However, the ever-alert Henri was there first. When the *patron* swung the door open, Holden was right behind him and saw a pathetically wet Fay Carroll standing in a dismal puddle of water.

Henri never had much patience with unescorted women after dark in Paris; after midnight, he had none at all. *"Fermé, madame,"* he snapped.

She protested in a voluble stream of French; he was about

56

to close the door on her when Holden intervened. "Hey, boss, she's a friend of mine."

Henri swung about in surprise. "This one, your friend?" After a moment's hesitation, he took another look at the latecomer. As he did so, Holden brushed past him and drew Fay inside. "What happened to you, honey?"

With a little cry of relief, she half-stumbled against him. "My cab broke down and I couldn't find another. Not even a bus. And I had no umbrella. The wind blew it right out of my hands and I had to walk all the way here without it." She made a mournful gesture and said to Henri in French, "You must excuse me, Monsieur Durand. You have not seen me before in this condition and perhaps you do not recognize me, but I have been here many times."

"Ah, but now I know you, madame," he replied in French. "It is Mrs. Bainbridge, is it not?"

While Holden knew no French, he could tell that *Bainbridge* was not in the dossier Fay had given him. "Her name's Fay Carroll," he corrected.

Fay let her hand rest in brief restraint on Holden's arm. To the *patron,* she said in English, out of consideration for Holden, "You have a good memory, Monsieur Durand, because it is almost four years since you've seen me. But I am no longer Mrs. Bainbridge. Mr. Holden is right. I am using my maiden name, Fay Carroll."

Just then the ever-practical Marie Durand descended on them with wrathful force. She said to Fay in French, pushing between the two men, "My poor child, you are wet and cold and starving and these stupid men debate your social credentials! Come with me!"

The *patronne* glared at her husband. "Sometimes I wonder about you, Henri Durand. If it is a woman who is in trouble, you are as insensitive as an American. But a man, ah, that would be different! Pah! Go back to your radio and your BBC!"

As she bore Fay off to the kitchen, both chattered in French. At the swinging kitchen door, however, Fay turned. "See you when I get dried off, Arch! Save me a drink, I'll need it!"

* * *

Henri muttered, looking fixedly over Holden's shoulder, "I did not know she was coming. . . . And the reporter, too. He just came in . . ."

Holden heard Pat Leary say behind him, "Never mind, Henri." When the pianist turned, he saw Leary, drink in hand, looking perturbed. The older man was about to say something else but stopped abruptly. Out of the corner of his eye, Holden caught a cautioning signal from Henri, a warning waggle of a forefinger.

"Gentlemen, I don't know what all this is about," Holden said, "but Miss Carroll is here because I invited her. Is anything wrong?"

"No . . . no, nothing wrong," Henri replied hastily. Then, recovering his poise, he said with a bland smile, "But, you see, we didn't expect her . . ."

Leary took up the burden of reassurance. "Of course we know her, and Gribov knows her too, from the time that her husband was the Public Affairs Officer at our embassy, so there is really no problem. She will be *our* guest tonight, too."

Henri and Leary looked at each other and smiled, but there was no doubt of their nervousness. Holden needed no seismograph reading to know that something had gone wrong—and he was properly apologetic. "If I've upset your plans—"

"Oh, no . . . no, my dear fellow, everything's *perfectly* all right," Leary assured him.

"Only, we had better make sure now that *she* is not surprised," Henri said with a significant raising of one eyebrow. And to Holden, "She does not know of the dinner for Gribov?"

"*I* didn't tell her," Holden replied. "Quite frankly, I didn't have any idea that she knew Gribov or"—and here he turned to Leary—"you and your family."

Henri tried hard to cover himself. "Had I known Mrs. Bainbridge—Miss Carroll, that is—was back in Paris, I would surely have invited her," he said to Holden. "You see, we all know each other, just as we know Gribov."

"Maybe I'd better have Amy go out in the kitchen and talk to her," Leary said, and drew his wife aside. The reporter, Saffron, meanwhile was watching the proceedings with a crooked little smile from his perch at the piano bar.

Henri, a hard note in his voice, jarred Holden out of his

confusion over the proceedings. "We must not neglect the piano, Mr. Holden."

Holden knew when he was being dismissed. The regulars at the piano bar watched him expectantly as he picked up his beer and settled himself again at the keyboard. Saffron, his crooked smile widening, said, "You sure stirred things up, Mac."

"Didn't mean to."

"Do you have any idea what's going on yet?"

"No, only the boss is pretty upset and I'm sorry about that."

"Don't be, Mac. He's got a lot of other surprises coming if he tries to go through with this little conspiracy."

"What conspiracy?"

"You'll find out."

The regulars had been talking among each other and had paid no attention to the conversation. But now, the big German broke in. "Arch, this girl you brought in . . ."

"Yes, what about her?" Holden was on edge.

"She has to be your girl from the Four Arts Ball, yes?"

The Italian teased Holden. "I give you my little place in the Forest of Fontainebleau for the weekend, if you are man enough."

"But for which girl?" asked the Frenchman.

The German asked with mock seriousness, "The question really is"—and he addressed Holden—"which one will be better for you, Arch? Catherine Vaillant, this new girl, or"—and he indicated Vivian Leary—"that thin little *maedl* over there with the big eyes and the expensive look?"

Holden tried to brush them off. "Don't confuse me, gentlemen. I can't handle more than one woman at a time." He set aside his beer glass and began fingering the keys in a tentative way.

"The new girl is so wet that you cannot tell about her," the German complained.

The Frenchman disagreed. "I know about her. She is good, very good. When she is dried out, you will see that she is a beauty."

"A beauty?" The Italian was incredulous. "That ragbag?"

"Before she married," the Frenchman explained, "she modeled while she was studying singing. She was an excellent

59

model, and cheap, too." Here he grinned. "Because she comes of a wealthy family and didn't need the money." He added, primarily for Holden's benefit, "She was a very fine nude, as you will see if you come to my studio and look at some of my paintings."

"You make him a good price for a nude of thees girl, Marcel?" the German asked.

"Sure." The Frenchman was cheerful. "I give him two nudes for the price of one."

Everybody stared hard at Holden and grinned, but he tried not to show his annoyance. It was shock enough for him to find out that Fay, far from being the lonely and neglected wife she had portrayed herself to be, was involved somehow in the mystery that now was entangling him. She had known Gribov, the renowned singer who seemed to be at the center of all the action. She had been a friend of the Learys, Gribov's American sponsors. And instead of being just another customer at Henri's, she seemed to have been one of the favored few. Here, she was not merely Fay Carroll. She was *Mrs. Bainbridge!*

But her career as a nude model seemed to be more upsetting to Holden than any of the other revelations about her. How could it be, he wondered, that she could be withdrawn and cold and even frigid with Bainbridge, then her husband, yet have no compunction about exhibiting her body for an artist's benefit? Could the whole pathetic scene before their liaison that early morning have been a contrived little shadow play to appeal to his sympathy and protective instinct? Was Fay a mere closet exhibitionist who enjoyed nudity for the effect it had on men but had difficulty responding to a sexual relationship?

So many questions about her crowded in Holden's mind that he almost forgot the doubts that Catherine Vaillant had aroused in him with her unexpected appearance at the restaurant and her equally unexpected departure. But between the two— Catherine and Fay—he felt he was being enmeshed in something complicated, perhaps even dangerous.

He ran his fingers over the keys aimlessly to cover his discomfiture. And meanwhile, the regulars wouldn't let up on him.

"So what happened to your beautiful nude, Marcel?" the German asked.

"After she married, this fellow at the embassy wouldn't let her pose for me anymore. Said it made her frigid!" The Frenchman smiled broadly. "Imagine! A woman who is a model becomes frigid because she is nude!"

"You warmed up thees model, hey, Marcel?" the German suggested.

Holden had just entertained the same disturbing thought. Valleau's rejoinder didn't make it any easier for the pianist, either. "A woman like this, with such a figure, must attract many men," the Frenchman observed. "But I," he protested virtuously, "I cannot think of such things. I am a painter."

"What is it with you painters?" the German inquired, winking at Holden, whose face was flushed in annoyance. "You say you do not get excited when you have a beautiful woman before you nude and all stretched out like this," he flung out his arms wide as he arched his back. "How can you paint such a one and not make love, I ask?"

"Don't be a fool, Eilers," the Italian observed coolly. "Sometimes they paint. And sometimes..." He paused with a leer. "Maybe they do not paint but do something else." He spread his hands as if to show how easily he had come to his not-unexpected conclusion.

Saffron saw how disturbed Holden was and tried to help him out. "Lay off, you guys. Here's Holden busting his ass at the piano to give you a good time, and you're all over him because he likes a girl he just met." The reporter paused and added, "Hell, maybe two girls for all we know."

"Oh, let 'em talk," Holden said with assumed professional assurance. He swung into an old Gershwin standard with modern overtones, "I Got Rhythm." For a little while, that and Saffron's intervention bought him time. But soon the regulars were on him again. He was too good a target to be ignored.

"Funny about that girl and her husband at the embassy," the Frenchman began.

The others, alert for more fun, perked up. "What about the husband at the embassy?" the Italian asked. "He had many rivals?"

"Nope, it was just the other way around," Saffron said. "This Spence Bainbridge figured he was a great lover." He elaborated with ironic intent, saying, "J. Spencer Bainbridge,

Yale man, Public Affairs Officer at the embassy here, man-about-town. Always playing around with somebody else's girl. And I felt sorry for the nice kid in the kitchen when she married him."

"But this Bainbridge and his wife, they make love, no?" the German asked.

"They act like lovers here at Henri's," the Frenchman added.

"What would you expect them to do, put on boxing gloves?" Saffron asked.

The Frenchman ignored Saffron. "I think these two, this Bainbridge and his former wife, were mixed up in the Gribov matter."

Holden couldn't contain himself now. He stopped playing. "What Gribov matter?" he demanded.

"This Nikolai Gribov, the Russian baritone, left the Bolshoi Opera when he was here in Paris and some friends helped him," the Frenchman explained. "I have a friend at the Quai d'Orsay, and he tells me this was the work of Americans, of the CIA."

Saffron roared with laughter. "The French Foreign Office thinks the CIA is under every bed."

"My friend heard it from the Sureté," the Frenchman insisted.

"So maybe the girl in the kitchen is with the CIA?" the German suggested.

"Sure, and that's what some say about Catherine Vaillant, too," Saffron added with a mocking air. "Holden here, he's just come to Paris. Is he CIA, too?"

Holden had to laugh when the Italian nodded and replied sagely, "Could be." The pianist turned to the Frenchman. "So what happened to Bainbridge?"

"After the Gribov business, Bainbridge went back to Washington with his wife," was the response. "And later, I heard about the divorce."

"But now, gentlemen, this lady has returned to Paris," Saffron said, intervening. In the manner of a Sherlock Holmes posing a question for a particularly obtuse Watson, he demanded, "What do you make of that?"

The Frenchman shrugged. "Who knows? With Americans, one must believe that anything is possible."

Saffron announced, with a wary eye on Holden, "I heard that the American embassy has made an urgent request for Bainbridge to work as Public Affairs Officer at the Special Session of the United Nations General Assembly here on disarmament next month."

Holden inadvertently hit a sour chord, then looked up from the keyboard in embarrassment. He couldn't keep quiet when the possibility was raised that Fay's ex-husband would be returning to Paris. "Are you kidding, Saffron?"

"Hell, no. It's God's truth." Saffron lifted one hand with palm outward as a sign of virtue. "The bid's in for him, sure enough, but we don't know yet if Washington will release him for temporary duty here. Anyway," he went on in an attempt to soothe the pianist, "if Bainbridge does show up, he's going to have a lot more on his mind than making trouble for you and his ex-wife. So relax, kid. Don't get in an uproar."

Holden protested faintly, "I'm not worried." But he skipped a few beats on the piano.

Just then Marie escorted Fay from the kitchen toward the piano bar. Dressed in a brown dressing gown many sizes too large for her, she looked like a refugee, but it didn't matter to Holden. The mere sight of her, despite all that he had heard, was immensely reassuring. The notion that he had to protect her came surging back, stronger than ever.

It didn't matter to him now whether Fay Carroll was a nude model, a singer, married or divorced, a CIA agent or an innocent bystander. All he knew was that he wanted her, loved her, and would not be discouraged even if her former husband did show up in Paris.

As Fay approached the piano bar, the Italian said, "Look how happy our friend is."

The German sighed. "He thinks he is in love."

Saffron raised his glass. "Gentlemen," he said, proposing a toast, "let's drink to love."

"Ah, go to hell," Holden muttered.

But when Fay came to him and let one small arm slide around his neck and briefly rested her cheek against his, she disposed of any remaining doubts he had. He asked in a low voice, barely audible above the patter of the piano, "Feel better, honey?"

63

She climbed on a bar stool next to him, disregarding the others. "I'm breathing," she said, "and I'm with you. And that's all that counts right now."

Marie Durand presented Fay with brandy in a wide-brimmed glass. "Drink, my child," Marie said in French. "It is to keep off the chill."

Fay took the glass in both hands. "A thousand thanks, madame."

"I only wish there was something nicer for you to wear," Marie went on. "But in a restaurant kitchen, one does not have a large wardrobe, is it not so?"

"It keeps me dry," Fay said. "The finest gown in all France could not do more."

As Marie returned to her usual post at the cash register, Holden reflected that the House of Henri had left no doubt where its sympathies lay between Fay Carroll and Catherine Vaillant. Fay was welcome, even under somewhat secretive circumstances; Catherine was not. And Holden, doing a few idle runs on the piano, couldn't help wondering what was behind the whole perplexing business.

Trying not to appear concerned, he asked Fay, "Did Amy Leary fill you in when she went to the kitchen?"

"Yes." She leaned toward him and continued in a low voice: "But I didn't know we were blundering into a supper for the Learys and Nikolai Gribov. Did you?"

With a humorous lift of his eyebrows, he said, "Honey, I don't know what the hell's going on."

Saffron overheard. "Take it easy, fella," he counseled. "We'll all know more when Gribov gets here."

Fay nodded. "That's my guess, too."

Holden nudged the conversation on a different track. "Where did you leave your things, honey?"

She ticked off the items on her fingers after putting down the brandy glass. "My shoes are in the oven. My stockings are drying behind the stove. And Joseph Citron, the chef, is ironing my dress. As for the rest of me, I'm well-baked and ready to serve."

Holden kept the piano going, but looked at her all the while he was playing. "You even looked good when you were wet."

"Now there's love for you," Saffron commented to nobody in particular.

The regulars were whispering together and weren't paying much attention just then. Fay murmured to Holden, "Now be honest, Arch. I must have been a horror when I came in, wet to the skin." She touched her head in dismay. "And my hair! I'd better hide before Nikolai Gribov sees me." She smiled reminiscently. "He used to say I was so-o-o-o beautiful." She mimicked the Russian's accent.

Holden couldn't help being disturbed at that. Like any lover, he was prone to torture himself with doubts over the slightest deviation in what he thought his beloved should be. And if Nikolai Gribov had thought her so-o-o-o beautiful, could it not be that their relationship was closer than he had been led to believe? "How well did you know Gribov?" he asked.

"Oh, my goodness!" she exclaimed. "First it was Dr. Beranger, and now poor old Gribov. You must think I've had a thousand lovers."

Saffron, who had been listening to the interchange with amusement, now interrupted. "Hey, you two, let's not have a fight when you've barely met. I'm supposed to know what's doing with Gribov and the Learys, but I don't. That's why I'm here. And I'll bet a plugged franc that that's why Catherine Vaillant showed up a little while ago." He chuckled. "Did you see old Marie give her the bum's rush? Hey, you can bet the Durands are in on anything Gribov is cooking up with the Learys."

Now it was Fay's turn to accuse Holden. "You didn't tell me Catherine Vaillant was here."

"Didn't think it was very important," he countered, wondering at the animosity between the two women. "What did she ever do to you?"

Fay said abruptly, "I don't like her, that's all."

"Lay it on, kid," Saffron muttered. "I'm with you all the way."

The whispering among the three regulars had ended, and they too now were interested observers at the piano bar. The painter, Marcel Valleau, was the first to speak. Nodding pleasantly toward Fay, he murmured, "You are looking well, madame."

She glanced up, apparently noticing him for the first time. "Marcel! How wonderful to see you again!" And in French, "A thousand pardons that I did not see you when I came in from the kitchen."

He came around to the side of the piano bar where she was perched on a stool and kissed her hand. *"Enchanté, madame. I thought I had forever lost my most beautiful model."*

She resumed in English, pretending to preen herself in her oversize brown dressing gown. "Don't you love this outfit? Right out of Givenchy's spring showing."

"You do yourself an injustice, madame," the Frenchman said. "You still have a figure."

The conversation tapered off. Holden, at Fay's prompting, swung into a reprise of the love songs he had been playing earlier.

"More stinking love songs?" Pastore asked sourly.

The Frenchman rebuked him. "Can you not understand, my friend? The American is making love to this young lady on the piano."

Pastore grumbled, "There are better ways to make love. In Italy, we do not hear of making love with a piano."

Fay nodded at the Italian. "But if one sings a love song?"

The Italian nodded in approval. "Singing of love is better."

"A friend of mine taught me a Parisian love song," Fay said. "The words were written long ago by Francois Villon . . ."

Marcel Valleau clapped his hands in delight. He quoted: *"Où sont les neiges d'antin?"*

She nodded. "Yes, 'Where are the snows of yesteryear?' . . . The old loves, the lost loves." She began singing softly in French, as if to herself, and the group fell silent. After a few bars, Holden caught the rhythm and embroidered on the melody with slow, haunting chords played *pianissimo* as background music.

She was pleased. Without pausing in her singing, she turned and sang to him as if they were alone, as if nothing else mattered to them. With the last words of the Villon poem, her voice melted into silence. There was a murmur of approval.

She drained her brandy glass, then glanced around the company, partly in pleasure, partly in embarrassment. "Thanks, but I don't sing very often."

Pat Leary, who had wandered over to the piano again to listen to her, wouldn't let her put herself down. "I think you did that very well, Fay." And to Holden, "You do a nice job of improvising. Had you ever heard that song before?"

Holden shook his head. "What the hell, professor, I just faked it."

"Pretty good faking, I'd say," the older man commented.

Impulsively, Fay leaned over the piano keyboard and murmured to Holden, "Now, play me a love song."

"I've run through just about all I know," he replied, then nodded toward the regulars. "They don't like love songs."

Marcel Valleau suggested, "Maybe *you* have written a love song, Holden?"

"I guess everybody in my business has written a love song at one time or another." He saw Pat Leary smiling and nodding. "How 'bout it, professor?"

"Sure," Leary said. "I wrote one the day after I met Amy." After a pause, he asked, "How about *your* love song, Holden?"

"Careful," Holden said. "I never heard of a piano player backing down when a composer asked him to show off."

Fay touched his arm. "Oh, please, Arch. I'd love to hear your song."

"Haven't played it in a long time," he said hedging.

But something in her manner, in the impulsive way in which she had appealed to him, touched him deeply. His tight, repressed mood softened and he finally nodded toward her. "Okay, honey. But remember, you asked for it!"

Pat Leary called from the edge of the circle around the piano bar, "C'mon, Holden. Let's hear it."

After a few introductory runs and chords, Holden leaned back, half closed his eyes and began singing in a clear if untrained baritone:

"I like a love song
    That's tender and slow;
Like it romantic
    —I do love you so;
Like happy music,
    A sweet melody
Fitted to lyrics

67

That rhyme tenderly;
Sing me a love song
    To remember you by;
A song that will thrill me
    Forever and aye."

Holden let his hands drift over the keys in a brief melodic reprise while Pat Leary boomed, "Bravo!" The three regulars, sated with love songs, were more restrained, as was Saffron. Not so Fay. With tears in her eyes, she whispered, "You wrote that for Caroline, didn't you?"

He nodded somberly. At long last, he thought, he had risen above his pain and loss. Singing Caroline's song had released him forever.

The *patron* barred the door after the three regulars finally left, and came to the piano bar, glancing at his watch. "Gribov is overdue," he remarked to Pat Leary.

"He'll show up, never fear," Leary replied as he listened to Holden with a little smile, nodding as he followed the pianist's improvising on a familiar theme. He objected at one point, "Don't do it that way, it's old hat. Do it some other way."

Holden didn't break rhythm, but looked up at the composer and grinned. "I took the easy way. You want to make it tough for me."

Leary blinked, then made a gentle gesture, a kind of salute, toward his wife. "Runs in the family." He rested one hand on Fay's shoulder, leaned over her and said quietly, "Haven't even had a chance to say hello to you or to ask how you are. Is everything all right?"

"Arch has taken good care of me," Fay replied. "But please, I don't want either of you to think that I barged in on your party for Nikolai Gribov."

Holden was so intrigued that he stopped playing momentarily. Fay nodded toward him. *"There's* the reason I'm here."

Leary said, "We're glad you're here, and we want you at the table with Nikolai when he finally arrives."

She was dubious. "If Arch doesn't mind . . ."

Holden was dismayed. His doubts, which he thought he had surmounted, came flooding back. And yet, he couldn't very well object to Fay's accepting the invitation. But he did want to find out why the company was so close-mouthed and why Gribov apparently had brought them together. And equally important, he desperately needed reassurance that Fay's meeting with her friends was indeed accidental; in all that she had told him about herself, she had very carefully omitted anything that referred to them, and he wanted to know why.

Once again, she seemed to have divined his doubting mood. Without explanation or prompting, she turned to him and sang the lyrics of the carefree little song they had put together in her apartment:

> "Wake me up in Paris
>> On a sunny, springy day;
> Let me feel the happiness
>> Of carefree youth at play.
> From the top of Butte Montmarte
>> To the islands of the Seine,
> From little yards to boulevards
>> I'll live and love again."

The song appealed to him. He accompanied her on the piano and bowed to her as they finished. "Didn't think you'd remember that," he said.

She came to him and kissed him. "Arch, darling, I don't forget things like that. It's part of a very happy time—and we're going to be a lot happier together."

Head down, he picked out chords in a minor key. "I sure hope so."

She stamped her foot. "Arch Holden, quit it! I'll not have you sulking." She pressed his face with both her hands. "Now please look at me and believe me. If you want us to go somewhere—just the two of us—say so and I'll bow out of this party at once."

She seemed so earnest, and the way she looked at him was so compelling that he had to believe her. Reluctantly, he replied, "No, guess we both had better stay here. But let's get away as soon as we can."

"It's a deal," she said. And with that he had to be satisfied.

* * *

Henri and the Learys had organized their party around the freshly decorated tables in the rear of the restaurant. The star of the evening, Nikolai Gribov, had not yet arrived. Holden, alone at the piano bar with Saffron, was still moody and had stopped with a riff after his latest set. He couldn't help watching Fay, in her grotesque brown robe, talking animatedly with her old friends in the rear.

Saffron called for another drink. Then he addressed Holden. "Hey Mac, what the hell's the matter with you?"

At first, Holden didn't want to come clean. "Just taking a break," he said.

"Want a drink?"

"No, thanks."

Both men fell silent. After a while, Saffron sampled a fresh drink a waiter had placed beside him. At about the same time, Holden absently let his fingers roam over the keyboard in his usual minor-chord routine, all the while watching Fay, the Learys, and Henri and his wife.

Saffron pushed his rain hat back on his head. "Hey fella, you got it bad."

Holden eyed him briefly. "What do you mean?"

"You've gone for that Bainbridge dame." The reporter nodded toward Fay.

"Is that *bad?*"

"Not if you know what you're doing, Mac."

"Name's Holden," he corrected good-humoredly. He didn't want to discuss his affairs with Saffron.

"Sure, Mac." The reporter took a long pull at his drink.

Holden made a hand-washing motion and rubbed his fingers. He was conscious that Saffron knew a lot that he didn't, and it bothered him. So he disregarded the reporter's prying manner and asked, "Why did you say awhile ago that it was strange I should know both Fay Carroll and Catherine Vaillant?"

The reporter grunted. "I didn't say that."

"Oh?" Holden was incredulous.

"I said," Saffron amended, "that it was funny you were mixed up with them two broads."

The pianist thought about that for a few moments, then asked bluntly, "Why?"

Saffron pursed his lips. "If you don't know, you better find out in a hurry, fella."

Holden persisted. "D'you know?"

Saffron nodded, but didn't say anything for a while. Holden had the distinct impression that the reporter was goading him to see how much he really knew. So he said, "Look, Saffron, let's quit playing games. I want to know what's going on."

"Okay." Saffron took off his rain hat and flopped it on the bar beside him. "But don't go jumping on me if you don't like what I tell you, see?"

"If all you're afraid of is a punch in the nose, forget it," Holden said, holding up both hands with fingers spread out. "I've got to earn a living with these—can't take a chance on bouncing them off that tough skull of yours." He did a few tentative runs on the piano and said to a passing waiter, "How'z about a beer?"

"Well, brace yourself, Mac." Saffron hunched over his drink. "You heard me say Vaillant was bad news, didn't you?"

"Yeah."

The reporter stared hard at his drink. "She's the one who broke up the Bainbridges' marriage...made that one down there," and he nodded briefly toward Fay, "go to a hospital ...mild breakdown or something like that, so I heard."

So his impression had been correct, Holden mused. Then, angrily, he taunted the reporter: "How do I know that's the truth?"

Saffron shrugged. "Ask anybody in that crowd down there." He indicated the group around the Learys. "Anyway," he went on, "why should I lie to you, Mac?"

Holden didn't respond at once. He recalled all too clearly how indignant Fay had been when she saw Catherine peering into the alcove at the Four Arts Ball; how poisonous Catherine had been in her references to Fay. If Fay had indeed been ill after the end of her marriage—as she had admitted and as Saffron now recalled—there probably was good reason for it. Fortunately, the damage had not been permanent.

Still, Holden was far from satisfied. He continued his probing. "And where does this Gribov fit in? Was Fay attracted to him? Was that part of her problem?"

"Hey, wait a minute, you're getting things all screwed up,"

Saffron protested. "Fact is, when Gribov defected from the Bolshoi troupe, it was Spence Bainbridge and his wife who hid him in their apartment; but that wasn't because of any romance between Gribov and this Fay you're so crazy about." He raised his glass, took a pull at it and set it down, then continued with great earnestness: "Now, I don't know this for a fact, but I always had a suspicion that the ambassador kind of hinted to Bainbridge to give the Russian a hideout but not to get caught."

"And did he get caught?" Holden asked.

Saffron nodded. "Yeah, somehow the Russians found out where Gribov was, raised hell with the French, and the ambassador had to send Bainbridge back to Washington. And some of the embassy crowd spread the story that Bainbridge got the heave-o over the Vaillant dame. But that just isn't so. Because, y'see, his wife went back with him, and I know for sure that both their families tried first to stop the divorce, then to hush it up. But when Bainbridge's wife began going to a psychiatrist and the psychiatrist absolutely recommended a divorce, that's when the split-up actually came."

"And now Bainbridge is coming back to Paris?" Holden again seemed almost to be talking to himself.

"Could be," the reporter said.

"Is Vaillant sleeping with Gribov?" Holden asked.

Saffron replied quickly, "I don't know that. But I wouldn't put it past her to try. I heard he used her as a translator a couple times. She sure knows about his movements; otherwise, why should she suddenly show up here tonight in a rainstorm?"

Holden's head was in a whirl. What he had heard about the Bainbridges and Catherine Vaillant fitted so well into what Fay herself had told him that he felt more protective of her than ever. And yet, was it mere happenstance that she, like Catherine Vaillant, had come to Henri's on this stormy night? True, Fay had insisted that he, Holden, was the only reason she had ventured out; and she did seem to have been surprised to learn that Gribov was expected. But then, as the pianist watched her while she was talking with Amy Leary just then, he couldn't help wondering about the rest of the puzzle.

He wondered how to take fuller advantage of Saffron's talkative mood. He thoughtfully sampled the beer the waiter brought him, then asked, "How did the Learys get into the act?"

Saffron lifted his empty glass, indicating to the waiter that he wanted a refill. He was now so well oiled that he talked rapidly with little prompting. "I know part of the story about the Learys, and I think I'm pretty accurate at guessing the rest," he began, "but you've got to understand that Gribov has kept his game plan so quiet that, even now, four years later, we still don't know all the details."

He broke off as Henri approached. "You will dine with us, M'sieu' Saffron?" the *patron* asked.

"Nah," the reporter said with a total lack of grace. "Think I'll just have another drink and bat the breeze."

"Ah, very well." Then Henri quietly broached the real reason for his intervention. "You must not forget that our guests like your piano, M'sieu' Holden."

"I'm just taking a break, having a beer," Holden replied.

Henri accepted that. "But of course you will play again?"

"Sure, boss." Obediently, Holden began a new set, but used such a soft touch that he could hear most of what Saffron said. The reporter, however, was beginning to slur his words. But that made it easier to lead him into more disclosures.

With a fresh drink before him, Saffron stumbled along with his story: "Y'know, Mac, Gribov really fooled th' KGB. He was singing in *Boris Godunov* th' night it happened. Lucky for him, the Bolshoi had cast him in a secondary role. Dunno if you ever heard *Boris,* but the baritone sings somebody . . . Damn, think the name is Tchelkalov . . ."

Holden didn't want to distract him. "C'mon, Saffron, you know I don't know *boris* from first base . . ."

Saffron swilled down his drink with relish. Now he was showing the effects of the liquor. He was sweating, his face was flushed and his speech was thickening rapidly. "Look, Mac. This Gribov ain't in 'Drop th' Handk'chief,' or suthin' like that, see? Thish's comp . . . complicated." He got the word out with an effort. "Y'see, the guy got out th' news he wants t' jump f'um th' goddam Bolshoi. But"—and he wavered on his bar stool—"he's also got to set time 'n' place once he gets to Paris, 'n' I gotta guess which people he used." He lifted one finger. "My guess, he used Amy Leary."

"Why Amy?" Holden asked.

"Becuz he knew her, thash why!" the reporter exclaimed in triumph. "Met her in the Brand . . . Brandon dance tour of Russia, see? Th' guy likes th' ladies, 'n' this Amy, hell, she musta been a cute dish." He nodded toward her. "Pretty cute dish still, huh?" he challenged. "Whaddya say, Mac?"

Holden was deliberately noncommittal. "Who steered the Learys onto Gribov?"

Saffron pulled at his drink and complained, "Mac, you got more goddam questions." He wiped his mouth with the back of his hand. "Now, like I say, th' Learys, they're in this, see? Mebbe the CIA paid 'em off, f'r all I know. *Anyway,*" and he rocked on his bar stool, "I figger Pat Leary gets to ol' Gribov first in Moscow. Checked at Yale, 'n' Yale tells me, sure, Leary got leave to go to Russia to do work on new opera, *Zhivago.* Y'know, *Zhivago?*"

"Pat Leary told me he wanted to do an opera based on the Zhivago story," Holden said, still keeping his piano routine going while he prodded the reporter. "How did Gribov figure in that?"

Saffron waved both hands. "Zhivago stuff was nonsense. But y'know? Bolshoi fell for it." He laughed shrilly, then took another drink. "Wha' happened? It got Leary to see Gribov, 'n' they fixed up scheme for Gribov to walk out in Paris: 's only way I c'n figger it, see?"

"And Gribov deserted his family in Moscow?"

Again, that waving of the hands to indicate Holden was on the wrong track. The reporter went on, "Gribov's got no family 'n Moscow, jus' his divorced wife. But . . . th' guy ran out on his sweetie. Name's Olga Var . . . Varen . . ." He gave up, not being able to pronounce the name and snorted, "Ah, th' hell with it. Gal's good, in th' Kirov Ballet. Y' know th' Kirov Ballet?"

Again, Holden nodded even though he knew as little about ballet as he did about opera. Saffron seemed satisfied. He hunched over the piano bar, continuing his disjointed story. "So now, Mac, Gribov comes t' Paris with th' goddam Bolshoi, see? An' he gets a tip to Amy tha' he's quitting th' night they put on *Boris.* Good opera, *Boris . . .*"

"But how did he do it?" Holden asked.

"Wait. I'll tell ya." The reporter swayed on his bar stool and lifted a forefinger to emphasize his revelation. "After th' second act, Gribov's s'posed t' be in his dressing room, see? But then, when th' third act starts, the guy's gone. Th' Bolshoi boss rushes to th' dressing room an', whaddya think? Gribov's dressed up a goddam dummy in his opera costume. Then, he skips. Amateur stuff, but he fooled th' KGB!"

"But Gribov must have had help."

"Nat'rly," Saffron went on. "My guess is our li'l Henri over there," and he nodded toward the *patron,* "steered him out from backstage . . . D'ja know Henri once sang in th' opera chorus jus' f'r th' hell of it?" The reporter paused, letting that sink in, then went on, "'s a fac'. An' I figger Henri got Gribov out the Rue Auber side door 'cuz it ain't ever watched, see? An' then, the Learys picked him up in a car, got him to th' Bainbridges' place an' that was it!"

"But the Russians found out Gribov was with Fay and her husband?" Holden prompted.

The reporter, whose eyelids by this time were drooping, delayed his answer while he fumbled with his wallet. As he produced a dog-eared clipping and began unfolding it with shaky fingers, he muttered, "Th' KGB's stupid, but not *that* stupid. Yeah, they found out, th' Russians squawked to th' French, 'n' somebody hustled Gribov by air to London. But," and now Saffron handed over the clipping to Holden, "jus' read this, willya?"

Holden took a chance on Henry's good nature and interrupted the set. He saw that the clipping was an announcement of the Kirov Ballet's visit to Paris in May, the following month— a routine bit of publicity except for the last line, which Saffron evidently had thought important enough to circle in black:

> The highlight of the tour will be three performances of *Giselle* in a new version choreographed for the Kirov Ballet, with Olga Varenka dancing the title role.

Holden passed back the clipping—which the reporter carefully restored to his wallet—and he asked, "Who's Varenka?"

"Thash Gribov's girl friend. An' he wants t' get her away

75

f'om th' Russians, see?" He waved a hand toward the group at the rear of the restaurant. "Thash why *they're* here."

"How d'ya know?" Seeing the *patron* frowning at him, Holden resumed his set.

"Got a good source at th' 'merican embassy, fella, thash how I know."

"Is this a CIA job?"

"Think th' CIA's crazy?" Saffron countered. "Jeez, y'gotta remember ol' de Gaulle tossed a lotta Americans in NATO outa France 'cuz he didn't like 'em. Th' French can be goddam independent, 'n' th' CIA knows it." He rocked back and forth in his chair. "Look, fella, thish's gonna be another amateur setup 'n' *you*"—he pointed a wavering finger at the pianist— "are gonna be the patsy, the fall guy if 'n y' don't watch out."

"Why me?" Now Holden was completely mystified.

Saffron pointed to Fay. "See *her?*"

"Sure."

"Well, fella, y' better watch out fer her, 'cuz she's a smart cookie. Knows a few tricks, too." The reporter grinned crookedly. Waving one hand, he added, "Y' got t' watch that other broad, too."

"Vaillant?" Holden prompted.

"Yeah, Vaillant," was the response in a hoarse whisper. *"Ma'mzelle* Poison, I call 'er."

Holden pressed Saffron hard for reasons why he should mistrust Fay as well as Vaillant, but received no satisfaction. The reporter, hard drinker though he was, seemed close to collapse. But before he passed out, Holden shamelessly urged him to disclose matters he ordinarily wouldn't have discussed in public with anybody. It was the only way he had to begin putting together the pieces of the puzzle before him to determine where he was supposed to fit in.

Still, the longer Saffron babbled on in his drunken stupor, the less sense he seemed to make. And instead of becoming more enlightened, Holden had the sense of being the innocent who had strayed into an intricate plot of which everybody had knowledge except him. Where he had been so sure of Fay before these complications began to unfold, he now felt himself being immersed in a quagmire of doubt. And as for Vaillant, he was more perplexed than ever over her role in the conspiracy.

He made one more attempt to clarify the position. He banged on the piano a few times with dissonance that temporarily, at least, brought the reporter out of his alcoholic stupor. "So wha'?" Saffron muttered, trying to focus his eyes on the pianist.

Holden demanded roughly, "Are you CIA?"

Saffron assumed a crafty and secretive air. "No, not me. But, thish is *my* story, see—"

As he babbled incoherently, Holden perceived that the reporter's main interest was to break the story of Olga Varenka's escape from the Russians and her reunion with Gribov when and if it happened. *"Gribov saves his Russian sweetie, see?"* Saffron mumbled at one point, drawing out an imaginary head-line with one hand in an uncertain horizontal movement. "Thash *my* story, *my* exclusive." He brought his glass to his lips through an erratic course and swallowed hard. Putting the glass down again, he assumed a drunkenly confidential air and assured Holden in a hoarse conspiratorial whisper, "Yer my pal, Mac. Won't let 'em do anything t' you 'n' yer girl, see? Y'gotta trust me..."

Holden tried to be soothing. "Sure... sure..."

The reporter went on, pointing a finger across the bar, "Look, Mac, th' KGBs got caught with their pants down last time." He shook a cautioning finger. "But not this time, see? They ain't complete fools, them KGBs, see?" He cautioned, "So button yer lip... fergit I told ja, hear?" With another wave of his hand, he managed to leave the bar stool without falling down, and lurched toward the inner recesses of Henri's. A waiter mercifully assisted him.

Fay came to the piano bar shortly afterward with two glasses of champagne. Having passed Saffron on the way, she was still laughing over something he had said to her. As she climbed on a bar stool, she handed one of the champagne glasses to Holden and announced, "I have strict instructions from Guy Saffron that I'm not to worry you."

He was instantly on guard. "Why would you want to worry me?"

She sensed it at once and reacted with spirit. "I don't know. Do you?"

"Well, you seem to know a lot that's going on here," he retorted in the same vein, hoping his unexpected directness

77

would surprise some answers. "But me, I'm way out in left field. I don't know a damn thing."

She was still holding the two champagne glasses. "Just for that, I won't drink with you." Her tone was crisp, but there was laughter in her eyes and he could tell she wasn't taking him too seriously.

Yet, Saffron's drunken conclusion that he might be involved in some kind of set-up had jarred Holden to such an extent that he wanted to test Fay once again. "How about a drink to no more secrets between us?" he challenged.

She set the glasses down on the piano bar, glanced about to make sure they were alone and replied in a low voice, "Arch Holden, I could *shake* you when you talk that way. Always hinting that I'm doing something awful—and I'm not."

He let his fingers drift over the keyboard. "What are you and Gribov up to?" he demanded.

She was soft-voiced but vehement. "You must believe me, Arch. Nikolai Gribov is an old friend who needs help, and he's asking for advice. We're trying to work something out for him. Is that so terrible?"

"What's his problem?"

"We'll all know more when he gets here."

He still thought she was fencing with him, and took a long chance because he wanted to see how she would react. "Do you know that Olga Varenka, his girl friend, is coming here with the Kirov Ballet?"

Fay glanced at him curiously. "How did you know that?"

"Read it in the paper," Holden said off-handedly, feeling it was only stretching the truth.

"And now you're trying to put two and two together, and it isn't going to be all that simple, darling." She was gentle, but reproachful; her words carried just a bit of sting to them. "You're just *too* suspicious."

He felt a touch of remorse. Even in that elephantine brown robe, he thought her wonderful; and the delights of the night with her flooded back through his consciousness.

"Do you *really* think I'd deliberately deceive you?" she asked softly, sensing a softening in him.

"No," he said carefully. "But I don't want you to get into trouble."

78

"Such as?"

"This Gribov business bothers me," he admitted with a calculated candor. "Do you *have* to be involved?"

She countered at once with another sharp question. "Do you want me to let down an old friend?"

"This Gribov means a lot to you, doesn't he?" he asked in return.

"Yes, but not in the way you suspect." Now her tone softened, but she didn't let up on him. "Nikolai Gribov was very kind to me at a time when I needed kindness and consideration, and I've never forgotten that. He treats me as if I were his own daughter."

Holden was surprised. "Daughter!"

She had to smile at his exclamation. "Oh, Arch! What am I going to do with you? You're so infernally jealous, and without any reason at all." She looked at him steadily, and there was laughter in her eyes. "Can't you believe that?"

He had to admire her spirit. If he had ever entertained the notion that she would be unable to fight her own battles because she had gone through an emotional crisis, he would have been dead wrong. She wasn't likely to yield to him merely because he was her lover.

He let his hands slip from the keyboard with an air of resignation, took up one of the champagne glasses and handed her another. "Here's to you," he toasted her respectfully.

She raised her glass, but changed the line. "No, Arch, here's to us."

They clinked glasses, drank champagne and held hands beside the piano keyboard until Henri approached. "Dinner is almost ready, madame," he said. "May I escort you?"

She pleaded prettily, "What about Mr. Holden? Can't he be with us, too?"

"Oh, most assuredly. But perhaps"—and to do the *patron* credit, he tried to be diplomatic about it—"Mr. Holden will not mind playing just a bit more on the piano until our guest of honor arrives."

"Then I'll keep him company, Henri," she said, quietly decisive. "He is all alone here."

The *patron* arched his eyebrows. "And Saffron, the reporter, he is gone?" he asked Holden.

Holden nodded toward the kitchen. "He's wandering about somewhere; maybe he needs help."

Henri caught the implication. "Ah yes, we shall take care of Mr. Saffron. Generally, Shukri finds a cab for him and sees him safely to his apartment. But perhaps, tonight, I can be of service."

As the *patron* departed on his rescue mission, Holden began playing some old Cole Porter standards with a steady, rhythmic beat. Fay, perched on a bar stool beside him, sang softly. They were interrupted by a great squealing of brakes outside followed by an imperious blasting on an auto horn. Next, Henri's stout front door reverberated with a tremendous banging. When the *patron* swung it open, in marched a dramatic figure with a leonine head of tousled black curls laced with gray and a long black cloak suspended from massive shoulders.

"Ah, Nikolai!" Henri exclaimed, embracing him.

At once the singer was surrounded by the four clamorous Learys. Fay and Marie Durand also came forward. Holden stopped playing the piano.

Gribov emerged laughingly from the onslaught of his friends and was about to take off his cloak when he noticed Fay. With three long steps he was beside her, caught her in his arms in a bear hug, whirled her off the ground as easily as if she had been a child, and kissed her.

"Still my precious little one!" He held her off and examined her, then pretended to scowl in displeasure. "But what has happened to all your pretty clothes?" He sniffed the air. "And your perfume? You always had such nice perfume."

"Oh, Nikolai, it's so good to see you again," she said, truly delighted. "And damn my clothes and damn my perfume. My clothes are hanging up to dry and my perfume washed away in the storm."

"What does it matter?" He embraced her again. "You are always beautiful."

She laughed out of sheer exuberance. "And you are always the same, Nikolai. You will always make me feel as if I'm sixteen even if I should live to be a hundred."

Almost unnoticed, Holden had resumed his Cole Porter medley. He was playing "It Was Just One of Those Things," and looking thoroughly bemused.

Chapter Three

Nobody should ever take a baritone for granted. He is a man of many faces, many moods. He seldom does what is expected of him. And he mightily enjoys springing a surprise.

Look at his roles. He may come on strong as Escamillo, the swaggering hero of a cigarette girl. Or he may materialize as Baron Scarpia, a heartless and despicable villain. Then, too, he is well able to play Figaro, the ingenious barber and super matchmaker of Seville. Or he may be a cunning, shriveled Rigoletto, the vengeful hunchback who kills the being he loves best.

All music-loving peoples prize their baritones. Among them, the Italians are the most cherished, the British the most over-rated, the Americans the least appreciated and the Russians the most sought-after.

For while Russian baritones obviously exist in sufficient numbers in their own motherland to fulfill operatic repertory, so few ever circulate freely in the Western world that they attain a special value. Even the critics occasionally are kinder to a visiting Russian baritone than he actually deserves.

This accounts in large measure for the recognition that came so swiftly and fully to Nikolai Gribov, the Bolshoi Opera's best-known baritone, when he defected to the West. Once he began singing at Covent Garden in London, with occasional forays into Paris, La Scala in Milan and the Metropolitan Opera in New York, he did the rest with the sheer power and brilliance of his voice.

Before long, with numerous appearances on the BBC and the American TV networks, his impressive head with its sharply aquiline features became familiar to operagoers everywhere.

His stocky, barrel-chested figure on its slender legs—the Babe Ruth of opera, one critic called him—became recognized on both sides of the Atlantic.

To the small party gathered at Henri's past midnight of that rainy spring evening in Paris, therefore, Nikolai Gribov's visit was an occasion.

On the surface, it was a fun evening. After Henri had seen two waiters load the incapacitated Saffron safely into a cab and head him for home, the party took shape.

Gribov was at the center table of the U with Fay Carroll, now in her dried clothes, at one side of him and Henri at the other. Holden, having finally been given a special dispensation to leave the piano, sat next to Fay, with Vivian Leary on the other side of him. Across from them, Amy Leary was next to Henri with her husband; Marie Durand and the gangling Gareth filled out the rest of the setup. The photographer, Stephanie, was taking pictures all the while dinner was served.

Henri made his guests comfortable, but until dinner was over, he thoughtfully relieved Gribov of the need to make conversation. He presided in an agreeable manner—recalling how long and favorably he had known Amy and Pat Leary, and exchanging anecdotes with them. It was all pleasant and good-humored, but after a while Holden began wondering where Henri was leading them.

Several times, Holden tried to strike up a conversation with Fay, but she and Gribov were intently conversing in low tones during most of the dinner, breaking off only when Gribov and Henri exchanged a few words.

It was on the tip of Holden's tongue to make a protest over being neglected, but a warning glance from Fay made him change his mind. He saw he couldn't have it both ways: either he had to believe in her and have faith in what she was doing or he had to forget about her. And, as he had long since realized, he couldn't forget about her.

At his elbow, he became conscious that Vivian Leary was restless. "Don't you ever talk?" she asked plaintively.

"What is there to say?"

She drew breath sharply in exasperation. "I do wish they'd let me talk to Mr. Gribov. He's so handsome."

Holden noted that Gribov had been looking at the pretty American girl part of the time Fay had been talking to him. "All in good time, Vivian," he counseled, amused and unimpressed. "I'm sure Mr. Gribov will get around to you."

She was staring at the Russian now, evidently having caught his eye. "Do you s'pose it's true that he was paid seventy-five thousand dollars for a single concert in Miami?" she asked, not shifting her gaze.

"Who told you that?"

"Read it in *Newsweek*."

"More power to him," Holden replied.

"He's earned millions of dollars since he defected from the Bolshoi," Vivian added, satisfied now that she had attracted his attention. "Isn't that wonderful?"

Holden grunted. "Even a Russian knows how to grab the main chance."

Then came the inevitable question. "Is he married?"

"Divorced."

"Oh." Vivian folded her hands and rested her chin on them, seemingly in deep thought. She said, half to herself, "He may be a little on the old side, but he's still good-looking."

Holden reflected that Vivian had grandiose ideas about Gribov that might eventually cause her embarrassment and grief. He repressed the urge to tell her about Olga Varenka. Let her find out for herself, he thought; it would be a part of the stern business of growing up.

Pat Leary, noticing his preoccupation, called from the opposite table, "Can you play *'Pari Siamo'* from *Rigoletto?* Maybe we can persuade our friend Gribov to sing for us."

Before Holden could reply, Gribov pinched the skin of his throat with thumb and forefinger and made hissing noises indicating hoarseness. "Tonight I was Scarpia in *Tosca*, my friends, and I must take time to recover. It is big part. Singing"—and he smiled to take the edge off his words—"is not like kicking soccer ball." He managed his English slowly, but spoke with a decided accent, pausing now and then to search for the English phrasing of what he was thinking in Russian.

Leary waved a hand good-naturedly. "Ah well, we tried."

Holden was grateful, at least, for that polite refusal which saved him from having to show his ignorance—both to Gribov and Leary.

Gribov, meanwhile, had inclined his head to listen to something Fay was saying; however, as he glanced up and again met Vivian's eyes, he smiled broadly. Fay seemed not to have noticed the byplay.

The meal, which had been one of Henri's best, was nearly over. It had been simple but satisfying to all at the tables except Holden, who was in no mood to appreciate it. The others had enjoyed a clear soup, *tournedos a la béarnaise* with vegetables underdone in the French mannner, some exquisite wines, a crisp salad, *a croûte à la lyonnais* for dessert and strong black chicory coffee.

Everyone was waiting expectantly for Henri. But when he arose to cap the evening, he played the genial host and carefully avoided, even indirectly, referring to the pending engagement of the Kirov Ballet. That, Holden suspected, must have been on everybody's mind.

Out of consideration for Gribov, Holden and the two young people, the *patron* spoke English. He was brief and circumspect, saying: "It was good of you to come to Henri's tonight, my friends, for this joyful reunion with our Nikolai. No doubt, we will all see each other again." Here, he permitted himself a discreet smile, but Holden noticed that Gribov faced forward and did not change expression. The *patron* concluded, "But before Marie and I say good night, our guest of honor has something to say to you."

Gribov arose, wineglass in hand, and proposed a toast to Henri and Marie, in which everybody joined. Just as the company was disposing of napkins and preparing to push back chairs, the singer remarked in an offhand manner, "Yes, as Henri has said, we will see each other again. I love Paris and . . ." He hesitated for a few moments. "I want to stay here after opera season. But"—he let his big voice slide into a softly confidential tone—"I need *dacha*, what we call summer place in Russian. It is for hot weather."

Holden suspected the *dacha* would be for almost anything except hot weather. Probably, he guessed, it would eventually be a hiding-place for Olga Varenka if she could be persuaded to defect.

Gribov was standing, surveying his friends with an affable smile. "Who has *dacha?*"

The company seemed unresponsive at first, then there was a buzz of speculation about friends who had summer places. But none of the suggestions seemed to please the big Russian baritone. He had special needs.

Holden recalled that the sad-faced Italian at the piano bar had offered him a place outside Paris for a liaison with Catherine Vaillant.

During a break in the conversation, he addressed Henri, "Y'know, Enzo Pastore has a place in the country. Heard him say it was in some kinda forest."

"Ah, yes." Henri made a fist, as if he were suddenly grasping this possibility. "In the Fontainebleau Forest, I believe, near Barbizon?"

Holden shrugged. "Could be. I just heard him chatter about it at the piano bar."

"This Pastore, who is he?" Gribov seemed uneasy as he turned to the *patron*. "You know him?"

Henri nodded. "He was here earlier tonight, comes often to the piano bar. He is an Italian, has a dancing academy."

"Oh-hoh!" The Russian seemed pleased. "An Italian dancing master. He will have good *dacha!*"

"I shall see him and make arrangements for you," Henri said.

With that, chairs were pushed back and the company arose. They said their good-byes and thanked their host and hostess. Holden hung back just a bit while Fay kissed Marie and took leave of Henri.

"We're going to Gribov's suite at the Crillon," she told him as they prepared to leave. "He wants to talk to us."

"The guy's been talking to you all night," Holden observed with just a touch of rancor. By this time, they were outside the restaurant and standing on the Place St. Michel, somewhat separated from the rest of the company. The rain had stopped. Only a few late passersby took notice of them.

"There are things we couldn't talk about at dinner," she said.

"Then go ahead and see him at the Crillon if you want."

He turned away, in an effort to curb his anger. The last place he wanted to spend the evening was with Gribov.

She plucked at his arm. "Where are you going?"

"Home. Where did you expect?" There was no reason for him to go to the Crillon, after all. Nor did he understand why Fay was so anxious to go.

However she wasn't going to permit him to stomp out of her life in anger. She tightened her hold on his arm and made him stop. "Don't be mean, Arch."

He tried to shake her off. "Look, Gribov wants you; he doesn't want me. And if that's the way you want to play it—"

"I'm not playing, Arch Holden," she said firmly, clinging to him. "And this isn't a question of what Nikolai Gribov wants. This was my idea, and I hope you'll help me."

"Do what?" He paused and regarded her suspiciously.

Alert to press her advantage, she tried to soothe him. "There are some things you can do that I can't possibly attempt to do. And both of us will have to talk it over with Nikolai before this affair goes any further."

"What affair?"

She glanced around to make sure she wasn't overheard. "It's about the ballet dancer—the one you mentioned to me, remember?"

"Olga Varenka?"

She put a finger to her lips. "Please . . . be careful. This has to be kept as quiet as possible."

She was in for a shock if she thought no one had linked the Kirov announcement with Gribov's appearance in Paris. "The reporter, Guy Saffron, already knows something's up," he told her flatly.

"That's dreadful." She drew her wrap about her and shivered just a little. "And if the Russians suspect—"

"Do they?"

She hesitated, then resumed in a low voice, "Nikolai says a friend told him that the KGB put a special guard on Olga before the Kirov company left Leningrad."

"Then there's no help for it and you'd better lay off," he said. "Honey, whatever you did for Gribov last time was enough. Don't try it again with Varenka. It's too damned dangerous."

"I can't let Nikolai down." She added impatiently, "And, Arch, you can't either. We're both in on this."

He shook his head slowly in disbelief. "Why me?"

"Because you can do things I can't do," she repeated.

"Oh?"

She indicated a big, chauffeur-driven Mercedes that was edging to the curb outside Henri's not far from where they were standing. "There's Nikolai's car, Arch. He'll be out in a minute. Please come with me."

She looked at him so urgently, so appealingly, that he swallowed all his doubts and suspicions. He told himself that he could go along to the Crillon with her amd merely listen. And if he didn't like what he heard, he could simply pull out.

As they turned and walked together toward the waiting Mercedes, Gribov emerged from Henri's shouting his good-byes, his black cape billowing about him. The Leary family was a short distance away, waiting for a cab. But when Vivian Leary saw the Russian, she ran to him with outstretched arms.

"It's been so marvelous being with you tonight, Mr. Gribov!" She stumbled and would have fallen, but he caught her just in time and roared at her, "I am Nikolai, my little one. Not 'mister.' Just Nikolai. Do you understand?"

"Oh, yes . . . yes, Nikolai." Vivian was almost breathless, and her eyes glistened in the wan light shed by the street lamps.

He patted her roguishly on the cheek. "We have old Russian saying, 'Better for man to run after woman, he catch her. But if woman run after man, he get away.'" He threw back his head and laughed, then with a courtly gesture kissed her hand. "I see you again, my little one."

By that time, Gribov had paused at the door of the Mercedes, which the chauffeur was holding open for him. He glanced around, saw Fay and Holden, and beckoned to them with an imperious wave of his arm. Gribov casually embraced Fay again and helped her into the car. Then both men got in beside her.

As the Mercedes edged off across the bridge to the right bank of the Seine, Gribov chuckled. Fay asked, "Why are you laughing, Nikolai?"

"This Vivian, this pretty little girl, she is so like her pretty mother," he replied in high good humor.

"It must be great to have a family fan club," Holden commented sourly.

Fay pinched his hand as if to say, "Behave yourself." But what she said aloud was, "Pay no attention to him, Nikolai. He is only joking."

The singer replied, "In Russia we have saying, 'When you cannot tell the truth, tell joke.'" He roared with delight, thrust an arm about Fay and hugged her until she called for mercy.

Not charmed by this display, Holden said half to himself, "I need a drink."

Once he had brought his guests to his suite on the top floor of the Hotel Crillon and slipped into a dark satin dressing gown, Gribov stood beside a window overlooking one of the great sights of Paris—the dimly lit Place de la Concorde. One by one, he pointed to the statues of women of heroic size along its perimeter and, under his breath, named the cities of France for which each one was a symbol. He had memorized the lot and was proud of his feat.

He concluded with a flourish, pointing to his right and announcing, "American Embassy"; to his left, "Ministry of Marine"; and off at an angle toward a small triumphal arch, "Champs Elysées." He clapped his hands, applauding himself, and concluded, "I am good tour guide, yes?" Neither disputed him. Satisfied, he turned to Fay. "And now, madame, you will have drink? Scotch highball with water? My memory is good, yes?"

She agreed. "You remember everything—statues, operas, even drinks . . ."

He beamed. To Holden, he proposed, "You want good drink?"

"Good and strong. I can stand it."

"Vodka and lemon soda? Plenty of vodka?"

"A Vodka Collins, we call it in America, and that will be fine."

Gribov busied himself at the small bar at one side of the Crillon apartment's elaborate living room. "My servants sleep, I tend bar for you," he explained. Evidently, he took pride in every small accomplishment, for he fussed over the drinks, chattering away in broken English all the while, and eventually handed a glass each to Fay and Holden.

For himself he poured a Coca-Cola. Lifting the glass, he explained, "After I sing, I drink no alcohol for at least twelve hours. Alcohol inflames throat, so I take good American drink." After a deep pull at his glass, he went on, "Many things good in America—opera house, concerts, big audiences, plenty of money. But American embassy?" He pointed to his right scornfully, then made an abrupt gesture of dismissal. "No good for me."

Fay elaborated for Holden's benefit. "Nikolai thinks it was unfair, after we took the risk of sheltering him after his defection, that the State Department recalled my former husband."

"They break up your marriage!" Gribov exclaimed wrathfully, sinking into an easy chair across from the couch on which they were sitting.

"You may blame the State Department for a lot of things, but not that," Fay observed quietly. "To be truthful, my marriage would have ended a lot sooner if we hadn't had a common interest in helping you."

"Ah, you are great lady, madame." Gribov nodded in approval. "But can you defend American Embassy now when I ask for help and they say no?"

"If there is another defection, the embassy doesn't want to be caught between the Russians and the French," Fay explained to Holden, "so the ambassador really wasn't very nice to Nikolai."

Holden nursed his drink, waiting to see how Gribov would react. It didn't take long. All at once, the Russian jumped up and began pacing the room. "My Olga Varenka comes soon to Paris with Kirov Ballet, it is in the newspapers," he began. "My friend, who comes from Moscow to Paris, tells me she wants to defect. I tell ambassador of your country..." And he whirled and pointed accusingly at Holden. He elaborated, "Your *free* country. But ambassador is frightened. He says he can do nothing, sends me to somebody else, maybe he is ambassador, too. I do not know."

Fay interjected, "From the description Nikolai gave me, it must have been Cary Wisner, who is in the political section and speaks Russian."

"His Russian!" Gribov commented. "Worse than my English!" His anger mounted. "Your Russian experts, what good are they? One day they say, 'Don't help Russia. Put more atom bombs in Europe.' And next day, they say, 'We make mistake, sell Russians wheat.' So you make business with them and they laugh at you." He drew breath. "Solzhenitsyn is right. You have mortal enemy and you do not know how to deal with him."

Fay responded patiently, "We can't change our government's policy, Nikolai, but as ordinary citizens maybe we can help you."

"Is a risk, a big risk," the Russian said. He turned to Holden. "You understand thees?"

Holden raised his hands palms upward in a gesture of helplessness. "I don't understand much of anything."

"Thees young man," Gribov said to Fay reproachfully, "is sensible, is afraid. Do not force him . . . *please*."

Fay protectively thrust her small hand in Holden's big one. "We can depend on Arch. He is with us."

"Like Bainbridge?" Gribov asked suddenly, whirling about. It was almost an accusation that Fay was trying to make do with someone of lesser ability.

"From what you say," Fay replied with an air of sweet reasonableness, "our government will not help us this time; and my *former husband*"—she stressed the description with a look of distaste—"couldn't help us at all now. He would be going against official policy."

"But he is returning to Paris, yes?" the Russian insisted.

"I don't know that. And I don't really care," she answered with complete indifference.

Holden now felt called upon to tell what little he knew. "Saffron says yes, the Paris embassy has asked for Bainbridge," he told Fay. "The embassy wants him to handle the press for the UN Special Assembly on disarmament, but Washington hasn't given its permission yet."

"Ho!" The Russian snapped his fingers. "We will see Bainbridge. For sure." He added earnestly for Fay's benefit, "Is very good man, my little one."

Now Fay openly pleaded for Holden. "Here's a better one," she said, linking arms with him. "Even if Spence Bainbridge were available, we wouldn't need him."

The Russian acknowledged defeat, waving one hand in a deprecating gesture and sinking into a nearby chair. "Is as you wish, my little one."

Holden began to comprehend dimly the reasons behind Fay's insistence on his involvement in the arrangements to spirit Olga Varenka away from the Kirov Ballet. Fay seemed to want to blot Bainbridge out of her life completely, to prove to herself that she did not need him now and never did. Having found Holden to be sympathetic, even protective, she seemed insistent now on drawing him completely into her life. To as capable and strong-minded a person as Fay, he had to be something more than someone to share her bed, someone to help her overcome her fears. He also had to have a courage and daring to match her own. Why? Somehow, she had decided that he must prove himself to be superior to Spence Bainbridge—and he'd never even seen Spence Bainbridge. He felt distinctly uncomfortable about that—it was like being matched with a ghost.

He had absolutely no desire to be a hero. His temperament was distinctly unheroic. As a musician, his fundamental training had always been to comply with the instructions of a conductor, to work in harmony with others in a band and leave the star performances—the solo efforts—to those more steeped in the need for self-expression. He was always the dependable operator in the rhythm section, carrying the beat, filling in the background with intricate keyboard improvisations but never getting in the way of the stars.

It went against his character as well as his training to be asked, as Fay now seemed to be suggesting, to smuggle a troublesome Russian ballet dancer out of the custody of the KGB. Why, in all reason, he asked himself, should he even try to make so foolhardy an attempt at what amounted to an international kidnapping? For Gribov? Certainly not. The big Russian's inflated ego repelled Holden quite naturally: what good operator in a rhythm section had much respect for a posturing, strutting star performer?

However, Holden realized, walking out on Gribov at this juncture also meant giving up Fay. It had been one thing to speculate that he could quit when he saw that the job would be unimaginably difficult. He saw now that he simply couldn't give up. He wanted Fay too much—more even than he had realized. After all that he had gone through with the death of his wife and baby in the past year, he found that he could not so easily give up a chance at ultimate happiness—with Fay. And if that meant he had to be a better man than Spence Bainbridge, he'd have to make the attempt.

Never was there a more reluctant hero than Holden. With amused resignation at his own lack of spirit, he felt like a buck private in the rear rank of some army unit who had suddenly been placed in charge of a raid to confound the enemy by rescuing a high-ranking prisoner.

But what, specifically, did Fay and Gribov want him to do, if he were enlisting for the duration? So far there had only been hints.

Would he be expected to barge backstage at the Paris Opera, fend off six husky Russians as if he were a great movie hero and walk off with the exquisitely beautiful ballet dancer resting cozily in his arms? Or was he to be provided with a submachine gun to confront a platoon of KGB operatives and force them to yield their fascinating prisoner? His imagination was running riot, but he had sense enough to repress these heroic images. "Well, let's get on with the job," he finally said to Fay, squeezing her hand to let her know that he was sticking with her.

She understood, and was grateful. "We'd better get Nikolai's ideas first," she murmured, never moving from Holden's side. "After all, he's sounded out the embassy."

"Embassy give no help, I tell you," Gribov, seeming discouraged, rested his brow in his hand as he sprawled in the chair opposite him. "They say only, 'We monitor.'" He appealed to them. "What is thees *monitor?* What they mean?"

Fay suggested, "I'm just guessing that the ambassador had you talk to the CIA people at the embassy. And what they do, if they can't handle an operation themselves, is to keep in touch with those who actually do the work. In this case, us."

Gribov shook his head, obviously puzzled. "What we do then? I report to the CIA and say, 'We do thees'? And they say, fine, go and get shot! Thees is monitoring?"

"Maybe not that bad, but you have the general idea," Fay responded. "Only, you cannot be the go-between, Nikolai. You are too well known and the KGB will be watching you."

He tossed his hands in the air as if he could see no end to the complications of rescuing Olga Varenka. "The CIA, they watch me also?" he suggested. "Everybody watch me?"

"It's possible," she agreed, but didn't seem to be dismayed by the notion. "Our go-between has to be somebody who's not at all known to either the diplomatic or the intelligence community, or even to the press."

It flashed through Holden's mind that Saffron had warned earlier in the evening about his role in Fay's scheme—and he had been sure there was one. Was this what the reporter meant? Uncomfortably, he muttered to Fay, "Is that what *I'm* s'posed to do—be the go-between?"

She gave his hand an impatient pat. "Hush." And to Gribov, she continued, "You needn't think the Americans are letting you sink or swim for yourself. The go-between may actually save you if all of a sudden you are caught in an impossible situation. I've seen it work before. When the CIA monitors a job, that means the Americans want it to be successful but they don't want to take responsibility."

"But thees is nonsense," Gribov protested. "If Americans want to help us against KGB, they should come out strong. Not hide. Not work with thees go-between."

Fay continued to argue warmly for acceptance of the American embassy's terms. "We can't have everything our way, Nikolai. At least, if our go-between shows the Americans they have to intervene, then maybe at the last minute they will help."

Gribov objected. "Is not sure."

"Nothing is sure," she countered. Turning to Holden, she said, "Arch, would you be willing to work with the people at the embassy for us?"

And there it was—the assignment. In a shaky voice that betrayed his panicky inner feeling, he asked, "Who am I supposed to see? What do I say?"

Fay was reassuring. "I'd try Wisner first." In her own quiet way, she seemed to have assumed command. To Gribov, she said, "Nikolai, we need a note from you identifying Arch as our liaison."

Gribov was thoroughly unimpressed. "How you spell thees 'liaison'?" He asked the question with a deprecating, half-humorous air.

93

Holden, in this instance, felt some sympathy for him. "And tell me what I say when the embassy guys tell me to go soak my head, they don't know me, they don't want to know me."

With a smile, she murmured, "Will I have to do this myself?"

Holden felt rebuked. "I said I'll give it a whirl. But I'm nobody in the diplomatic league, don't forget that."

"Just be sensible and protect us," Fay replied. "That's all you *can* do."

Gribov raised another difficulty just as Holden realized that, as Saffron predicted, he had been neatly positioned to be blamed if the plot failed. "So many people know about thees now," the Russian complained. "Learys know, Henri and Marie know, Americans know, Russians maybe know, even reporter knows. Maybe KGB kills my Olga, then say, 'Suicide.'" He pursed his lips and nodded somberly. "Is possible, no?"

"A lot of people also knew you wanted to defect," Fay retorted warmly. "You told me yourself the KGB said they'd shoot to kill if you tried it. And still, we got you out of there, didn't we?"

He remained gloomy about their prospects for snatching Olga Varenka. "Is different now."

"No," she insisted, "the chances are about the same, about even. The Russians may suspect, but they still don't know how or when the attempt will be made—and that's our advantage. We call the time, just as we did in your case."

"They have guard on Olga," Gribov reminded her.

"They had guards on you, too." She crossed the room impulsively, stood by him and tried to rally his sagging spirits. "Don't be so negative about everything, Nikolai. You want Olga, don't you?"

"Want her alive, not dead," he responded.

"The KGB won't dare harm her, not after the Kirov announced she would be the special performer during the Paris engagement," Fay assured him. "How would it look if all of a sudden Olga Varenka does not appear in Paris, or if she is injured in such a way she can't dance? No" — and she presented herself at her appealing best before him—"the only thing the Russians could do to stop us is cancel the Kirov Ballet's engagement in Paris; and if they did that, the French would take it as a mortal insult."

Holden was more than ever impressed with the way she was taking charge. With Fay resolving each difficulty as it was raised, the thing seemed to him to be risky—very risky, in fact—but *do-able* if everything broke well.

Still, he hardly agreed that the chances for success or failure were about even, which was her estimate.

On balance, he felt a bit more hopeful about his own projected role as a go-between with the CIA in this wholly amateur conspiracy. He still didn't know what to expect, or how or when the attempted delivery would be arranged.

While he was thus preoccupied, Gribov was at a desk off in a corner, at Fay's prompting, scribbling on blue Hotel Crillon notepaper. Then he folded the paper in a blue Hotel Crillon envelope, crossed the room with a few big strides and presented it to Holden with a flourish.

"Your credentials," Gribov explained. "It say you represent me, Nikolai Gribov." And he tapped himself proudly on the chest with an operatic gesture.

Holden took the envelope and stared blankly at it. He asked Fay, "What do I do with it?"

"Show it at the embassy," she said. "I'll make an appointment for you as soon as possible."

Gribov escorted them to the door, showering them with thanks. And as they waited for the elevator, Holden asked, "Will it be my place tonight?" She lifted her face to be kissed. "My place," she answered. "Why change when everything's going so well?" He was still kissing her when the elevator stopped at their floor and the doors clicked open.

Holden scarcely expected to overcome Fay's fears of frigidity at the very beginning of their relationship. He knew it would take time, care and sympathy—and a lot of encouragement. Moreover, having seen how decisively she was able to handle herself under stress, he dismissed out of hand any feeling he had that the failure of her marriage had caused her to shrink from responsibility. The problems of sexual maturity, however they may have affected Fay, did not seem to have interfered with her intellectual competence. And for that, he admired her all the more. Despite her show of strength in their talk with Gribov that night, Holden could tell that she still looked to him for protection. Why else would she have wanted him to be the one to sound the alarm at the American embassy if their attempt to deliver Olga Varenka involved them in deep personal danger?

It heartened him now to feel that she had confidence in him. And for that reason, he did not worry quite so much as he had at the outset about Saffron's warning that the conspirators might be looking for a fall guy. That, Holden decided, was a remote possibility now. If it did develop, he would have to deal with it. But for the present, it did not worry him.

His greatest concern, on reentering Fay's apartment with her that night, was her preoccupation with the notion that she still had to get Spence Bainbridge out of her life. Holden didn't mind that she seemed to be making him appear larger than life so that she could expunge Bainbridge's image from her consciousness. Holden was so used to underrating himself that he actually enjoyed being thought of as a superman.

Fay seemed to want him because he had a sense of compassion, of sympathy, even of love. And in her bedroom that night, Holden felt more protective of her than ever, for it was here that she seemed to need him the most. Outside, as she had shown him, she was able to handle the serious problems of daily living with far more competence than most people.

Where love play had made her timid and even withdrawn that first night, she seemed to be a bit more relaxed after their return from the meeting with Gribov at the Crillon. She let Holden kiss her, embrace her, even undress her; but he couldn't help feeling that she still was forcing herself. So he tried very hard to be calm and steady so that she wouldn't be frightened, and withdraw from him. For a long time they lay in bed and embraced and kissed each other. And yet, he felt her body trembling against his in a way that distracted, even unnerved him.

He tried to remind himself that this had happened, too, the very first time they had gone to bed together. Then, too, there had been this sense of forced accommodation, of a kind of passive resistance, then that same fit of trembling. But at last, when he had thought he would be unable to keep from throwing off all self-restraint, the trembling stopped and she had almost thrown herself at him. So by sheer force of will, he held back once again and waited. And the trembling stopped this time too. With a half-strangled cry and a joy that was fierce in its intensity, she came at him as if *he* had been the frigid one, as if *she* were the one who had to arouse her partner.

This time, once she was able to forget herself and her fears, he would never have known that she was laboring to overcome an obsession. It was easy now for him to bring her to a climax with him. And when they fell back happily, he knew that she never had had any basis for being afraid that she was cold.

Yet, unaccountably, she was anxious. "Was I all right, darling?"

"You were fine."

"And you didn't think I was frigid?"

Her lack of belief in herself disturbed him. "Honey, it's my guess you *never* were frigid."

"Never?" When she echoed him, she sounded as if she couldn't bring herself to believe him.

He took her in his arms once more and kissed her repeatedly, avidly, until she responded to him. "This is the real you," he whispered.

She was breathing hard, couldn't seem to control herself. All he heard her say was a muffled, "Love you."

After a while, when they were resting, he said, "This coldness, this frigidity, was something Bainbridge dreamed up."

"He got so he didn't want to touch me," she said.

"Sure, he needed an excuse at home. He was playing around outside."

"How can you be sure?"

"Just take a good look at Vaillant sometime," he said. "Once she gets into a man, she's not going to let go."

He saw that Fay had closed her eyes and hidden her face against his chest. She didn't say anything. He asked, "What's the matter?"

"I don't want to talk about Catherine Vaillant," she answered, again in that muffled, almost hoarse voice.

"You don't have to, honey," he said. "As far as you're concerned, Catherine is ancient history."

"But she came after you at the Four Arts Ball." Fay's voice

sounded distant, almost disembodied. "I know. I saw her when she found us together there while we were drinking champagne, remember?"

"Sure." He recalled how Catherine had taken the senator back to the hotel, then returned to the ball, and was troubled. Then Fay forced that disturbing image out of his mind because he saw that she was crying.

He snatched her and held her roughly against him. "Stop it now, honey. You're safe with me."

More tears. "And you don't think me cold?"

"How could I?"

"And you think I'm good?"

"You're wonderful," he said, and meant it.

The weeping stopped and she held her face up to be kissed. "I want to do the best for you."

That is the way it was all night until, at last, they fell asleep in each other's arms out of sheer exhaustion. And when Holden awoke with the noonday sun streaming into the open window beside their bed, he thought that he was more in love than he had ever been before. For a long time, he watched her as she slept, a tiny smile on her lips, then kissed her awake. At first she was startled; but, seeing his face and watching him looking down at her, she gave a joyful cry and pulled him to her. As he had been telling her all along, she was just fine.

Off a corner of the Place de la Concorde at the head of the Avenue Gabriel, the American embassy sits like a querulous *grande dame*. Even touring Americans who approach its gates are regarded with suspicion. And to strangers like Arch Holden, who don't know their way around and are uncertain of their business, the Marine guards are icily polite but firm in demanding requisite explanations.

It doesn't matter who the ambassador is, whether he is a competent Foreign Service career man or a fat cat who bought his way into the elect of diplomacy with campaign contributions. The routine has been the same for much of this century. In consequence, when Holden entered those hallowed precincts later that day, he found that he was almost immediately categorized as a character who would bear watching.

Even to someone unversed in diplomatic routine, it seemed

unnecessary to Holden at first to display the note Gribov had scribbled hastily the night before at the Crillon. He saw that it was addressed to nobody in particular. And even more to the point, Holden didn't consider himself to be very good at making explanations. So acting on Fay's suggestion, he asked a guard where he could find Cary Wisner, in the political section.

There followed a consultation by telephone with someone within the upper reaches of the embassy who, of course, had never heard of Arch Holden, didn't have him listed for an appointment and wasn't sure what his business with Wisner would be. Nor was Holden able to offer satisfactory answers to routine questions.

As is the case with such strays who come off the streets into an American embassy, he was asked to wait. And he waited, patiently at first; then, as an hour passed, he grew a trifle indignant. Neither a woman receptionist nor a Marine guard was able to explain the delay. Just that "Mr. Wisner is in conference."

Eventually, Holden decided that he would have to use the note; he gave it to the receptionist for delivery to the man Fay had advised him to see in the political section. The reaction was not long in coming this time. An older woman, a secretarial type, appeared within a few minutes and abruptly asked him to accompany her, which he did. Once past the guards, he hazarded a remark, "Mr. Wisner must know Nikolai Gribov."

The woman stopped, turned and studied him through her thick eyeglasses. "I doubt if Mr. Wisner knows Nikolai Gribov, but he's certainly heard of him. Anyway," and she seemed to hesitate for a moment, "I'm to take you to Mr. McKelvey's office, and Mr. Wisner will be there."

"Who's Mr. McKelvey?"

She didn't reply. Eventually, after taking an elevator and walking around corridors in a particularly quiet part of the embassy, they came to a door that was unmarked except for a number. His guide turned him over to a cheerful young secretary in a blue cotton dress, then left without explanation.

The young secretary advised him, "Mr. McKelvey and Mr. Wisner are in conference, but I'm sure they'll see you in a few minutes. Do you mind waiting?" She gave him a pasteboard container of bitter coffee and the morning's *Paris Press,* neither of which helped him very much. There was nothing in the paper about Gribov. Under his breath Holden cursed the evil moment when he had agreed to hand-carry the note from Gribov to the embassy.

After another half-hour or so had passed, an inner door swung open and a stout man with a black-bearded red face and a forced air of joviality approached him. "Sorry about all the delay, Mr. Holden. I'm Cleveland McKelvey. Won't you come in?"

Holden wondered whether he shouldn't ask McKelvey who he was, but decided against it. It didn't seem politic. But from the drabness of the office and the lack of identification on its affiliation, he concluded that he was dealing with an investigative unit, perhaps an affiliate of the CIA or that formidable organization itself.

When he reached the inner office, he was introduced to Cary Wisner, a scrawny-looking old-grad type in an Oxford-gray Brooks Brothers suit with a Phi Beta Kappa key hanging from a gold chain across his vest. Wisner didn't bother to rise from his uncomfortable-looking straight-backed chair, merely extended a limp hand in a wet-fish handshake.

The interrogation, which is what it turned out to be, began in a way Holden hadn't expected. McKelvey regarded him and Wisner with his irritating pose of phony good humor. "You two fellas don't know each other, do you?"

"Never laid eyes on him in my life," Wisner responded, very much on the defensive. It was almost as if he suspected Holden of being a KGB agent in the guise of an American visitor.

Holden didn't make matters any better. "Never heard of the guy until last night," he agreed, nodding toward Wisner.

"And what happened last night?" McKelvey acted as if he were highly amused at some situation of which only he had knowledge.

"Gribov gave me a note to take to the American embassy."

McKelvey held up a bit of blue notepaper on which there was what seemed to be an illegible scrawl and a large signature, written with a flourish. "What is your relationship to Mr. Gribov?" McKelvey seemed to be enjoying his cross-examination of the visitor.

"None. I only met him last night." When he saw McKelvey and Wisner exchanging looks, he explained, "I handle the piano at Henri's on the Place St. Michel, and Gribov was the guest of honor at a party there."

At this point, Wisner arose abruptly, strode to McKelvey's desk and whispered earnestly to him. McKelvey kept nodding and smiling as if to show Holden that what was being said was of little consequence. The stout man picked up the blue notepaper again and read aloud, "This is to introduce Mr. Arch Holden. He will represent me." McKelvey put down the note and asked, "How are you going to represent Mr. Gribov and why?"

Holden's patience was wearing thin. "I thought you fellows knew all about it."

"About what?"

"Gribov wants to help a dancer named Olga defect to the United States."

Wisner nodded and for the first time tried to ease the burden of what had become an irksome interrogation. "It's as I told you, McKelvey. Gribov told the ambassador some time ago that Olga Varenka was ready to defect from the Kirov Ballet during its engagement here beginning next month. And the ambassador, after telling Gribov we couldn't help him, shipped him to me."

"And your instructions?" McKelvey demanded.

"We take no part in this operation, but as a general policy, we'd like to be informed of what's going on," Wisner replied. "So I assume Gribov wants Mr. Holden to be our informant."

"That right, Holden?" McKelvey demanded.

Holden nodded. More than ever he felt like an odd man out, the innocent who had been caught up in a mystery for which he had no responsibility and thrust among characters who seemed to know everything while he knew nothing. He resented this Wisner, hated McKelvey for his phony good humor. Either one or both, he concluded, were heartless enough to do him in if it suited their purpose. That made Holden angry, if for no other reason than that Fay had depended on him to negotiate a reasonable attitude of helpfulness at the American embassy, plus a pledge to step in if the conspiracy threatened to backfire on its prime movers.

But Holden kept his thoughts to himself and managed a mild protest. "As I understand it, the embassy wants to be helpful in what we're doing, but you two don't seem to have gotten the word."

Wisner nodded blankly toward McKelvey. "This is your man. I'm just political."

McKelvey scowled, dropping his pose of phony good humor for the first time. "No you don't, Wisner. We don't want any part of this operation."

Holden couldn't help asking, "Who's 'we'?"

McKelvey ignored him and continued to Wisner, "If this man reports to anybody at the embassy, he reports to you. He's your baby, and this operation has to be monitored by the political section, not by us. Count us out. And that's final."

Wisner looked miserable but made no comment.

Without addressing either one in particular, Holden posed the question that had been bothering him all along. "Let's say one of us gets into trouble in this operation. Maybe Professor Leary or his wife, or maybe Fay Carroll . . ."

Wisner caught him up quickly. "Who's Fay Carroll?"

In a dry, humorless manner, McKelvey reminded him, "Spence Bainbridge's former wife. She's resumed her maiden name." And to Holden, he added, "What kind of trouble do you anticipate?"

Once again, Holden felt a surge of anger against the two embassy men and the bloodless machine they represented, but he controlled himself with an effort. "Gribov told us last night that he'd heard the KGB had put a guard on Olga Varenka for this trip. What if the KGB gets tough with us?"

McKelvey was abrupt. "It's your ass, Holden, not ours."

"And you wouldn't get us help and protect us if we were in danger?" Holden surprised even himself with the sharpness of his question. But then, he had been thinking of Fay being in danger and expecting that he, a go-between with the embassy, could call in immediate support.

"*We* can't get into a showdown with the KGB in Paris," McKelvey replied, "and I'd say the embassy as a whole has to be damned careful not to get involved. The French are in no mood for shenanigans."

Wisner got up and stood with his back to them, looking out the window and absently jingling a few coins in his pants pocket. After a while, he turned and said to Holden, "I agree. We can't promise anything, but you must keep me posted on what's going on. What we *can* do and what we *must* do"—here he cast a reproachful glance at McKelvey—"is to protect the lives of American citizens abroad as long as they are not involved in criminal activity."

Holden caught the qualification immediately. "Is *this* what you call a criminal activity?"

Wisner figuratively ran for cover. "Depends on how you go about it. If you let me know what you plan to do, I can at least tell you if you're likely to violate French law. And in that case"—he gazed out the window for a moment before concluding half to himself—"I'm going to deny I ever saw you or talked to you."

"And you still hope we'll kidnap Olga Varenka and make the Russians look bad," Holden observed sardonically. Now he was done with wavering about the project, with wondering whether he should back out. He couldn't leave Fay at the mercy of circumstances over which she might have no control. He was in this to the finish, whatever happened.

McKelvey didn't look at him, but waved a fat hand in the air. "About all we can do is wish you luck."

"Thanks," Holden said, and arose. He'd had enough. "Guess I'll be on my way." And to Wisner, "If you want to hear from me, let me have a phone number, will you?"

Wisner stepped away from the window. "Just call the embassy daytimes and ask for me. At night, the duty officer will put you through to me. But," and he added a caveat, "don't be surprised if I tell you that I can't talk to you. That means you are to wait awhile and call me back."

"Playing games, huh?" Holden let his anger show through. "You two guys wouldn't be of much help in a fight, would you?" He turned away from them.

McKelvey reassumed his pose as a jolly fat man and opened his office door for Holden and Wisner. "Good to see you, gentlemen," he called out, evidently for the benefit of two men who were waiting near the secretary. And yet, Holden had the impression that McKelvey also had been displeased with their meeting. "Who's this McKelvey? What does he do?" he asked Wisner as they strode along the corridor toward an elevator.

"I'm not supposed to identify him," Wisner replied, automatically glancing behind him for a furtive shadower, "but he handles everything having to do with the Russians for the station chief."

"Station chief?" Holden looked blank.

Wisner glanced at him, as if in wonder at his ignorance, then said, "CIA." He added, "I'll show you out."

An American embassy is like an iceberg. Holden felt, upon emerging from the one in Paris into the cloudy chill of an April morning, that he had gained but a few inches in ascending a slippery slope, only to fall back repeatedly to a hard and unyielding earth. But the experience had done one thing for him: he had made up his mind to go through with whatever arrangements Fay made with Gribov about rescuing Olga Varenka. He knew now that the embassy's approach to so risky an undertaking would be covert at best; he wondered how anybody could ever have hoped that it would be otherwise.

As he headed toward the Metro station at the Place de la Concorde with long, quick strides, he heard a woman's voice behind him calling, "Arch! Wait!" There was a flurry of light footsteps, and as he wheeled about, he saw Catherine Vaillant approaching. She was in a belted tan raincoat, very much in the military manner, with a silken printed scarf in brown and white over her dark hair. She was carrying her big leather translator's bag. In spite of himself, he felt enormously attracted to her even though he had schooled himself by now into mistrust of her motives.

She stopped beside him and said accusingly, "You passed right by me in the lobby of the embassy without even looking at me."

He was apologetic. "Guess I was in too much of a hurry."

She proceeded to thrust him even deeper in the wrong by making him more uncomfortable. "I thought you were going to call me for lunch today."

Under this methodical attack, he became wary and defensive. "Something came up," he said, determined to tell her nothing.

"Such as?" She was merciless in pursuing her advantage. "Remember, you *did* promise."

He looked her up and down, and smiled. "I had some business at the embassy."

"I have no doubt." She was mildly but not rudely sarcastic. Her next question was sufficient to keep him off balance. "With whom?"

Now she was definitely fishing for the information, and he felt curiously powerful at being able to frustrate her. "Just some routine business."

She tucked one hand under his arm. "You and I aren't on the same wavelength and we ought to be," she remarked lightly. "Let's have coffee, shall we?"

There was no escaping Catherine Vaillant this time. That was evident to Holden quickly enough as he felt her gentle pressure on his arm. Rather than appear to be pulled along unwillingly as Catherine's captive, he gave in to her. "Sure, why not?" But he wondered as they walked along together why she was so insistent and what she really wanted of him. She gave him not a clue, just chattered on lightly in the confident manner of a sophisticated *Parisienne*.

This time, because Holden was with someone attached to the embassy, the guards didn't challenge him. Nor did the receptionist pay any attention to them. She gave them a bored look as they entered, then went back to her perusal of that morning's *Le Monde*.

Soon he found himself with Catherine in a long line of elderly American tourists in the embassy cafeteria, most of them hungry for apple pie, hamburgers, toasted English muffins and decaf in the American manner, with an artificial sweetener. Even at that off-hour, the cafeteria was comfortably full: Americans on tour seemed eternally to flock to the cheap and the familiar rather than experiment with the treacherous and often expensive unknowns of the midday French cuisine.

Catherine asked if he liked the typical French coffee and provided herself and Holden with a cup each. She led the way to a small cafeteria table somewhat removed from the crowd and plumped down beside him. She drew off her scarf, fluffed out her hair and opened her raincoat to display a neat dress of soft brown silk. With a glint of humor in her dark eyes, she demanded, "Now, Arch, let's have it. What are you up to?"

He wasn't ready to oblige her, but countered with, "Why do you want to know?"

She smiled, then gave him that big look, so searching and so compelling. "You interest me," she said.

It was a come-on, but he also couldn't help thinking of Fay's warning about her. So he raised a question. "How come? You're Charley Fourier's girl, aren't you?"

"Charley's thousands of miles away," she replied with a careless air. "Anyway, I can't let him run my life forever. And," she went on with emphasis, "you oughtn't let Fay Bainbridge run yours."

"What do you know about Fay and me?" It annoyed him that she would dare to warn him openly about Fay and expect him to believe her.

She seemed not a bit put out, but laughed easily and retorted, "We translators are like computers. We remember everything we are told and everything we read, because we are expected to have instant recall." She sipped her coffee thoughtfully. "You know," and she was almost studiously offhand in manner as she went on, "Nikolai Gribov is one of my clients."

He sat up, instantly alert. It was as if she had applied an electric shock to him, which seemed to be exactly what she had wanted to do. He tried to match her casual air, but wasn't very successful. "You know Gribov well?" he asked.

She didn't answer at once but studied herself in a pocket mirror she took from the shoulder bag. "Sometimes," she replied, still preoccupied with her mirror image, "one gets a bit tired of being with older men." Satisfied, she snapped the mirror shut, put it in her bag and concentrated all her attention on him, murmuring, "It isn't often I meet an attractive young man."

Had he just met this disturbing woman, he reflected that he could have been thoroughly infatuated with her by now. But, never for a moment forgetting what Fay had told him about Catherine, he refused to let her draw him closer to her. Instead, he pursued his own inquiry. "How come you can translate for

106

Gribov? I thought you embassy translators weren't supposed to have any private clients."

She explained, "We contract translators don't work regularly, so it's none of the embassy's business who our outside clients are."

He pointed to the big shoulder bag. "So this is really no clue as to whether you're working or not."

She laughed. "You remember everything, don't you?" She added in a confidential manner, "I wish my memory were better, but I have to depend a lot on my steno pads in the bag."

"But you speak two languages," he said. "That takes memory work."

She corrected him. *"Three* languages, and"—she seemed quite proud to say so—"I'm good at them. But I have to keep notes in each language—French, English and Russian—on what people say. It's not easy."

He asked idly, "How come Russian?"

Again she laughed. "My mother was Russian, was married to my father when he worked at the French embassy in Moscow, and Nikolai Gribov remembered it and came to me after his defection. He pays well, but"—she made a roguish little mouth—"he's difficult to teach." In that insinuating manner of hers, she went on, "Young men are easier to handle."

Holden met her cool, inquiring gaze, but shifted uncomfortably in the hard cafeteria chair. It was, he thought, time for him to leave as politely as possible. She could not help noticing how perturbed he was, and quickly changed her manner. Instead of questioning, searching, probing, she became soothing and even charming almost at once.

She rested one hand lightly on his just as he shoved back his chair in a tentative move to get away from her. "You mustn't mind me, Arch," she said. "I don't mean any harm. But when I meet an attractive man, and particularly someone who's new to Paris..." Here she smiled at him reassuringly. "I hate to see people take advantage of him." She gave his hand an affectionate little pat. "I'm only trying to protect you."

Even though the alarm bells were ringing in his head, he asked, "What do you think you're protecting me from?"

She raised her head and gave him a long look. "You'd be surprised."

"I don't like playing games, Catherine," he said sharply. "Whatever you've got on your mind, spill it."

She knew she had his attention once again, and she was elaborately casual. "You don't know it, but you're in very deep water, Arch," she murmured.

"Why do you say that?"

She delayed her reply and her manner was tantalizing. "Because you're so very vulnerable."

"I don't understand."

She had been circling around him for some time, but now she came boldly and swiftly to the point. "I couldn't help noticing that you were with Fay Bainbridge the other night when I came back to the Four Arts Ball."

He froze. "You mean Fay Carroll?"

"I knew her as Mrs. Bainbridge." Catherine Vaillant was fastidious about pronouncing Fay's married name. "And you must know that she seems to have an unfortunate effect on some of the people about her."

It shocked him that she had opened such a deliberate attack on Fay. His immediate reaction was resentment. "You'd damn well better know what you're talking about, Catherine," he retorted with a show of anger.

Catherine Vaillant was undeterred but thoughtful. "Mrs. Bainbridge is a very clever woman and I can see that she's made quite an impression on you already, but you'd best be careful."

He mocked her. "Careful! You'd think Fay was going to take a gun to me!" He pushed back his chair now. "Catherine, I'm not going to listen to a lot of nonsense."

But before he could get up to leave, she stopped him cold. "Arch, watch out for Fay Bainbridge and Gribov."

He stared at her for a few moments, seemingly unable to comprehend, than sank back slowly in his chair. What did Catherine know? And how did she know it? Could Gribov have drawn her too into his conspiracy to pluck Olga Varenka from the Kirov Ballet? Or had Catherine gotten wind of what was up through her work as a translator for the Russian?

Holden felt that he had to know whose side Catherine Vaillant was on: was she working with Gribov or was she against him and resentful of Fay's influence over him? He was careful about posing his next question because he instinctively felt a deep distrust of this fascinating but ruthless woman. "Let's quit hinting," he said sharply. "Whatever you want to tell me, put it on the table."

"Very well," she replied coolly. "Mrs. Bainbridge is a very old and very dear friend of Gribov's and I want you to know that. Anybody who knew her at the embassy will confirm what I say. And maybe . . ." After a moment's seeming reflection, she went on: "If Mrs. Bainbridge had not been such an *old friend*," here she emphasized the term, "she might have preserved her marriage to Spencer Bainbridge."

That rocked Holden, for it was exactly the opposite of what Fay had led him to believe. He started to say something in Fay's defense, but Catherine anticipated him. She glanced at her watch. "Oh, goodness, I must go! I'm late for my appointment with the DCM!"

"DCM?" he asked, mystified.

"Deputy Chief of Mission." She was almost patronizing. As she circled behind his chair, she let one hand pass smoothly and lightly over his shoulders and the back of his neck, riffling his hair. "Wish I could tell you more, but I must run. If you get into trouble, though, I'll do everything I can to help you." She paused, seemingly on impulse, then drew a small notebook from her purse and scribbled on it quickly with a pencil stub. "Here's my address and phone number. And maybe"—this as a parting shot—"you'll want to call me for dinner."

She thrust the slip of paper into his hand, arose and sauntered from the cafeteria before he could pull himself together. For a brief time, he stared at her as she left, then folded the slip of paper and put it in his wallet. If she hadn't made a convert, she had at least given him pause.

Chapter Four

The events of the morning had so disturbed Holden that Fay had taken him on a tour of Paris to distract him. "We'll have to protect each other," she had said. "Nobody else will do it."

And so, that afternoon, they stood before the gleaming white Basilica of Sacré Coeur. The shadows were lengthening on the Butte Montmartre. Below them, Paris shimmered in the golden haze of April—a splendid tapestry of stone and steel.

"What happened at the embassy this morning," she was saying, "is not what Paris is all about. It was merely American bureaucracy at work. Spence Bainbridge used to call it, 'The Committee for Getting Out from Under.' Embassy people don't want to take responsibility for anything."

"And Catherine Vaillant? What about her?" He kept his head down, still thinking of how cruel she had been about Fay.

"I can't explain her." She glanced at him curiously. "She's very, very complicated. What do you make of her?"

Holden was blunt. "She has her claws out for any man she can get."

"Including you?" she asked.

He agreed. "Including me."

She didn't say anything right away. Their footsteps clicked almost in unison on the path beside Sacré Coeur as they continued their stroll together. At last she volunteered, "My psychiatrist, Dr. Beranger, always said Catherine envied me and wanted me to like her. But I couldn't."

"I don't understand that," he said. "Wasn't she having an affair with your husband?"

"Oh, it was before that," was the low response. "It was when I first met her—when she was giving my husband and me French lessons." She bit her lip. "She always used to want to go to lunch with me, and I couldn't. And I think that was when she started saying around the embassy that I was cold and unresponsive." She sighed. "She got Spence to believe it."

He stopped, put both his hands at her elbows and made her face him. As they looked into each other's eyes, he thought her very beautiful. *"You* mustn't believe it, Fay." His voice was low but firm. "It's not true."

"You're sweet," she said, and smiled.

As they resumed their walk along the steep brow of the Butte Montmarte, he couldn't help reflecting on how lucky he was to have found her so early in his Paris adventure. Only a little more than a week before, he had arrived in Paris feeling desolate and abandoned. The thought of performing every night in a saloon atmosphere, even as genteel a saloon as Henri's, had made him squirm: to be pawing over half-forgotten old songs before a partly- and sometimes non-attentive drinking crowd scarcely seemed to him to be worth doing. And to do it for six months, feeling as he did, seemed impossible.

Fay had changed all that from the moment he first looked up at her on the swaying ladder at the Four Arts Ball. Where he once had little or no hope of ever loving again, he now dared to hope and to love. That was why, upon leaving the embassy that day, he had hurried to the Ile St. Louis and again had been lucky enough to find Fay just returning from her semi-weekly singing lesson at the Paris Conservatory.

With her sympathetic encouragement, he had told her the story of his frustration and his anger over his meeting with the two embassy officials, and his unexpected run-in with Catherine Vaillant.

"You did the best you could," Fay had said. "There's nothing to worry about. You made the contact and you set up liaison with Wisner, which was all you were expected to do."

"But Catherine's all over Gribov, and pretends to know everything that's going on," he objected. "Could she give away the whole business?"

"That's a chance we'll have to take," Fay had said.

Then, she had proposed a drive around Paris in Dr. Beranger's Citroën. "Let me show you the sights. . . . You've been here more than a week, and you've seen nothing of Paris."

He had understood that she wanted him to get his experience at the American embassy out of his mind, and he had accompanied her gratefully on the rounds of the postcard Paris—the Eiffel Tower and the Champs Elysees, the Tuileries Gardens and the Louvre, and all the other familiar spots that have drawn millions of tourists. Now, standing on the rim of the Butte Montmartre, they held hands and viewed the city below as though it were part of a dream.

Tourists brushed past them, chatting in a dozen languages about mundane matters. A uniformed policeman who strolled by smiled slightly, and put a finger to his cap, a small Parisian tribute to lovers. All around them, people were taking pictures of the city below, and Sacré Coeur above.

Sated with the scenery and relaxed at last, Holden said, "That ends the tour for the afternoon, madame. Now may I buy you a drink?"

"Just so I have a little privacy."

"You name it."

She took his hand, leading him away from Sacré Coeur. "Down at the Place du Tertre, I'm sure we can find a nice shady table in front of Mère Catherine's."

"And then?" he asked.

"We can decide later." She stood on tiptoe and kissed him. "Oh, darling, it's been such a fun afternoon."

The shadows were now a velvety black. Tourists were scattering like a flock of frightened sparrows. Through the budding green of the chestnut trees in the Place du Tertre, the jeweled rays of the setting sun sparkled in longish patterns. And around the outside of the cobbled square, the mottled rows of square-faced buildings, shops and houses squatted in silence like grateful old men dozing at the end of another spring day.

Along with many another traveler who has spent a carefree day wandering about the immensely human theater that is Paris, Holden let the images of all those precious idle hours flood back in his memory. He felt deeply in Fay's debt, as he walked beside her along the cobbled Place du Tertre toward Mère Catherine's.

Holden interrupted the play of memories as they took chairs at a table outside Mère Catherine's. After giving their drink orders to a waiter, they held hands beside the table and settled back to watch the passing scene.

"Have I succeeded?" she asked shyly.

"In what?"

"In making you forget about your troubles at the American embassy?"

"Oh, that!" He laughed. "I guess I did take it too seriously." He lifted her hand and kissed it. "But thanks for giving me the grand tour . . . loved every minute of it."

"So did I," she said.

"But it must be old stuff to you by now," he went on. "You and your husband must have done a lot of this."

She shook her head in regret. "No, he always said he had too many important things to do . . . stayed out late at night . . . seemed to catch up on his sleep most weekends." She concluded, "As I told you, I was by myself an awful lot. Too much, really, and it finally got to me."

When he saw that she was downcast and seemingly reliving a bad experience, he cautioned, "Don't think about it anymore."

"Oh, but I want to . . . I'm not afraid now." She squeezed his hand. "That's what you've done for me." While the waiter put their drinks on the table, she was silent. But as soon as he had turned away, her feelings came out in a rush of words. "At first, I couldn't understand what was happening to me. At the American Hospital here, Dr. Beranger did his best for me. But at that time, he couldn't bring me around. Nobody could bring me around. So, because the ambassador knew a psychiatrist at St. Elizabeth's back home, they shipped me there. More trouble, but no progress. I was sent to two different private sanitariums before I began coming to, seeing that I still had a life to live even if I was separated from Spence Bainbridge. Throughout, my wonderful mother stuck with me, praise be, or I wouldn't be here now. And old friends like Pat and Amy Leary helped when they heard about me. But not the embassy crowd." Her voice trailed off and she grew silent and pensive.

Holden knew perfectly well that she didn't want to talk about her former husband any more than he wanted to discuss that last agonizing illness of his late wife. And yet, some quirk in his makeup caused him to edge onto what should have been forbidden ground.

"Your husband..." he began tentatively. "The embassy crowd stuck with him?"

She nodded slowly. "It figures. If one man is caught out having an affair and his marriage breaks up, the rest stick with him. Why? Maybe the next guy's marriage will break up too, and he'll need a friend."

"Is that the way it was with Bainbridge?"

"What can I say?" She sipped her drink, and there was a far-off look in her eyes. "He played the game." She winced just a little as she said it. "Y'know," and the tone of her voice changed as if she had just thought of something, "I bumped into him completely by accident shortly before I returned here. It was in a restaurant in Georgetown, and I'd gone there with friends. Well!" She drew breath sharply after the exclamation. "It was just as if nothing at all had happened, as if we'd been sweethearts all over again. Before I knew it, he was holding my hand and kissing my cheek and telling me how gorgeous I looked." She half-closed her eyes. "I suppose"—and now she stared directly at him—"that I should have slapped his face or stamped on his toes or done something else to show him exactly how I felt about him, but I didn't."

Holden shook his head. "It's a strange game we play, isn't it?"

"Particularly in the Foreign Service," she said. "We're trained, all of us, officers and spouses, never to make a scene, to hold in, to suppress emotions. And you smile and pretend nothing has happened."

There was a harsh note of urgency in his voice as he swept on. "But now Bainbridge is coming back to Paris. Do you still play the game, Fay?"

She sighed. "I just don't know."

"Why can't you tell him off?"

"I may have to," she answered. "Amy Leary said last night that she'd heard he told friends that the divorce was a mistake, that he wants to marry me again."

"Oh, nonsense!" he exclaimed angrily.

A brisk wind had sprung up with the coming of dusk, and

Holden saw that she looked chilled. "I wish I could say the same thing, Arch."

He stopped short, stared at her. "You wouldn't think—"

"No, *I* wouldn't," she cut in quickly, "but I have others to think of."

"Others?"

"My mother's last two letters have been very hard to take," she explained in a low voice. "My stepfather has always blamed her for encouraging me to get a divorce, says she was crazy and I was too. I never paid any attention to him at the time. But now . . ." Her voice broke and she turned away from him.

Holden grasped her arm and made her face him. If he had been stunned at first by the turn of events, he was impatient now to the point of rudeness. "Look, Fay, let's get this straight. I've got to know where you stand. You owe me that much."

She gave a piteous little cry. "Don't leave me."

"I'm not leaving," he retorted roughly, but tightened his grip on her arm, even shook it just a bit for emphasis as he went on. "But you must level with me."

"You're hurting me," she protested.

He released her, insisting, "Tell me the story."

"There isn't much to tell," she began in a voice that was low and strained. She related her unhappiness about the death of her father, Selden Deak, and her mother's subsequent remarriage to a blustering oilman, Waco Texas Carroll. It was Carroll, she said, who had persuaded her to marry his nephew, Spencer Bainbridge. She blamed Carroll, too, for opposing her divorce until Dr. Beranger, the chief psychiatrist at the American Hospital in Paris, warned that it would have to be done to preserve her sanity. And now, she continued, Carroll was campaigning for her remarriage to Bainbridge by browbeating her mother, even threatening to have her mother committed to a psychiatric institution.

"But your mother must have decent legal advice," Holden protested. "Why does she let him get away with it?"

"Mother can't help herself," Fay confided wearily. "At the time of her remarriage, she foolishly gave power of attorney over my father's estate to my stepfather; and by this time she and I receive only what little money he doles out to us." She halted awkwardly, fought off tears and concluded, "Lord knows what he's done with father's estate."

"Your mother ought to go into court, demand an accounting," Holden argued in indignation.

"And have my stepfather's psychiatrists declare her insane and authorize her commitment to some awful place?" Fay seemed surer of herself at this juncture. "No, Arch, I can't let that happen. We'll just have to find some other way of stopping my stepfather. I have a friend at the embassy checking into what kind of deals Spencer Bainbridge is in with his uncle."

"Deals?"

She lifted one hand and dropped it in her lap in a gesture of resignation. "All I know is that Spence, during our marriage, spent a lot of time with some of the Arab oil people from the Persian Gulf states and then used to hang on the phone three or four nights a week making long-distance calls to my stepfather."

Holden was puzzled. "Now what kind of a game would they be playing? Stock-market deals, maybe?"

"I don't know. All I can tell you is that Bartley Crandell, the DCM at the embassy here, thought it was important enough to look into when I told him about it." She rose and turned to him in sudden appeal. "Let's get out of here, Arch, shall we? The place depresses me."

He motioned to a waiter that he wanted to pay the bill. "Where do you want to go?"

"How about the Ritz Bar?" she suggested. "If we're lucky, maybe we'll see Pat and Amy Leary. They were going there after taking Vivian and a friend to tea at Maxim's."

He shoved money on the table for the bill and a tip, then joined her. "Maxim's," he mused. "I once saw it on the late-late show in an old movie. Is it for real?"

"Oh, it still exists," she assured him as they walked off toward Dr. Beranger's Citroën, which she was driving.

"I wonder if *we're* for real?" he asked.

She kept her head down and her face was pale. "What do you mean?"

He couldn't get Spencer Bainbridge out of his mind; nor, for that matter, could he help being worried about the lengths to which Fay's stepfather was going to press his campaign for

116

her remarriage. "Can you give me your word that you won't marry Bainbridge again?" Holden demanded.

Her voice rose. "Arch, I'll do everything I can to avoid it, believe me, but I can't let my mother suffer for what I will or won't do."

He stood there indecisively for a few moments. Then, seeing her tilt her face toward him with tears on her cheeks, he kissed her. Arm in arm, they walked down the hill together, each deeply troubled, each unwilling to be separated from the other.

The unsettling part of Holden's affair with Fay, to him, was the suddenness with which his passion for her had taken possession of him. For a few moments, after she had told him about Bainbridge's unexpected advances and her stepfather's campaign for a remarriage, Holden had felt so despairing that he thought himself foolish to be so mistrustful of what Catherine Vaillant had told him.

But then, he was unable to resist Fay's tearful appeal. He felt he was moving helplessly through a nightmare. He wanted out but at the same time he couldn't even summon up the will to leave her. "Can we go to my place now?" he proposed.

Momentarily, the sadness left her eyes and she even managed a tight little smile. "I thought we'd go to the Ritz Bar first."

"But I don't have all that much time, and I'll have to be at work at Henri's until late."

"We have tomorrow, darling," she said.

He had to be content with that for a while. Until he had met her, he hadn't thought of himself as a passionate man. Yet, whenever he was unsure of her—and his uncertainty had now returned—all he could think of was that he had to take her to bed with him.

Nothing like that had happened to him during his marriage to Caroline. Now, he felt himself carried away by an overwhelming desire to lie with Fay in some secluded place.

Walking with her across the Place du Tertre to the Citroën, which was parked under a wavering line of chestnut trees in the gathering April dusk, he felt once again that unreasoning urge. He halted, and made her face him. He touched her hair,

117

stroked her cheek, then kissed her. "I love you very, very much," he whispered.

She held the hand with which he had stroked her cheek and murmured, "All those people out there," nodding toward a group of elderly Americans who were trooping toward a tour bus, "are watching us."

He kissed her again and embraced her.

"To my place," he urged softly.

She shook her head smilingly, took his hand in her own and drew him after her like a graceful sailing craft towing a stocky rowboat in a choppy sea. "We won't stay at the Ritz Bar very long," she said.

This, he reflected as he followed her without further diversions, was the public Fay, the intensely practical person, the competent manager, self-assured in everything she did. The shyness, the hesitation and then the swift abandon that so excited him in their private moments seemed to come from an entirely different person. When she faced the world, she could be as impersonal as any model showing off a new handbag, a hat, a dress.

How, he wondered, could she have seemed so provocative to him at the Four Arts Ball, a nymph in a red veil; and now, so much the self-possessed woman of affairs? It was difficult for him to believe that she was the same person.

He opened the Critoën's door on the driver's side, let her in, then slid beside her through the opposite door. "How about meeting at Henri's tonight when I get off and going to my place?" Perhaps making love would heal the gap that was developing between them.

She released the brake and let the Citroën roll down the steep incline from the Butte Montmartre. "You don't give up, do you, darling?" She gave him an amused sidelong glance. "There are so many nights ahead for both of us. I'm not going to disappear, really I'm not." Keeping one hand on the wheel, she reached over and patted his knee comfortingly with the other. "I've given you a bad time, and I'm sorry."

"You can make it better."

"All right, darling, I will."

"Good!" For the time being, he felt relieved. "I think Henri

118

will let me off around one in the morning. Is that going to be awkward for you?"

"No, I'll make it."

He settled back in the car seat, puzzling over the varied facets of her personality. Seated beside her, looking at her, often touching her, he couldn't divert his mind to the scenery. He was too full of the thoughts of her, too impatient for what would happen after he left Henri's that night.

Was she truly two such different people somehow fitted together in the same lovely body? Sometimes it seemed that way to him. Yet, he discerned that their coming together had aroused as many conflicting emotions in her as it had in him.

While he had borne up through Caroline's long illness and her death, Fay had had to survive the indifference of an unfaithful husband. And she hadn't been able to tolerate that.

What his own experience had done to him was to create an ineffable sense of loneliness, a groping—even a craving—for the care and sympathy a beautiful woman could give him. He wasn't so sure what Fay's experience had done to her beyond the nervous breakdown that seemed still to bother her at times. But her anxiety over being thought of as cold and unemotional, the reaction to the reproaches her husband had flung at her, was painfully apparent.

He stared at her with unabashed admiration, but scarcely listened to her running commentary on the Parisian scenes past which they were driving. They had come out now behind the soaring columns of the Madeleine and she was driving by the stalls of the flower sellers, each a beautiful blending of color. Something moved him to ask her to stop, which she did; as always, she seemed to want to fall in with his moods.

He darted from the car, extracting a wad of franc notes from his billfold and waving it at a vase of red roses. There was a flurry of sign language between him and an old woman in a kerchief who presided over the field of roses scattered in vases along the sidewalk. After a few minutes, he ran back to the car, bearing a dozen red roses which he presented to Fay with a flourish.

"Allow me, madame!"

She selected one and arranged it in the buttonhole of his sport coat. "That's the first rose, and it goes to you," she said.

Then she felt around in the glove compartment of the car for a pin, which she used to fasten two roses on the front left shoulder of her dress. "And these," she added gaily, "are to remind me of the two of us. As if," she said as an afterthought, "we needed any reminder."

She laughed; seeing that he was going to kiss her, she bent forward; at this time there was no protest about making a scene in front of a crowd. Her lips met his eagerly.

He felt better. He saw that she was trying to yield to him when she might have had little desire to do so, to come closer to his life at the expense of her own. Unlike Catherine Vaillant, there was nothing about Fay that was demanding. Nor was there even a trace of narcissism to mar her.

Fay asked little of him except trust. She seemed to be asking him to love her as she was, not as he might want her to be. And to try to understand her because she had been deeply hurt. If he judged her character correctly, he was more certain than ever that he could please her.

But could she tolerate him? Sometimes, in the nature of his own deprivation, he showed an excessive sexuality that must have been frightening to someone as restrained in her normal behavior as she was. That night and early morning after the Four Arts Ball, she had tried not to show it in her apartment. But he sensed that her later play at wild abandon was a pose.

Again and again, he could hear that small, pleading voice: "You don't think I'm cold, do you? . . . Or frigid?" He wanted to make love to her and reassure her, "You're exactly what I want!"

By this time, she had maneuvered the Citroën along the classic beauty of the Rue de la Paix and swung into the brooding vastness of the Place Vendome. After parking there, they headed toward the main entrance of the Ritz where, by chance, they met young Gareth Leary and Henri's photographer, Stephanie Rivet, who had just emerged from a small Renault Elf.

"Hey, Arch!" Gareth called. "Can we buy you a drink?"

"Sounds good," Holden said.

The uniformed doorman smiled, and gave the two couples a small salute as they entered the old hotel. "Makes you feel important," Holden said.

120

Fay linked arms with him. "But you *are* important, darling," she murmured. "You are very important to me."

At that cocktail hour, as at others, the Ritz Bar resembled a small American colony. Not that Americans overran it or even dominated it. But it remained for them a place where they could gather in a familiar atmosphere—at least part of a home away from home.

For the relatively modest American business establishment, the Ritz Bar was a refuge from the frustrations of dealing with the often irascible French. For the youthful American intellectuals now resident at the Sorbonne, it was a temporary relief from homesickness. And for the thirsty tourist from the States, it was a Valhalla of good Scotch whiskey, superior French brandy and imported beer.

Whatever glamour there was about this polyglot gathering place, it existed mainly in the mind. For whether the patrons took their liquor standing at the bar or sitting around nearby tables, they resembled any other mass of congealed, star-spangled humanity sealed into a haze of alcohol and choking cigarette smoke. It might as well have been New York City, San Francisco or Dubuque as the Ritz Bar in Paris.

Unless the French had urgent business that kept them, they fled what they felt was an uncongenial atmosphere at the first opportunity. But less fastidious members of the foreign colony in Paris found the Ritz Bar both useful and amusing, particularly when it was necessary for them to make an impression on a resident American.

So it turned out, as Holden escorted Fay into this amiable Babel of confusion, that they saw the Learys and their guests crowded about two tables in a corner. Vivian was with her parents and looked sinuous in a clinging silver dress. Beside her was a young man with the shoulders of a shot-putter and the waist of a ballet dancer, with restless blue eyes and big white teeth that flashed continually in a mirthless smile. They were listening at the moment to Gareth, who was standing beside his father with Stephanie between them, her arms closely linked with those of the two men.

Holden heard Fay sigh beside him. "Oh, if I could only be like Stephanie."

He glanced down at her, his eyes crinkling in amusement. "Are you feeling deprived?"

She made a face at him. "You know what I mean, Arch. Just look at her; so relaxed, so self-possessed, so proprietary about both Gareth and his father."

"Yes, and Amy Leary will tell her off in about two minutes," Holden replied, nodding toward the little Englishwoman who was eyeing Stephanie.

"That won't bother Stephanie," Fay said. "The women may not like her, but she knows how to play to men."

"And you don't?"

Another sigh. "I wish I did."

As they approached the Learys' party, they heard Gareth tell his father that he had proposed drinks for them. But Holden, by this time, wanted to get Fay off in a corner and keep her to himself. It would be a long, lonely evening at Henri's without her. However, Pat Leary insisted, and the pianist accepted two Scotches, one of which he handed to Fay.

Leary proceeded to introduce her and Holden to the stranger who had arisen and now waited to be presented.

"This is Baron Rudolf von Norden, counselor at the West German Embassy."

Von Norden clicked his heels, bowed, and kissed Fay's hand. "Enchanté, madame."

Fay reacted with the breathless pleasure of a little girl at a costume party. With her other hand at the neckline of her dress, she smiled tremulously at Leary. "A real baron?"

"The genuine article," Leary assured her. "Right out of an old Erich von Stroheim movie."

Von Norden released Fay's hand and drew himself easily erect. "Without the monocle, my dear professor," he admonished Leary. He spoke with a crisp approximation of a British accent and flashed his big teeth to indicate a tolerant good humor. To Fay, he went on, "You and your young man must join us for dinner later. I've arranged for all of us to go to an excellent little restaurant in the Rue de Grenelle."

"Wish I could," Holden said regretfully. "But I'm due at work soon."

"Arch's on piano at Henri's in the Place St. Michel," Leary explained.

"Ah, so." The German nodded without interest.

"But I'll come along," Fay announced. "You're sure you don't mind, darling?"

Holden put up as good a front as he could under the circumstances.

"Then I'll see you later?" he asked Fay, vaguely upset that she should have jumped at von Norden's invitation.

"I'll be at Henri's," she assured him.

"We'll take good care of her and deliver her safely," von Norden assured him.

Holden was not at all reassured, and delayed his departure. He couldn't fight down a surge of jealousy as Fay made conversation with the German. "Where did you learn your excellent English?"

Von Norden chuckled, showing his teeth. "My father was a career diplomat assigned to London when I was a child. I was very fortunate. But," and his deep voice was tinged with regret, "I'm having a devil of a lot of trouble learning French."

"Who's your teacher?" Fay asked.

"I've a good one—Catherine Vaillant, a translator at the American embassy."

There was a sweet-and-sour quality about Fay's voice as she observed, "I should have known. Catherine is everybody's French teacher."

"Oh, really?" Von Norden simulated surprise. "Who else?"

Holden, having been put out by Fay's show of interest in von Norden, wasn't at all averse to adding to the German's discomfiture. "Well, there's Nikolai Gribov for one."

The German replied ruefully, "I hope she has better luck with him than me." He continued, shaking his head, "Of course, you can't expect to turn a German into a Frenchman overnight."

"If anybody can do it, Catherine can," Amy Leary remarked. She turned to von Norden. "Don't you find her fascinating?"

The German played at being the gallant courtier. "Of course. However," he added to Vivian, who had been sitting beside him without paying much attention to the banter, "she isn't as attractive as your daughter."

Vivian's wooden expression remained unchanged, "You're just saying that," she commented, as if it were a highly original observation.

Amy took her daughter's part. "She's very young, Baron."

"The young are often very good at languages," he said, turning to Vivian. "When we went to Lasserre for dinner the other night, you ordered quite professionally."

Her father had no illusions. "If it's expensive, she can handle it."

"Oh, *Daddy!*" Vivian objected, then seemed to cuddle up protectively beside the German as she said, "Don't pay any attention to *him.*"

Whatever Holden had thought about Vivian before, he felt somewhat better because she wouldn't let the German monopolize Fay, whom he seemed to prefer. He tossed off a drink as it was handed to him. "Well, guess I'd better be going." To Fay he added, "I'll see you at Henri's later?"

She laughed at his evident concern. "Sure thing, Arch."

A gravelly voice interrupted behind them. "Don't be too sure."

They turned and saw Guy Saffron, the *Paris Press* reporter, in soiled brown slacks, an old tweed coat and a white shirt open at the collar. He was standing beside Pat Leary, drink in hand—having apparently separated himself from the crowd around the bar—and wandered over to join the party.

He waved his free hand around the circle of upturned faces. "Hi, folks. Just wanted to tell Fay here that she's got a little surprise comin'."

Fay tried to pass off the interruption. "Is the surprise pleasant or unpleasant?"

"Depends entirely on how you feel, sweetie," Saffron said.

Von Norden saw that the newcomer was less pleasing than annoying to his guests, and stood up. With a formal air, he asked, "And you are . . . ?"

"The professor here will tell you all about me, Baron," was the cool response.

"Saffron of the *Paris Press*," Leary interjected for von Norden's benefit, "and an old friend from New Haven."

"But nobody has to introduce you to me, Baron," the reporter resumed. "You're the big gun from Bonn. Met you at General Teschner's headquarters at the last NATO maneuvers."

"Ah, you were with the foreign press group," von Norden said, simulating sudden recognition. "I should have remembered." But he indicated no pleasure, and renewed his pressure on the newcomer. "So you have a surprise, Mr. Saffron?"

"Not so much for you but maybe for some of the rest," was the teasing response. "Especially"—and he lifted his glass in Fay's direction—"for Madame."

"Get on with it, Saffron," Leary said with an air of indulgence. "We've a dinner date with the baron."

"Okay." The reporter turned and motioned to someone in the crowd around the bar. "Here we go."

A sluggish, sleepy-eyed young man with thinning red hair and a close-cropped red beard separated himself from the bar crowd as if he were acting on cue. Although he was neatly dressed in a dark suit, white shirt and regimental striped tie, there was a suggestion of power and ruthlessness about him. His movements were slow but deliberate, almost like those of a trip-hammer. And when he stood before them, glass in hand, he stared directly at Fay with heavy-lidded pale blue eyes. "We meet again, my dear."

She gave an unhappy little cry. "Spence!"

Holden remained rooted where he stood, his face mirroring both his surprise and his dismay. He had not imagined that Fay, for all her assumption of inner strength, could be so unnerved by the mere presence of her former husband.

Pat Leary was the first to recover. With a few quick strides, he reached the side of the red-bearded young man and grasped his hand, pumping it vigorously. "Good to see you again, Bainbridge. When did you get in?"

Still staring directly at Fay, Bainbridge replied, "Couple hours ago. Came here directly from Charles de Gaulle Airport to see what was stirring." He advanced toward Fay with continued deliberation, bent over and brushed her cheek with his lips, and took her hand. "So good to see you again, and looking so well. You must excuse Saffron's dramatics. If a journalist can't kick up a big fuss, I guess he has to create a small one. But I don't want to interrupt." Bainbridge released Fay's hand, stood erect and glanced about the little company, greeting each in turn except for Holden and stopping with the German. "Glad to see you're in such good hands, Baron."

Von Norden arose and smiled. "We've missed you, Spence. Coming back to the diplomatic corps?"

"Not right away." Now Bainbridge was gazing at Holden with something more than mere curiosity. "Thought I'd take my leave in Paris before going to work on the UN project. It's a temporary reassignment."

"Maybe the State Department can be persuaded to make it permanent," the German said. "You were the best doubles partner I've had here."

Bainbridge bowed slightly in acknowledgment. "Glad somebody appreciates my special talent." He seemed to be wavering for a few moments, then appeared to have made a decision. He moved toward Holden. "Don't think we've met."

"Arch Holden's new to Paris," Pat Leary explained.

Bainbridge seized the pianist's sensitive right hand in a bone-crushing grip that made him grimace in pain and draw back slightly. "Spencer Bainbridge." The red-bearded newcomer nodded toward Fay, who was watching the encounter between the two men with flushed cheeks. "I hear from Saffron that my former wife speaks well of you."

Holden tried to free his hand without seeming to be rude about it, retorting, "I think well of her, too."

Amy Leary apparently decided the confrontation had gone far enough. She rose, looked around at the company and said, "If we're ever going to dinner, we'd better start."

Everybody gathered around her in evident relief. Pat Leary took his wife's arm. Gareth, who had been nuzzling Stephanie, now put one big arm around her and drew her along beside his mother. Vivian, still expressionless, tagged along beside von Norden. And Fay, although she stood up, seemed at a loss as to what to do next.

Von Norden pretended not to have noticed Fay's indecision. "Why don't you come along to dinner with us, Spence?"

Bainbridge looked at her fixedly. "If Fay doesn't mind."

She seemed to force herself into politeness. "Oh, not at all," she said, but her voice was faint and she stared fixedly at the carpet, avoiding the directness of her former husband's gaze.

The party drifted toward the Place Vendome entrance to the Ritz, brushing past Holden who hadn't moved. He was watching Fay, wondering about her, hoping to catch her eye, wanting to draw her aside and tell her he loved her. But when the opportunity came, as she was passing him, the exchange was painfully commonplace.

"Oh, Arch, I forgot, you don't have a car. I must take you to work."

"That's all right."

"But what are you going to do?" She glanced at her watch. "You have to be at the Place St. Michel in fifteen minutes."

"I'll take a cab." He wanted to hold her and kiss her, but he froze as he saw Bainbridge coming up behind her. "See you later, then?"

"Sure." A tremulous moment as their eyes met. "G'bye."

"'Bye."

As she moved off with the crowd, he heard Bainbridge rumble, "You take up with the strangest men, my dear."

To which she replied firmly, "You go to hell."

Her show of spirit heartened Holden. But as he turned away to go out the Rue Cambon entrance and find a cab, he saw Guy Saffron standing nearby, watching him with a twisted grin. "You got yourself a problem, fella."

Holden was irritated. At first, he didn't want to talk to Saffron at all but his curiosity got the better of him. "What do you mean?"

"It's not so good when your girl's ex shows up, is it?"

Holden shrugged indifferently. "It's her problem."

Saffron wasn't deterred. His twisted grin widened. "Maybe it's his problem, too. He sure didn't turn his back on *her*."

Holden relapsed into silence, but the reporter fell into step with him as they left the bar and headed for the Rue Cambon entrance. Saffron prodded him, using much the same bald technique as a small boy who thrusts a stick into a bear's cage to annoy the animal. "Actually," he said, with an air of sufferance, "Spence Bainbridge isn't such a bad guy."

"Yeah?"

They strode along together in silence for a few moments. Saffron suggested, "Maybe, if it hadn't been for Catherine Vaillant, they might still be together. Y'know, their marriage was one of the events of the season not so long ago."

Holden was in no mood to be tormented. He demanded, "What are you trying to do, Saffron? Get me to poke Bainbridge in the nose?"

Saffron was hopeful. "It'd make a story." But he quickly added, as if to show he hadn't been serious, "I thought you'd be interested. Because, y'see, this kid you're going with pretends to be just a simple little doll, but actually her stepfather has a lot of clout at the White House."

Holden was nonplussed. "Look, I'm just a piano player. Her stepfather's clout doesn't mean much to me."

"Maybe not, but Bainbridge has been doing some thinking about that situation since his divorce." They emerged from the hotel into the cool evening air. The reporter added, "For a guy in the diplomatic service, he just wasn't very smart to be caught out in Paris with a French dame."

An old cab, summoned by the doorman, drew up at the curb and the poorly dressed, elderly driver touched his cap in a casual salute. Holden edged toward the open door of the cab. "Can I give you a lift?"

Saffron wasn't paying attention. He had recognized the driver, and spoke with him briefly before turning to Holden. "This is Andrei Pedenko, Mac, an old-timer at the Ritz cabstand. He'll take you where you want to go. Me, I'm headed the other way." He jerked a thumb over his shoulder. "Out to Neuilly, where the paper is."

Holden was relieved. His only thought at the moment was to get away from the Ritz Bar, from the *Paris Press* reporter, from all the other visiting Americans coming and going into the old hotel. As the cab took off with a disagreeable jerk for the Rue de Rivoli and the bridge across the Seine most convenient to the Place St. Michel, he slumped back on the well-worn seat cushions and wearily closed his eyes. He didn't want to think any more about Fay and Spencer Bainbridge. But try as he might, he couldn't shut out of his mind the memory of her taut and troubled face when she saw her ex-husband standing before her.

Henri studied his watch in the manner of an irritable drillmaster when Holden walked in five minutes late, glanced about the well-nigh deserted establishment and headed for the piano bar. "We keep precise hours here, Mr. Holden," the *patron* said, meaningfully, glancing at his watch.

"Couldn't help it, boss." Holden tried to pass off the five-minute infraction lightly. "I was with the Learys and some other people at the Ritz Bar..."

"Ah, yes, Stephanie was there too, with the young Leary boy?"

Holden took another look about the sparsely filled restaurant. "Guess she's late, too."

"My friend, Stephanie took the precaution of telephoning me, and I gave her *permission*"—the *patron* emphasized the word—"to go on to dinner with the Learys as the guest of Baron von Norden." He summed up in the manner of a man who didn't want to make too much of a small though necessary point of conduct. "You will not find me unreasonable as long as you keep me informed, Mr. Holden. I appreciate it, truly, when my employees take an interest in our good customers."

Because he had been brooding over the incident at the Ritz Bar, Holden couldn't resist asking, "Then what do you expect me to do about Spencer Bainbridge?"

"Mr. Bainbridge, who was formerly with the American embassy? He has returned?"

Holden nodded glumly. "He's with the baron's crowd and the Learys, and so is his former wife."

"A difficult situation." Henri stroked his mustache thoughtfully, then brightened. "But we must be agreeable to all our customers, Mr. Holden. Is it not so?" He motioned with one arm toward the piano bar. "Including that one," he added.

Holden peered into the dim light and made out the figure of Catherine Vaillant, perched on a bar stool next to the sad-faced Italian dancing master, Enzo Pastore. She seemed slim and very sophisticated tonight in a black suit and white silk blouse, pearls and four-inch heels, a mink coat carelessly flung across the bar beside her.

Although she didn't notice him at first, he felt drawn to her again more strongly than ever. He was laboring under a storm of conflicting emotions. It had been bad enough for Fay to seem to be attracted to the German, von Norden, but now she could be under quite different and even more direct pressure from Spencer Bainbridge, her ex-husband. And after what she already had told him about her stepfather's campaign for a remarriage to Bainbridge, Holden was by turn angered, uncertain and despairing. Even ignoring the petty rebuke Henri had given him for being five minutes late, he quite literally felt drained of feeling at the notion that Fay now was at dinner with not only one serious rival, but two.

Holden cursed himself for having been so simple-minded as to believe that he could solve all his problems merely by taking Fay to bed with him. Now, an intense fit of jealousy and resentment at Fay's meek acceptance of her ex-husband's sudden reappearance tore at his feelings. He stood there between Henri and the piano, clenching and unclenching his fists, trying desperately to maintain at least an appearance of calmness.

The *patron*, evidently attributing Holden's emotional fit to the rebuke for his tardiness, had misgivings. "You must not think that I do not appreciate what you are doing for us, Mr. Holden," he interjected in a soothing manner. "Because I expect promptness, do not think that I have failed to appreciate both your talent and your devotion to your work for me."

Holden, however, could not be appeased. He was on the piano bench in three strides, pounding out *fortissimo* the first tune that came to his mind, which happened to be Cole Porter's old standard, "It Was Just One of Those Things."

Catherine Vaillant, unable to continue her conversation with Pastore, turned meditatively to watch him as he agitatedly flung his hands about the keyboard. And when he finally had thumped out the last chords with painful loudness, she commented briefly, "Gracious, Arch!"

He stared at her with fierce intensity. "You don't like it?"

"I don't mind," she replied, choosing her words carefully, "but why all the noise?" Unlike Henri, she seemed to have a more sensitive feeling about the cause of Holden's disturbance. In dealing with men, she rarely made a foolish mistake.

"That's the way I feel, goddamit." He ripped out the answer with savage fervor.

"Excuse me," she said in a low voice to Pastore. Without another word to him, she calmly draped her fur over her arm, came slowly around the piano bar and took over a part of the piano bench beside Holden. He caught the faintly exotic scent so typical of her, felt the gentle pressure of her body against his and had to admire the proud manner in which she held her beautiful face in three-quarters profile.

"What's the trouble, Arch?" Her voice was low, sympathetic, appealing.

For a moment, he was wildly moved by impulse to let her lead him wherever she wished. She was here beside him, inviting, even seductive—a powerfully emotional antidote to the storm seething within him. To divert him, she dangled a small white beaded bag before him. "I'm off tonight," she said lightly. "No big translator's bag over my shoulder tonight, Arch."

He smiled. "Good!"

"It's playtime, Arch," she announced. "Don't be so serious." Few women could be as charming as Catherine Vaillant when she wanted to make the effort. And she was trying now. As Holden realized from the night he first saw her, she was deeply interested in him, for reasons he didn't understand.

Yet, even as he felt so powerfully drawn to her, he held back. She rested her small bag on the piano, and he felt her hand stroking his, then withdrawing. "You're upset, Arch," she said in a low voice. "What's the trouble? Tell me."

"I didn't like Henri bawling me out in public," he evaded.

Her direct gaze never wavered, even though he didn't abandon his fixed stare at the keyboard. "Sure there isn't something else?" Her tone was casual, but he could sense intensity in her question. He held back, however; whatever Catherine wanted of him tonight, he sensed an ulterior purpose. He said harshly, "There's nothing else," and forced himself into his usual routine—a new song or two, something from show business, some standard oldies, and perhaps a novelty number—all judiciously mixed but held together with brief improvisations of his own.

She shrugged, draped her fur over her shoulders and returned to her bar stool next to Pastore. The Italian had been watching the little drama on the piano bench with mild amusement. "You want him, signora?" he asked, nodding toward Holden.

She touched the glass before her to her lips, showing no sign either of impatience or displeasure. "Scarcely. I'm waiting for Nikolai Gribov."

"I rent him my hunting lodge in Fontainebleau," Pastore said. "He tells me it is his *dacha*. Pays me well."

She consulted her wristwatch. "Gribov should be here by now. Why is it that these singers and musicians"—here she smiled briefly at Holden—"are usually late?"

131

Holden didn't say anything. He was calmer now, methodical in his playing, as he used her gambit to change the subject. "Gribov is a great man. He can afford to be late, unlike a poor piano player."

"He should not be late, especially when the signora is so beautiful, so elegant tonight," Pastore objected.

"Madame is always beautiful," Holden said, nodding and continuing his improvisations.

She considered his compliment with that direct, unwavering look in her dark eyes—her big look. "One day," she observed quietly, "you will believe that."

With a melancholy smile, the Italian said, "One day it will hit him like this," and he smacked his hands together, at the same time exclaiming, *"Colpo!"*

Holden continued his theme *pianissimo* without a break. He wasn't sure why he had drawn back from Catherine Vaillant at that critical moment when he had been so overcome by anger at Fay. Perhaps something in her manner had turned him off. Perhaps it had been her expensive dress—expensive, certainly, for a professional translator—that made him suspect somebody was keeping her. And now that he had heard she was waiting for Gribov, and that Gribov had rented Pastore's hunting lodge at Fontainebleau, Holden felt relieved. His instincts had been right. Fay's indecision still rankled. But he suspected that he could have been even more disturbed had he responded to Catherine.

Charley Fourier had told him, "You can't satisfy Catherine, in bed or out of it. And you'd better not try it."

When Holden wanted to know what Fourier meant, his friend evaded a direct answer but went on, "I never saw a woman who could ask more damn-fool questions at the worst possible times. Always wanted to know what people were doing—and why."

Holden could get nothing more out of his predecessor, which didn't go very far toward explaining Catherine Vaillant. It only increased Holden's wariness of her. And that was why she was now on one side of the piano bar and he remained on the other. It was, he thought, just as well. Regardless of what Fay said or did, he was more at ease with her than he was with Catherine.

Holden felt more like himself now. He was in command of

his emotions and no longer inclined to give way to either anger or despair. But he did want to test Catherine, to find out, if he could, what she might know of Spencer Bainbridge's return and his uncle's campaign to force Fay into a remarriage.

He remarked in an offhand way to Catherine as he ran his hands over the keyboard, "Met another of your students tonight."

Her reaction was bland to the point of indifference. "Yes, which one?"

"The German baron, von Norden."

"Ah yes, Rudi. So charming. Sometimes I almost want to forgive him for being German. Where did you meet him?" she asked.

The nonchalant reply, without a break in the piano routine: "At the Ritz Bar. He was with the Learys' daughter, Vivian."

She looked boredly into her tall glass. "Rudi is always after the young ones, the younger the better."

Holden enlarged on his theme, slightly increasing the tempo. "Spencer Bainbridge was there, too." He said it carelessly, but he was quite deliberate about watching her reaction.

She affected indifference. "I knew the embassy had asked him to do the P.R. work at the UN Special Assembly. So now he's arrived?"

"Large as life." He was very much in control now, feeding her brief questions and seemingly idle remarks in an offhand manner.

She was even more careful than he was. "Somebody at the embassy was saying the Bainbridges might remarry."

He didn't even blink, recognizing that now she was testing him. All he said was, "Oh?"

With instinctive grace, the Italian slipped from his bar stool with a brief, *"Scusa."* It was a special virtue of Henri's barflies, Holden thought, that they became bored with conversation they didn't understand.

Catherine sipped her drink and eyed him speculatively. "You ought to know something about that marriage business, seeing as much of Mrs. Bainbridge as you do."

He smiled and shook his head. "She minds her own business."

Catherine was disinclined at the moment to say much more.

To cover the silence, he made casual music. He always did that very well. "Doodling," he called it; it was his way of disparaging his own gift for improvisation.

Presently, Catherine asked another question. "Think I should tell Gribov about the Bainbridges?"

"Tell him anything you like," he said.

"You know," she went on, "he has a special fondness for the Bainbridges. They hid him for a while after he defected."

Holden kept playing without a break. "That's ancient history now, isn't it?"

With a great appearance of openness, she began chattering about the Bainbridges. "I was so surprised when they were divorced. Spencer didn't want it, even *told me at the embassy,*" and she emphasized that with virtuous solemnity, "that he was still very much in love with his wife. But she seemed to want it, and that was the end of it."

Catherine seemed to want Holden to believe that she was blameless and waited for him to say something. When he didn't respond, she went on with just a trace of indignation, "Even her parents didn't want her to get a divorce. Why, her stepfather told the ambassador that he wanted to persuade his daughter not to do such a senseless thing. You know"—and it was almost an aside—"Spencer is a nephew of Mrs. Bainbridge's stepfather."

"The stepfather has the clout to get the ambassador's attention?" Holden asked skeptically.

"Goodness, yes!" She played with her tall glass, then glanced at him. "You didn't know?"

"Don't even know who the guy is," Holden said.

"You won't find many politicians in your country or mine who haven't heard of Waco Texas Carroll," she replied warmly. "A very rich and powerful man, rich in oil and cattle. And a big man," she added, "big even for Texas."

Holden softened the music to hear her better. "But in spite of his influence, the Bainbridges were divorced. Is that the whole story?"

"Part of it." She continued, "Mrs. Bainbridge is not the helpless girl she may seem to be, Arch. She got the psychiatrist at the American Hospital here, Dr. Beranger, to recommend the divorce, and I think her mother actually paid for it." She paused, seemingly to gather her thoughts. "You know, I find it strange that just when there is talk at the embassy of a reconciliation between the Bainbridges, Mrs. Bainbridge suddenly returns to Paris and takes up living in Dr. Beranger's apartment on the Ile St. Louis." She caught her breath. "And now Spencer Bainbridge, too, is here."

"What does that mean?" Holden was trying to egg her on.

She needed no urging. "Then, the Learys are here, too. Everybody, in fact, who had something to do with Nikolai Gribov's defection."

"And what do you make of that?" Holden was inwardly amused because she was obviously leading up to a conclusion.

But she held off, saying vaguely, "There's a lot going on that we don't know about." All at once she leaned across the piano bar toward him. "Arch, be careful and don't get involved. You could be in great danger!"

She didn't get a chance to elaborate on her cryptic warning, because just then Nikolai Gribov entered the restaurant. But, thinking back over the conversation later, Holden was morally certain that she either knew or had guessed something of the plans for snatching Olga Varenka from the Russians.

However, at the moment nobody could have failed to notice that Gribov had, in effect, taken center stage. He was dramatically dressed, as always, in a wide-brimmed floppy black fedora, a billowing black cloak and a theatrical costume of open-necked white shirt and tight black pants underneath. He gave a happy roar as he smothered Henri in a bear hug. *"Mon ami, mon cher ami!"*

Enzo Pastore, who had been talking animatedly with the *patron* until the Russian entered, now slipped back to the piano bar and mounted a stool. To Catherine, he remarked with a slight frown, "What a noise this Russian makes."

She said, as if that explained everything, "He is a great singer."

"But not as great as Pavarotti, signora," the Italian rejoined.

"We all have our preferences," she said, with feigned indifference, but glanced over her shoulder to see what Gribov was doing.

Pastore noticed. With a grin, he announced, "The Russian comes to you now, signora. He is in a big hurry."

"He is always in a big hurry," she observed, taking a small sip from her glass. "You will remember, when we were at the little restaurant in Barbizon where we went over the rental contract for your hunting lodge, he did not even want to listen to my translation of the contract. All he wanted to do was sign."

Pastore nodded. "He pays well."

She agreed. "I have no complaint."

The Russian was upon them now, bellowing at Catherine, "Ah, my dear, how beautiful!" She turned her cheek and leaned toward him to let him kiss her, which he did with an elaborate display of affection. "You have been waiting long?" he asked as he mounted a bar stool beside her.

"Not long, Nikolai," she replied. She nodded toward her glass. "Drink?"

"No, madame, we do not stay here," he said.

"You have other plans?"

"For you, big plans!" he exclaimed with a roar of delight. "Now I have *dacha*." He nodded toward the Italian. "Signor Pastore's *dacha* at Fontainebleau, and we must inspect it."

Catherine was dubious. "It is a long drive."

"But tonight, I do not sing opera, I am free, madame," he explained. "We have dinner at our little cafe in Barbizon, yes? Is not long drive, you will see. Anyway, my chauffeur takes us in my car." He slipped from the bar stool and held out his arm. "Come, my little one."

Holden had to admire Catherine's self-possession. "A moment, Nikolai," she said, inspecting herself briefly in her handbag mirror and expertly touching up a fancied blemish on one lip.

He exhaled breath sharply in a monumental show of impatience and then stood back with folded arms to await her pleasure. She took no notice, Holden saw, except to glance at the Russian once out of the corner of her eyes. And when she was finally ready, she seemed to take special pleasure in making him pay further attention to her leisurely departure by giving him her mink coat to hold, and smiling up at him prettily. "Perhaps I should wear my coat, Nikolai," she said. "The ride to Fontainebleau may be chilly."

Again, she tried his patience by making an elaborate show

of struggling into her coat as he held it for her, then giving him a small reward with a negligent pat of one hand on his bearded cheek. "Thank you, Nikolai."

"We go now, yes?" he prompted loudly.

"As you wish."

"And maybe," he roared, as he escorted her from the restaurant, "we study French tonight at *dacha!*" He gave a bellow of laughter, as Shukri, the doorman, swung the door shut behind him.

Holden reflected on how far Catherine had been able to push her work as Gribov's translator by insinuating herself into his personal life. How much would she find out tonight at the hunting lodge about Olga Varenka? Or would she, perhaps, even supplant Olga Varenka in Gribov's affections and nullify his plans to rescue his Russian mistress?

The Italian evidently was also speculating on Catherine's apparent success with Gribov, for he said, "This is much woman, this Catherine. Maybe," and he smiled whimsically, "she is too much for our Russian friend."

Holden doodled on the keyboard. "He will study French with her."

"Ah yes," the Italian agreed, "she will give him some fancy lessons, that one. Some lessons he will not forget."

"You know her that well?" Holden asked, inwardly amused.

Pastore murmured, as if to himself, "To know the *signora* well? Ha!" He added for Holden's particular benefit, "When a man studies French with the *signora,* he learns many things." And he repeated, "Many, many things."

Chapter Five

There's no accounting for piano players or lovers. And when the two are combined, you can expect lightning flashes on a lot of personal horizons.

That's the way it was for the regulars at the piano bar in Henri's after Spencer Bainbridge's reappearance in Paris. For Arch Holden wasn't taking Fay's courtship by her former husband lightly. He was playing detective in his off-hours. He saw them, lost them. Once he even confronted Fay, after he had come across her unexpectedly at the embassy, and was on the point of making a scene when she pleaded with him,

"Don't, Arch. It's bad enough as it is. Don't make it worse."

"Then why are you doing this to me?" he demanded. "Why can't I see you when I want to?"

She was on the point of tears. "Let me handle this in my own way," she begged him. "If I had only myself to consider, maybe everything would be different. But my stepfather..." She never did finish what she was going to say about that formidable personage, but broke off and fairly ran from Holden before he could stop her.

Yet, he remained convinced, for all his frustrations and disappointments, that he could win her back; and he made every effort to do so. As a mark of his faithfulness, he would walk in fine weather from his own flat in the St. Germain des Près district on the Left Bank to the Ile St. Louis, directly behind Notre Dame, to see what had become of her. But gradually, after the elderly concierge at her apartment building reported the American lady had not been seen for some time, Holden realized she was deliberately avoiding him.

That angered him. He could not believe that she was giving

up their relationship of her own volition. He could recall all too well those delicious moments in bed with her when, finally overcoming her fears and her distractions, she gave herself to him freely, lovingly, even fiercely. The memory heartened him, made him believe that eventually he could overcome whatever pressures she now was under to force her back into marriage with Spencer Bainbridge.

It helped him to talk to Pat and Amy Leary about his feelings whenever he felt down. When they came to Henri's, which was fairly frequent, he always sat with them during a break in his routine at the piano and told them what little he knew of Fay's whereabouts and his own quest to solve the riddle of her disappearance. While they couldn't help him very much, they were at least sympathetic. The *patron* didn't even want to talk to him about Fay, being afraid it might alienate some of his American trade. And Henri, being an eminently practical Parisian, knew he couldn't afford to take sides in these interminable clashes of temperament and purpose among the Americans on whose business he depended.

And so, when the Learys appeared at Henri's for a late supper while they were in Paris, it was always heartening to Holden to have coffee with them during breaks in his routine and exchange whatever information they had about Fay and the former husband who seemed to have such power over her. Bit by bit, pieces of the puzzle fitted together, and both the Learys and Holden began to understand that there was nothing very mysterious about the reasons Fay was avoiding them and the other regulars at Henri's. It appeared well-nigh certain that Waco Texas Carroll, Fay's stepfather, was dictating every move in the campaign to force Fay into remarriage with his nephew, Bainbridge. First, Carroll's power over Fay's inheritance, as well as her mother's source of income, was absolute, as Fay had confided to friends at the embassy. And through the ambassador's deferential acceptance of Carroll's demands to make sure that Fay was not subject to "pernicious influences," meaning mainly Holden, it also appeared that Carroll had political clout that he applied ruthlessly in Washington, D.C. As for the relationship between Carroll and his nephew, Bainbridge, that seemed to be as close and as mutually advantageous as ever, although the scope and nature of their activities continued to be confined to disturbing rumors.

Holden had his own suspicions about Bainbridge's operations in Paris, based on what he had picked up from regulars at Henri's piano bar. As Charley Fourier had told him, the piano bar was a good listening post because its largely American clientele was usually well-informed and unusually indiscreet.

Bainbridge hadn't been in Paris very long before rumors spread through the American colony in Paris about his intimate relations with Arabs from the oil-rich Persian Gulf states who were accustomed to meeting him at the Ritz Bar of a late afternoon or early evening. While none of the regulars at Henri's could prove that money changed hands at these meetings, it was a virtual certainty that information did. And to people who invested in oil stocks, good information on Arab operations was hard to come by; therefore, a reliable source was, as one of the regulars at Henri's put it, as "good as gold."

The one element in Bainbridge's activities on which Holden couldn't get much of a fix was his relations with Catherine Vaillant. For Catherine and Nikolai Gribov now were being seen together constantly, and as one regular from the American embassy reported, they seemed to be spending a lot of their evenings together at the hunting lodge in Fontainebleau Forest. "As a contract translator, she used to be around regularly for work, so we began to depend on her; but now she's almost useless to us," the embassy man remarked one evening when the gossip had reached barroom level.

At any rate, Holden saw nothing of Catherine, either, and could only speculate on whether Gribov still meant to rescue Olga Varenka during the Kirov Ballet's Paris engagement. If Gribov again intended to involve Bainbridge, there was no sign of it so far. And if Bainbridge yearned for a renewed liaison with Catherine Vaillant, he didn't seem sufficiently motivated to leave the Arabs at the Ritz Bar to look her up. For that matter, she seemed to have pretty well settled on Gribov.

Under these circumstances, what would happen to Olga Varenka, in Holden's estimation, could very well depend on the intensity of the ballet dancer's own feeling for separating herself from Soviet influence. In fact, the pianist concluded, if Olga found out about Gribov's liaison with Catherine Vaillant, Paris might not be large enough to hold the three of them, let alone Fay and Bainbridge in the bargain.

One evening, not long after Catherine Vaillant had become Gribov's mistress, a familiar brooding face appeared above one of the piano bar stools at Henri's. It was early evening, and the newcomer was the first to take up a position there. At first, Holden tried to guess the early customer's identity by cautiously sounding him out for a clue as to where they had met. But the man saved him the trouble by muttering into his beer, "I'm Cary Wisner. Saw you at the embassy, remember?"

Holden remembered and was not overly cordial.

Wisner was patient. He nursed his beer, accepted repeated rebuffs from Holden without showing temper and finally came to the point of his unexpected visit while he was still alone with the pianist. "What do you hear about the Kirov Ballet matter?"

Holden shrugged as he let his fingers idly roam over the keyboard. "Nothing."

"Is everything still on 'go'?"

"Didn't know it had gone that far," he commented.

"Seen the big Russky lately?"

Holden understood the reference to Gribov, but wasn't in a mood to offer a tidbit about one of his contract translators. If the embassy couldn't keep up with Catherine Vaillant, he thought, then the embassy didn't deserve to be given the latest gossip about her.

So it went for the better part of the half-hour or so that Wisner spent at the piano bar with Holden. Regardless of how many questions he asked, the result was the same: no information, no speculation, no progress. As he climbed off the bar stool, the visitor gave the subject his parting shot:

"Think anything will ever come of this business?"

Holden frowned. "Don't know what you mean."

"Well, do you think anything will ever happen?"

"Can't say." He shrugged, as if he hadn't been burdened by that very question.

Wisner finished his beer without comment, but as he left,

he gave Holden something to think about. "Y'know Spence Bainbridge?"

"Saw him once."

"Well, he's saying around the embassy that he's getting married again this June."

Holden's fingers froze on the keyboard. "Who to?" he asked, in a cracked voice.

Wisner was buttoning his raincoat. "The guy's not very original. I hear the bride's his ex-wife." He pulled his battered hat down over his forehead. "Well, see y' around." And he wandered casually from the bistro.

For the rest of the evening, Holden couldn't apply himself to his work. He messed up even the familiar old standards that he used to get older Americans in a sentimental mood suitable for prolonged reminiscence and drinking. As soon as he could get away from Henri's, which was shortly after that midnight, he took a cab to the Ile St. Louis and mounted the steep stairs two at a time when he saw Fay's apartment aglow with light. He pounded on the door.

A man's shrill voice demanded in French to know the late caller's identity. The voice was unfamiliar. Holden was so upset, however, that he wouldn't have cared if the voice had turned out to be Bainbridge's. So he yelled in English, "Hey, it's Arch Holden, the piano player at Henri's. Open up!"

A long pause, during which nothing happened.

In sheer desperation, Holden kicked at the bottom of the door. "Open up, damn you!"

A key turned in the lock. The door creaked open slightly and Holden saw a small, thin-faced man with bushy white hair and a flowing white mustache peering at him through thick eyeglasses. "What do you want?"

"I want to see Fay Carroll," Holden demanded. He had no idea who the man was and didn't care at that particular moment. After muffling his feelings for so long, he was throwing off all restraint.

"She's not here." The older man guarded the door.

"Where is she?"

"I'm not sure. Somewhere around the Pantheon, I think." A pause, while the thin-faced man studied Holden through the partly open door. He added, not unkindly, "If you'll call me tomorrow, I think I can get you the address from the people at the embassy. They know more about it than I do."

Holden gritted his teeth. "I can't wait until tomorrow." He almost shouted, "I've got to see Fay."

"I hear you perfectly well, you needn't yell." The man assumed a crisp, professional tone. "I think you'd better come in here and let me take a look at you, Mr. Holden." He opened the door wider.

"Why? Who are you?" Holden drew back.

The man pointed to a small sign above a green outside doorbell. "I'm Dr. Beranger. This is my office, as well as my apartment."

Holden stood his ground, refusing the psychiatrist's invitation to enter the apartment. "But Fay was living here, wasn't she?"

The psychiatrist said abruptly, "She is not here now." He would have closed the door, but Holden thrust his foot over the threshold with a quick movement, and challenged the psychiatrist: "You're going to be held responsible for whatever happens to her, I'll see to that!"

Dr. Beranger protested mildly, "Fay Carroll was my patient, still is, and I've always done the best I could for her." He had given up trying to close the door but, pointing to Holden's foot projecting over the threshold, said, "If you don't mind, I'd like to lock up as long as you won't come in. It's late."

Holden wouldn't budge. He shook a finger at the older man and almost shouted, "Let me tell you something, doctor. Because you abandoned Fay's care, because you went off to America and let her shift for herself, she's right back now where all this started. Bainbridge is telling people at the American embassy that he's going to marry her again in June."

"How do you know that?" The psychiatrist was clearly distressed.

"One of the embassy officials told me only tonight," Holden added, again raising his voice. "And damn it all, doctor, if you don't stop this marriage, I will."

The psychiatrist studied Holden for a few moments. "You seem to be under great stress, Mr. Holden." He again opened the door wider. "I think you'd better come in and we'll talk things over."

This time Holden did not refuse. He entered the hall, blinking at the harsh overhead lights, and let his host lead him into what he took to be an office for consultation. The living quarters were in the rear.

Dr. Beranger motioned to Holden to seat himself on a chair beside a big desk, obviously the one reserved for patients. The psychiatrist then slipped into the desk chair, smiled encouragingly at the younger man and suggested, "Now, let's talk."

It was late. Holden was feeling contrite; the psychiatrist had been talking to him for some time about matters of little consequence to soothe him. And yet, even in his somewhat less aggressive mood, he was still determined to find out when he could see Fay. "Where can I find Fay, doctor?" He was calmer than he had been, and his voice was under control.

"Truly, I wish I could help you tonight, but I can't," Dr. Beranger observed with mild regret, subtly restating his original position. He went on, "Tomorrow morning, as soon as the embassy opens, I'm sure I'll be able to locate her for you." With a reassuring air, he advised, "Whatever you have to say to her will keep for just a few hours, won't it?"

It seemed so reasonable that Holden had to agree. And yet, he felt as if he were being put off. "The embassy crowd is going to stick with Bainbridge," he said. "I know that. So what help can I expect from them?"

"But I'm not part of the embassy crowd," the psychiatrist reminded him. "I'm on *your* side."

At once, Holden was resentful. "Supposedly, you were on Fay's side, too, but look at the fix she's in now."

Dr. Beranger leaned back in his office chair and pursed his lips, tilting his head sidewise as he studied the younger man. "I think you misunderstood the circumstances, Mr. Holden. May I review them, please?"

Holden nodded reluctantly.

"Very well," the psychiatrist began. "I want you to know that I did not abandon Fay, as you put it when you were out there in the hall shouting at me. I have never in my life abandoned any patient. Let me first assure you of that."

Dr. Beranger paused to note Holden's reaction. The younger man merely gave him a noncommittal nod. "Perhaps I shouldn't have shouted," he said, but made no apology and waited for the psychiatrist to resume.

Dr. Beranger, with a slight shaking of his head, continued. "I do suppose it is difficult for a layman to understand how delicately some of these cases have to be handled, but let me try to explain.

"My principal recommendation, once I had studied Fay's case, was to expedite her divorce from Bainbridge to the extent that our American judicial processes permit," Dr. Beranger said in a low voice. "Fortunately, even though her stepfather opposed me, her mother was strongly in favor of her divorce— and paid for it, in fact. Even more fortunate, Bainbridge did not contest the divorce suit when it was filed. Consequently, when Fay returned to America to be with her mother, it seemed that there was a very good chance for both to resume the normal processes of life." Almost as an aside, the psychiatrist commented, "Actually, Fay's mother, for a number of reasons, had been under an even greater strain than her daughter had been, but I'll come to that later. Right now, let me deal with Fay. You have followed me so far?"

When the older man paused, Holden again nodded without comment.

"Under the circumstances, as long as the marital conflict had been resolved," the psychiatrist resumed, "I felt I might safely take my twice-postponed leave from the American Hospital here and proceed to the Menninger Clinic in the United States. But I made it a point to keep in touch with both Fay and her mother weekly by telephone to be sure that all was well. I didn't advertise this then, nor do I intend to do so now, but I must answer your accusation of neglecting a patient, Mr. Holden."

Holden was not in the least abashed. "I understand your position. I'd like to hear more."

"Naturally." The psychiatrist proceeded in an even voice. "Eventually, Fay felt so secure that she telephoned me not long ago at the Menninger Clinic and asked me whether I would approve of her return to Paris to resume her studies at the Paris Conservatory. Of course I did. It seemed to me to be a signal that she was on course and taking up the part of her life that she had been obliged to give up under the strain of her misfortune. And so I not only gave her my blessing but also offered her the use of my apartment and my car while she was in Paris. I could not know then that her stepfather had gained such ascendancy over her mother that he was in a position to try to force a remarriage and that Bainbridge would agree."

Holden, out of curiosity, raised the one question that had been troubling him. "If Bainbridge never opposed the divorce in the first place, what changed his mind so that he wants to remarry Fay?"

Dr. Beranger removed his glasses and busied himself by wiping them with his handkerchief. "Until Fay's mother came to me and spoke to me privately at my hotel while I was on my way back to Paris, I did not realize that Fay Carroll, in a few years, will come into a great deal of money that has been held in trust for her under her father's will." He replaced his glasses and leaned forward with a troubled air. "For reasons of their own, Fay's parents had maintained secrecy over this part of his will, but her stepfather, for his reasons, made the disclosure to Bainbridge in arguing the case for remarriage."

"Why didn't Carroll use that to stop the divorce?" Holden asked.

The psychiatrist turned up the palms of both hands in a gesture of helplessness. "I can only speculate on what was in his mind. I know now, because of what Fay's mother told me that night, that Carroll had obtained power of attorney over the mother's assets by threatening to have her declared incompetent. Evidently, that provided him for a time with sufficient funds to satisfy him. But somehow, and in some fashion as yet undisclosed, Carroll needed more money and now seems to have persuaded his nephew to work with him in what I deduce will be an effort to take over Fay's inheritance as well."

"Does Fay know this?"

The psychiatrist bowed his head. "Unfortunately, yes. She learned of it from her mother, which complicates everything. Because, you see, Fay has now been led to believe that, if she resists her stepfather and Bainbridge, her mother will be forced into a mental institution."

"These crooks will have to be stopped!" Holden exclaimed, jumping to his feet.

"Careful, you'll have to prove conspiracy; and lawyers tell

me it is a very difficult charge to sustain in American courts," Dr. Beranger cautioned.

"But we can't just sit still and do nothing. Fay deserves better than that of us." Almost unconsciously, Holden had put himself in league with the psychiatrist.

Dr. Beranger took notice at once of the changed position. "Now I'd like to ask *you* some questions, Mr. Holden."

"Go ahead." While he didn't raise his voice, there was defiance in his attitude. He wanted the psychiatrist to know that the fight on Carroll and Bainbridge was to be carried on regardless of consequences.

Dr. Beranger looked at him gravely. "Before you hammered on my door tonight, Mr. Holden, I didn't know you existed. Fay didn't say anything to me about you when I cut short my research at the Menninger Clinic and returned here to be with her." He paused meditatively, then asked, "Would you mind telling me what your interest is in this matter?"

Holden said simply, "I'm in love with Fay."

"From the way you burst in here, I assumed it was something like that. But you cannot have known her very long."

"That's true. We only met."

"Didn't you suspect that she came of wealthy parents?"

"No."

"And yet"—the psychiatrist chose his words carefully— "you could see at once that she wasn't without resources."

Holden was openly resentful. "So you think that I too am after Fay's money?"

The older man shrugged. "You'll have to admit that's a possibility."

For the first time in the conversation, Holden felt that he had to defend himself. Although he was outraged by the doctor's suggestion, he tried hard to keep his voice low and his emotions under control. "Dr. Beranger, there is no reason for you to trust me or even to believe me, but let me tell you that this is one case in which a man is attracted to a woman for no other reason than his love for her."

"Ah yes, the romantic urge," was the sardonic comment.

Irritated by the psychiatrist's deliberately offensive manner, Holden kept himself in check. "I didn't know Fay had anything to her name when I first saw her. I didn't know until you told me that she stands to inherit a fortune and that it may be taken away from her; but one way or another that doesn't in the least account for the way I feel about her. I don't need her money or anybody else's. I've been self-supporting since I was fifteen years old..."

"Are you thinking of marriage?" the psychiatrist interrupted.

Holden stared hard at the thin-faced little man before him. "You're way ahead of me, Dr. Beranger. Fay and I have just met. What will happen to us eventually, I can't say and I doubt if she can say."

"You're very convincing, Mr. Holden. Sorry if I've been a little rough on you, but I suspect that you've involved yourself in a situation that is far more difficult than you believe it to be. No matter how pure your motives may be"—and here the psychiatrist couldn't repress a small, professional smile—"I'm sure you know by this time that Fay Carroll is a very complex person."

Holden paused, then flared at the psychiatrist, "What do you mean when you say Fay is a complex person?"

The psychiatrist didn't answer directly but stared off in the distance somewhere over Holden's head. "You're having an affair with this young woman." It wasn't stated as a question, but as a fact.

"Yes."

"And you know that she is the product of a broken home and a broken marriage."

"All I know is that she and Bainbridge were married and divorced, and that she has been under a strain." Holden was going to say something else, but suddenly decided he didn't want to go into Fay's fears of being thought cold and unresponsive.

Despite the assurance of his manner, he wasn't at all prepared for the next question. It hit him with the impact of an unexpected blow: "Have you had a satisfactory sexual relationship with Fay?"

He felt himself redden. He evaded the issue. "Satisfactory? Just how do you want me to take that?"

"Well, is she responsive?"

"I think so."

"Do you always initiate the sexual act, or does she sometimes take the lead?"

"Both."

"Could you be more explicit?"

Holden felt embarrassed. "I've never talked about things like that before. . . ."

"Of course." There was just a trace of impatience in the psychiatrist's manner. "That's one of the problems with most sexual relationships. People keep their feelings bottled up inside them when, very often, it would be better to discuss them with their partners." Seeing Holden was still reluctant to go into detail, Dr. Beranger took another tack. "Let me see if I can make it a bit easier for you. When you first met Fay, did it occur to you that you were seducing her?"

"It wasn't like that at all." The response was sudden and almost instinctive, for all at once Holden felt free of restraint. "I didn't seduce her, she didn't seduce me. It just . . . well, it just happened, that's all."

"What we call mutual consent among reasonable, normal people?"

"Yes."

"She exhibited no sense of deprivation?"

"Deprivation of what?"

"Ah well, never mind." The psychiatrist rephrased his question. "She seemed satisfied after the sexual act?"

"At first we were both happy about it, doctor."

"And then?"

"After a while, she began asking me whether I thought she was . . ." He paused, again in embarrassment.

". . . frigid?" Dr. Beranger suggested.

"Yes, that was it. She said"—and here Holden regained confidence as he recalled Fay's distress—"that her husband had so often called her cold and unresponsive that she'd begun to believe it."

"Indeed, she did believe it, Mr. Holden. That was part of her trouble." The psychiatrist leaned forward and regarded his visitor intently. "But you don't think it is so?"

"Not at all."

"Have you ever found her to be unresponsive?"

"No." Again, Holden surprised himself with the additional

149

comment that seemed to slip out of him. "If anything, I had trouble keeping up with her, doctor."

"But you saw nothing abnormal about her responsiveness to you?"

"No."

Dr. Beranger chose his words carefully. "You must not be offended when I say that you are giving me the kind of judgments I'd expect from a man who has a good deal of experience in these matters. Is that so?"

Holden replied quietly, "I was married for three years to a wonderful woman who died in childbirth. The baby died, too."

The psychiatrist bowed his head. "I'm sorry." He offered an excuse. "In our efforts to help our patients, we psychiatrists never know when we are likely to come up against the deepest personal feelings of others. You must forgive me."

Holden inclined his head. "It's okay, doctor."

"How long ago did you lose your family?"

"More than a year. That's why I came here."

"But you haven't forgotten?"

"You never forget something like that, doctor." Holden took a deep breath. "But when I met Fay, I thought that maybe there still was a chance for me to start all over again."

"And you told her?"

"Yes."

"Do you still believe it?"

With fervent conviction, Holden replied, "Doctor, I've got to believe. But now that Bainbridge's back, I have the feeling that he's taking her away from me.

"Fay's been avoiding me, she doesn't let me know where she is, and she won't even send me a note of explanation."

The psychiatrist rose from his chair, set aside his drink and put a steady hand on the younger man's bowed shoulders. "Don't give up so easily, Mr. Holden. Fay's future is very far from settled. First of all, we know that this proposed remarriage to Spencer Bainbridge is being forced on her mainly by her stepfather and by Bainbridge himself. And second, I have an urgent commission from her mother to tell her certain things of which she is not now aware. That is precisely what has brought me back to Paris at this time. So you see, a lot of things can change." He paused, almost forcing his visitor to

150

look up directly at him. They both relaxed then. "There, that's better," the psychiatrist said, returning to his chair.

Holden felt renewed courage. "Thanks, doctor."

"But remember," the psychiatrist went on, "even though Fay has the outward appearance of a perfectly normal, conventional person, she is a bundle of complex contradictions that we are going to have to straighten out for her somehow. This condition, as I have told her, wasn't created yesterday or even during a relatively short marriage that fell apart. It grew on her, unnoticed by everybody except her mother, from the time she was a little girl and lost her father."

Holden said doggedly, "Whatever she was, whatever she now is, that's not going to change my feeling about her. I must find her."

Dr. Beranger nodded. "Good! I'll see that you get to her as soon as possible."

"And I'd like to know from you," Holden continued, "if I ought to have a talk with Bainbridge."

The psychiatrist frowned. "Now why would you want to do that?"

"I want to tell him to lay off Fay," he said simply.

"Yes, and what if he refuses?"

"Then I'm going to fight him." Holden looked grim and determined.

Dr. Beranger shook his head. "That will do no good at all. It will only make things worse." He sighed. "I think I'd better fill you in on the background of Fay's relationships. You know some of it, but a lot of it you don't. And maybe you'll understand her position better if I start at the very beginning."

The psychiatrist made himself comfortable behind his big desk. "Except for the matters I must discuss privately with Fay, the things that her mother has told me, I'll try not to leave out anything of importance," he said.

Fay (the psychiatrist began) was brought up to believe that her natural father, Selden Deak, commuted daily from their Long Island home to a modest law office in New York; and that her mother, a small and abnormally nervous woman, was an average housewife who had to struggle to make ends meet.

That was Deak's way. He was the product of an older society.

In his family, with wealth amassed over generations of western mining operations, it was the fashion to pretend that money didn't matter. If wealth could not be concealed, at least it was not to be put on crass display. And that was how Selden Deak ordered his family life.

While he lived, he guided Fay's education with painstaking care. He refused to put her in private schools in the middle-class Long Island community in which they lived; instead, he saw to it that she faithfully attended the grammar school and high school to which the other neighborhood children went. He never intended for her to know that one day she would inherit a large amount of money.

She was taught very early in her childhood to appreciate the value of money. A five-cent ice cream cone was denied to her, more than once, because it was termed too expensive. And she was encouraged to believe that one day she would have to work to be self-supporting.

All this might have developed into excellent training in responsibility for a growing child, but two things happened to change everything. First, Selden Deak was killed in an auto-mobile accident while Fay was still in her teens. And, as a result, Sarah Deak suffered a nervous collapse that caused her to spend much of the rest of her life under psychiatric care.

Even when Fay's mother felt up to running a small house and keeping Fay in a public school, there were difficulties. Sarah Deak simply didn't have it in her, without the strength of Selden Deak's presence, to keep up the myth that theirs was just another family in modest circumstances. Yet, under Deak's will, the bank that was his executor doled out funds to her with so little consideration for her actual needs that she was often on the brink of despair.

All that changed when Waco Texas Carroll entered her life and Fay's. Carroll, a Texan, was a distant relative of Selden Deak's and had come to Long Island to call on his widow some years after his death. A widower himself, Carroll convinced Sarah that they had common interests and eventually they were married.

No one was ever quite certain whether Carroll's sudden display of wealth was due to his success as an oil prospector, as he led people to believe, or the somewhat more believable speculation that he made a deal with Sarah Deak's bank to release more of her late husband's funds to meet her needs and Fay's. At any rate, Fay's life—and her mother's as well—underwent wrenching changes.

First of all, they moved to a much larger home in the wealthy community of Glen Cove, with a live-in couple to take housekeeping off Sarah's mind. Probably, considering her condition, that was all for the best. But next, Fay was separated from her mother by being shipped off to a private school to which she was confined except for carefully spaced weekends and vacations. And finally, both she and her mother found it almost impossible to live their lives in the Deak tradition; instead, they had to give in to Waco Texas Carroll's distasteful ideas about flaunting their wealth.

But it was not entirely Carroll's boisterous manner or his showy way of life that made the difference for Fay and her mother. Rather, it was his bullying manner, his insistence on making them symbols of a superior status in life that made them both cringe. To have his way, he often threatened to have Sarah Deak declared incompetent. For that reason, neither she nor Fay resisted him.

When Fay was home during Christmas vacations and had to be overdressed for some social function at her stepfather's insistence, she would cry sometimes and ask her mother why she had to comply when she felt so foolish in those awful clothes. Sarah Deak Carroll was sympathetic but helpless. She never dared cross Waco Texas Carroll. Even so, her nature was such that she had to be placed in a sanitarium from time to time—because she couldn't summon up enough strength to do the many things her second husband demanded.

It was no surprise, therefore, that Fay chose to marry almost as soon as she was graduated from Sweet Briar College in Virginia. Her bridegroom, Spencer Bainbridge, was a Yale man, the son of a retired Foreign Service officer, and Carroll's nephew with whom he seemed to have a business relationship. Carroll was delighted. He lavished a fortune on the ceremony which he made into a social event. He invited hundreds of people to his estate and reveled in the publicity that was generated.

Thereafter, through the judicious distribution of political

153

contributions, he saw to it that his son-in-law received suitable promotions in the Foreign Service and, in a relatively short time, was assigned to the American embassy in Paris. Bainbridge's career background helped, of course: where the Foreign Service had once been dominated by "Europe-ists," those officers whose careers were based on American-European relations, it now was somewhat more under the influence of the "Arab-ists," of whom Bainbridge was one. Under Carroll's prompting, his nephew had specialized in Arab studies and the economics of the oil business at Yale. Then, through fortunate circumstance, Bainbridge was in a key post where Arab contacts counted for a great deal.

It did not completely escape public notice that Waco Texas Carroll was a heavy investor in oil stocks. In the financial journals, from time to time he received respectful mention as a judicious appraiser of the potential of Persian Gulf oil developments, one who had excellent information on American involvement in the region. To older Foreign Service people, there was little doubt about the source of Carroll's information and the advice he was receiving on his investments. In Paris, Bainbridge's reputation as an "Arab-ist" was second to none.

But what was wrong with that? Even if it had been proved that Bainbridge continually leaked information about American oil deals with the Arabs to his uncle and profited thereby, both were considered politically untouchable. True, issuing top-secret information was a crime, but that wasn't part of the Bainbridge-Carroll relationship when it had to be made public for the benefit of inquiring congressional committees. To know what was coming out a few days or even a few hours before a formal announcement, however, was an obvious advantage to any large investor. And thus, older Foreign Service people grumbled about Bainbridge's supposed ethical violations but they couldn't prove anything.

So, for a time, Carroll prospered and so did his nephew. The Texan's fortunes continued to rise as long as he stuck with known quantities such as Arabian-American Oil shares and similar stocks. But like all gamblers—and essentially this is what Carroll was—he inevitably swung to high-risk oil shares because he wanted ever larger profits; and that marked a drastic change in both his income and his reputation.

Now the financial gossip sheets referred to him as a "plunger" who had suffered dramatic reversals in his investments and was trying to recoup. It did not escape the notice of the older Foreign Service officers in Paris that Bainbridge was frequently seen, at around this time, with somewhat less savory Arab characters whom he would meet, not at the Ritz Bar, but at suspicious hangouts on the Left Bank. Worse still, there were rumors inside and outside the embassy that Bainbridge's marriage to Fay Carroll was falling apart because he had become infatuated with a contract translator at the embassy, Catherine Vaillant.

Temporarily, the gossips' judgment about Bainbridge's marriage turned out to be premature. For at the time of Nikolai Gribov's defection from the Bolshoi Opera in Paris, it was, as everybody knew, Bainbridge and Fay who hid him in their apartment until he was obliged to seek more security in London. But once that heady adventure was over, there was nothing to bind the couple together. Bainbridge went back to the fascinating Catherine. And Fay broke under the strain and became Dr. Beranger's patient. Though it was difficult for her mother and for her, once she returned home to America, Fay rallied sufficiently to survive her stepfather's badgering and obtained a divorce. Evidently, Bainbridge was so preoccupied with Catherine at the time that he didn't care whether he was divorced or not and raised no objection to the proceedings.

Speculation as to what happened thereafter was often based more on supposition than on fact. The basic change in position was that Sarah Deak Carroll had to be committed to a sanitarium to recover from the strain under which her husband had placed her once Fay's divorce went through. And soon afterward the financial community noticed that Waco Texas Carroll had somehow obtained access to a fresh source of funds for his high-risk oil investments. At the same time, Bainbridge received a change of station. He was posted as Public Affairs Officer for the American delegation to the United Nations in New York City, and soon was spreading the story that he intended to remarry Fay.

All manner of rumors circulated among Foreign Service people to account for what was going on. And, strangely, some of the most poisonous gossip came from Catherine Vaillant, whom Bainbridge seemed to have hastily and even rudely abandoned in the sudden reversal of his life-style. Eventually, when all this came to Dr. Beranger's attention, he sketched out a credible scenario, admittedly without a shred of proof to support his theory:

Once Waco Texas Carroll and Sarah Deak were married and he discovered that she had to undergo treatment in a sanitarium from time to time for a chronic nervous disorder, it became a simple matter for him to persuade her to give him power of attorney over her large inheritance from her first husband.

At first, she was thankful that she had been relieved of that responsibility; however, as banking officials and lawyers both began expressing concern about Carroll's large withdrawals of her funds for unspecified purposes, she had to question her husband. And at that time, he began threatening to commit her for life to an institution for the mentally unstable. The threat was credible enough; at any time he wished, Carroll could have found psychiatrists who would recommend such a commitment on the basis of his wife's medical record.

For as long as Carroll stayed with his solid investments of his wife's money in Arabian-American oil shares and others like it, nobody questioned what he was doing in the various financial markets. But once he began losing, and taking more and more of her funds for what appeared to be his own purposes, the financial community came to the conclusion that the supposedly successful Texas oil "wild-catter" had been mostly bluffing.

Sadly, Sarah Deak Carroll received just such an assessment from her lawyers. But instead of authorizing them to sue Carroll for an accounting in order to stop him from draining her inheritance, she begged them not to do so. She was convinced that he would be able to carry out his threat to have her committed.

Sarah Deak Carroll did try to safeguard the inheritance which Fay was due to receive on her thirtieth birthday and of which she had had no previous knowledge. Now Fay learned from her mother that within a very few years she would inherit many millions of dollars. And yet, because of the broadness of Waco Texas Carroll's power of attorney over his wife's affairs, there

156

already was alarm among her advisers that he was dipping into the funds that had been set aside for Fay.

The lawyers were all for intervening in Fay's behalf. But seeing the absolute panic in her mother's eyes over any action that would be taken against her stepfather, Fay could not bring herself to approve. Even so, Carroll was wary enough to set up a strong defense for himself rather than continue to rely on threats.

That apparently was how he persuaded Bainbridge to break off his love affair with Catherine Vaillant and propose to re-marry Fay. Very likely, Fay's stepfather also was using Bain-bridge to abet his scheme to obtain control over what remained of Fay's inheritance.

Exactly how Carroll drew Bainbridge into the affair was uncertain for a long time. Sarah Deak Carroll was shrewd enough to guess that her husband had baited Bainbridge with word of Fay's coming inheritance in order to persuade him to remarry her. In any event, Bainbridge returned to the Carroll estate on Long Island soon afterward and openly courted his former wife. It served only to depress Fay.

Sarah Deak Carroll tried to send Bainbridge on his way, pleading that her daughter needed more time to herself, but it didn't work. Waco Texas Carroll was outraged when he heard of it. He let it be known that he approved of Bainbridge's courting Fay, and was angry with his wife and stepdaughter for not welcoming the young man back to the family fold.

Under these circumstances, mother and daughter appealed to Dr. Beranger at the Menninger Clinic for help, and rejoiced when he eventually approved of Fay's return to Paris. It was reassuring to both women, too, that he let Fay use his apartment and car in Paris and agreed to return at once in the event of an emergency.

Carroll, of course, was furious, because Fay's planned departure would effectively block Bainbridge's plan to remarry her. This time, his wife was able to resist all the arguments her husband raised and she stood up at last against his usual threat to have her committed. She wanted Fay removed from Bainbridge's immediate presence, and this was how it was to be done: She was to resume voice study in Paris.

However, Carroll did win one concession from mother and

daughter. If Fay couldn't stand the pressures of the daily routine of Parisian life and the voice study she was to resume at the Conservatory, she would return home. However, she refused flatly to consider remarriage to Bainbridge. And this time, her stepfather had to give way, much as he hated to do so.

At first, everything seemed to go well for Fay on her return to Paris. While her affair with Holden did not figure in her frequent telephone talks with her mother, Sarah Deak Carroll was reasonably sure that someone was making her daughter happy—and she suspected, not without good cause, that it was a young man. And so, for a relatively short time, mother and daughter felt more secure than they had since Carroll had come into their lives.

They couldn't have anticipated the State Department's decision to return to Bainbridge temporarily to Paris for the UN Special Assembly on disarmament. Whether or not Carroll had had anything to do with the change in plan, Bainbridge's reappearance in Paris was upsetting to Fay. And, since he arrived at a time when Gribov was at least talking about helping Olga Varenka to defect from the Kirov Ballet, Fay's former husband was in a position to upset everybody's plans.

Fay had been discouraged enough watching Catherine Vaillant, the immediate cause of her marital failure, capture the attentions of Nikolai Gribov. It was even worse when Catherine was the undoubted source of a lot of poisonous gossip about the reasons for Bainbridge's renewed attentiveness to Fay.

That was how matters stood when Dr. Beranger returned to Paris and Fay impulsively decided she no longer could see Arch Holden. It could only mean Fay was so concerned about renewed threats to her mother that she was willing to make the sacrifice of remarriage to Bainbridge.

"...so you can see," the psychiatrist concluded, nodding to Holden, "that you've come into Fay's life at a very critical period. What do you intend to do about it?"

Holden got up. "I'll stop her from marrying Bainbridge again."

"How?"

"I don't know, but I'll find a way to do it." He turned to

the psychiatrist grimly. "If you're in Fay's corner, Dr. Beranger, you'll help me."

The older man arose. "What can I do?"

"First of all, find Fay for me."

The psychiatrist nodded. "In the morning, first thing. As I said, I think she's staying with friends somewhere near the Pantheon. It's not far from here."

"I'll call you," Holden said. "I have rooms just off the Place St. Sulpice."

They had sealed their alliance. But Dr. Beranger cautioned, "Don't try to settle this by fighting with Bainbridge. That would be the height of foolishness."

There was a note of urgency in Holden's voice. "Doctor, how *can* Fay even think of going back to Bainbridge, feeling as she does about him and knowing he's in on a scheme to defraud her?"

"She must feel that she has to protect her mother. Frankly," the psychiatrist went on, "I haven't had a chance to talk to her about it since I came back. As soon as she received my cable that I was returning, she moved out and I haven't heard from her since."

"But how can her mother accept Fay's sacrifice?" Holden persisted. "It's almost inhuman."

"Mrs. Carroll can and does resist up to a point," Dr. Beranger said. "But there are two things against her indefinite resistance. The first and most important is the fear of a permanent commitment to a mental institution, and don't think that Carroll couldn't make it stick. In her condition, she might break right in the courtroom if her lawyers wanted to contest that kind of thing. I'm a psychiatrist, and I know something about her situation."

Holden pressed him. "You said there were two considerations. What's the other?"

"The human condition," the psychiatrist continued mildly. "You mustn't forget that Mrs. Carroll is a very lonely woman. She has no relatives except her daughter, and very few friends. No matter how much she may deplore and even fear her husband, she seems to feel bound to him in a way that younger people simply can't understand. I know that Fay doesn't understand it."

159

Holden pursued his inquiry with vehemence. "Mrs. Carroll is a woman of means. She has the advice of good lawyers. Why can't she simply file suit for divorce? In most states, she'd have adequate grounds."

"Agreed." But Dr. Beranger gently shook his head. "I doubt if she'll ever do it."

"Because she's afraid of him?"

"Perhaps so. And yet," the psychiatrist went on, "I think I could make out a pretty good case as well for her absolute horror of living alone." He explained, with a slight inclination of his head, "You'd be surprised at how many marriages continue entirely because one partner or the other, and sometimes both, don't want to be alone very possibly for the rest of their lives. No matter what you young people may think," and here he returned to his dry, professional manner, "we are not a gregarious society. The individual very often tends to be isolated, and very few can stand it. The lonely life is seldom a good life."

"Still, she has a lot of weapons against Carroll that she isn't even using," Holden protested.

"There's a limit to how far she can go and still retain her sanity," the psychiatrist replied, and added heavily, "And I think she knows it." He blinked at the younger man. "I'd be interested to know what you intend to do once you see Fay again."

Holden stood up and plunged his hands into his coat pockets. He had been so wrapped up in the search for Fay that he hadn't even considered what he'd do when he found her. "After what you told me, I suppose I'll feel like a damn fortune hunter when I catch up with her," he commented sourly.

"Bainbridge isn't letting that stop him."

"Well, he *is* a fortune hunter, isn't he?"

"We all are, more or less," was the older man's quiet response.

"What do you mean?"

"Just this." Dr. Beranger ticked off his points on his fingers. "We're all looking for *something* from a partner. Some want happiness, others money. Some look for contentment, others peace of mind. And sometimes"—he seemed regretful—"all we look for is sexual satisfaction, the crudity of the orgasm."

160

The psychiatrist permitted himself a small smile to ease the harshness of his words. "No, Mr. Holden, we can't afford to strike noble attitudes when we think of the motivations behind most human relationships. Not many of us are heroes or villains. All most of us want to do is to survive the struggle through another day in our lives."

Holden bit his lip. "Still, I wish you hadn't told me that she's going to be filthy rich."

"It shouldn't make much difference to either of you. The money's going to be hers, not yours."

Holden squeezed his hands together in an agony of self-doubt. "Don't know if I could stand a rich wife."

The psychiatrist reacted sharply. "Are you afraid she'd put you down if she has all the money, and the power that goes with it?"

Holden protested, "That's not fair."

"Why not?"

"Because, doctor, I don't think that way. And anyway, Fay's not ruthless enough to use the power that goes with big money."

The psychiatrist resumed his appearance of imperturbable good humor. "Most people who worry about money don't have any. Is that your situation?"

"Just about."

"All right, that's Fay's situation, too. Don't forget she learned only a little while ago about her inheritance."

"I don't think she had to try very hard to make a living," Holden objected. "I should think her mother always saw to it that she had a generous allowance."

"Probably so," the psychiatrist agreed. "And yet you ought to give her credit for trying to support herself after she left college. She did, you know."

Holden nodded. "Oh, I'm not putting Fay down. I know she modeled for some artists and was good at it. Also, she once told me she did part-time art and music criticism for the *Paris Press*."

The psychiatrist sighed. "I guess it's just as well that she knows how to make a living. It seems as if there won't be much left of her inheritance."

Holden jumped up. "I'll stop them!" Then, all at once, he

turned to Dr. Beranger in an appeal. "Think she'll listen to me?"

"Oh, I doubt if you'll have to worry about that," was the reassuring reply. "Remember, I have something pretty important to say to her, too, something that her mother has instructed me to tell her. And maybe that'll make the difference."

"Sure hope so," Holden said.

What Fay wanted most of all was to see Holden. She had had a difficult time, too, beginning with that afternoon at the Ritz Bar when Spencer Bainbridge had come back into her life. At first, his renewed attentions had only annoyed her. But when he tagged along with Baron von Norden's party and showed up for dinner at the little restaurant in the Rue de Grenelle, she became concerned. And finally, she was frightened.

Her unhappiness was so apparent that Amy Leary whispered to her late in the evening, "We'll be going home soon. Can we give you a lift?"

"Oh, please!" It was almost a plea, rather than a polite expression of gratitude.

"Is that man annoying you?" Amy looked severely in the direction of Spencer Bainbridge, who at the moment was talking with Baron von Norden at the head of the dinner table.

"No, he's all right, but I want to get away from him," Fay said.

Amy was comforting. "We'll take care of you."

That disposed of Bainbridge as a problem for one evening, but it didn't solve Fay's dilemma. Before Bainbridge's return she had been warned by her mother of her stepfather's plans for her, and she knew it wouldn't be easy to stand up to him. On top of that, she was enormously attracted to Arch Holden and didn't want to discourage him by taking flight because of her problems.

So it turned out, for a short time at least, that while she remained in Dr. Beranger's apartment on the Ile St. Louis, she tried to carry on with things as they had been before Bainbridge's arrival. But she soon learned that she'd have to avoid Henri's, because Bainbridge did as much of his drinking and dining there as he could.

However, when he discovered that Fay no longer came to Henri's regularly, he made several unannounced trips to her apartment at the Ile St. Louis. The first time it happened, she was just leaving for the Conservatory and begged off. After that, on her instructions, the concierge announced to all callers that Madame was not at home. And that was why Holden, as well as Bainbridge, found it was almost impossible to see her. Moreover, she completed her isolation by refusing to answer the telephone.

Then she received Dr. Beranger's cable announcing his arrival. She had to move quickly or go home. In her desperation she had at first considered moving in with Holden in his small apartment in the Rue Bonaparte. But her fear of her stepfather, who almost certainly would have vented his anger on her mother, caused her to give up that idea.

Instead, she appealed once again to the ever-practical Amy Leary, who quickly made room for her in the Leary's exchange apartment in the Rue Soufflot, not far from the Place St. Michel.

The change to accommodate Fay was easily made. Gareth, under protest, was moved out of his bedroom and assigned to the living room couch, which enabled Fay to take over his room and bath. Through Pat Leary's intercession, she was given a certain amount of time every morning after breakfast to practice her singing lessons; occasionally, when Pat had the time, he would take over the Dessaix' piano and work with her. As things turned out, it was an eminently satisfactory arrangement for all concerned, including the ever-demanding Gribov. The only ones to be put out were Bainbridge, who began using the embassy's resources to track her down, and Holden, who was both confused and dismayed by the unhappy turn of events.

Very soon, it became evident to Fay that she couldn't hold herself aloof from Holden. And she didn't want to. So she risked spreading word of her whereabouts by sending a message to Holden through Gareth and Stephanie Rivet at Henri's: "Come see me, I'm at the Learys' place." He received it the day after his call on Dr. Beranger.

After a restless night, Holden set out for the Rue Soufflot. The Dessaix apartment was partway up the hill of St. Genevieve, with the awesome gray pile of the Pantheon at its peak.

It was a section of Paris that was crusted with history, and the Dessaix apartment reflected its influence. As Holden was admitted, he walked among period furniture and art objects of great value that had been gathered over a lifetime. But neither art nor history engaged his attention at that moment. All he could see was Fay's slender figure waiting for him beside the piano. She was alone, Pat Leary having tactfully interrupted singing practice as soon as the concierge announced Holden's presence over the house phone.

The reunion was joyous. Without a word, Holden caught Fay in his arms, kissed her, let his hands stray over her hair, her cheeks, felt her arms encircling his neck, kissed her again. He couldn't get enough of her. And she was content to be in his arms.

After a while, Holden found his voice. "Why did you run away? I've missed you so."

"I couldn't help it."

"Didn't you *want* to see me?"

"That wasn't it at all, darling." She held him off to look at him. "You know that now, don't you?"

"Yes." He drew her to him. "But you can't keep on hiding. It's no good. You can't live that way."

"I have to. I can't *stand* Bainbridge!" She was vehement, flaring into anger. "I don't want to see him."

"Then tell him so, Fay."

In a choked voice, she said, "I can't."

"Why? Don't you have the guts?" He was sorry he had said it the moment the words were out of his mouth, because she seemed to cringe. He apologized immediately.

"That's all right," she murmured. "But . . . it's hard to explain. You'll just have to let me work it out my way."

Now he was determined to force a change in her attitude. He led her to the couch that sat in a splashy pattern of morning sunlight that cast a soft glow about the room. "I'm not going to let you hide, Fay. It's not normal. It's not right."

She drew him down beside her and held his hands in her own. "Of course, darling. I agree with everything you say. But I can't face up to seeing Spencer Bainbridge and listening to him tell me how much he loves me. And knowing all the time that it's a lie."

"Will you let me tell him off?" Holden's eyes glittered. "I can do it, believe me. It would give me a lot of satisfaction just to take a swing at him."

"You stay out of it. I'll not have you fighting. First thing you know, Saffron will get hold of the story; it'll be in the *Paris Press* and I'll be embarrassed to tears."

Now Holden was troubled. "But we can't go on this way, just waiting for Bainbridge to give up and go home."

"I can't think of anything else to do."

"Maybe he'll get into trouble over Gribov again," he suggested.

"Nikolai has trouble enough without bringing him into this," she answered. "He's going to have to make up his mind between Catherine Vaillant and Olga. He thinks he can have both, but he can't."

Holden was somber. "You have a choice to make, too."

"Don't push me, darling." She softened her words with a little smile and squeezed his hands. "I have a lot to think over."

"Surely you're not going to change your mind about Bainbridge," he protested.

She didn't answer him directly. "You've never met my stepfather, and he's the one who's pushing this idea of remarriage. You don't know how violent and ruthless a man my stepfather is."

"But he's there and you're here."

"True, but I'm very much afraid of what he's going to do to my mother if I tell Spencer Bainbridge that I can't even think of remarrying him." She withdrew her hands from Holden's. "That's my problem."

"Yes, and avoiding Bainbridge isn't going to solve it," Holden said. "Sooner or later, you're going to have to tell him that's the way you feel about it."

"That *is* the way I feel," she said.

He tried another tack. "Have you seen Dr. Beranger yet?"

"Not since he's returned."

"Are you going to?"

"Eventually."

"I've seen him," Holden said. "He has a message for you from your mother. It's important."

"My mother's already told me about that," and she shook

her head. "One of our friends has tipped the Securities and Exchange Commission in Washington to look into my step-father's financial dealings, but that's a long shot. Anyway, my mother won't prosecute, and that puts everything back to square one." She sighed. "I'll just have to duck seeing Bainbridge for as long as I can to avert a crisis back home."

"But *please* listen to Dr. Beranger," he pleaded. "You *must* see him and let him try to help you."

She seemed fatalistic. "There's nothing he can do to help me right now, Arch."

"Can I?" Holden's tone was appealing.

She kissed him. "Yes, darling, you can help a lot if you'll see me whenever you can and love me and be patient with me." Somewhere in the apartment, a buzzer sounded and they heard Amy Leary's voice in the distance. Apparently, she was talking with the concierge over the house telephone in French. As they listened without comprehension to the distant voice, it suddenly halted. Amy bustled into the living room. "Sorry to interrupt, people, but Nikolai Gribov's on his way up here and he's in a pet."

"What about?" Fay asked.

"Olga, of course."

"What's happened to her?"

"Nothing. The trouble is that she's shown up in Paris and Nikolai hasn't the faintest idea of what to do about her."

Amy rolled her eyes in mock despair. "Honestly, one never knows what this family is going to be involved in next. Almost anything can happen as long as Nikolai insists on playing around with Catherine Vaillant and talking about abducting Olga. Sometimes I think the man is out of his mind."

The front door buzzer sounded just then. In a few moments, Gribov's rich baritone could be heard in the hall with Pat Leary's softer voice in the background as *obligato*.

"They guard Olga," Gribov was saying, his voice growing louder as he and Leary approached. "I tell you, they guard Olga like she was in the Kremlin."

To which Leary responded in soothing tones, "Be calm, Nikolai."

"Be calm, be calm!" Gribov expostulated. "This is all Americans know, to be calm. And the Soviet Union does anything

166

it wants while Americans are calm. You should be angry, you Americans! Anger! This is what the Soviet Union understands." He clapped his hands together to emphasize what he was saying as he strode into the living room.

Seeing Fay and Holden sitting together on the couch, the singer halted in the middle of the room and exclaimed, "Fay, my little one!" He flung his arms wide and hugged her as she arose to greet him. "What a surprise! So nice to see you!"

"It's good to see you again, Nikolai," she said.

He pointed to the piano. "You practice your singing, yes?"

"Every morning."

"Good! Very good! But you must do scales," and he emphasized his suggestion by running a C-major scale on the piano as if it were a treasured operatic aria. He halted as Holden stood up and attracted his attention. "Ah, my little one, your friend is here! Your friend from Henri's!" He advanced and shook hands with Holden. "You are lucky," the singer said. "Always, piano players are lucky!"

Amy was unimpressed. "Nikolai, you will be lucky, too, if you were not followed here."

"By KGB?" He chuckled. "Ha, I watch for KGB when I leave taxi, but I see nobody." He turned to Fay, still in good humor. "But my little one, tell me, do you see poor Bainbridge now?"

There was an embarrassed silence that Amy Leary finally broke with a tactful, "Fay has her problems too, Nikolai. But let us first discuss your problem?"

He nodded. "My Amy is so wise. She thinks of everything!"

Chapter Six

There was a gloomy silence in the Learys' luxury apartment in the Rue Soufflot that morning. Gribov had postured and ranted to no avail to try to mobilize his amateur conspirators into a group capable of separating Olga Varenka from the Kirov Ballet. Looking about the room as he sat in a secluded corner with Fay, Holden saw without surprise that the Learys were heart and soul with the large Russian in trying to help him devise a plan for the delivery of his sweetheart. The Learys, after all, had had important roles in Gribov's own defection, so he knew he could trust them.

Yet, as Holden quickly sensed, the members of the conspiracy were nervous, even jumpy, about the considerable problem of outwitting the formidable KGB. There was a morbid sense of secrecy that blanketed the group; not one, clearly, trusted the others sufficiently to advance a plan to wrest Olga from her captors. Was it because they all knew of Gribov's dalliance with his French mistress, Catherine Vaillant? Or were they merely unenthusiastic about plotting in the absence of any real encouragement from Olga herself?

There was no doubt that what the conspirators needed more than anything else was leadership.

Holden glanced around the room once more at the Learys, at Gribov, and at last at Fay sitting beside him in a low-cut white blouse, short black skirt and high-heeled patent leather slippers that gave her legs an elegant look. He adored watching Fay; evidently, she enjoyed his attentiveness too, for she squeezed his hand.

"Don't you have any bright ideas about Olga?" she murmured.

He had to be honest with her. "Honey, I wouldn't know a *pas de deux* from third base. There has to be a better plotter around here than I am."

"All this should be very conspiratorial, dark and secretive, shouldn't it?" she went on lightly.

"Sure, if we were professionals and knew what we were doing," he agreed. "But we're not the CIA. What the hell, even a guy like Saffron might make a difference here."

"Sh-h-h-h," and she suddenly put a finger to her lips. "Amy Leary's got an idea."

Everybody else was just as hopeful when Amy finally broke the silence, but it soon became evident that she was only trying to stimulate responses from the rest. "Why are we just sitting here?" she began. "By this time, we each should have an assignment and be on our way. We're not going to help Olga very much if we just stare at each other and wait for something to happen."

"Is right," Gribov conceded.

"Amy is always right," Pat Leary agreed. "But at the moment I can't think of a damn thing that makes sense, and I guess that's the problem with all of us. Now, if you want me to compose a song..."

Gribov rocked his head from one side to the other in a sardonic approximation of impatience. "You compose, I sing, Amy dances, Holden plays piano..." He glanced around, his gaze fixed on Gareth—by far the largest and strongest male in the room—and added, "The young man here makes love ... what good is it? It does not help my Olga."

"Let's begin at the beginning," Amy proposed. "Come, Nikolai, tell us again *how* Olga arrived at Charles de Gaulle Airport, and maybe somebody will come up with a good idea."

It was, as everybody in the room realized, a despairing gesture, this process of groping for a miracle to deliver a ballet dancer from the Russians. They fell silent, waiting expectantly for Gribov to review what they already knew.

The big Russian seemed pained, but he complied: "Somebody call me yesterday, maybe CIA, and say, 'Go to Charles de Gaulle Airport at eight o'clock tonight.' I say, 'Why I go, tell me?' So this voice, this man, say, 'Go. Is important.'" He shrugged, letting his gaze wander about the room. "So I go to airport. I ask myself, Who can be at the airport? Kirov Ballet will not come until later. But I hear at eight o'clock announcement that Aeroflot plane comes in from Leningrad." A smile lit up the singer's somber features. "I go to Aeroflot gate, and who comes in?" Even though he already had told the story once, his sense of the dramatic overcame him and he arose with upraised hand. "I see my Olga." He paused as if he were trying to create a feeling of suspense, then went on in a low, well-modulated voice, "But Olga is not alone. She moves in crowd of big men. But *big.*" He emphasized the point with a gesture. "And I see under coats they have guns." He clapped his hands together for emphasis. "Is KGB. Eight men, all KGB."

"And she saw you, Nikolai?" Pat Leary asked, as if to reassure himself.

Gribov nodded. "I see Olga, I wave." He smiled. "She see me, she wave too. But KGB take her away quick. I follow. But they take her in big black Russian automobile—whoosh!—on highway to Paris."

"She's probably at the Russian embassy right now," Pat Leary said, "and still surrounded by KGB agents." He shook his head. "That's what makes it so tough to plan. I can't even guess at where they'll take her or what they'll do with her until the Kirov Ballet arrives."

"Kirov is here tomorrow," Gribov announced. "Next day is rehearsal. Next night after that Olga dances in *Giselle.*"

"I should think we will have very little chance of penetrating the Russian embassy," Amy concluded.

Gribov nodded. "We wait. When Olga is in Paris Opera, then we move. I get her. Not KGB, not French police, nobody stops me."

Pat Leary asked hopefully, "You have a plan, Nikolai?"

The Russian thrust out both arms for silence. The group watched him raptly. "When Olga dances in *Giselle,*" the singer suggested, "I call out, 'Fire!' Is panic in house. Company runs from stage. I go in from orchestra, I carry Olga away in crowd." Gribov looked around him, beaming, expecting immediate approval.

Instead, there was an embarrassed silence. Pat Leary finally explained gently, "It won't work, Nikolai. And if you start a panic in the opera house, some people may be killed. And the French police will arrest you."

Gribov dropped to a seat on the piano bench, his spirits deflated. "All right, what we do?"

Leary said, "Let's try to figure this out. If the KGB brought Olga in ahead of the Kirov Ballet company, then they already know or at least suspect that something's afoot in Paris. And they're very much on their guard."

"Is right, KGB knows," Gribov agreed. "My friend from Leningrad tells me KGB will not trust Paris police, so Olga comes in ahead with separate guard. But I get Olga anyway."

Again Amy challenged him. "How, Nikolai?"

In half-humorous protest, Gribov mimicked her. "How, how? My Amy, you always ask how. What should I say?"

Leary came to his wife's defense. "We'll have to face the facts, Nikolai. If we don't have a plan, and if the KGB suspects that Olga may try to defect, we are in for a very difficult time. And so is she."

There were other meetings about Varenka, all of them just as futile. Sometimes Henri Durand and his wife, Marie, joined the group. Once, to Fay's consternation, Gribov announced that he was bringing Spencer Bainbridge. That day, Fay absented herself and made Holden stay away, too.

But essentially, the situation did not change. The Kirov Ballet began its Parisian engagement at the opera house in a burst of favorable publicity. Full houses nightly applauded the visitors. And after Varenka's first triumphal appearance in *Giselle*, there were columns of laudatory articles in the French press.

It all added to Varenka's reputation, but her prestige gave Gribov little consolation. Nor did Catherine Vaillant's devoted attention make him feel any better. Instead of taking her to Pastore's lodge in the Forest of Fontainebleau, the Russian singer now saw her only occasionally at Henri's.

Still, fashionable Paris was diverted by rumors that Varenka was about to defect. In every salon and cafe frequented by artists, musicians and writers, people pondered imaginary plots to separate the *prima ballerina* from the KGB. All the while, of course, nobody could get to her to ask about her intentions.

Why the excitement about Varenka?

Even to someone like Holden, who would just as soon have been shot into orbit instead of being forced into attendance at a ballet, interest in the fate of the dancer was understandable. She was a world figure, held under close guard by the KGB, the Russian intelligence service. And being in Paris added to her prominence.

It wouldn't have made much difference if a Bulgarian shot-putter or a Ukrainian balalaika player had sought asylum in the West. But when artistic Paris echoed with rumors that a Russian ballet dancer was about to desert the ranks of the proletariat for the riches of America, that was news.

Dancers of the prominence of Mikhail Baryshnikov, Natalia Makarova and Rudolf Nureyev already had found ways to break out of Russian custody. The longer the Kirov remained in Paris, the more interested Paris became in what Varenka would do and how she would do it.

The Kirov, after all, was not just another touring ballet company. Once, it had been the Imperial Russian Ballet of St. Petersburg, the pride of the Czar's court, the initiator of Tchaikovsky's *Sleeping Beauty* and the beneficiary of the genius of the great choreographer Marius Petipa. Now, along with the Bolshoi Ballet, it was an ornament of Communist Russia in its home city of Leningrad, as St. Petersburg had been renamed.

Actually, if Varenka and the Kirov had not been of such importance, the Russians might have had an easier time of it in Paris. But as the rumors mounted, the French press began to raise questions and, eventually, diplomatic inquiries descended on the Russian embassy. Was it true that Olga Varenka was being held in protective custody? Had the dancer been forced to remain with the Kirov when she in fact wanted to defect to the West?

At first, the Russians issued angry denials. It was all nonsense, an American plot fabricated by the CIA. Newspaper talk. As anybody could see who wished to attend a performance of *Giselle*, Olga Varenka was happy with her artistic career and at the top of her form as a *prima ballerina*. So the Russians said.

The denials weren't good enough. The rumors spread, as did the questions. And the diplomatic representations from the

172

Quai d'Orsay, seat of the French Foreign Office, grew sharper. Eventually, the Russian ambassador took the extraordinary step of announcing that Olga Varenka would hold a news conference at the Hotel Crillon, adjoining the American embassy, to silence the rumor-mongers.

That night, Gribov was jubilant. By coincidence, he had taken the Learys, their children, Fay Carroll and Baron von Norden to see the Kirov's *Sleeping Beauty* ballet. Then, after midnight when Henri's closed early, the rest of the conspirators joined them at the Rue Soufflot apartment—Holden, Henri and Marie Durand, and the photographer, Stephanie Rivet. It would have been unthinkable, Fay told Holden, to proceed without Henri, who had helped Gribov escape the Russians.

The atmosphere at the outset was more hopeful. "Now we have them!" Gribov proclaimed. "They cannot hold Varenka any longer. World opinion is against them."

Henri was philosophical. "What do the Russians care for world opinion? No, my friend, you will not live to see the KGB escorting your Olga to your door at the Crillon."

"I will pay the staff at the Crillon to bring her to me," Gribov said. "She will come directly from her news conference."

Henri whistled in a minor key but said nothing. Leary's response was a melancholy smile. But Amy Leary chided the singer. "Nikolai, you are out of your mind. Such things do not happen. The Russians will not let them happen."

Gribov turned expectantly to Henri. "You have a friend at the opera, can he not leave open the little door? That one I used?"

"It will not do," Henri replied. "I have already asked Robert Clement. The door has been sealed."

"Then let us give this Clement a black wig for Olga," Gribov proposed. "Between acts, she dresses, puts on wig to fool KGB, she walks out, we pick her up outside, presto!" He smiled expectantly, waiting for comment.

Nobody was impressed.

"It will not be that simple, my friend," Henri said. "The people of the KGB are no fools. If you disguise your Olga, she must be thoroughly disguised." He addressed Holden. "This

173

man from the American embassy, this Wisner, telephoned for you today, and I am sorry I did not tell you. Can he help us?"

"Afraid not," Holden said. "All he wants me to do is to let him know what's going on."

"That's easy," Amy Leary said. "Nothing's going on."

"Oh, I don't know," her husband added. "We're trying."

The German, von Norden, had been sitting beside Vivian Leary and taking all this in. Now he assumed an amused expression and called attention to his presence by saying, "I must say that you Americans aren't very good at making plots."

Henri, carefully muffling his dismay over the presence of an unexpected auditor, nodded gravely and addressed the German with exquisite courtesy. "But we Europeans who sympathize with the Americans have not distinguished ourselves either, Baron von Norden." It was perfectly obvious that the *patron* did not want to antagonize a good customer. And yet, at the same time, he also did not particularly like an outsider to be listening in on the details of this amateur plot and laughing at the participants.

Henri might have saved himself the trouble of worrying over where von Norden stood. The German chuckled. *"Touché!"* he exclaimed. "You have me there, M'sieu' Durand, for I have contributed exactly nothing so far to this enterprise. And I really should, if I intend to sit here and offer you unasked-for criticism."

Pat Leary was a good deal more blunt than the *patron* in trying to resolve the difficulty of the German's presence. "Look, von Norden, you don't have to be so damnably polite about this business. We know you're a diplomat, and a West German diplomat at that. It is understandable that you may feel uncomfortable because you find yourself involved with us and," he added thoughtfully, "in an entirely accidental way."

"Oh, I feel perfectly comfortable with you," von Norden said; then went on with a slight bow in Vivian's direction, "even flattered to be in such company."

Vivian gave him a regretful smile. "But Daddy's trying to chase you away, Rudi." Impulsively, she squeezed his arm between her elbow and side. "Don't you let him!"

"No danger." The German grinned cheerfully. "I find myself

quite intrigued both by the company and the situation in which we find ourselves. But if my presence embarrasses you . . ."

"No, no, Baron," Henri protested at once, anxious to placate von Norden. "We thought only that *we* were an embarrassment to *you.*"

"Indeed not," von Norden responded with a broad smile. "Whatever we Germans can do to make it difficult for the Russians simply supports our national policies, although"—and here he dropped in a deprecating caveat—"I must say that I can't appear in this matter officially." He glanced at Vivian with admiration. "But you all understand that, so please proceed, my friends, and rest easily. I am with you."

Gribov, who had been listening to the exchange without comment, now strode to the German's side and grasped his hand. "Is good, Baron. But Russians are not bad people, please. Only Communist government is bad."

Von Norden's reply was fervent. "Agreed, Nikolai! You and I, we understand each other."

Gribov turned quickly to a less complex topic. "You have seen Varenka dance in *Giselle,* Baron?"

"Not yet. But tonight, she was simply marvelous in *Sleeping Beauty.*"

"You see her in *Giselle,* Baron. I get tickets for final performance, yes?" He waved a hand around the room to include everybody. "This time, we all go?"

Henri said, "One of us, Marie or myself, must stay here. But," he continued, with a gesture toward Holden and Stephanie Rivet, "we will not stand in the way of our photographer and our pianist."

Holden wasn't so sure he wanted to go, but Fay pinched him before he could say anything to get out of the ballet party. And Stephanie, standing arm in arm with Gareth at one side of the room, murmured her thanks to the *patron* in French.

Henri addressed another idea to Holden. "Why don't you go to the American embassy tomorrow and see this Wisner? Let him know exactly how we stand now. It will do no harm."

Leary agreed. "Sure, maybe he'll have a suggestion."

Von Nordon laughed. "Poor Wisner, he hasn't had an original idea in the three years he's been here. I know him well."

But Gribov, by this time, was willing to grasp for help in

any direction, no matter how little promise there was of anything substantial. "Yes, go to embassy. Maybe"—and he glanced about the room—"maybe your Americans will be ashamed."

"It's rather difficult to shame Americans," von Norden observed. "But of course, try it." There was a twinkle in his eyes. "Perhaps we will be given one of the CIA's famous worst-case scenarios."

Fay finally put the pressure on Holden, who had sat beside her with a wooden expression during the banter. "Why don't you go first thing tomorrow?"

There was no help for it. Everyone nodded agreement. But all Holden could think of was the abysmal reception the regulars had given him at his first venture to the embassy. To Fay, he suggested, "Why not go with me? You know your way around."

In a faint voice, she demurred. "I'd rather not. There'd be too many complications."

Holden had his assignment and hated it.

One of the most familiar methods of handling a problem in the higher reaches of diplomacy is to deny that it exists. Nor is this necessarily a bald negation of the truth. As the veriest beginner in the Foreign Service knows, it sometimes becomes expedient to bend the truth a trifle without actually lying.

Consequently, Holden, like the rest of the conspirators, had the feeling of groping in a fog toward some distant goal. Yet, he, like all the others, was determined to push on with or without official help.

When he saw Cary Wisner, his contact, that official was both suspicious and withdrawn. "What do you want?" he demanded.

"Just advice," Holden said. "It's about Olga Varenka."

Wisner, unlike his posturing colleagues, was openly hostile. "We can't have anything to do with the Varenka matter."

Holden held his temper. "But we need help."

"I told you that the embassy can't be involved."

Holden arose stiffly, considering that he had made the attempt, and headed for the door. He was heartily disgusted with the impracticality of Gribov's operation.

With a few quick steps, Wisner headed him off. "What's your hurry?"

"No point in staying here."

"Don't get sore."

It was Holden's turn to be exasperated. "Look, Wisner, you told me you wanted to be kept informed. You came to Henri's while I was at work, but I couldn't tell you anything. I still can't. So let's forget the whole business."

Wisner's attitude softened. "Did Gribov send you here?"

"Gribov, Professor and Mrs. Leary, Henri Durand and his wife, and..." He hesitated briefly. "Some of the rest of us who are interested in the Varenka business."

"Let me see what I can do." The diplomat fingered his Phi Beta Kappa key and warily eyed his visitor. "Will you wait?"

Holden was in no mood to be put down again. "Not very long," he said.

Within a few minutes, he was escorted to the office of Cleveland McKelvey of the CIA. The stout, red-faced agent got up from his desk, pumped Holden's hand and exclaimed with a phony show of hearty good humor, "Good to see you again, Mr. Holden. What can we do for you?" He indicated a chair beside Wisner in front of the desk.

Holden remained standing. "Wisner tells me the embassy can't give us any help if Olga Varenka wants to defect."

"That's true. We can't be involved," McKelvey replied, stroking his black beard but appearing unperturbed. "You see, it's not our problem. In fact," he went on, "there's no problem at all unless and until Varenka actually defects. Do you know if she will?"

"Gribov says she will."

"But how does he know?" McKelvey persisted. "Did she tell him?"

Holden felt as if he had hit a clinker on the keyboard—and looked it. "You guys aren't talking sense."

McKelvey's manner was soothing. "What I'm trying to tell you, Holden, is that you'd better get a message to Olga Varenka before you do anything else." He turned to Wisner. "First principles—right, Wisner?"

Wisner blinked. "Maybe they can't do it."

"But they can try," McKelvey argued. "If she doesn't know they're waiting for her, she's not going to make a move."

Holden was incredulous. "Do you expect her to walk out of the opera house?"

McKelvey spread his hands, still pretending to be good-humored. "She can't fly and she won't crawl. One way or another, she's the one who will have to walk out when the time comes."

"But the Russian guards will stop her."

"That's her problem," McKelvey said. "Your people won't be able to get to her, she's going to have to get to you. Do you have anybody waiting outside the Crillon for her, just in case she gets away from the KBG after her press conference?"

"Nobody's thought of that," Holden admitted.

"And do you have any arrangements for keeping people outside the opera house on the nights she's performing?"

"No."

The CIA man leaned back in his chair, quite pleased with himself. "Suppose she does get out and you pick her up. Do you know where to take her?"

Holden was able to answer that. "Gribov has a place in the Fontainebleau Forest."

"Suppose the KGB people follow her there and try to take her back? Do you put up a fight?"

The shower of questions wearied Holden. "We haven't even gone that far."

"Well, you'd better if you're going to be serious about this." McKelvey hunched over his desk now and stared at Holden. He was no longer pretending. "I'll bet you'd never even thought of having armed guards around your hideout if you get Varenka into it."

"You've got the troops and the guns; we don't," Holden said.

McKelvey shook his head. "Remember, we stay out of it. The CIA never heard of you, knows nothing about Varenka or Gribov. Understand?"

"No, I don't understand," Holden said.

A secretary entered discreetly and murmured something to McKelvey that couldn't be overheard. "Thank you." He arose as the secretary left. "Gentlemen, the DCM is ready for us." And to Holden, "Just follow me."

The Deputy Chief of Mission, Bartley Crandell, occupied

a large, bright office on a lower floor of the embassy. He was an old pro in the Foreign Service and looked it—a tall, thin figure in somber brown, with drooping shoulders, a large head with a shiny, pinkish skull and expressionless eyes behind tinted glasses. The ambassador, being a fat-cat political contributor who had been given status in Paris for services rendered, took the bows for whatever slight gains the embassy made in Franco-American relations; but the DCM, as the real operating head, took the blame for everything else.

Holden wasn't in Crandell's office more than two minutes before he became aware that he was being given final instructions, but in such a way that the embassy could deny any involvement in a sticky situation.

Unlike McKelvey and Wisner, who sat on either side of Holden, the DCM didn't pretend that Gribov's venture was something outside the embassy's knowledge. Without bothering to shake hands or waste time on other amenities, he addressed his visitor:

"Mr. Holden, we're obliged to you for coming here and most apologetic because we can't do anything for you and your friends that will become a matter of record. The French right now are very sensitive about their relations with Moscow, and they're walking a chalk line between us and the Russians. So you'll have to take the burden for success or failure in the Varenka matter on yourselves. Do you understand?"

Holden nodded, wondering what was coming next. He didn't have long to wait.

The DCM continued, "I want you to give me your word that you'll do nothing to involve this embassy or embarrass us if Varenka does defect and you're able to pick her up."

Holden wasn't sure of Crandell's meaning, and shifted uneasily in his chair. "But I don't know what will involve you or embarrass you."

McKelvey glanced inquiringly at the DCM, as if to request permission to speak, and received a curt nod. "It's just as I said in my office, Mr. Holden. The CIA doesn't know you and has never heard of you or the ones who work with you. That goes for the embassy too."

Holden couldn't repress a grin. "You mean that I'm not

actually here now, talking to you guys? That I'm only dreaming it?"

"You can't even dream," McKelvey said. "We can't be involved, or the French will come down so hard on the ambassador that he'll have to clean house and a lot of heads will roll around here."

"You speak for the CIA, McKelvey," the DCM objected. "I'll speak for the embassy. I think Mr. Holden appreciates that we're asking him and his people for the utmost discretion."

"What happens if we get into a fight with the KGB?" Holden asked.

"You're on your own," the DCM said. "It'll be between you and the KGB and, I daresay, the French police." He arose and shook Holden's hand. "Please understand that we know of the risks you and your friends are taking, Mr. Holden."

It was small comfort. "Thanks," Holden said dryly. "Appreciate that."

"Oh, and by the way," the DCM added as if in afterthought, "I hear you're a friend of Fay Bainbridge."

"You mean Fay Carroll?" Holden was blunt about the correction.

The DCM permitted himself a small smile. "As you wish. My wife and I knew her when she was married to Spencer Bainbridge, and were very fond of her. Please give her our best wishes."

"I shall."

"And if you please"—now the DCM dropped his official manner and spoke with the urgency of a personal appeal—"try to keep her out of trouble, will you?" He seemed apologetic as he went on. "I can't permit Bainbridge to be in on this, as he was in the Gribov defection. Besides, he has his hands full with the UN Special Assembly."

Holden stared hard at Crandell. "We can get along very nicely without Mr. Bainbridge."

On the way out, just before he left Wisner and McKelvey, the CIA man slapped him on the shoulder. "If a few packages should be delivered to Henri's in your name, don't be surprised."

"After what I've heard this morning," Holden said, "nothing will surprise me."

The packages were waiting for him when he went to work at Henri's that day. In one were four crinkly new brown hunting costumes of various sizes, complete to bright little feathers in the bands of the four velour hunting hats. In the other package were four guns of a type generally used by huntsmen, with enough rounds of ammunition to slaughter every rabbit in the Fontainebleau Forest.

"What is this?" Henri asked in wonderment, surveying the yield of the surprise packages. "Who wishes to outfit *chasseurs*, hunters, in *Chez Henri?*"

"If Olga Varenka escapes, someone must guard her," Holden explained.

Henri's face assumed a knowing expression. "Ah, yes." He surveyed the regulars at the bar—Eilers, Valleau and Pastore—who were having their first drinks of the evening and passing the time with the house girls, Toinette and Josette. "Do you think these will fit our friends?" And he nodded toward the regulars.

"We can try," Holden said. "All they need is boots if they want to go hunting."

"But there are four costumes," Henri suggested, "and we have only three at the bar."

"Maybe," Holden said, "the fourth will fit me."

Gribov was indignant when he learned that the CIA had expressed doubt that his Olga really wanted to escape from her Russian masters. "But this I know!" he exclaimed wrathfully when he joined his friends at Henri's that night to hear Holden's report. "She has told my friend. She will defect."

"Even so," Pat Leary argued, "the embassy people are quite correct, from what Holden has told us, when they say we must get word to Olga that we will pick her up if she escapes. But when? And where?"

For reply, Henri said, "Let us see." He cleared a table in the rear, well away from the few others who were still lingering over drinks or food at that late hour, and began sketching a large map on the marble top. The company gathered around him—Pat Leary and his Amy, Gareth and Stephanie, Baron von Norden and Vivian, Holden and Fay. Only Marie Durand, presiding over the distant cash register as always, could not be compelled to move.

Henri explained as he drew: "Here we have the Opera itself, facing the Place de l'Opera, the public entrance. And in the rear, the Boulevard Haussmann entrance for the administration and the artists."

Now he sketched in the streets around the sides of the building, calling them off as he worked, "Here we have the streets of the composers, the Rue Auber, the Rue Gluck and the Rue Halévy, and over here," a long diagonal mark, "the street of the librettist and novelist Eugène Scribe." He glanced up with a smile. "The street of the American Express.'

He continued, "Now across the Rue Auber, as we know, is the Grand Hotel and here, on the corner, is the Cafe de l'Opera on the Boulevard des Capucines." He stood back. "My friends, as you can see, it will not be easy for Olga to find anybody in such a busy place in the very heart of Paris, even if she can escape backstage. There are twenty-two hundred people in the audience at the opera for every performance. They come and go, and there is constant confusion."

Leary nodded. "What do you suggest, Henri?"

"We must inform Olga that there will be a diversion backstage on the last night that she dances in *Giselle,* that she must come to the Rue Auber and someone will pick her up."

Baron von Norden wanted to know, "What kind of a diversion, Henri?"

The *patron* lifted a cautioning finger. "It is my secret."

"I will wait for her outside," Gribov announced.

"No, my friend." Henri was polite but firm. "It would be the same as moving the Eiffel Tower to the Place de l'Opera. If you will permit, I shall go."

"You will need a bodyguard," Amy Leary warned. "The KGB could make a fight of it, and not only in Fontainebleau."

"I have thought of this," Henri replied. "Shukri, my Tunisian giant who guards my door, will go with me."

"I'll go, too," Gareth proposed eagerly.

"No, Gareth, you and my Stephanie will drive Olga to the Forest of Fontainebleau when I bring her here," Henri said. "And our four *chasseurs,* our hunters, will wait for you there."

"You seem to have thought of everything, Henri," Amy said. "But how do we give Olga the word?"

Von Norden suggested, "Maybe the reporter, Saffron, could slip her a note at the Russian news conference at the Hotel Crillon."

Leary objected. "Saffron knows too much already."

Holden felt Fay's hand tighten on his arm. "I could do it." she whispered.

He shook his head. "Stay out of it, Fay."

"But I want to."

"Wish you wouldn't." And he thought of Dr. Beranger's doubts about her condition. "If something should go wrong . . ."

But before he could finish his sentence, she faced the company. "I'll do it."

"How, madame?" Henri was skeptical. "Do you have access to the Crillon?"

"Sometimes I work with Saffron, I do part-time criticism," she explained. "I could ask him to let me go with him, and I'm sure he wouldn't object."

"But can you get to Olga?" Henri was far from convinced.

"I can try."

"Put a note in a bouquet of roses for Olga," Amy proposed.

"Roses at a news conference?" Her husband laughed. "Generally, the reporters throw brickbats."

"Ah, but that is in America," Henri said. "In France, we are different."

A news conference at the Hotel Crillon in Paris is like putting on a circus in a museum. The transmission of news at such a function is purely coincidental. What really counts is the demeanor of the participants and the artistry of the performance. It is, in the language of journalism, a pseudo-event.

The Russians, as hosts, understood this quite as well as the assembled reporters and hangers-on when they produced Olga Varenka in the grand ballroom of the Crillon to give public expression to their denials that she sought to defect. The glistening rows of spindly, gilded chairs were almost filled as Guy Saffron of the *Paris Press* entered with Fay and Holden that morning. On a dais draped with dark green cloth, a row of impassive Russians sat behind bare tables placed end to end with a speaker's stand complete with reading light and microphone in the middle.

"They're putting on a show for us this morning," Saffron said as he headed for three seats in the front row, directly below the dais. Fay slipped in between the two men and glanced about nervously.

"Where's Varenka?" she asked.

"Oh, they'll bring her on soon like a captive queen being fed to the lions," Saffron said.

Holden jerked a thumb over his shoulder at the people behind him. "Didn't know there were this many reporters in Paris."

"There aren't," Saffron responded. "The Russians have papered the house. I just spotted the receptionist in their embassy on the Rue de Grenelle, and a lot of the people around her have familiar faces. They're here to applaud."

"Is that part of the act?" Holden asked.

"Not really. Theoretically, we're here to get news, not to give three cheers. But the Russians have their own way of doing things."

"Think we'll be able to say hello to Varenka after it's over?" Fay wanted to know.

Saffron gave her a curious look. "What for? She doesn't understand much English and is only a little better at French. If you look over there," and he nodded in the direction of two men with white stenographic pads and a stack of pencils before them, "you'll see that the Russians have brought on translators, so I'd guess whatever she says will be in Russian."

"I'd just like to meet her," Fay said. "She's such a marvelous dancer."

Holden, well aware that Saffron didn't know Fay had a message for Varenka, added for his benefit, "We don't want to interfere, but maybe we can just take a chance on shaking hands with her when she's done."

"You might get clobbered by the KGB," Saffron said. He waved a hand toward the dais and around the corners of the ballroom. "They're all over the place."

Olga Varenka appeared just then at the end of the ballroom with an escort of three large, grim-faced Russians in dark suits. It wouldn't be quite right to say that she walked down the center aisle between sections of the audience on either side. Rather, in an ample gray gown that billowed about her, she gave the impression of floating. She was quite tall and very thin and held her blond head with exquisite grace. While her heavy-footed escorts tramped up the stairs to the dais, she seemed to spring lightly without apparent effort. But as she stood beside the speaker's stand to be introduced by a flat-faced Soviet functionary, her oval face was pale and her lips worked nervously.

The rudimentary applause, which started from the back of the room and splattered forward by degrees, didn't help much. It was fairly apparent that the Russians were applauding; the news people were not. Finally, some of the audience stood up and held their hands above their heads to show rapid enthusiasm as they continued to clap, but no stampede developed. Within a very short time, order was restored and the Soviet functionary explained in French that the purpose of the meeting was to dispel false rumors that Olga Varenka was being held at the Soviet embassy against her will. She was introduced without flourishes:

"Mesdames, messieurs, Madame Varenka."

Once again, the Russians in the audience tried to create the atmosphere for an ovation, but nothing like that followed. Those who had applauded before tried again, swinging their hands in rhythm above their heads, but soon gave up. The slender dancer gripped the podium on either side with hands so tense that, as Holden could see directly below, the knuckles showed white.

She spoke Russian in a voice so low that even the sensitive Crillon public-address system couldn't amplify it to make it distinguishable all over the room. Everybody could tell that she was reading from a sheet of paper on the podium. The row of Russians on the dais stared straight ahead, stony-faced. And the escorting group remained behind her, two on either side. When she had finished, which didn't take very long, she was shown to a seat on the dais while a translator gave the sense of her remarks in French. Then, an English translation followed, which was notable for its bluntness and brevity:

"Madame Varenka says that there is no truth to rumors that she wishes to leave the Kirov Ballet and her family and friends

185

in the Soviet Union. She also denies malicious statements made in recent days that she is being detained by force in the embassy of the Soviet Union here in Paris. She rejects these slanders against herself and her country and she believes them to be the work of the American CIA, whose notorious concoctions are well known. She thanks the people of Paris for the generous reception she has been given during the current engagement of the Kirov Ballet at the Paris Opera and wishes them well."

After more applause, now barely perfunctory, the Soviet master of ceremonies stifled an attempt by several reporters, Saffron among them, to ask questions. Madame Varenka, it appeared, had an important engagement and would not have time for further remarks. It was clear enough that the dancer would be hustled out of the ballroom as quickly as possible, but before she had descended from the dais Fay had managed to work her way along the front row to the aisle.

Holden, who had kept up with her, saw that she had a small square of folded paper in her right hand. As the dancer descended from the dais, Fay smiled, said something rapidly in French and held out her hand. Varenka paused in uncertainty, then timidly grasped Fay's hand. A Russian escort officer barked a command, pushed her ahead roughly and snapped off the handshake. But Fay turned excitedly to Holden, who was still behind her: "She got it, she took it."

Holden was well aware that people around them had heard Fay's remark, and some might have been able to guess at its meaning. He felt cold perspiration standing on his forehead. Glancing about the room, he saw that the Russians had advanced Varenka well along the aisle although other people also were grasping at her hand to shake it. Maybe, he told himself, everything would turn out well.

But Saffron, beside him, growled close to his ear, "Whatever you guys are trying to do, you'd better take care."

Holden looked ahead and saw that Fay was smiling cheerfully. When he caught up with her, he said, "Let's get back to the Rue Soufflot."

"Didn't I do well, darling?" she asked.

"You sure did," he said. Saffron, directly behind them, grinned but said nothing.

* * *

There comes a time in every new enterprise—good or bad, safe or risky—when some of its participants feel that they'd like to spin off. That was how Gribov's hapless attempts to rescue Olga from the Russians were affecting Fay Carroll and Holden. Whenever they could, they absented themselves from meetings with Gribov and made free with the handsome apartment in the Rue Soufflot, which the Learys left to them.

In spite of all the disadvantages of their position, Fay and Holden were happy with each other. True, Fay's stepfather was still insisting on her remarriage to Spencer Bainbridge and badgering her mother to support him. But once Dr. Beranger had revealed to Fay the source of Bainbridge's revival of interest in her, her will to resist seemed to have been strengthened. As Holden observed to her one afternoon when they were alone in the apartment on the Rue Soufflot, "It sure helps to know that you're going to inherit a lot of money when you're thirty."

"Does it interest you?" she asked idly.

"It scares hell out of me."

"Do you fear for your immortal soul?"

"It's not my soul I'm worried about," was the frank response. "If I'm still around when you're thirty, you'll be splashing mud on me with your Rolls-Royce when you dash by on your way to the bank. You won't even know me."

She snuggled close to him. "You think of the most impossible things."

"Well, it's true," he insisted, and he was quite serious about it. "Anybody who picks up a few million dollars all of a sudden is never going to be the same again."

"You have almost five years to worry about that, darling," she said, and lifted her head. "Kiss me."

It was her way of ending an argument, one of which Holden thoroughly approved. After he first met her, he had worried unnecessarily about any man who seemed to take an interest in her. He felt a little foolish now to think that he had worried because she had returned to Paris at Gribov's invitation. And he was shamefaced when he thought of how he had suspected her when he saw men's clothes in her closet while she occupied Dr. Beranger's apartment on the Ile St. Louis. Nor could he understand now why he had felt uncomfortable because of the polite interest people like Baron von Norden and Guy Saffron took in her.

As for Spencer Bainbridge, the American embassy was keeping him thoroughly occupied with arrangements for the Special United Nations Assembly. And, as had been pointed out by Bartley Crandell, the DCM, Bainbridge was under orders to avoid involvement with Nikolai Gribov.

Holden, however, was under no illusions that Bainbridge had given up his campaign to persuade Fay to marry him. At that particular time, circumstances had given her only a temporary respite. And one morning, when Holden awoke to a tattoo of small fists outside his apartment door in the Rue Bonaparte, he had a premonition of disaster. For when he swung the door open, Fay brushed past him in a panicky mood.

As he closed the door, she flung her arms about him. "You've got to help me, Arch."

"Sure, honey, I'll do anything I can. But," and he was mystified, "what's the trouble?" He saw she had been weeping.

"My mother's just called me from Long Island. My stepfather wants to see me; says I'm not being fair to Spence Bainbridge."

"Are you going home?"

"No." She added vehemently, "And he can't make me go home."

"Then don't be afraid of him."

She released her fear in a torrent of words:

"I'm not, but my mother is. She's afraid that Carroll will commit her to a mental institution for life if she crosses him. And it could happen. Right now, her record of treatment in various sanitariums goes back years. And even her own doctors can't predict when or if mental instability will make her permanently incompetent to handle her affairs. It's serious."

"But is it really in Carroll's interest to try to do away with her—to put her in an institution for life?" Holden asked. "Isn't there a chance that her lawyers could prove to a court that he's acting to cover up misappropriation of funds?"

"The lawyers already have tried that approach," Fay replied. "And when my mother turned them down, they came to me and showed me where it would be in mother's interest and mine to act now against Carroll."

"And why don't you?"

"We've both been afraid of what would happen if Carroll beats the indictment. And he could." She sat on the bed beside him and seemed very small and defenseless. He put his arms around her. She lifted her face to his to be kissed. "Oh, Arch, it's so good being with you again."

As they continued kissing each other, he pulled her down beside him on the bed, then took her in his arms. He couldn't think of lawyers and doctors, of her mother's plight, even of the menace of Carroll just then. All he knew was that he had missed Fay, ached for her, wanted her. And now that she lay beside him, he didn't want to think of anything other than the sheer delight of what she had meant to him before, and what she would be again. He began pulling off her dress, but she anticipated him. The zipper was undone in the back, and now she quickly slipped off the dress, shed her underthings, stockings and slippers, and came to him. He was waiting for her on the bed.

"Oh, darling, it's been such a long time," she said. And she flung her arms about him and let him take possession of her. There was a fierce joy about her when she let herself go that aroused him and made him forget himself completely in the ecstasy of the moment. And so they embraced and kissed and loved each other—and thought of nothing else for a long time.

The lovemaking gave both of them renewed confidence in each other, an influx of courage and a strengthening of will. She murmured to him as they lay together in the delicious relaxation and recovery after an overflow of passion, "I can't give you up, Arch. I want to help Mother, but I can't give you up."

"Who wants you to?"

"I had a lot of noble ideas of sacrificing myself." She smiled at the notion. "Of going through with marrying Bainbridge again and letting my stepfather do whatever he wanted to with my father's estate. Anything, so he would quit persecuting my mother. But it would be foolish. I can't do it. Not to you. Not to myself."

"There's no reason for you to do it, honey," he said.

"But Carroll's coming to Paris to have it out with me, to

189

tell me that I must marry Bainbridge again—or else," she went on.

"How do you know?"

"Mother told me when I talked to her the other night on the telephone. She says he's in a devilish mood. She's afraid of what he'll do to her if I cross him."

"What do the lawyers say about his position?" Holden asked. "Do they know enough to get a court order against him and make him show what he's done with your father's estate?"

"They suspect; they have no proof yet."

"But if they do?"

She snuggled up to him and kissed him. "Oh, Arch, it's much better just to be you and me and think only of ourselves. Everything else is so mean and ugly . . ."

Holden tried to get her to be practical. "Yes, honey, but we can't let Carroll run wild. We've got to stop him."

"Stop him?" she echoed. "He's a devil, won't stop until he has his way. Wants me married to Bainbridge and Bainbridge in control of whatever's left of my share of father's estate. So then the two of them will think they're safe. But," and she stirred beside him and sat up all at once, "I've got news for Spence Bainbridge. I'm not afraid of him this time; whatever happens, I won't let him take advantage of me." She put her hand on Holden's chest and looked down at him fondly. "That's what you've done for me, Arch. I'm going to fight them as long as you're willing to stick with me."

He sat beside her and took her in his arms. "You couldn't drive me away. There isn't anything I wouldn't do to help you."

"Then," she decided, looking up at him wide-eyed, "I'm going to tell the lawyers to go ahead with their investigation, but keep it as quiet as they can. And I'm going to pretend to do what Carroll and Bainbridge want me to do, just to keep Carroll from doing something drastic to mother."

"But what if it doesn't work?" Holden asked. "What if the evidence just isn't there to prosecute, and Carroll gets off clean? You're in the middle, honey."

She did not flinch. "That's a risk I'll have to take. It's the only chance I have of beating them, of keeping mother out of commitment for life to a mental institution."

He liked her flash of courage, but he couldn't help being concerned about letting her put herself under the control of Bainbridge and his uncle, even for a short time. "Suppose Bainbridge suspects you're not on the level?" he demanded. "He could make things tough for you and your mother."

"Maybe so, but he isn't so solid at the State Department, although he thinks he is." In a burst of confidence, she went on, "Bartley Crandell, the DCM, and his wife are old friends of mine and they know what's going on."

"How so?"

"I've kept in touch with them. Bart insisted on it."

"And what can he do?" Holden asked, still skeptical about her plan to take covert action against Carroll and Bainbridge.

Her eyes flashed. "Plenty! Just let the lawyers come up with enough evidence to show that there's been a lot of hanky-panky in the handling of father's estate, and a great many things are likely to happen."

Now her mood had completely shifted. She felt so good about the two of them as they sat on the bed together that she laughed and suddenly pulled him down beside her. She wouldn't let him talk, just continued to kiss him and quickly and tenderly made him respond to her. Before he quite realized it, he had been thoroughly aroused once again and had forgotten all else except the sheer joy of being with her.

A lot of things were likely to change in the days ahead, and both of them might be in danger. But he was certain of one thing now, and that was their love for each other. That, he knew, would never change.

Henri Durand, too, was making plans for the safe delivery of Olga Varenka when and if she escaped from the Russians. Once he was able to pick her up, he proposed to bring her to the Place St. Michel. There, Gareth and Stephanie, with Holden's help, were to be waiting to drive the fugitive to the hunting lodge in the Forest of Fontainebleau in Stephanie's car.

There, Pat Leary would be stationed with Amy and Fay, to receive her. Upon his arrival, Holden was to slip into his role as a hunter and join the three regulars—Karl Eilers, Marcel Valleau and Enzo Pastore—in guarding against intruders.

In briefing them, Henri warned them all to be careful, to maintain absolute security over their plans, to discuss them with no one. As for Gribov, the titular head of the conspiracy, he cloaked his own moves in the deepest mystery. Nobody except Gribov and Henri knew how the group planned to spirit Varenka out of the opera house, and both simply refused to talk about it. That was their secret and they would confide it to no one.

So the conspirators prepared to attend the Paris opera for the Kirov Ballet's third and final performance of *Giselle,* with Olga Varenka dancing the title role. It attracted a brilliant gathering. Honoring a singer of the first magnitude, Gribov had his private box. While the others took up their stations outside the opera house, Gribov, the Learys and Vivian, with Baron von Norden, Henri, Fay and Holden watched the ballet from there.

From Varenka's initial appearance in the first act, the audience was delighted. The applause was tumultuous. And Gribov, sitting in the front row of the box, glowed with pride at his sweetheart's accomplishments. If anything, the enthusiasm was even greater as the second act progressed. When Varenka had caught everyone else's attention, Henri gently touched Holden's arm in the darkness and whispered, "When you see the curtain descend, come to the Rue Auber. I will be waiting." He slipped out, preparing for the climactic moment.

Fay pressed Holden's hand. "What's Varenka going to do?"

"I don't know," he said.

Henri had kept his secret well. As the curtain was about to descend for the second act, there was a distinct haze that spread about the giant stage from the right wing. Some of the members of the cast began coughing. Others stopped dancing. The orchestra faltered, but rallied as the conductor shook his baton to command attention.

Frightened murmurs spread through the audience as the haze thickened on the stage and spread to the house itself. The smell of pungent smoke seemed almost suffocating to the cast.

Remembering his instructions, Holden took Fay by the hand. "We're getting out of here," he said. "Follow me." As he brushed by Baron von Norden, he heard the German say, "I didn't think Henri would do anything like this." To which Pat

Leary replied, turning about with an air of earnestness, "Don't be afraid. There's no fire."

"How can you be sure?" Von Norden arose in the box, peering at the stage through the smoke.

Leary tried to calm the German. "All I can say is that Henri thought there might be smoke but no fire."

Von Norden was angry. "This is madness."

"Please, Rudi!" Amy got up quickly and went to him.

He shook her off roughly. "I can't be associated with anything like this. I must leave..."

That was the last Holden heard as he left the Gribov box with Fay. The Russian, alone, was not disconcerted. He sat in the front of the box, raptly watching the stage, as if he expected Olga to be delivered to him momentarily. But the curtain was descending, the orchestra had stopped playing and people were choking the aisles of the great auditorium.

As Holden led Fay through the excited operagoers who were filtering into the lobby, he heard someone call his name once, then again. He turned briefly, saw Guy Saffron some distance off and resolutely looked away. Saffron was the last person he wanted to talk to at the moment; fortunately, the reporter was blocked off by people who were streaming into the lobby for fresh air.

Emerging on the Place de l'Opera, Holden swung left on the Rue Auber. Fay had to take a few jogging steps to keep up with him, now and then, as they hurried along. Except for traffic, the street seemed quiet. The night was misty, and there was a distinct feeling of rain in the air.

Fay was almost out of breath. "I can't keep up, Arch..."

"Just a few steps more," he urged, not turning around.

"I'm tired..."

"That's them, right up there."

In the eerie half-light cast by street lamps into the darkness that shrouded the side of the opera house, Holden made out the massive figure of Henri's doorman, Shukri the Tunisian. He was standing on the sidewalk in his shiny yellow slicker, one arm beckoning to the approaching couple. Across the street, Holden saw Henri's Peugeot, its dimmers on, and made out the shape of the *patron* sitting behind the wheel. The car was headed south toward the Place de l'Opera and was standing in a No Parking zone, its engine running, with traffic swinging around it.

As they halted beside Shukri, who greeted them with a broad smile, Fay asked him in French what had happened. He replied, shaking his head, *"Rien."* Then he laughed, pointed across the street to Henri's car and made an observation to Fay in French. She translated for Holden's benefit: "He says Henri may be losing money out here for nothing, and he thinks I should get into the car."

"Good idea," Holden said, took her hand and picked his way across the street. As he came abreast of the car, he said to Henri, "You'd better keep Fay with you," and almost shoved her into the backseat of the car. "If Olga gets out, swing the car across the street and we'll put her in the front seat next to you."

"But is there any sign of her?"

"No, but there's hell to pay inside the opera," Holden replied. "The place was filled with smoke just as the curtain started to come down for the second act. What did you do?"

"I did nothing," Henri said. "I left it to my friend, Clement, to create a diversion. He told me he would pull the switch and throw the house into darkness if he could reach the fuse box backstage. If not, he had a smoke bomb." Then, anxiously, "Was it very bad?"

"Suffocating. Everyone got panicky and von Norden made a scene in the box."

"Ah, then we are in trouble." Henri was morose, his head bowed over the wheel, his chin touching his chest. "I told Clement that the smoke bomb was not a good idea, but he is such a ferocious anti-Communist. He said the Russians would be lucky if he didn't blow up the stage."

"You shouldn't have trusted him," Holden said. "Too excitable."

Henri shrugged and spread his hands. *"Que voulez vous?* I had to take help where I could get it. But if Clement should talk now..." He broke off as they both heard the thump of heavy boots on the sidewalk across the street and a cry of warning from Shukri.

Three large Russians, bareheaded and in conventional dress, had come pounding around the back of the opera from the

Boulevard Haussmann. They now flung themselves without warning on Shukri, but the giant already had sent one sprawling with a kick and was swinging on the others. In the distance, at the Place de l'Opera, police whistles could be heard. The shrieking sirens of ambulances rose and fell as they approached the front of the building.

"You've got to get out of here," Holden shouted to Henri, thinking only of Fay.

Henri protested, "We must help Shukri."

Fay called from the backseat, "Get in the car, Arch."

"I can't," he yelled. "Got to help Shukri."

He ducked and bobbed between the cars that kept coming down the street. The drivers ignored the fighting on the sidewalk and the flashing lights of police vehicles and the ambulance sirens ahead in the Place de l'Opera. Shukri had downed another opponent in the gutter with a ham-handed swing to the stomach and was taking on the third Russian when Holden dashed up. Between them, they were able to overpower the last man. But by that time, one of the Russians had revived, pulled a gun from a shoulder holster and was about to aim when Holden called a warning and kicked the gun out of his hand.

Henri, having pulled himself together, now swung the Peugeot across the street and called to Holden and Shukri to get in. They needed no urging. The Tunisian crammed himself in the front beside the *patron* while Holden pushed into the rear with Fay. One of the Russians fired a wild shot at the car as it moved off in traffic, but missed. Weaving through the pileup of police, fire and hospital vehicles in the Place de l'Opera, Henri was lucky to get his car away unchallenged.

As he drove the car toward the Seine bridges and the safety of the Place St. Michel, he chattered in French with Shukri. The Tunisian was laughing over the affair and seemed to be unhurt. "Shukri thinks the Russians were expecting us," Henri said. "They were asking no questions. All they wanted to do was to fight."

"And shoot," Fay added. To Holden she said, "If you hadn't kicked the gun out of that man's hand, he would have shot you."

Holden hugged her. "Honey, it's lucky I played soccer in school. I can kick better than I can punch."

Henri was intensely serious. "Ah yes, it is easy to joke now, but it was a very near thing." He stared directly ahead, seeming dejected, as he stopped the car for a red light near the Louvre. "If we are not involved with the police in this matter, we will be very lucky." He shook his head. "It is not good."

His mood did not improve when they reached the Place St. Michel and entered his establishment. For Marie, sitting behind her cash register, noted their dispirited manner and Shukri's torn yellow slicker and drew appropriate conclusions. Nobody, least of all Holden, needed any translation when she directed a stream of sharp-voiced French at her husband. Nor was Fay able to improve her disposition by trying to explain everything.

Henri interrupted the proceedings by breaking out a bottle of choice Calvados and passing around a jigger each to his companions. "To better times," he proposed, raising his glass in a mordant toast.

"We couldn't have done much worse," Holden said.

As he took his accustomed place at the piano and let random runs and chords ripple from his fingers, he nodded to the regulars and Gareth Leary who had been waiting there. Presumably, they would have been charged with guarding Olga on the way to the Forest of Fontainebleau had she been safely delivered from the opera that night. But there was no Olga, no sign of Gribov. And there seemed to be no particular need to talk about it.

There were more people than usual in Henri's that night, and they stayed later, eating and drinking, so the misspent heroics around the opera soon overlaid with a dull patina of routine. With Shukri at the door in a more serviceable raincoat, Henri greeting new arrivals and Holden at the piano, there was a semblance of irreproachable order about the place. No one could have guessed anything about the evening's events from the leisurely atmosphere.

The first break in the artificial calm came toward midnight, when Guy Saffron sauntered in and climbed on a bar stool near Fay at the piano. He proceeded with an elaborate display of barfly ennui and made small talk with Fay and Holden. Henri came over for a short while, pretending to be just as casual,

196

but went back to the door when he saw that the reporter wasn't prepared just yet to discuss the events of the evening.

But after a while, Saffron edged gingerly into the affair at the opera. "Saw you leaving the opera house tonight," he said to Fay. "Everything okay?"

Her face was a mask. "Sure." But neither she nor Holden knew precisely what to expect. He tried to divert Saffron's attention, saying, "We weren't hurt. Was anybody else?"

"A coupla old ladies fell down after they got outside," Saffron replied lazily, "and some of the members of the cast were treated for smoke inhalation. Three went to the hospital." He took a drink from his highball, stared at the glass and muttered, "It was a silly thing to do, tossing a smoke bomb."

Holden pretended surprise. "Was that it?"

Out of the corner of his mouth, the reporter said in a low voice, "Oh, come on. Don't try to kid me."

Holden put on a show of virtuous astonishment. "But I got Fay out of there because I thought there was a fire."

Saffron's reply was soft-voiced and controlled, but skeptical. "And you were in Gribov's box, and Gribov came backstage after the second-act curtain and demanded to see Varenka? *He* knew damn well there was no fire, just a smoke bomb."

"I didn't know what Gribov did," Holden said, and tried to divert everybody by ripping out some loud rock music, expressly against Henri's instructions. All he did was to bring Henri back to the piano, appearing at the reporter's elbow.

Saffron was saying just then, "Well, whatever you guys planned, you didn't get Olga. The Russians hustled her away and called off the performance after the second act."

"But we planned nothing, it was not our doing," Henri announced blandly.

"You guys didn't get into a fight with the Russians outside?" Saffron was grinning and needling them now.

"A fight?" Henri smiled with a superior air. "What is there to fight about?"

"The Russians told the French police that there was a gang of the CIA outside the opera on the Rue Auber, waiting to kidnap Olga; but the attempt was broken up by Olga's guards." He added, his grin widening, "And the leader of this CIA gang was a big black man in a yellow slicker. That wouldn't be old Shukri outside, would it?"

Henri managed a nervous little laugh. "Shukri has been on duty all evening as usual. He is not of the CIA."

Holden saw that Saffron was getting uncomfortably close to the truth, and again tried to divert his line of questioning. "Did they get the guy who threw the smoke bomb?"

"The police aren't sure who did it, but the Russians blame the chief carpenter, a Frenchman named Robert Clement," the reporter responded, "and he is missing." He turned to Henri. "There used to be a Clement who came in here, an old man who fought with the Maquis in the Second World War. Could it be the same man?"

"This I do not know," Henri said. "Clement of the Maquis must be a very old man now. Anyway, since he has not been here for a long time, maybe he is dead."

Saffron shoved his hat back on his head. "You guys kill me. You don't know anything, do you?"

"Why should we?" Henri answered. "This should be Gribov's concern, not ours. Perhaps you have seen him?"

Saffron stopped a waiter and paid his bill. "Yeah, I've seen Gribov, and he swears he had nothing to do with it." He chuckled. "I must say the guy's convincing. He got together a helluva cover story."

"Cover story?" Holden asked, not interrupting his piano-playing.

Saffron slipped from his bar stool. "You'd have to see it to believe it, Mac, but between the time I heard him roaring for right and justice backstage at the opera and the time I saw him coming out the Hotel Crillon a little while ago, he'd rounded up one of the most gorgeous women I've ever seen in my life. Just to show he wasn't really interested in Olga."

"Amy Leary, the professor's wife, was with us tonight," Fay suggested.

"That little old butterball? I've known her for years and I love her, but she's not gorgeous," Saffron said, buttoning up his raincoat. "No, this one was in a long gown with white sequins and a white fox coat and she looked like a movie star when Gribov handed her into his limousine."

Fay was amused. "Nikolai Gribov has many gorgeous women."

"But he doesn't take them all to his private hangout. No, this woman is the one he's been dating for quite a while, and it can't be much of a surprise to you if he was with her tonight."

"Not Catherine Vaillant!" Holden exclaimed.

"You hit it, brother," and Saffron slouched out of the bar.

Holden looked at Henri and Fay. "So," he said with a touch of irony, "Catherine has won the consolation prize."

What the French press called the smoke-bomb attack at the Paris opera was soon forgotten by all but the immediate participants. The French police inquiry was lackadaisical. An inspector routinely interviewed Henri and his associates, made note of their denials and gravely apologized for having taken up their time. If there was any hint that the French government was aware of what really had happened, it came sometime afterward. Shukri, the Tunisian, was summoned to the immigration office and informed that he could not continue to claim asylum in France if he indulged in political activity.

Gribov, being a world figure, was handled quite differently. Once a decent interval had passed and Russian ire over the incident had been dispelled, a functionary from the Quai d'Orsay made a formal call on the Russian singer at the Hotel Crillon and asked politely whether he had any hard evidence that Olga Varenka was being held by the Russians against her will. Gribov, of course, presented only broken French rhetoric in reply. He was therefore assured, in fulsome terms, of the French government's interest in the rights of man (and women); and that if, in the future, he came into possession of the necessary evidence he would be welcomed at the Foreign Office. Meantime, he was reminded in silken terms, the laws of France applied to all who were within its borders, regardless of nationality. It was a suave performance, but its meaning was unmistakable. Gribov had been put on notice that his campaign to detach Olga Varenka from the Kirov Ballet would have to be abandoned.

The Russians, quite understandably, were the only ones who continued to be upset. When they asked for the arrest of the chief carpenter at the opera, Robert Clement, they were informed that at least a score of members of his union had sworn that he had not been backstage at the opera on the night of the smoke-bomb attack. So Clement, after an appropriate interval, returned to his regular job and continued to serve during the remainder of the Kirov Ballet's engagement. Nor did the Russians make an issue out of his presence, since it was evident that the French wanted to gloss over the incident as quickly and expeditiously as possible.

As for the Americans, they were discreetly silent throughout the investigation. It was accepted as a matter of routine that the CIA would be blamed for any untoward event that unsettled the Russians; all that was possible, under the circumstances, was an official denial. But for the ambassador, the notion that the CIA had instituted so clumsy a plot seemed thoroughly absurd, and he refused to dignify the charge with a denial. However, after the Kirov Ballet resumed its engagement, it became known to the American embassy that the Russians had two pieces of evidence about the smoke-bombing. One was a note that the Varenka's guards had taken from her, directing her to the Rue Auber after the second act of *Giselle* and instructing her to telephone Henri's if she needed assistance. The other was the license-plate number of the car in which the supposed gang in the Rue Auber had escaped, which had been traced to Henri Durand.

Holden found out about it when he came to work one evening about a week after the incident and saw that Cary Wisner, his contact at the American embassy, was on a bar stool waiting for him. They were alone. While Wisner talked in a low voice, Holden let his fingers roam over the keys without attempting any coherent performance. He kept his head down, wondering what was coming next. When Wisner avoided the issue, Holden asked, "Assuming all this is true, what am I supposed to do about it?"

"You and your friends had better keep your guard up," was the dry response. "We were told that the Russians wanted to send some goons over here to wreck this joint, but the French got lucky and found out about the project in time to head it off."

"What's to prevent the Russians from doing it anyway?"

"Can't say. But"—and here Wisner became cautious—"I

don't think they want to offend the French any more than we do." He waited a few moments, then faced Holden directly. "Do you know if any further attempt will be made to help Olga Varenka?"

Holden smiled. "That was our Bay of Pigs, Wisner. We took a licking and I haven't heard that anybody wants to try again."

"Even Gribov?"

"Even Gribov. As far as I know, he has a girl."

Wisner sighed. "Yes, we know about her. Vaillant, one of our contract translators, and she tells us the same thing you do." He drummed on the surface of the piano with impatient fingers. "Look, Holden, we can't afford any more nonsense about Gribov and Varenka. You guys better lay off."

"I didn't want to do anything in the first place," Holden said. "But"—and he was thinking primarily of Fay—"what if some innocent people are hurt if the Russians get tough?"

Wisner was patient. "As I told you, I don't think the Russians want to get the French sore at them. And you'd better realize that we don't want to have the Russians and French yapping at us, either."

"I thought we hated the Russians."

"Sure, officially we do. It's good politics to hate the Russians. But just take a tip from me, Holden. Don't be surprised if you hear that we've assured the Russians that we won't give Varenka political asylum if she defects." He climbed from the bar stool. "Take care." It was his sign-off.

When Holden reported the conversation to Henri later, the *patron* nodded sadly. "I feared as much. We must warn Gribov."

"Do you think he cares? He has Catherine, doesn't he?"

"You do not understand. Gribov makes love to Catherine. He makes war on the Russians, and Olga is the cause of the war."

"But he's already lost the war."

"He will not admit it, which is dangerous." Henri fingered his mustache, deep in thought. After a few moments, he went on, "And you must remember that we have absolutely no control over what Olga Varenka may do. That is even more dangerous."

The Learys entered just then with Vivian and Gareth, evidently to take advantage of Henri's early dining hour. As they approached the piano bar, Pat Leary called out, "What's the matter with you two? You look as if the fate of the world was about to be decided."

"Perhaps not the fate of the world," Henri replied, "but more likely the fate of my own little establishment. If we are not careful, we may provoke a Russian invasion."

The Learys took possession of bar stools. "Fear not," Amy Leary said, "there will be no invasion."

Pat Leary added, "Baron von Norden says the Americans won't give Varenka asylum if she defects, and the Russians are satisfied with that."

"I would like to talk to von Norden," Henri said. "On the night of the smoke-bombing, I am told he was very angry with us."

Vivian, her pretty face a blank, responded, "He got over it."

Stephanie Rivet, the photographer, had just come on duty, and Gareth waved to her. "Now *there's* somebody worth getting excited about," he said with a show of spirit. "Let's just forget about all the Russians."

Henri's response had a melancholy ring to it. "I wish we could."

Chapter Seven

The failure to free Olga Varenka deeply affected Fay. Somehow, she had linked her attempts to free herself from her tyrannical stepfather with Olga's efforts to shake off the restraints of a dictatorial government. When Olga was denied freedom, Fay seemed to lose confidence in her own cause.

At first, Holden had thought that Fay's fit of depression would be temporary; that she would rally. Then he counted on life with the Learys at the Rue Soufflot apartment to bring her around. It didn't work. Nothing that Holden could think of now seemed to divert her. The only truly hopeful aspect of their relationship was that their love for each other remained steadfast.

Under these circumstances, Holden didn't dare push her about her pretending to agree to remarry Bainbridge. Nor did he mention it to Dr. Beranger, whom he visited several times to talk about Fay's state of mind after the failure of the attempt to deliver Olga.

At one point, he confided to the psychiatrist:

"What will happen to Fay when Carroll and her mother reach Paris scares hell out of me."

"Do you know they both will be here?" Dr. Beranger asked.

Holden nodded. "Any day now. I checked at the Ritz, and they have reservations. The manager seems to think Carroll is important enough to be taken in whenever he shows up."

"Fay's mother hasn't let me know," the psychiatrist said. He added, as an afterthought, "Perhaps she couldn't."

"Do you think it's dangerous to let Fay continue to be mixed up in the Varenka matter?" Holden asked, not being very certain himself of how to proceed.

"Anything that distracts her, that keeps her interested, is worth doing," was the quiet reply. "As for the dangers involved, I just don't know about that. You'd be the better judge. Is anything being planned now that would put renewed pressure on Fay?"

"Not that I know of."

That, indeed, was the case. Often, in the painful interval before the arrival of her mother and stepfather in Paris, Fay asked Holden what was happening to Olga. The Russians had hidden her well. So he had to confess, quite honestly, that the conspiracy was at a standstill. As for Gribov, he seemed to have lost interest for the time being; now and then he came to Henri's with Catherine Vaillant.

It was small comfort for Holden when Guy Saffron announced one evening at Henri's that Olga Varenka had been seen in the fenced-in garden of a Russian-owned estate at St. Denis, a property used by its embassy people. Fay, who happened to be at the piano bar with Holden at the time, brightened at the news.

"Do you suppose we could get to her?" she asked.

Saffron laughed harshly. "You won't get close enough to her to slip her another note, baby. Not this time. They beat up one of our photographers who tried to sneak a picture of Varenka in the garden."

After that, none of the group around Gribov and the Learys had the heart to suggest they even try. Fay's burst of hope was followed by an even deeper despondency, particularly after her parents arrived at the Ritz. "I can't face them," she confessed.

"Want me to go along?" Holden suggested.

"Would you?" She seemed to grasp at almost any chance to avert a scene.

"Sure, honey," Holden said. "I hope it'll help."

Waco Texas Carroll was the kind of man who wore his ten-gallon Stetson hat to dinner at the Ritz in Paris. He devoutly believed that he could make French people understand his brand of English by shouting at them. But he made himself an acceptable guest, nevertheless, by handing out American money lavishly.

Despite all that, Sarah Deak Carroll meekly accepted him

204

for what he was. She did try in an ineffectual way to defend Fay from her stepfather's bullying. But she was a small woman, quiet in manner, and suffered violent headaches very often after her husband had an argument with her.

It never paid to argue with Waco Texas Carroll, in any case. Sometimes, if he was displeased by something as impersonal as a TV weather forecast, he would push over the TV set. He could become violent if he ordered soft-boiled eggs from room service for an early breakfast (he was invariably up and about by 6:00 A.M.) and they arrived in a slightly different state. He would splatter the sedate walls of his Ritz suite with the offending eggs.

Carroll was a large man, standing well over six feet and weighing more than two hundred pounds. By effete French standards, he was old; yet, his face was tanned by sun and wind and relatively unwrinkled, and his thicket of rather unkempt black hair—when he removed his Stetson—showed few traces of gray. No one could say that he moved about in a conventional way; even if he left the ancient French elevator to head for the bar, he made a great show of stomping about in his high-heeled Texas boots.

And yet, on the first day after his arrival with Sarah Deak Carroll and mountains of luggage, the American embassy was solicitous enough to inquire whether he was well settled and satisfied. Even more important, a military attaché in uniform was sent to call on the new arrival and present the compliments of the ambassador since Carroll had been commissioned a noncombat brigadier general in charge of nothing in particular at the Pentagon during World War II. It was taken for granted, therefore, that if he wanted Spencer Bainbridge in his suite rather than at the United Nations conference in the Palais de Chaillot, Bainbridge would be detached from duty as often as necessary.

So Bainbridge wound up spending a lot of time either in the stiffly proper lobby of the Ritz or in the bar, awaiting Carroll's convenience. Following the instructions of the ambassador, Bainbridge did whatever he could to please his uncle. And while Bartley Crandell, the DCM, was less than pleased over what he considered an improper assignment, there was little he could do about it. The ambassador, a political appointee, vividly recalled that he was overruled by the Secretary of State when he sought to keep Bainbridge in Paris after Gribov's defection. Carroll, being a large contributor to the coffers of the party in power, had to be pleased. Thus, he decided Bainbridge's assignments.

This was the situation into which Fay Carroll was thrust with the arrival of her mother and stepfather at the Ritz. Waco Texas Carroll was outraged that she had no permanent place to stay in Paris; as the first business of his visit, he personally supervised her removal from the pleasant apartment occupied by the Learys in the Rue Soufflot to a bedroom attached to his suite at the Ritz. For Pat Leary and Amy, who sought to appease the Texan, there was only frustration.

"Thanks for taking care of my daughter," Carroll said in a loud voice as he took her out the door at the Rue Soufflot, "but I don't want her to be a bother to anybody."

"She wasn't a bother," Amy Leary replied in her most charming manner. "We loved having her and we wish you'd let her stay."

"You're very kind, Ma'am. Come see us at the Ritz, y'hear?"

As a special mark of his approval of Amy Leary, the Texan momentarily removed his Stetson hat. Then, slamming it down hard over his head, he clutched Fay's elbow with one ham-size hand. "Now you come along, Missy. There'll be no more nonsense, y'hear?"

That was the last Holden saw of Fay for some time; nor, for that matter, was he able to establish communication with her, much as he tried. She was as surely Carroll's prisoner at the luxurious Ritz as Olga was caught in the custody of the KGB at St. Denis.

Holden learned within the hour of Fay's enforced removal from the Rue Soufflot to the Ritz. Amy Leary telephoned the news just before he left his untidy little flat in the Rue Bonaparte for Henri's late that afternoon. "But don't try to do anything foolish," she cautioned. "This fellow Carroll is big and mean, and he won't hesitate to use force."

Amy might have spared herself the show of concern. Holden's philosophy was to accept what he could not change and he considered useless demonstrations a waste of time. If he made a nuisance of himself at the Ritz, he knew that he would be ejected at Carroll's orders; worse still, Fay would be punished and perhaps even roughed up.

It particularly worried Holden that he didn't know if Fay had gone through with the plan she had formulated so hastily to pretend to fall in with Carroll's wishes and accept Bainbridge. Or was she too frightened to attempt it? And even if she did, it was still possible that events would overtake her, and nobody would be able to show evidence of Carroll's wrongdoing. In that case, both she and her mother could remain under his influence indefinitely. Reluctantly, he faced the fact that the odds were not in Fay's favor.

Except for his nightly routine at Henri's, Holden was inactive for days on end. The regulars at the piano bar would ask about Fay to show their sympathy for her, but as they realized that Holden was cut off from her as surely as they were, they turned their attention to other matters.

Holden eventually psyched himself into action. At first, he would break into his evening's routine at the piano by playing Fay's favorite songs. He would try to remember how she looked as she sang their love song, or the François Villon love poem, or the jaunty tune he had fitted to "Wake Me Up in Paris." That kind of thing didn't last very long, however. The regulars would give him peculiar looks, then turn away and concentrate on their drinking.

Once he heard Marcel Valleau observe laughingly to his colleagues, after listening to a *pianissimo* version of the love song, "Our American Cyrano is a poet also but—how do Americans say it?—he has no fire in his belly."

It hurt.

He excused his dilatory attitude toward Fay by remarking to Henri, "There's something we should do for Fay, but I don't know what." And Henri, in his deprecating way, would reply sadly, "There is also something we should do for Olga, but I don't know what."

Once, Henri tried to comfort him when they were discussing Fay's captivity. "You are not one of her family," the *patron* said. "And these are not the Middle Ages. You cannot climb up the walls of the Ritz with a sword in your teeth and do battle with Fay's stepfather."

Then the *patron* would pat him on the shoulder and gently advise him, "We can only do what we know, my friend. Anatole France's juggler honored Our Holy Lady by juggling before her altar. You must do what you can at the piano." In other words, Holden thought, "Keep out of trouble. Do not interfere."

Yet, inactivity palled on him. He began to lose sleep. His appetite almost vanished. Instead of staying in his little flat on the Rue Bonaparte, he took long, aimless walks along the crowded boulevards of Montparnasse and across the bridges of the Seine to less familiar places along the right bank of the river.

On one such lonely expedition, early in the afternoon of a fine day in late spring, he paused on the Ile de la Cité and on sheer impulse had the concierge announce him at Dr. Beranger's apartment. The psychiatrist was home and readily admitted him. As Holden entered, he saw that suitcases, packing cases and even trunks stood open all about the place and were in the process of being filled.

"Sorry to interrupt, Dr. Beranger." Holden was apologetic at once. "I didn't know you were moving."

The psychiatrist motioned to him to sit on the piano bench. "That's all right. Make yourself as comfortable as you can. I'm glad to see you, especially since I'll be leaving Paris soon."

"Where to this time?"

"Back to Topeka, but now I'm going to stay for two years, maybe more," Dr. Beranger replied. "It will be too expensive to maintain this apartment for so long, so the things I can't take with me are going into storage."

Was it a signal? Holden wasn't sure. So he asked, and tried to keep his voice from shaking, "Are you giving up on Fay?"

"Fay, I'm afraid, is giving up on me. That is," he quickly amended, "she's being forced to give up on me."

"Have you tried to see her?"

"Oh, yes. Mrs. Carroll telephoned only yesterday, telling me that Fay was in bad shape and asking me to come to the Ritz. But when I did," and he spread his hands in a gesture of futility, "Fay's stepfather was there to tell me that my services were not needed."

"Then you've not seen Fay?"

"Regrettably, no."

Holden hesitated. "Do you think I should try?"

"I wish you luck," the psychiatrist said. "But don't ask me to go with you." He perched on the side of a packing case that had been nailed shut. "If there was anything I could do for Fay, I give you my word that I would stay here. I like her very much and I think she's being forced into an impossible position. But what is there for me to do?" He shook his head.

Holden ran his hands through his mass of taffy-colored hair and tried not to appear distraught. "When you say Fay's being forced into an impossible position, what do you mean?"

"Remarriage to Spencer Bainbridge."

"Do you know that for a fact?"

"Well, I can't give you the time and place, but Fay's mother told me that's why her stepfather's holding her at the Ritz. More often than not, she says he brings Fay and Bainbridge together at the Ritz and tells them both what he wants."

Holden protested. "Fay's no child. She's twenty-five years old and she can do as she pleases legally. In not too many years, she's going to be independently wealthy."

The psychiatrist nodded. "All very true. But Fay is very close to her mother, knows her mother is repeatedly threatened with commitment to a mental institution for life. Fay herself already has been under a strain and I think it's asking too much to expect her to resist her stepfather much longer."

"Isn't it possible," Holden suggested, "that she could merely be playing along with her stepfather to give him the feeling that she'll do what he wants, but at the end she'll refuse?"

Dr. Beranger shrugged. "A very pretty notion, but not very practical. If Carroll sets a date for her wedding to Bainbridge, Fay will have to say yes or no. And if it's no, then I'm convinced that Carroll will make good his threats against both her mother and her. What does he have to lose?"

"But if somebody can stop him?" Holden suggested.

"With what, a gun?" The psychiatrist glanced up sharply. "Is that your idea, to shoot the man?"

It hadn't occurred to Holden before; but now, when every other way of helping Fay was being closed to him, he hesitated.

Dr. Beranger snapped. "Forget it, Holden. That's the one thing you *cannot* do."

"But here's someone who's being held captive against her will," Holden objected. "Can't *something* be done about it?"

"Not illegally," Dr. Beranger responded coldly. "I can't advise that."

Holden grasped at the slenderest possiblity of all. "When word got around about the Russians holding Olga Varenka, there were diplomatic inquiries from both the French and American governments. Isn't this case even worse?"

"No government is holding Fay," the psychiatrist replied. "It's her family. And with her stepfather's money and political influence, I doubt if any inquiry by the embassy would amount to much—if that's what you're driving at."

Holden stood. "Guess I'd better get moving."

"What are you going to do?" Although Dr. Beranger was old and much smaller than Holden, he blocked the door.

"Oh, I'm not going to shoot anybody, doctor," Holden said reassuringly, "but I think I'd better have a talk with somebody at the American embassy."

Dr. Beranger stood aside. "I wish you luck."

Bartley Crandell, the DCM, received Holden at the American embassy as soon as he was announced. "I think I know why you've come by," he said, indicating a chair on the opposite side of his desk to his unexpected visitor.

"It's about Fay Carroll," Holden said, slumping into the chair.

Crandell nodded. "I expected it."

"Do you know that she's a virtual prisoner at the Ritz, that her stepfather won't even let her go out for a breath of air?" Holden demanded sharply.

Crandell's face became a diplomatic blank. "Our Mr. Wisner called on Mr. Carroll yesterday at the Ritz to convey the ambassador's respects, said he saw Fay and that she looked well. She didn't say anything to him about being held against her will."

"Of course not, she couldn't," Holden exploded. "Not with

her stepfather right there listening to every word she was saying."

Crandell held up one hand in a calming gesture. "Let's not get excited, Mr. Holden. All I'm trying to tell you is that this embassy can't act for or against any American citizen on mere supposition. Do you have proof that Fay Carroll cannot leave the Ritz whenever she pleases?"

The questions jarred Holden. "Well, *I* can't see her," he said tensely.

Crandell relaxed and his voice became softer.

"Have you tried?"

"No."

"Have you talked with Fay by telephone recently?"

Now Holden was abashed and looked it. "No."

Crandell leaned back in his chair and gazed out the window for a few moments in silent reflection. Without changing his position, he observed, "You needn't think I'm cold or unresponsive, Holden. Mrs. Crandell and I are old friends of Fay's, and we have been concerned about her for some time. But"— and here he swung back and hunched over the desk, looking directly at the younger man—"you must remember that I am in an official position and have rules and regulations by which I must abide. I can't proceed on mere supposition."

"Then what do you suggest?" Holden felt himself redden with suppressed anger over the futility of an appeal to the American government in these circumstances.

"Go see Fay," Crandell advised in a low voice. "Tell her of your concern. Tell her that she has friends at the embassy who are worried about her, too. And let her know"—here he stopped and chose his words carefully—"that certain inquiries are under way by the Securities and Exchange Commission." He halted abruptly, as if he felt that he already had said too much.

Holden glanced up, alert at once. "What does that mean?"

"It may mean anything or nothing, I can't say," Crandell responded. He arose, rounded the desk and held out his hand. "Thank you so much for coming to see me."

Holden shook it wonderingly. "I didn't do anything."

"That's just it," was the quiet response. "I would suppose that you were under great provocation, but so far it seems to me that you've handled everything very well." As Holden arose to go, the DCM added, "Oh, and by the way, keep in touch with Wisner, will you?"

When Holden glanced back in puzzlement, he saw that Crandell already was back at his desk, fiercely intent on an official-looking document he had selected from the pile before him on his desk. But through the maze of officialdom, the DCM had permitted a glimmer of light to filter through the darkness that enshrouded Fay Carroll's future. And for that, Holden was profoundly grateful.

By good fortune, Holden arrived at the Ritz that afternoon during cocktail time when Waco Texas Carroll was at the bar with Spencer Bainbridge. Fay and her mother were alone in their suite. It occurred to Holden to go there directly, rather than to invite an immediate rebuff by announcing himself over the house phone.

When he pressed the buzzer and Fay herself opened the door, therefore, he was at first surprised, then overjoyed. He pushed past her into the room, embraced her and kissed her. It took him a little while to realize that she was unresponsive. But then, as he looked over her shoulder, saw why. Someone had shut the door behind them and was saying in an agitated voice, "Fay, be careful. Your stepfather will be back at any moment."

For Holden, it smothered all the joy of seeing her again. He released her and stood aside. Facing him was a small, frightened woman in black, her gray hair neatly coiled in a bun at the back of her head.

He heard Fay saying, "This is Arch Holden, Mother."

Holden murmured polite acknowledgement, but couldn't help being chilled by the older woman's attitude.

She noticed how reserved he was. "Forgive us, Mr. Holden. As you can see, we're under some strain."

He didn't say anything, but reached out with one hand as if to touch Fay, who held herself aloof from him.

Mrs. Carroll, her dark eyes shifting in distress from Holden to her daughter, stood beside them, her thin hands squeezed together. She floundered, trying to be polite to the unexpected guest. "Fay has told me so much about you, Mr. Holden. . . . You've been so good for each other." She hesitated, then burst out, "Oh, but I wish we'd been able to meet at a better time. Everything is so very, very difficult for us now." She broke off, overcome by emotion.

"Mother's not been well, Arch," Fay said.

The older woman went on, "I'm so afraid—"

"She doesn't want my stepfather to find us together here," Fay said. "He'll be very angry."

Holden froze. "What difference does that make?"

"You don't know what he can do when he's angry." Fay put a protective arm about her mother. "Please don't worry about Arch, Mother."

Mrs. Carroll said, "I don't like to tell you this, Mr. Holden, but you'd better go." And she hid her head against her daughter's shoulder.

Now Holden was stunned. "But I want to talk to Fay."

"Some other time," the older woman replied, her voice muffled. "Mr. Carroll will be returning any minute."

Somehow, Holden found the courage to say, "I want to talk to him, too."

Fay was despairing. "It isn't going to do any good, Arch. Can't you understand?"

"No, I don't."

Fay lowered her voice, let her arm slip about her mother's waist and led her toward an inner room. "It's better that I talk to Arch alone, Mother." The older woman was still protesting Holden's presence in a broken voice when an inner door clicked shut behind them.

Soon afterward, Fay returned, unsmiling. Her face was set, as if she were confronting someone not particularly agreeable to her, and certainly not a cherished friend and lover. She drew him aside to a small settee and sat beside him as if they had been strangers. "Everything's changed, Arch," she began.

"Not unless you want it to be." He reached out to take her hand, but she drew back. "Why, what's the trouble?"

"I can't go into it, there's not time."

"But you love me, I know you love me." This was the one thing he was sure of, the appeal she had to heed.

She bent her head and didn't reply at once. "I don't want to think about it. It's no use."

He lowered his voice. "What about something you told me you might do when we were at the Rue Bonaparte?"

She bit her lip. "I tried it once, but I just couldn't go through with it. My stepfather would have seen through it right away." She pressed her hands together until the knuckles showed white. "I'm just not a very good liar."

He tried another tack, trying to put heart into her. "I've just come from the American embassy, saw the DCM."

She showed mild interest. "How's Bart?"

"Fine."

"We were always good friends. Give him my best." She was moving away, as if she wanted to break up their all-too-brief meeting.

In desperation, he put up one hand and motioned to her to approach him. When she did, he whispered, "Crandell says there's an inquiry under way at the Securities and Exchange Commission."

She seemed unmoved. "I know about it. So does my stepfather."

"What does it mean?"

"I'm not sure. One of mother's lawyers flew here from New York and tried to see us yesterday, but my stepfather wouldn't admit him."

Holden clenched his fists in a sudden surge of hope. "Then it *does* mean something! An illegal stock deal, maybe?"

She touched her forehead wearily with the back of one hand. "I just don't know, Arch. But whatever it is, my stepfather will bear it. His influence is unbelievable."

Fay's mother could be heard calling from an inner room, "Has Mr. Holden gone yet?"

Fay responded quickly. "He's just leaving."

But Holden remained firmly seated. "You can't do this, Fay."

"Sorry."

"Come on, let's get out of here!" He grasped her by both hands. "We'll go to my place, to the Rue Bonaparte."

"Forgive me." Clearly it hurt her to do it, but she disengaged herself.

Just then, the outer door to the suite opened, men's voices were heard and then the door slammed shut. Waco Texas Carroll tramped into the room in his high-heeled boots, his Stetson shoved on the back of his head. Behind him came Spencer Bainbridge, like a darkened shadow of the big Texan.

Carroll planted himself in the center of the room and whirled on Fay. She was balanced on the edge of the settee, chin up, with lines of weariness etched on her face. "Aren't you going to introduce me to your guest?" Carroll demanded.

"It's my friend, Arch Holden," was the quiet reply. And to Holden, "My stepfather, Mr. Carroll."

The two men stared at each other without speaking. Bainbridge broke the silence. "That's the fella I've been telling you about, Waco, the piano player Fay's been seeing."

"That right, Fay?" Carroll glowered at her.

"I told you that Mr. Holden and I are friends," she repeated without raising her voice.

"And you invited him here?"

She didn't answer directly. "I'm glad he's here."

Carroll turned to Holden. "I'd rather you didn't call on my daughter."

Somehow, Holden found his voice and tried to make it sound natural. But his words came out in a panicky rush. "Your daughter will tell me if she doesn't want to see me."

"Perhaps so, but right now you'd better leave."

Holden protested, "You can't keep Fay a prisoner."

"I'm her father," Carroll snapped. "I'll do whatever I think is necessary for her best interests."

Fay pleaded, "Please, Arch, don't push him. It'll do no good."

Noting Fay's very real distress, Holden paused irresolutely. There was, he realized, no way in which he could contest Carroll's dominance at that moment, but he hated the prospect of leaving the suite. At that point, Bainbridge suddenly walked past him and opened the door in silent invitation.

Carroll said, "Now, get out."

But Holden didn't want to go without giving Carroll and Bainbridge some cause for hesitation, however slight. Sheer force was out of the question. Carroll, despite his age, was so big and strong that he could have pushed his unwelcome visitor out the door without much effort. Nor would it have done any good to protest to the hotel or call the police—other possibilities that flashed through Holden's mind. But as he faced his tormentor, he thought of a small bit of comfort for Fay and acted at once.

"A lot of people are thinking of you, honey," he said, going to her as if to say good-bye. "You're not alone and you mustn't think you're alone."

"Thanks, Arch." She didn't dare look at him. "Tell the Learys I wish them all the best, and give Henri and Marie my love."

"And there are friends at the embassy . . ."

Here, Bainbridge broke into a laugh.

Taking no notice, Holden went on, "Bartley Crandell and his wife haven't forgotten you, and send their regards." Over his shoulder, he said to Bainbridge, "The DCM hasn't forgotten you, either, and you'd better take notice of it." The warning was just a chance shot, something to toss at his grinning rival. But the effect on Bainbridge was remarkable.

"Crandell doesn't know what the hell he's talking about," Bainbridge replied shrilly. "Whatever I do is my own personal business and he has no right to interfere."

Carroll was instantly alert. He growled at his nephew, "What's all this?"

Bainbridge was sullen. "There's a guy at the embassy who's getting in my way. Says I'm spending too much time with nonessential informants. Actually"—and here he seemed to be appealing to Carroll for support—"they're all representatives of some of the Arab oil people who are important to us." He said "us" with a significant look at his uncle, and there was no doubt that he was referring to Carroll and himself, not the embassy or the United States.

"Who's this guy?" Carroll was in an irascible mood. "Just tell me, and I'll fix his wagon."

"It's that Crandell, the DCM."

"Yeah." Carroll stopped short for a few moments, then mused, "The guy who called me the other day about that goddam SEC investigation."

Holden couldn't help risking a small jibe at his enemy's expense. "So they're catching up with you, huh?"

Carroll made a furious motion with one big arm. "Get outta here!"

216

Ignoring Carroll's irritation, Holden went to Fay and let his lips brush against her cheek. "Don't let them scare you, honey," he said, assuming an air of confidence that he didn't really feel. "Because actually," he went on, looking boldly at Carroll and Bainbridge, "these guys are scared themselves."

Both men glared at him.

Outside, Holden signaled for a cab, and a familiar rickety vehicle drew up, driven by Saffron's friend, the elderly Andrei Pedenko. He gave his usual weary military salute. *"Au Cafe Henri?"* he asked courteously but unnecessarily. By this time he recognized Holden because of his journeys to and from the Ritz. Holden waved one hand and nodded in dejection. All of a sudden, he felt as if he'd been beaten.

It had seemed even less possible that afternoon that Olga Varenka could be delivered safely from the Russians who guarded her so closely at the estate in St. Denis. The Kirov Ballet had concluded its French engagement the previous evening, and the vanguard of the corps already had taken off from Charles de Gaulle Airport early that morning in an Aeroflot plane bound for Leningrad. The main contingent was to follow.

But, early in the afternoon, without advance notice, a motor cavalcade formed outside the estate in St. Denis. In the van were a dozen French police on motorcycles. Curious passersby, had they been alert, would have seen a slender, pale-faced woman in a voluminous fur coat being hustled from the house into a black Citröen sedan bearing diplomatic license plates. She was placed in the backseat, one guard beside her and another in front next to the driver.

Directly behind that sedan was another, a Mercedes, in which there were four other guards and a driver. But that wasn't all, for, as the procession set out with warning blasts from police motorcycle sirens, a large two-toned gray Rolls-Royce flying French and Russian flags on its front fenders brought up the rear. Beside a stiffly uniformed driver sat a beribboned elderly man in the uniform of a Soviet army officer. And in the backseat, the only passenger was an impressive-looking diplomatic type swathed in a black cape with a black homburg set squarely in the middle of his large head.

Traffic gave way readily for that official-looking motorcade as it swung into the well-traveled highway around the perimeter of Paris. But instead of turning off at Charles de Gaulle Airport, it continued on around the perimeter road, and even picked up a rear guard of French motorcycle police who followed the three official-looking vehicles. It wasn't long, however, before the destination of the motorcade became clear, for it turned toward Le Bourget, the historic field where Charles A. Lindbergh had landed in 1927 on the first solo flight from the United States across the Atlantic.

Le Bourget, once the main air terminal for Parisian flights, now was little used. And yet, that afternoon it fairly teemed with French police, French customs people and French and Russian diplomatic representatives. Far off, at the western end of an east-west runway, a large Soviet airliner could be seen, with French airport personnel making their final checks on fuel and loading provisions aboard for takeoff. Russian guards stood beside the steps leading to the cabin, brandishing Kalashnikov automatic rifles.

It was testimony to the importance of the lone passenger who was being escorted to Le Bourget with such an overwhelming display of armed might.

As the motorcade raced past the entrance to Le Bourget, the field's guards waved on the three cars sandwiched between the motorcycle police and drew a grave salute from the elderly man in the beribboned Soviet army officer's uniform, riding in the Rolls-Royce.

Before the terminal building, there was a dramatic scene. All the guards in the first two cars tumbled out and formed double lines. Then, after a pause of a minute or more, the tall, thin woman swathed in the fur coat stepped from the Citröen sedan and slowly walked between the lines of her guards into the terminal building. There, waiting Russians from Aeroflot gathered about her, evidently to speed her through the formalities of departure from France. Others unloaded her baggage from the first two cars and hurried it into the terminal building.

The third and last car, the Rolls-Royce with its uniformed driver and official-looking military and diplomatic representatives, meanwhile swung around the outside of the terminal building, its French and Russian flags whipping in a stiff breeze, and drew up beside the exit. Evidently, it was to pick up the lone passenger and ride her in state along the tarmac to the Aeroflot liner at the edge of the runway. As a token of respect, the uniformed officer stood beside the open rear door of the Rolls-Royce to see the woman safely inside.

It wasn't long before the formalities of departure were completed. The passenger, with her Aeroflot escort, emerged from the terminal building; seeing the Rolls-Royce waiting with a military figure beside the open rear door, the escorting group quickly hustled her to the car and put her inside. The uniformed officer resumed the front seat with another salute, the diplomat in the rear waved a negligent hand forward toward the Aeroflot liner and the car slowly started along the tarmac.

But all at once, the Rolls-Royce swerved back around the side of the terminal building, gathered speed and raced out the gates of Le Bourget before either the French motorcycle police—lounging beside their vehicles—or the massed Russian guards were quite aware of what was happening. All that followed as the Rolls-Royce spurted out of sight was that a few people shouted warnings; an alert guard at the Aeroflot liner shot off a few rounds from his Kalashnikov gun but hit nothing; and people inside the terminal building began milling about to try to decide what to do.

It wasn't long, however, before the police radio crackled with warnings that Olga Varenka had been kidnapped from Le Bourget, and an all-points alarm was issued for the fugitive Rolls-Royce. To this, Tass, the Soviet news service, contributed an announcement that the brigands of the CIA, in a criminal enterprise, had abducted Olga Varenka as she was about to leave for Leningrad and were bent on smuggling her into America.

As Holden approached Henri's at the early dinner hour that day after leaving the Ritz, he saw the *patron* standing beside the giant Tunisian doorman, Shukri. The sun was setting behind the great twin towers of Notre Dame, tinting the sluggish Seine with its radiance. Along the sidewalks beside the river, booksellers were closing up at the end of a fine spring day. And in the Place St. Michel, pedestrians dodged through the traffic with skill and daring.

Everything seemed the same. Nothing appeared to have changed. But to Holden, after his frustrating time with Fay, the *patron's* presence outside his establishment seemed to be a foretaste of something different.

As he approached, Henri waved him to one side. "Quickly, my friend! Go across the Pont St. Michel and the Pont au Change." Here he referred to the two bridges spanning the Seine as it divides past the Ile de la Cite. "You will find a car waiting for you close by at the Place du Chatelet. Stephanie and Gareth Leary are there."

Holden wavered in surprise. "What's up, boss?"

"You will find out. But" —the *patron* added a precaution— "do not show emotion of any kind, if you please. This is a dangerous and difficult business." He lowered his voice almost to a whisper. "You are to let Stephanie and Gareth transfer someone from their car to your own."

"Who is it?"

Henri gestured in impatience. *"Attendez!"* Although he strove to remain calm, he could not help for a moment breaking into excitable French and waving his hands as he did so. "You are to permit Stephanie and Gareth to drive you to the Pastore hunting lodge in the Forest of Fontainebleau."

Holden stood bewildered. "You want me to go right now?"

Henri gave him a little shove. "At once! Do not ask questions!"

He was red-faced. Perspiration stood out on his forehead in tiny beads as he grasped his pianist by the arm and marched him into the Place St. Michel, then pointed to a taxi. "Tell the driver, Place du Chatelet!"

Still wondering at what had so excited the usually placid *patron,* Holden did as he was told and was transported across the Ile de la Cite in an ancient cab to the Place du Chatelet, where Stephanie Rivet, camera held at the ready, was waiting on a corner.

The elderly driver rolled his eyes in romantic ecstasy as he was paid. Holden added a generous tip and waved the cab onward; then, as naturally as possible, he joined Stephanie.

She ceased her pretense at once and grasped his arm, fairly shoving him along until she had deposited him in the backseat of her car; then she climbed in beside Gareth, who was driving.

All she knew, she explained to Holden—while Gareth made the best time he could in Parisian traffic—was that the *patron* had told her to pick up Holden, get plenty of film for her camera and have Gareth drive them to Pastore's lodge.

"And what do they expect us to do at the lodge?" Holden asked, thoroughly mystified.

Gareth, who by now had headed the car toward the highway to Fontainebleau, offered the additional information: "Henri started Pastore, Valleau and Eilers toward the lodge an hour ago in his own car. They'd gotten themselves up as hunters, and they had guns and he told them to expect you."

Holden snapped his fingers, having suddenly acquired a theory to explain these moves. "Gribov's at the lodge and he's in trouble, that's what's up. I'll bet anything."

Stephanie glanced around at him and shook her head. "Yes, M'sieu' Gribov is in trouble—I heard Henri say the police were questioning him—but he is not in Fontainebleau. He is at the Crillon."

"If it's not Gribov, then who is at the lodge?" Holden asked.

Neither Stephanie nor Gareth could give him an adequate answer. "Patience. Soon we will know," Stephanie counseled, and that was the best any of them could offer.

Holden devoted himself to watching the street signs that flashed past, and admired the easy way Gareth nosed the car through heavy traffic toward the Fontainebleau road. By the time they arrived in the town of Barbizon and swerved to the less-traveled highway through the Forest of Fontainebleau to Pastore's lodge, it was dark. There was no moon. The car's headlights sent two narrow beams slashing through the gloom of the forest, but Gareth could not speed. There were too many twists and turns in the road.

Soon they came to the clearing in which the lodge stood. They could see its dim lights in the distance as the car skidded to a halt before a barrier of fallen trees that had been placed across the road. Gareth jumped out. "Hey, what's going on here?" he called.

In reply, shadowy figures with guns emerged from the woods before them, giving orders in French for the new arrivals to stand before the car with their hands up. Holden emulated the others until there was mutual recognition between him and

Pastore, Valleau and Eilers in their hunters' costumes. Valleau and Stephanie chattered together in French as the photographer examined her camera before the car's headlights to make sure of her film and checked her purse to be certain that she had an extra roll for emergencies.

Finally, when Stephanie returned to Holden and Gareth, who had been waiting for her, she said, "Come, they want us inside the lodge."

"Who's there?" Holden asked.

Although this was scarcely a place for eavesdroppers, Stephanie self-consciously lowered her voice in the manner of a conspirator. "Marcel has told me that they are guarding Olga Varenka."

"Varenka!" Holden couldn't help being startled. "How did she get away from the Russians?"

"Quiet!" Stephanie put a finger to his lips and choked back a little laugh. "Marcel tell me that Varenka is not happy, that she makes trouble. We are not to upset her."

Gareth muttered, as if to himself, "These Russkys beat hell out of me. You never know what they want."

Stephanie handled him with more assurance. She took him by the hand and led him around the barrier of fallen logs in the road after switching off the car's headlights. To Holden she said, "Come to the lodge. I must photograph Varenka."

They saw an ancient French taxi outside. Inside, when they reached the lodge, they found Pat and Amy Leary talking with the reporter, Saffron, in the outer of three rooms. The Learys were sitting on a humpbacked couch. Saffron was in a wicker chair opposite them. Standing at one side and seeming quite out of place was a poorly dressed elderly man who held a battered chauffeur's cap in one hand.

"Where've you been?" Saffron called out as they entered. "We've waited for you more'n two hours."

The two younger people deferred to Holden. "We got here as fast as we could," he said, trying to seem self-assured. He couldn't resist asking, "Where's Varenka?"

The reporter nodded toward an inner room. "In there, raising hell." He held up one hand for silence so that they could hear the angry murmur of Russian spoken rapidly and excitedly.

"What does she want?" Stephanie asked.

"Don't know what the hell she wants," Saffron responded cheerfully. "But ain't it just like a dame? You break your ass for her and still you can't satisfy her. Ah, well" —and he grinned philosophically— "maybe she was tougher on the Russians."

The elderly man said something in French, which Saffron promptly translated. "Andrei says she's not mad at us, she's mad at Gribov. She wants him here right now." There was more French conversation between the two men, after which Saffron added, "Andrei says she's got a lot of questions for Gribov. Is he on his way, does anybody know?"

Holden, turning to Stephanie with a look of inquiry, received a nod and answered, "Stephanie heard that Gribov is being questioned by the French police at the Crillon."

Saffron guffawed. "If you guys had waited for Gribov to put the snatch on her, you'd have had zilch." He clapped his hands and addressed Stephanie. "Look, babe, part of the deal I made with Henri to get Varenka away from the Russians was for you to take pictures of her for the *Paris Press*, tomorrow's edition, so get the hell in there and start moving, willya? We don't have a lot of time."

As Stephanie moved into the bedroom, the angry flow of Russian ceased. Then, the photographer could be heard explaining in very basic French that she needed some pictures. The storm of Russian broke again, to be succeeded by a flow of soothing French, and at length there was silence. Then the click of the shutter could be heard.

Holden turned to the Learys with a trace of impatience. "Would you mind telling us how Varenka got here and what we're supposed to do now?"

Amy held out one hand toward Saffron. "There's the man who knows."

Saffron in turn pointed to the poorly dressed elderly man whom he introduced as Andrei Pedenko, an émigré from the Ukraine who had been a cab driver for almost forty years. At Pedenko's suggestion, a Rolls-Royce limousine had been rented by friends using assumed names, and a fellow émigré had been fitted out with a fancy chauffeur's uniform to drive it. Pedenko himself had obtained a Russian military uniform.

Saffron, in a homburg and striped pants, had posed as a

diplomat. The Rolls-Royce, with French and Russian flags flying from the fenders, had no difficulty in following the official procession that took Varenka to the airport. Nobody questioned the authenticity of such official-looking personages in such an official-looking car.

Nor had there been much trouble in determining when Varenka would be taken from the St. Denis estate once Saffron had located her hiding place. Employees on the estate gossiped interminably about their Russian charge, especially at their favorite drinking place in the neighborhood. So Saffron, who made it his business to hang out there as a bar fly, knew the approximate departure time two days in advance and was able to make his plans accordingly.

"But actually," he explained, "everything depended on making us look very official and Russian; and, without Pedenko, we couldn't have worked it. When they saw the ribbons and medals and Andrei's way of saluting, they fell for the ruse."

"You took a long chance, Saffron," Pat Leary said. "What if you'd been caught?"

"We weren't," Saffron replied easily. "I was betting that the Rolls-Royce and Colonel Pedenko" —here he nodded to the cabdriver— "would look so authentic that the Russkys would be afraid to stop us. And they were." He laughed for sheer relief. "For a while, we even fooled Olga. But when we changed from the Rolls to Pedenko's taxi—about a mile from Le Bourget—and Pedenko and I had to dump our uniforms, she caught on."

"And she was satisfied?" Leary asked.

Saffron cocked his head at a doubtful slant. "She was suspicious; kept asking Pedenko if the Rolls and the chauffeur were from the American embassy. What could we say? The chauffeur, Pedenko's friend, had instructions to abandon the car, get out of his uniform and go home, and I guess that's what he did. But we couldn't tell Olga that. Maybe," and he nodded to the bedroom with a wink, "she still thinks we're from the CIA."

"And Henri was in on this and wouldn't tell us," Amy Leary murmured.

Saffron brushed her objection aside. "Actually, Henri didn't know much and had to take me on faith. But he came through.

224

Last week, when I asked him for the key to Pastore's lodge, he got it from Gribov. And when I phoned this afternoon after we reached the lodge and asked for Stephanie and her camera, he didn't even ask a question."

"Why Stephanie?" Amy Leary pressed him.

Saffron arose and stretched. "My dear, if this story holds and they don't find us for a few hours, the *Paris Press* has a big, beautiful exclusive story with Stephanie's pictures of Olga on page one." He gestured to indicate a banner headline and quoted, "'Saved from the Russians.'"

But just then, outraged cries burst from the bedroom.

Stephanie came rushing out, her camera held in her right hand like a football, with Olga Varenka in vengeful pursuit. The Russian woman, still in her voluminous fur coat, was throwing various articles of feminine apparel at the photographer—nightgowns, panties, hose, even a few dresses and a handbag.

Pedenko, the only one in the room who understood Russian, turned to Saffron in agitation. "We must stop her. She wants to run away."

Saffron and Holden reacted at once, catching a furious Olga on either side. Stephanie paused near the door, still protecting her camera. Over his shoulder, Saffron asked, "What's the trouble, Andrei?"

"These clothes, they make Olga very angry. She say this lady," indicating Stephanie, "left them here because she was living here with Gribov."

"Tell her it's a lie," Saffron ordered. But even after Pedenko tried to be reassuring, the dancer still struggled against Saffron and Holden. She continued to shout at everybody in Russian.

Amy Leary picked up some of the clothes, examined them and then smiled. "Of course they're not Stephanie's," she said. "Stephanie's far too thin to fit into those dresses and nightgown. And besides, we're perfectly certain she was never here with Gribov."

Although Stephanie murmured her thanks in French for Amy's intervention, the little Englishwoman was busy now with the contents of the handbag with a convenient shoulder strap. As Amy dumped the contents on the table, the bag seemed to have held everything a woman needed, from perfume and a supply of ballpoint pens to a regulation stenographer's notebook.

While Pedenko continued to explore Varenka's feelings in staccato bursts of Russian, Amy leafed through the notebook with every appearance of idle curiosity. Her husband asked her, "What have you found, dear?"

"It looks like Catherine Vaillant's notebook, mainly what appears to be a translation in French and English of what various people were saying at the American embassy..." She continued her explorations as her voice faded away.

"Vaillant, huh?" Saffron said. "Guess we can figure out now who was in this place with Gribov."

Amy looked up briefly from the notebook and nodded. "Makes sense. These clothes would fit Vaillant, and she's just mean enough to keep them lying around in case Gribov decided to bring somebody else here in her absence." She resumed her examination of the notebook.

Varenka, who had held her peace while all this was going on, now pointed an accusing finger at Pedenko and appeared to be challenging him in Russian. There was a rapid exchange of Russian between the dancer and the elderly cabdriver. Saffron demanded of Pedenko, "What's her trouble now, Andrei?"

Pedenko was apologetic. "The lady say, 'This lady,' and he nodded toward Stephanie, 'was with Gribov,' and I tell her again, 'No, it was someone else.' She ask who, and I say it was woman with French name, but she is gone now. Now she want name.... She will accuse Gribov. What I tell her now?"

Amy interrupted with a little cry of excitement. "Why, here's some Russian in this notebook." She hurried to Pedenko and showed him what she had found. "It *is* Russian, isn't it?"

Pedenko glanced at it briefly. "Is Russian." Then, with a sudden show of interest, he snatched the notebook. "This lady, she talk on telephone with Russian, she makes notes..."

"Maybe she and Gribov spoke Russian together," Amy suggested, trying to be helpful.

"No, is not Gribov," Pedenko objected with a vigorous shake of his head. He examined the notebook closely and announced, "Is another name, could be Mikhailov..." He turned to Varenka, who had become intensely interested as she heard the name "Mikhailov," and separated herself with great dignity

226

from her captors. She and Pedenko spoke briefly in Russian; then the cabdriver announced, "This lady say Mikhailov is second secretary at embassy of Soviet Union in Paris—"

Varenka interrupted him with another brief blast of Russian, after which Pedenko resumed, "She say Mikhailov was chief at St. Denis, was in charge of guards, maybe KGB?" He looked questioningly at the dancer, apparently asking her to confirm this. She nodded vigorously. He concluded, "Yes, this lady say Mikhailov is chief, KGB, Paris."

"*Well!*" It was Leary's turn now to be astonished. "If Mikhailov had the telephone number of Catherine Vaillant and spoke with her, then she must be a Russian agent."

"Maybe even a double agent," his wife added. "I had always thought she worked for the CIA as well as the embassy. She was always so interested in what all of us who helped Gribov defect were planning to do next."

"Whatever she is," Leary added, glancing at his watch, "we've been here too long already, and we'd better move out. Because if Mikhailov knows what Vaillant is doing, then he also knows she was being kept here by Gribov. . . ."

There was an agonized wail from Varenka, who had been poring over the Russian notes in the notebook with Pedenko and exchanging animated remarks with the old cabdriver. The dancer slapped the back of her hand against the notebook as if it had offended her, and turned to Pedenko with a show of emotion. After he listened to her carefully, he turned to the assembled company and tried to keep his voice from trembling.

"This lady was spy for KGB, made fool of Gribov, took orders from Mikhailov, put down note" —here he slapped the notebook— "that she must leave Fontainebleau tonight."

Now Leary took charge. In a low voice, he said, "Ladies and gentlemen, we must leave at once. I've heard enough to convince me that the Russians know about Pastore's lodge. They might suspect that we've brought Varenka here, and they could even come back here tonight with Catherine Vaillant . . ." He paused. "Everybody clear out. And let's get the hunters out, too."

Holden, conscious of his own assignment as the American embassy's contact, broke in as the company quickly went about preparing for immediate departure: "Don't you think I'd better let the people at the American embassy in on this?"

Leary again checked his watch. "You'll get nobody there at this hour except the duty office, Holden, and he'll be worse than useless. No, whatever we've learned will have to keep until morning." To Pedenko, he said, "Please tell Miss Varenka that we are asking her to come with us to our apartment."

As Pedenko transmitted the request in Russian, Varenka nodded in agreement, then appeared to be asking the cabdriver a question. He translated, "She say she is sorry for Gribov making such a fool of himself, but she must tell him Catherine is KGB spy."

Leary didn't let that bother him. "All in good time, but now we must first make sure that the KGB doesn't surprise *us*. Please tell her that," After Pedenko translated, Varenka had no further comment but came to Amy Leary with the notebook and expressed her thanks to the Englishwoman in broken French. "It's all right, dear," Amy replied complacently, just as if the Russian understood what she was saying. "We all have to discipline our menfolk, don't we?" And she gave the dancer an understanding hug and a kiss.

Pat Leary now made the final disposition of his forces with the aplomb of a general. Holden and the regulars—Pastore, Eilers and Valleau—would post themselves in the wooded area about the hunting lodge and note the activities of the KGB. As Leary ordered everybody else into Stephanie's car and Pedenko's cab for a quick getaway, he explained, "Let's not give the KGB a chance to recapture Olga Varenka." Seemingly, she understood his concern, for she and Pedenko had a brief exchange in Russian, then nodded and smiled at each other.

Almost as an afterthought, Leary instructed his wife, "You'd better put Catherine Vaillant's clothes back where you found them and make sure that all her papers are put back in her shoulder bag. We can't let anybody suspect that we know she is a Soviet agent—and maybe a double agent at that."

"You think of everything, dear," Amy commented, but she quickly and efficiently followed his instructions.

Within a few minutes, Holden was alone with the three regulars, who insisted that he also must get into his hunter's costume and carry a gun for purposes of self-defense. "But we're not going to fight the KGB," he protested.

"Maybe KGB fights us," Pastore suggested.

Soon the lodge was dark and deserted. The four observers were posted in the woods some distance away, safely concealed by thick underbrush and darkness.

Leary had moved Olga Varenka and the bulk of his party none too soon. Within no more than thirty minutes, three carloads of Russians slammed to a halt in front of the tree-trunk barricade on the road to the lodge. Perhaps a dozen or more men carrying guns tramped through the underbrush to the cabin. There was a shouted exchange between the leader, who was tall and thin and muffled in a raincoat and a big hat with a flaring turned-down brim, and someone in the lead car. Because none of the hidden observers understood Russian, they could only guess that the leader was reporting the cabin was dark, deserted and locked up.

Two big men banged their shoulders against the stout cabin door, but it resisted their efforts. Beside Holden, Pastore was swearing under his breath in mingled French and Italian and fingering his gun. Alarmed, Holden gripped his arm, bent down and whispered in his ear, "Forget it, Pastore. They'll kill us."

"I kill them if they ruin my lodge," Pastore swore in a muffled voice.

"Forget it," Holden insisted, and motioned to the other two to grab Pastore and restrain him, which they did with efficient but silent force. However, further trouble was avoided when another figure left the lead car—a woman who walked with a graceful, swaying movement toward the cabin. While Holden couldn't see her, he was convinced that it must be Catherine Vaillant. When he heard her voice, responding to the lead Russian's questions, he knew without doubt that it was she.

Her role, evidently, had been that of a guide. Moreover, when she produced a key and opened the lodge door for the intruders, she was the first to go inside and turn on the lights. But the Russian party did not remain on the premises very long. Nor did they do anything to the lodge to excite the recumbent Pastore. By this time, Valleau and Eilers were sitting on him and gagging him with a handkerchief to make certain that he didn't do anything rash.

In a somber procession, the invaders left the lodge single file after rummaging through it without taking anything. The only one who departed with anything of substance was Catherine Vaillant. After she had turned off the lights and locked the door, Holden could tell that she had a bundle under her arm—very possibly, the clothes that she had left in the bedroom—and over one shoulder he recognized her familiar translator's leather bag. If the conspirators' luck held good, Catherine might not suspect that her role as a concealed Russian agent had been discovered.

Once the three Russian cars left the forest, the four observers emerged from their hiding place. Pastore, still upset because he had been forcibly restrained by his companions, would not leave until he had made a careful inspection of his lodge. When he rejoined them, he appeared more at ease. "All okay," he reported. "Everything in order, nothing stolen. But that Vaillant!" He shook his head. "She fool me!"

As he got into Pastore's car with his two companions, Holden could not help feeling that a kindly providence had spared him from involvement with Catherine Vaillant and directed him instead toward Fay Carroll.

It isn't often, in this electronic era, that a newspaper can spring an international sensation, particularly a rag like the *Paris Press*. But the removal of Olga Varenka from the homebound Kirov Ballet, which the *Press* somewhat smugly called a defection, was such a story.

Predictably, when the paper appeared next morning with Varenka's picture on page one under flaring headlines, the assembled French press deplored the enterprise of the English-language daily. It was, *Le Monde* maintained, a barefaced violation of journalistic ethics. And *Le Figaro*, which had to make over page one to get in the story, called it a kidnapping that should be prosecuted once the culprits could be found. *La Croix* vowed that Charles de Gaulle would never have approved, and the Communist *L'Humanite* denounced it as an insult to a great and friendly power.

The *Press* was defiant. To the government investigators who swarmed into its disorderly newsroom, its managers and staff offered no information. This affair, so the editorial rubric went, concerned itself with human rights. To invade a newspaper was, naturally, a violation of press freedom. And if it happened to add to circulation and interest in the paper because it was a good story, what was wrong with that?

Accordingly, Guy Saffron became a journalistic hero for a day—to some; to others, chiefly his colleagues on the French press, he was a villain who would do anything to get a story. And, of course, the opposition wondered exactly how he had managed to spirit so famous a personage out of the combined guard of the French police and the KGB.

Eventually, some details of Saffron's operation did leak out by way of the *Paris Press* newsroom. And some very old survivors of a bolder if not better time recalled that one Herbert Bayard Swope, a nosy American, had tricked the French police in 1919 by hiring a chauffeured limousine, dressing up in diplomatic costume and having himself driven through the closely guarded gates at Versailles to listen in on a secret conference of the Big Four of that day. But by the time Saffron's methods became known, it was far too late to do anything about it.

In the interim, Olga Varenka, although restless and embittered, remained with the Learys in their apartment in the Rue Soufflot. Both Pat and Amy Leary had decided, early on, that they would make no attempt to stop her if she decided to return to the Soviet Union. However, they did their best to keep her hiding place a secret until she had made up her mind what she wanted to do.

Having no means of communicating with their guest except in a few broken French phrases, the Learys could only guess at her state of mind. But, as matters turned out, Amy Leary's guess was eminently correct: "Olga is going to have it out with Gribov before she decides on anything." And, since Gribov was closely watched by the police, not to overlook operatives of various international agencies, he had little chance to shake off pursuit and venture into the Rue Soufflot.

It is an axiom of diplomacy that a secret known to more than two persons will in time become no secret at all. So it was remarkable, in a way, that Olga's presence in the Rue Soufflot did not attract attention. Out of loyalty to Stephanie, whom he wanted to protect, Gareth Leary did no talking about his family's famous guest. But Vivian, who was dispossessed from her bedroom for Olga's sake and had to be content with a living-room couch, had no such inhibitions. She took it with poor grace that her constant escort, Baron von Norden, had been asked for the time being to begin his dates with Vivian at Henri's rather than at the Rue Soufflot. Noting her sour attitude, the German didn't have to be a mind reader to guess that something rather strange was going on at home.

But as others either guessed or were informed of Olga Varenka's whereabouts, the secret of the Rue Soufflot became known in high places without any ensuing flap. The reasons for maintaining secrecy about Varenka's hiding place were evident enough. The French, already embarrassed because of her deliverance from an armed Franco-Russian escort, preferred to forget about the incident as long as possible. The Russians, knowing where their quarry was hiding, were content to keep watch over her and not raise another outcry. The British, West Germans and others in the diplomatic corps who became privy to the secret simply looked on in amusement. And the French newspapers, having unanimously denounced the *Paris Press* in the first place, would scarcely wish to revive the issue.

The only place where the Varenka story still was hot, as nearly as anybody could determine, was at the American embassy. However often the CIA had been blamed for high crimes and misdemeanors in which it had no part, it still rankled with the State Department that Americans remained Europe's favorite whipping boys. Routine denials by the CIA of complicity in the Varenka affair were taken as affirmations, and *Tass's* charges that Varenka was the victim of an American plot were widely believed.

Under these circumstances, Holden was asked to see his contact, Cary Wisner, at the American embassy next day. Having seen that Gribov had turned out to be the patsy, the fall guy, in the amateur conspiracy, Holden wasn't quite as guarded as he had been in his role as the go-between. As he rather expected, Wisner escorted him soon enough to McKelvey's office after hearing a brief, factual account of the events of the night before.

For once, McKelvey did not put on his phony show of heartiness. Instead, he assumed the role of the responsible CIA official he really was and closely questioned Holden about Catherine Vaillant's extracurricular activities outside the embassy and the manner in which she had insinuated herself into Gribov's life. Finally, the CIA official arose and looked out the window, deep in thought, then turned back to Holden. "There's no chance you could be mistaken about your identification of Vaillant last night?"

"I'm sure," Holden said. "And even if I'd made a mistake, I doubt if Pastore, Eilers and Valleau also could be wrong. They saw her, too, and recognized her. And who else known to the Russians would be their guide to Pastore's lodge and then have a key to open the door for them?"

McKelvey didn't say anything but was obviously disturbed. "Do you think she knows she's been found out?"

"I can't say. I haven't seen her," Holden replied. "But I do know that we did everything we could not to make her suspicious. We left her shoulder bag in the lodge and made it look as if nobody had been into it, even put back the translator's notebook and her ballpoint pens. I noticed she had the bag on her shoulder when she left with the Russians. And she took her clothes with her, too, so maybe she's moved out on Gribov."

McKelvey drummed on his desk with anxious fingers. "What do you think, Wisner? Has she been alerted and pulled off the job by the Russians?"

Wisner picked up the desk phone. "We'll soon find out." After he dialed an in-house number, he asked, "Translation section? . . . Cary Wisner here. Can you tell me if Catherine Vaillant has called in for an assignment today? . . . She has? Oh, then she will be at the UN conference. Thank you." As he replaced the phone, he reported without emotion, "Vaillant calls in for work every day as a contract translator, and today they assigned her to work with the American delegation at the UN conference. One of the regular translators is sick."

McKelvey resumed his seat at his desk. "Guess she can't do any harm at the UN. Anyway, it's the last day of the conference, so what the hell. The main idea is," and here he seemed to be talking to himself, "to keep everything going along normally and don't let her get the wind up." He glanced at Holden. "Anything else? I'll have to leave you guys and see the station chief in a couple minutes."

Holden was going to say something, then thought better of it. McKelvey, noticing his hesitation, asked irritably, "Let's not waffle about this, Holden. If you've got something on your mind, let's have it."

"I'm just curious." Holden felt apologetic. With McKelvey staring at him, the pianist went on haltingly, "You see, this Vaillant was Charley Fourier's girl—the pianist at Henri's who's in the States. And I took Charley's place..."

"Yes?" McKelvey's face was tinged with red as he tried to suppress his impatience. "Get to the point, Holden, will you?"

The younger man felt embarrassed and had trouble finding words to express himself. "Well, after Charley moved out, this Vaillant—and mind you, I didn't know her before—made a play for me." He shifted in his chair uncomfortably and stared at the desk.

Wisner snorted. "So you fell for her, huh, Holden?"

"Nope, I didn't." Somehow, Holden managed to steady himself. "But see, I wondered... why would this dame make a play for *two* piano players at Henri's?"

McKelvey answered briefly, "Because a lot of Americans come to Henri's and some of them are fairly important. Mikhailov, who must have been Vaillant's control officer, probably figures that it might be a pretty good listening post. As for spending her spare time in bed with a piano player, I guess that was *her* idea." He arose. "Thanks for coming in, Holden. For a bunch of amateurs, I must say you guys handled yourselves pretty well in the Varenka matter. And now," he cautioned, lowering his voice, "not one word outside this building about Catherine Vaillant." He walked to the door of his office, then turned. "Just by the way, if you were thinking of laying her, forget it."

As he and Wisner were walking away from McKelvey's office, Holden hazarded a guess. "Would you say that Vaillant was really a double agent?"

"Probably." Wisner kept talking in a low voice as they proceeded along the empty corridor. "I've always figured she was a CIA informant, because she isn't the world's greatest translator, and she either forgets or deliberately leaves out some things that should be included in the record. So somebody, or some agency, must have had enough clout to have the translation section keep her on as a contract worker. She wasn't good enough for staff."

"And do you think McKelvey was aware she was working for the Russians, and was just pretending he didn't know?"

Wisner gave the pianist a sharp look. "You're pretty cute, Holden. You know damn well McKelvey was rocked right back on his heels by what you told him. He didn't even pretend that he'd known about Vaillant all along. Fact is," and he forced back a small smile, "he called me one day about her background, but all he really seemed interested in was her home address and telephone number."

"And *he* told *me* to forget about laying her," Holden commented.

Wisner was philosophical. "Ah well, we're all human and that Vaillant is well-stacked. So what the hell." As they reached his office, the embassy official held out a limp hand. "Thanks for coming by. You've helped us a lot."

But Holden wasn't satisfied with that. "As long as I'm here, Wisner, d'ya think I could have a few words with Bartley Crandell?" He added hastily, "Nothing official, strictly personal."

"You know him that well?" Wisner was dubious.

"Not exactly, but we have some mutual friends," Holden said.

Wisner nodded. "Sure, the Bainbridges and the Learys, that crowd."

"Actually," Holden confessed, "I want to ask about Fay Carroll."

Wisner's manner changed abruptly. He indicated an office down the hall with one bent index finger. "You'll find Crandell down there. Just see his secretary and say you've just been talking with McKelvey and me. That ought to get you by her."

"Thanks," Holden said.

The outburst of activity at Pastore's lodge in the Fontainebleau Forest the night before evidently had aroused Bartley Crandall's interest, too, for the Deputy Chief of Mission saw Holden as soon as he was announced. The DCM began pleasantly enough, "I hear you've had a pretty busy time."

Holden slipped into a chair beside the DCM's big desk and

nodded. "Varenka's holed up right now over at the Learys' apartment on the Rue Soufflot, and I guess the Russians have an alarm out for her."

"The French Foreign Office has been querying us all morning," Crandell said, "but of course we're not involved." The older man stood up, he was tall and thin and fitted out in a fuzzy suit of stone-quarry gray. "Let's go over here next to the window, Holden, and have some coffee."

With his large head and pinkish skull, and his gimlet-like eyes behind their tinted glasses, Crandell was a basically unsympathetic presence. And yet, seeing a young man before him fairly bursting with unspoken desires, something caused the DCM to try to draw him out.

An elderly secretary brought them coffee, which she placed on an oval brass table before the couch on which they were sitting, then she withdrew. Crandell waited patiently. Holden sipped his coffee, not knowing precisely how to begin his inquiries about Fay.

The diplomat suggested, "Are the Learys going to be able to keep Olga Varenka at the Rue Soufflot without too much trouble?"

"I hope so," Holden said. But from his detached attitude it was evident enough to Crandell, an old pro in the State Department, that his visitor was concerned with matters other than the defecting Russian ballet dancer.

However, the Varenka case had brought them together currently, and Crandell pursued it without particular purpose, hoping that eventually Holden would come around to his real reason for seeking an interview. The diplomat said, "I'm sure the Learys realize that it would be out of the question for us right now to grant Varenka a visa to come to the United States."

Holden hazarded a guess. "I don't think she wants to travel right now. She has something to straighten out with Nikolai Gribov."

"Oh?"

"She knows now that Gribov has been having an affair with one of your translators, Catherine Vaillant, and she's upset about it."

Crandell leaned back on the couch. "We're not very happy about Vaillant, either," he said. "The station chief was just

236

giving me a summary of her activities. And" —he nodded in recognition of Holden's services— "we're very thankful to you and your friends for putting us onto her. Now we'll just have to watch her and wait for developments."

"I'm glad I'm not in Gribov's shoes," Holden said. "That Varenka has a mean temper."

Crandell acted as if he hadn't heard. "Funny thing about the Russians," he mused. "They make such a fuss about defectors, and all the time I suspect they're glad to be rid of them." He let a smile flit across his thin, bloodless lips. "It would serve them right if Varenka changed her mind."

Because Holden was so preoccupied with his anxiety over Fay, he exploded, "At least Varenka has a choice. She can stay with us in Paris or she can go back to the Soviet Union."

The diplomat seemed amused. "Well, not exactly. Although I suppose the French might let your friends keep her for a while longer if the Russians don't raise too much hell."

"That's what I mean. Varenka has a choice," Holden repeated, with considerable heat.

Crandell didn't seem disconcerted. "Sometimes, if you give people too many choices," he suggested, "they get in out of their depth. Now take young Bainbridge, for example." Out of the corner of his eye, the DCM caught a glimpse of Holden, suddenly alert, but pretended not to notice. He resumed, "Here's a fella only a few years out of Yale being pushed along by a rich and politically important relative. Well, he gets into the Foreign Service, has a good assignment in Paris right off, then the United Nations, comes back to Paris on temporary assignment and now he's down in the dumps because he's being given an assignment he doesn't want. What do you think of that?"

Holden asked faintly, knowing that Fay's future was involved, "What's the assignment?"

"Katmandu." The DCM snapped it out. Seeing Holden didn't have the faintest idea of where Katmandu was, he explained without seeming to give instruction, "Actually, I think it's a very relaxing assignment for a young man in the Foreign Service to be sent out to Nepal for three years. Up there in the high Himalayas, life is a lot less complicated than it is in Paris or New York, and I think young Bainbridge will find it agreeable. But both he and his uncle, Waco Carroll, have been in the embassy to protest to the ambassador."

"When is Bainbridge due to go?" Holden asked, wondering all the while how Fay was taking the news and what she would do about it.

"Well, unless Carroll can get somebody to change the assignment, and he won't get much encouragement here, Bainbridge will be off pretty quick after the United Nations Ball tomorrow night. That's the formal end of the UN Special Assembly, you see." The DCM was quite matter-of-fact in what he said and how he said it, but all the while he was darting sharp glances at the young man beside him.

Holden was downcast. "I'm worried about Fay," he confessed at last, clasping and unclasping his hands.

The older man murmured, "I thought that was it." Then to Holden, "Mrs. Crandell and I are concerned, too. We were over at the Carrolls' apartment in the Ritz only yesterday, and I thought both Fay and her mother didn't look at all well. Mainly, I'd guess they're worried."

"I wish I could see Fay," the younger man said.

Crandell's voice softened. "Why don't you?"

"Her stepfather will run me out."

"He isn't there."

Holden shifted in his chair and surveyed the diplomat, who was poker-faced. "Anything bad happen to him . . . I hope?"

"Can't say, as of now," Crandell said. "When he found he couldn't change Bainbridge's assignment to Katmandu by protesting to the ambassador, he decided to take off for Washington. And just about that time, something else happened—" He caught himself and bit off the last sentence, as if he thought he'd said too much.

Holden pressed him. "Was he hurt?"

"Not so I noticed, but he could be." Crandell leaned toward the younger man and lowered his voice, although nobody was around to overhear what was said. "Look here, Holden. I don't want you gossiping about this or drawing inferences—because nothing may come of it—but the Nassau County Grand Jury in Mineola, New York, is investigating the administration of Fay's inheritance and her mother's."

Holden was mystified. "What does that mean?"

238

"Right now, nothing; but if the grand jury happens to come across some hanky-panky, then the federal tax people get into the act and that means really big trouble." Crandell was going to say something else, but changed his mind. He concluded, "Waco Carroll may have a few things on his mind other than forcing the remarriage of his stepdaughter."

"Does Fay know about this?" Holden asked.

"Vaguely, I suppose, but her mother knows a lot more." Crandell got up. With a show of sympathy, he shook hands with the younger man. "I'm overdue at the ambassador's office, so you'll have to excuse me." As they walked to the door together, the DCM's manner became urgent. "Mrs. Crandell and I saw Fay and her mother yesterday at the Ritz for a little while. If you decently can, Holden, try to get over there. Every aspect of this affair has been hard on both of them. They need the support of every friend they have."

Crandell walked off after giving Holden's shoulder an encouraging slap, and vanished around a bend in the corridor. The silence outside the DCM's office was oppressive. Head down, Holden made his way to the elevator. All he could think of was that he would soon be seeing Fay. And that thrilled him.

Unfortunately, it wasn't a happy reunion. Even though Waco Carroll had hurried back to the United States to handle the various legal inquiries into his affairs, the showy luxury of his suite at the Ritz was depressing to Holden. It was a suffocating reminder of who Carroll was and how he ordered his life, as well as the lives of those around him. No one, coming into the living room of his expensive suite at the Ritz, could fail to be affected by the sadness, the impoverished spirit, even the despair of the two women he had left behind him.

Because of his feeling for Fay, Holden was even more sensitive to such an atmosphere than others. Subconsciously, he held himself under rigid control and kept his voice low as he talked to her at one side of the museum-like living room. Nearby, her mother stood beside a window and looked out over the Place Vendome. She was a study in melancholy.

Fay had confirmed for Holden all that Crandell had told him, but neither Carroll's legal involvement in the United States nor Bainbridge's coming assignment to Nepal seemed to make much difference to her. "My stepfather has beaten every rap so far, and I doubt if they'll be able to catch him this time," she said. "No, I'll be going to Katmandu with Bainbridge, I'm afraid."

Holden burst out indignantly, "You *can't* do it, Fay."

"I wish you were right," she replied quietly, showing only suppressed emotion. "But I must think of Mother."

Hearing this, the older woman turned from the window. "It makes me feel dreadful when you say things like that, Fay."

Now Fay became agitated. "I can't do it to you, Mother. I can't just go away, have a good time and make a different life for myself. Although" —and she reached out and held Holden's hand briefly— "I think it would be a wonderful experience. But I must think of what my stepfather would do to you."

"What can he do to me beyond commit me to an institution? He's threatened me so often that I'm prepared for it." She continued with spirit, "But he's still not going to do it to me without a struggle. You know that I've told the lawyers to go ahead and take every necessary action to protect the both of us and our inheritances."

Holden desperately wanted Fay to believe that Carroll couldn't force through his plans for her. "You see?" He faced her and spread his hands palms upward in a gesture of appeal. "There's still time. You can stall Bainbridge. And if they get something on Carroll . . ."

Fay was far from hopeful. "That's been tried before, but Waco Carroll has too much political clout. He's gotten out of a lot worse jams than the one he's in now." She sighed and shook her head. "Arch, I'm sorry. I feel the way this is going to wind up for me is a quick civil marriage to Bainbridge, then off we go to Katmandu."

Holden's voice quivered with anger. "If Bainbridge is willing to force you into this, then he's just gambling that he can stop you from testifying against his uncle. And if commitment papers can be sworn out for your mother, then Carroll and Bainbridge simply take over your inheritance. Give in to them, and that's exactly what's going to happen."

"Let's not go over that again, *please*." She was restrained, even pained, but there was a sense of finality about her words.

"You can tell me again and again that Bainbridge isn't in love with me, that he and his uncle are just after my money and my mother's, and you're probably right. But we can't hold out against them, don't you understand? We're defenseless, both of us."

"If I had never met you . . ." His voice drifted off, but she caught his meaning and their hands clasped briefly.

"Don't say that."

"But Fay, it's true. Everything would be different if I had never met you."

She inclined her head. "Well, yes. I'd still think I was incapable of love, of having a normal sexual relationship. And you'd be off somewhere by yourself, lonely and bitter." She looked at him through half-closed eyes. "Don't think I've forgotten, and don't think I've not cherished the beautiful time we've had together, short as it's been. When we met on that blessed ladder at the Four Arts Ball, it was the best moment of my life."

Her mother couldn't restrain herself. "Run away, the two of you," she said in a shrill voice. "Take your chance while Carroll's gone!"

Holden jumped up and held out both hands. "C'mon, Fay."

She didn't move. To her mother, she said, "And if I'm gone, what will you do when *he* comes back? You know how he terrifies you when he rages and shouts and makes threats. You can't stand it."

The older woman seemed beside herself. "Then I'll run away, too."

"You can't."

"Oh, yes I can. Dr. Berenger pleaded with me before he left Paris to have me go to the Menninger Clinic. He said they could help me."

Fay put her arms around her mother to quiet her. "Maybe you should have taken Dr. Berenger's advice."

Mrs. Carroll choked back a sob. "Carroll wouldn't let me."

Still holding her mother in her arms, Fay said to Holden, "You see? I can't leave her. Not now."

Holden suggested, "We'll take her with us."

"Where would we go?" Fay asked. "How long could we hide?"

"You have to get away. You can't take much more of this."

"I'll have to do it on my stepfather's terms, or he'll turn on mother." She made a gesture of helplessness. "Arch, I'd give anything if I didn't have to tell you this, but I'm going to the United Nations Ball tomorrow with Spence Bainbridge."

He was stunned. "I can't believe you're doing this."

"There's no help for it. My stepfather's made all the arrangements. And Spence has been telling all our friends that we're engaged again."

"Are you?"

"Yes."

With a wail of protest, her mother struggled out of her embrace and ran to the bedroom, slamming the door behind her.

Fay now stood beside Holden, calm and white-faced. She seemed very slim and tall in her dark silk dress. And when she spoke, she was completely self-possessed. "Will you be at the Palais de Chaillot tomorrow?"

He forced himself to match her composure. "I doubt it."

"Then I don't know when we'll see each other again."

"Good luck," he said.

In a small voice, she asked, "You'll be at Henri's?"

He nodded. A sense of frustration, even anger, possessed him at the thought that she would be marrying Spencer Bainbridge again. He was conscious now of wanting to hurt her because he, too, had been hurt. But there was really nothing more he could say to reach her, not even in spite.

Her eyes filled with tears. "Good-bye, Arch."

She turned her cheek, his lips brushed lightly against it and he stepped back. Before she could say anything else, he turned on his heel in blind rage and rushed out the door.

Olga Varenka's situation in the Learys' apartment on the Rue Soufflot wasn't any better, as Holden discovered when he came to Henri's that night for his usual session at the piano bar. The regulars already were buzzing with whispers about complications in Gribov's romance with his Russian mistress, which they attributed mainly to his dalliance in Paris with Catherine Vaillant.

Amy Leary, with her husband's assistance, had gone to the

242

trouble that afternoon of setting up a meeting between Olga and Gribov at a small but comfortable hotel, the d'Iena, not far from the Palais de Chaillot. Olga had been driven there reluctantly. And Amy had gone to the Crillon to bring Gribov to the ballet dancer. He had postured, sighed, proclaimed his love for Olga, but in the end he had not gone to her. And that complicated matters considerably.

That evening at Henri's, when Holden appeared to preside at the piano bar, he saw the Learys taking counsel with Henri at a nearby table. In unspoken accord, when they saw Holden, they moved to the empty stools about the piano bar and included him in their strategy session. He was little interested, for he was still furious over Fay's refusal to break off with Bainbridge. Bit by bit, the Learys drew him into their consideration of Gribov's difficult relationship with Olga.

"I think Gribov is afraid of Olga," Henri said.

Pat Leary suggested, "Maybe he likes Catherine Vaillant better?"

"Not so, Pat," Amy replied. "Catherine would like to have Olga think so. Why else did she leave some pretty fancy underthings around the lodge in the Fontainebleau Forest? I'm satisfied that Nikolai really wants Olga."

"Then why, after we arranged a rendezvous for them at the Hotel d'Iena, didn't he come?"

Amy hesitated, then seemed to have made a decision to speak up. "I can guess. You see, Gribov actually *has* talked with Varenka."

Her husband reproached her. "He came to the apartment? Why didn't you tell me?"

"No, he wasn't at the apartment," Amy responded, "but he did go to a pay telephone and call her. You must remember," and here she relaxed and permitted herself a little laugh, "that Nikolai has a conspiratorial disposition. He imagines he's being followed if he goes out for cigarettes, and is convinced his telephone is tapped."

"It could be so," Henri commented.

"Anyway," Amy went on, "I suppose I should have told you that Gribov and Olga had talked, but of course I didn't know what was said—I'd long ago forgotten what little Russian

243

I knew—and Olga refused to tell me anything in her few words of French..."

Leary interrupted. "But you do know something, Amy. Get to the point, *please*."

"As I said," she resumed, "I have to guess."

"Well, then, let's have your guess. Usually, you're pretty close to being right."

"The first time Gribov called this afternoon," Amy said to her husband in a soothing voice, "you'd taken the children out to Longchamps for the races and I didn't want to bother you. Because, frankly, I didn't have to be a mind reader to tell that they weren't getting along. Olga wound up screaming into the telephone and disconnecting."

"But Gribov tried again?" Henri asked, trying to prod her into giving a bit more information.

"Yes," Amy said, "and again it was from a pay telephone a little later, and Olga and I were alone in the apartment and I had trouble even getting her to talk to him. When she did, she had very little to say. He did most of the talking and she just listened. She seemed angry."

"Was that all?" her husband asked.

"No, because I then called Nikolai myself and went to see him at the Crillon." She turned to her husband. "I did intend to tell you, dear, but it didn't come off very well. First of all, Gribov was hurt. He said Olga was making all kinds of accusations because she had found Vaillant's underthings at the lodge. He couldn't make her listen to reason. And then, when I tried to set up another rendezvous for them, he told me that we'd have to wait. He made all kinds of excuses. He was being watched. Olga was angry. Anyway," she concluded with a sigh, "I couldn't get him to move."

Holden, thinking of his own difficulty in seeing Fay, suggested, "Maybe there's something we don't know about that's complicating things. Maybe they already know Varenka can't get a visa and go to the United States."

"That wouldn't bother them," Amy said. "Varenka doesn't have to dance in New York. Someone with her reputation and ability would be welcome anywhere. No," and she looked up at her husband, "I'm afraid we may have a permanent guest for as long as we stay in the Rue Soufflot."

"That isn't going to be much longer," Pat Leary observed. "I heard only yesterday from Professor Dessaix that he didn't want to spend the summer in New Haven, and I can't blame him for that. He wants his apartment. So we'll be shoving off soon, and Varenka has to be told about it."

Henri registered a mild protest. "But aren't you staying for the United Nations Ball at the Palais de Chaillot tomorrow night?"

"Of course, dear. Don't you remember?" Amy was all sweet reasonableness. "We gave Vivian permission to go. Baron von Norden asked her. It's the event of the season—the end of the UN Special Assembly."

Leary saw that he had to give in. But with husbandly persistence, he clung to his point. "Right after that, we must go, and Gribov and Varenka will have to come to terms or make other arrangements. It would be rude if we were still at Professor Dessaix's apartment when he returns."

"Poor Nikolai," Amy said. "Too many women. Too little time."

Chapter Eight

On the night of the United Nations Ball at the Palais de Chaillot, it was understandably quiet at Henri's. Too quiet, Marie Durand decided. She had a distinct aversion to nights like this because the cash register played a languorous tune. Many of her best customers would be celebrating at the Palais de Chaillot.

At the moment, surveying her establishment from behind the cash register, Marie noted only the three regulars and Saffron at the piano bar facing the ever-dependable Holden. That was bad. Worse still, Henri was having two waiters put together a special table in the rear.

Marie sighed. Henri, she was sure, had given way once again to his weakness for grandiose ideas. And when the special table had been set up, complete with roses in the middle, Henri came to her and confessed.

Naturally, it had to be pried out of him bit by bit.

"You prepare for special guests tonight, Henri?"

"Yes."

"They will come soon?"

"No, my dear. After hours."

Marie sighed. She had feared as much. "And do the guests pay us, or do we pay for the guests?"

Henri fingered his mustache nervously. "It is a dinner in honor of our friends, the Learys. They have been good customers."

"And why should they not pay?"

"Impossible, my dear." Henri seemed perturbed. "It is their last night out in Paris. Perhaps we will not see them again."

Marie was unmoved. She considered farewell dinners both

foolish and impractical. If guests were leaving her board for good, why was that a cause for celebration at the expense of Henri and Marie Durand?

But, from hard experience, she knew that Henri could not be dissuaded from playing the generous host. With a long-suffering air, she asked, "How many will there be?"

"We will be eight."

It seemed to be a modest number. But, knowing Henri's bent for inviting every stray to his celebrations, she asked, "You are sure?"

"Positive. The Learys are four—the professor and Madame with the two children. And, of course, Baron von Norden for the daughter, Vivian, and our own Stephanie for the son, Gareth. And you and I make eight."

"A dinner for Stephanie, who is our photographer, our employee?" To Marie, it seemed unnecessary.

Henri was quick to defend himself. "Tonight, Stephanie works not for us. She had time off coming to her, and she is the guest of the Learys. So you see" —he spread his hands in gentle supplication as if to show how helpless he was to turn against his own logic— "if the Learys are our guests, then their guests become our guests."

Marie was unimpressed. "And what if the Learys produce five or six additional guests, they will be our guests, too?"

"It is not possible, my dear. The Learys are attending the United Nations Ball at the Palais de Chaillot tonight; but the tickets come from Baron von Norden, who has a fixed allotment of five in addition to his own. He was most apologetic because he could not take care of us."

"What happens at the United Nations is a matter of indifference to me," Marie responded. "My place is here," and she tapped the cash register delicately with the point of her ever-present pencil.

Henri agreed. "It is what I told Baron von Norden—that you and I cannot dance the night away as long as we have a business. And yet" —he appeared regretful— "I would not mind being at the United Nations Ball tonight."

"Then you are more of a fool than anyone can imagine, Henri Durand."

"Oh, but I would not dance, Marie."

"No? Then you would no doubt send yourself into an alcoholic stupor?"

"Not that, either." Henri preened himself and adopted a slightly superior air. "For as the whole world will soon know, there will be excitement at the Palais de Chaillot tonight, my dear."

"Excitement?" Clearly enough, Marie thought the prospect absurd. "The Security Council will perhaps vote once again to rebuke Israel? Or perhaps some country thousands of miles away that is even smaller?" She did not bother to conceal her contempt for the powers of the United Nations. "No, Henri, you must not pretend that the United Nations is capable of producing excitement."

Still, Henri was patient. "I said there would be excitement *at* the United Nations, not necessarily *by* the United Nations."

"Then I have married a seer, a prophet," she replied. "And what is it that you are predicting for tonight, if you please?"

Henri, his face flushed, could hold back no longer. "It is not a prediction, Marie, but a fact. Our friend Gribov will escort his Olga to the United Nations Ball."

"If Gribov makes such a scene, then he is an idiot."

"He is wiser than you think."

"Wise? An opera singer wise?" Marie paused briefly to total up a bill in her spidery handwriting for a waiter who was standing nearby but out of earshot. "How did this remarkable transformation come about?"

"Our government," Henri announced, "has granted political asylum to Olga Varenka. So it is possible, even practical," and now he assumed a triumphant air, "for Nikolai Gribov to present her before the world. It is what the Americans call surfacing, what the British term 'coming in from the cold.'"

"So!" Marie exclaimed with a sardonic expression. "Now my Henri has a direct channel to the Quai d'Orsay! What the Americans no doubt call a pipeline, and what the British call it doesn't matter."

But Henri was far from flustered. "The information comes from the Quai d'Orsay, naturally, but the channel, the pipeline, is one of the regular guests." He nodded toward the piano bar. "The reporter, Saffron."

248

"Then why is Saffron here when there is such excitement at the Palais de Chaillot?" Marie demanded.

"Because the arrival has been arranged for midnight. Gribov is no fool. He wishes the American television networks to display the pictures of him with Olga on their evening news programs." He consulted his watch. "Saffron no doubt will soon be departing, and eventually we will hear all about it from our friends, the Learys."

Marie made a mouth, then indicated with a brief gesture that Shukri, the doorman, was admitting a guest—always an event on a slow evening. Looking over Henri's shoulder at the newcomer, his wife said, "I wonder what that one will think of Gribov's presentation of Olga before the United Nations tonight."

As Henri turned, he saw Catherine Vaillant approaching. Whatever she was, double agent or not, she compelled attention. Taking note of her handsome black evening gown and the jacket she had slung over one arm, Marie said, "You are very fashionable tonight, madame."

"When one escorts an American general, one must dress the part," Catherine observed. And to Henri, "I must meet my general soon at the Palais de Chaillot, and I am famished. May I have supper?"

"Most assuredly, madame," Henri replied, and thought that she was truly magnificent. He saw not a sign that she feared her undercover activities were known. She was completely self-assured.

As the newcomer moved off toward the piano bar, Marie observed her stately, slightly swaying walk, then remarked to her husband, "She will be an armful for that American general tonight, that one."

To which Henri responded gravely, "She is capable of many things."

In silent agreement, Marie turned her attention to the bills and the cash register and began doing something far more practical—adding the charges on the bills of the few customers who had dined that evening.

The regulars at the piano bar already had teased Holden about Catherine Vaillant's presence. As she exchanged the compliments of the evening with Henri and Marie Durand, Marcel Valleau had said, "There she is, Holden, our own mysterious lady."

Pastore, turning slightly for a better look, had rolled his eyes. "Ah, to have a night with this one at my lodge in the Fontainebleau Forest. I would wrap her around me."

And Eilers observed sagely, "Who needs your lodge? With someone like that, I take her to a *stundenhotel.*" He clapped his hands together smartly. "Quick, like that!"

Saffron, who was sitting between Josette and Toinette—for whom he had bought beers—was derisive. "All you guys are big talk, no action. Here, you got two of the cutest girls in the business," and he indicated the two house operatives, "but I don't see you making any moves."

Holden, who hadn't been listening too carefully, committed the tactical error just then of breaking into an old standard, "You Made Me Love You." It aroused a small chorus of derisive hoots, particularly when the group noticed the approach of Catherine Vaillant.

Eilers was delighted. "See? He salutes Catherine with a love song. He wants Catherine."

"Okay, Arch, I give you my lodge for tonight," Pastore said.

Valleau objected. "Maybe he can't wait for the lodge."

"Shut up, you guys," Holden said good-naturedly. And to Vaillant, as she took over a bar stool at the top of the piano keyboard, "Don't pay any attention to them, Catherine."

"I never do," she said in her precise English. "The greatest product of their intellectual effort is an indecent proposal."

Valleau registered mild objection. "You do not care for indecent proposals, Catherine?"

"It depends on who makes them," she said tartly. A waiter put a brandy and soda before her, and she tilted her glass toward the assembly with a derisive, "Cheers."

Saffron tried to turn the bar talk into less offensive channels. "Going to the United Nations Ball tonight, madame?"

"I can't very well avoid it."

"How's that?"

"One of your two-star American generals is here on leave from Bitburg Air Base in Germany and I'm assigned to escort him. It barely got away from him tonight to change clothes, and I'm due to pick him up soon as I can at the United Nations Ball."

Eilers leered at her. "Do American generals make indecent proposals?"

It didn't bother her. "It wouldn't do him much good if he did. Although," she reflected, "I can't say that goes for all generals. I've seen one or two nice ones at the American embassy."

"So if Charles de Gaulle hadn't tossed NATO out of France, you'd probably see more," Saffron observed. "Do I know the guy from Bitburg?"

"His name's Ferrender. He's small and bowlegged."

"Sure, Charley Ferrender," Saffron said. "An old World War Two fighter-pilot type, crazy as they come."

"Crazy or not, he's my man until midnight. He said he'd let me off then."

"Midnight?"

"Well, maybe a few minutes before." Catherine sipped her drink. "What's so important about midnight?"

Saffron seemed embarrassed. "Guess you haven't heard," he muttered.

"Heard what?" Catherine's reply was mechanical. She didn't seem overly interested.

Saffron had the air of a man who had just spilled soft-boiled egg on a new necktie. "Big show at midnight. Gribov's alerted the media that he's bringing Olga Varenka to the Palais de Chaillot at midnight."

"Interesting." Catherine displayed no emotion.

Holden, fingering the piano keys with small improvisations between numbers, rather admired her composure. He thought of Varenka's outrage when she had discovered Catherine's underthings in Pastore's lodge. Without dropping a note, he asked indolently, "Do you know Varenka?"

Catherine shook her head. "I hope to tonight." She added with just a touch of condescension, "She's a marvelous dancer, too good for the Russians."

"Guess that's why the French are giving her asylum," Saffron remarked. "She'll be a sensation here."

"Not if Gribov keeps screaming at her," Catherine said. "They're not good for each other."

Saffron, who had been leaning lazily over the bar, slowly straightened up. "How d'ya know that?"

"I don't. That's what people are saying around the American embassy." She said it with a markedly defensive air.

"How would they know?" Saffron persisted.

Catherine shrugged. "Maybe wiretaps, maybe bugs. Who knows? There are plenty of ways of getting that kind of information."

Henri approached just then. With a deferential air, he announced to Catherine, "Your supper is ready, madame."

Without another word, she slipped from her bar stool and walked to a corner booth, taking her drink with her.

Saffron sat for a moment staring after her, almost as though he were going over the previous conversation word for word in his mind. Holden could almost see his nose twitch. Suddenly, Saffron climbed off his bar stool. "This bears investigation."

Holden was just finishing his set. "Where are you going?"

"Time to talk things over with Vaillant," Saffron said. Then, urgently, "You'd better come along."

Holden fell in beside the reporter as they both left the piano bar. "What's so important about talking to *her?*" her asked.

In a low voice, Saffron replied, "Ferrender, the guy she's with, is in charge of intelligence at Bitburg and she must know it."

"Think she suspects we're onto her?"

"She has to," was the whispered reply. "But just look at her, not a nerve in her body." Saffron waved toward her and was encouraged when she waved in return. "Look at that! She's really *something!*"

Saffron wasted little time on formalities as he slid into the corner booth next to Catherine Vaillant. "What are you going to do about Gribov tonight?"

She paused briefly over her plate of *entrecote* and green string beans. "I think that's beside the point. What is he going to do about me?"

Holden, who had moved in on the opposite side, saw a glint of amusement in her eyes. Before he was quite prepared, she flung a question at him. Still addressing Saffron, she went on, "And what about our friend Holden? What's he going to do about Spencer Bainbridge? That's a pretty question, too."

Saffron grinned and deferred to Holden, who could think of nothing but a play for time. "What's so important about Bainbridge?"

"I hear he's taking off for his new post in Nepal right after he winds up his UN job here; and he's taking your girl, Fay, with him." There was a glint of mockery in her eyes. She had made Holden feel uncomfortable as she intended, and diverted them from their purpose for a moment. She resumed dining. "You must pardon me, I'm starved." Then, after a brief interval, "Won't you have something?"

After both men had ordered sandwiches and coffee, Saffron went back to the subject of Gribov. "Look, Catherine, anybody who's been around Gribov recently for more than two minutes knows he's interested in you. But now, here comes his Russian sweetie . . ."

She interrupted with a murmured, "You're a born trouble-maker, M'sieu' Saffron."

"You haven't answered my question," the reporter said. "You must have *some* feeling about what Gribov is doing."

"What shall I say?" she mused. "That I love Gribov, that it is breaking my heart to give him up?" She smiled. "It will look good in your newspaper, yes, but I will not say it. I am not so foolish, so stupid."

Holden had to respect Catherine Vaillant. She labored under no romantic illusions. Nor was she impressed with either appearances or the dictates of middle-class morality. And, of course, she was well aware that Saffron's only interest in her was the newsman's everlasting pursuit of his story.

Saffron wouldn't quit, however. "But you do admit to having an affair with Gribov, don't you?"

Catherine calmly finished her meal, savored a glass of wine and then sat back with an amused expression. "Really, gentlemen, I am not your typical journalistic heroine. I do not beat my breast, I do not weep, I do not proclaim my everlasting love."

"All right, all right." Now Saffron seemed to be verging

on impatience. "But you must admit that you are impressed by Nikolai Gribov."

She agreed. "Who would not be? He is the most famous baritone in the world, probably the greatest singer since Enrico Caruso."

"Many women are in love with him."

"Millions, no doubt," she said. "That golden voice is thrilling wherever it is heard."

"And now," Saffron suggested, "you are giving it up."

She leaned back and laughed. "You reporters are impossible. You think of life in terms of a bad short story and try to invent characters to fit. But, M'sieu' Saffron, I am not an invention. I am real. Here!" With a mischievous look, she pinched him and he howled, "Quit it!"

"Now you understand the difference between a real person and your invention."

Saffron nursed his injured wrist. "Did anybody ever give you a punch in the nose?"

Holden saw that Saffron was thoroughly discomfited, but Catherine chose not to pursue her advantage. Instead, she chattered away at nonessentials while she finished her supper and the two men had their sandwiches and coffee. But once the table was cleared, she resumed her barbed assault on Saffron without preliminaries.

"You know everything, don't you?" she began.

The reporter wasn't disturbed. "Not really."

"But you think you know all about Gribov and Olga Varenka, don't you?"

"I'm going to be at Palais de Chaillot at midnight to find out," he said. "In the news business, you never take anything for granted."

"Luckily for you," she commented dryly.

He whirled on her. "Damn you, Catherine, you know something. Now out with it."

She chided him. *"Doucement, doucement."*

Attracted by the outburst, Henri sidled toward the little group. "Is everything all right, my friends?"

"Your supper was wonderful, but now I must go to meet my general," Catherine said. She made a great show of pulling her wrap on and picking up her bag and gloves. As she arose

254

to leave, she turned to the *patron* almost as if in afterthought. "You're having a party tonight?" And she nodded toward the festive table that had been set up in the rear.

"A farewell for the *famille* Leary," he responded. "They will be leaving Paris shortly and they have been good friends."

Over her shoulder, she asked, "Why the Learys alone? Others will be leaving, other friends..."

Saffron was at her in a moment, one big hand on her arm. "Quit hinting, Catherine. Let's have the story."

With a dainty gesture she freed herself. "Come with me to the Palais de Chaillot, gentlemen. You will not regret it." She have Holden her big look. "And especially you," she added, then departed with that graceful, swaying walk so typical of her.

Henri furrowed his brow. "This means trouble tonight."

"Sure, wherever that baby goes, she means big trouble."

But all Holden could think of was the possibility that she was trying to tell him something about Fay. On impulse, he asked the *patron,* "Would you mind if I went to the Palais for a little while? I'll be back in time to play for the crowd after the ball."

Henri fumed, as he always did when there was a threatened break in the routine at his establishment. But in the end he said, "But not for long, M'sieu' Holden. We have a special party tonight."

On the spur of the moment, the pianist suggested, "If there is to be trouble, maybe I should bring the Learys back with me."

That made the difference. The *patron* brightened. "Very well." Then he added, "And if you will call for the *famille* Leary, you may take my car."

Saffron clapped Holden on the shoulder. "C'mon, Mac. Let's get going before he changes his mind."

The United Nations still exists as a world organization because it is able to celebrate its defeats. And nowhere are such events marked with greater pomp than in Paris. For it is here that all good diplomats hope to spend their lives discussing the fate of the world and solemnly agreeing to do nothing whatever about it.

Thus, when the United Nations Special Assembly adjourned that night in a blaze of inaction, the delegates saluted their disagreements with a monumental popping of champagne corks and the consumption of small mountains of the best caviar.

No conquering army ever marched up the Champs Elysées toward the Arc de Triomphe with greater élan. In consequence, they brought with them an avid host of Parisians.

From early evening on, the Place du Trocadero drew ragged phalanxes of the curious, attracted by the glaring white lights of the television crews, the bustle of traffic, the comings and goings of people who looked important. But it was not until much later that the stars of the diplomatic firmament descended from the embassies and allowed themselves to go on display before the white marble pillars of the Palais.

The lights of the television crews flashed on and off, first on one celebrity, then on another. The great black limousines swung to the curb in front of the Palais to discharge their passengers—the women in the best of Paris high fashion, the men slashed with colored ribbons across their white shirt fronts, and rows of medals for those in uniform. And if the watchers did not know that these were personages from Suriname, Upper Volta, Fiji and the Malagasy Republic, among others, what did it matter? The public illusion was that all who paraded before the television lights were movie stars and nothing at the Palais dispelled the dream or the excitement.

But there was grandeur, too, for as the ranks of the élite advanced along the white sugarloaf base of the Palais, moonlight glinted on the polished helmets and drawn swords of the Garde Republicaine, that superbly theatrical unit of French arms. And as the guests approached the grand staircase leading to the ballroom of the Palais below ground, the soldiers of the Garde drew up in double ranks facing each other on either side of the red-carpeted marble staircase. Colorful feathers trailed from the silvered helmets, drawn swords were held at rigid salute.

This was the best theatre in all France, a spectacle of limousines, bright lights, the ultra in fashion and uniforms, crossed swords and banners, gaping crowds alternating between bistros and pressure on police barriers.

On the basis of Saffron's press credentials and his voluble

identification in bad French of Holden as his assistant, French police waved them through the checkpoint outside the Palais after they had parked Henri's car. Just ahead of them, they noticed Catherine Vaillant, who had stepped from a taxi and had turned to wait for them.

"So you changed your mind," she said to Holden. "Good!"

"Now, when's the big break?" Saffron demanded.

"Nikolai Gribov is expected at midnight with Varenka," she said

He fidgeted. "C'mon, Catherine, you know what I mean. What else happens and when does it happen? What d'ya know?"

She drew back and smiled. "Oh, I know nothing beyond what is planned, M'sieu' Saffron."

Three abreast, they advanced across the broad white marble surface of the palatial terrace. Then, they mingled with others in a glorified processional down the red-carpeted marble stairway of the Palais between a double line of the brilliantly uniformed Garde Republicaine.

At the entrance to the ballroom, Catherine left them. General Ferrender, her escort for the evening, was waiting there to claim her. Taking no notice of her companions, who seemed faintly disreputable in their rumpled business suits, the general announced, "Just in time. We're tapped to take a turn in the receiving line." With scant ceremony, he hustled her off.

Saffron pulled Holden to one side, where they could be by themselves and still see what was going on in the ballroom. "Our baby's flying high tonight," the reporter said.

"But why the receiving line?" Holden asked.

"Oh, that doesn't mean much. The big shots always take turns there, and believe me, Charley Ferrender is a big shot. If they got him out of Bitburg and put him on Catherine tonight, then they must be ready to move."

"Move?" Holden was hazy.

"Sure, sooner or later they've got to grab her and she probably knows it," Saffron remarked in a low voice. "But that dame's got class. Looking at her, you couldn't tell she had a care in the world."

Together, the two men entered the ballroom, which was probably the only place in Paris where people could still waltz without being self-conscious. It was too hot. The lights were too bright. The orchestra was too loud. The dancers seemed thoroughly uncomfortable. But everybody who was there had a sense of participating in a bit of history, and nowhere was this more evident than in the receiving line. The Secretary General of the United Nations had long since given way to a succession of his staff people, and protocol officers seemed to be eternally busy fitting others into the line through which newcomers were expected to pass.

Saffron and Holden, of course, were exceptions. Not being in evening dress, they were unceremoniously shoved into a roped-off space for reporters and cameramen directly opposite the receiving line. There they saw Catherine and her general politely shaking hands with other new arrivals and murmuring greetings to those they knew. Also in the line were an Indian in his Congress uniform, a Russian marshal, several Africans in native costume, a British admiral and a retinue of anonymous Europeans and their ladies.

The members of the assembled press, quite frankly, were bored. They were too far off to hear what was being said, too close to relax in the event of something happening. And so the reporters languidly made notes now and then; the still cameramen would take a picture just for luck; and the television people, with their minicams balanced on their shoulders, ran a few feet of videotape mainly to check their equipment.

Saffron soon saw that nothing was to be gained by watching people pass down the receiving line. "Let's get outta here."

Holden, however, was holding back. "Wait awhile. Gimme a chance to look around."

Saffron was impatient. "If you want to see Fay Carroll, she's over in a corner with the American ambassador and his crew."

A sense of anger swept over Holden because Fay had given in to her stepfather, and he had let her. When he had rushed out of the Carroll suite at the Ritz, he thought that he might never see her again. But now, he had to admit to himself that he had joined Saffron on the trip to the Palais only because he wanted to see her once more. But he did not want to face her just yet; it would only hurt him more to know he couldn't have her.

"I'll see her later," he said offhandedly.

"Then let's have a drink." Saffron steered his companion away from the roped-off press section.

Threading their way through the dancers on the way to the bar, they noticed Baron von Norden, awesomely formal in his diplomatic attire, waltzing sedately with a rather bored Vivian. A few steps beyond, they came across Gareth boisterously dancing in the modern manner with Stephanie while elderly couples about them gave them severe looks of disapproval.

"Glad somebody's having a good time here," Holden muttered.

Saffron broke into his crooked grin. "You're just set on making yourself unhappy, aren't you?"

At the bar, they met Pat and Amy Leary and retired to a quiet alcove to join them in a drink. Like most people on the fringes of the diplomatic community, they had heard of the French decision to give Olga Varenka asylum and of Gribov's victorious gesture in announcing her attendance at the ball. No one really knew if they would appear, but everybody was waiting, including the little circle of Americans who had gathered around the ambassador some distance off.

Amy said wistfully to Holden, nodding toward the American array, "You know, Arch, Fay's down there with the ambassador." She added with animation, "She looks simply beautiful."

Holden tried to be casual. "I heard she'd be here with Spence Bainbridge."

Amy took no notice of the comment about Bainbridge. "Arch, I'm sure Fay would like very much to see you."

Pat Leary, in a low voice, asked, "Why not let Arch alone, Amy? Don't you see how he feels?"

Her reply was vigorous. "But, Pat, I'm trying to help him. I'm sure he doesn't know that Fay has been left all alone in that great big suite at the Ritz."

Holden froze, not knowing what to make of the information. "Alone? How so?"

"She called me from the Ritz this morning and begged me to come over," Amy said. "When I got there, she said Carroll had called her mother last night from New York, but she didn't know what it was about. Anyway, her mother got a cab to

259

Charles de Gaulle Airport this morning before Fay was up and took off for New York."

Saffron gave a low whistle. "No explanation?"

"Not a word," Amy said.

"Something's sure happened to that combo between Waco Carroll and Spence Bainbridge," Saffron muttered. "Waco in New York, Spence headed for diplomatic burial in the high Himalayas..."

Pat Leary broke in. "What are you getting at, Saffron?"

"Hell, I wish I knew." The reporter grinned. "But maybe I'll call the office and see if there's something on the Associated Press..."

"Oh, yes," Amy added eagerly. "While I was at the Ritz this morning, an Associated Press reporter telephoned Fay and asked her for comment on something, but she refused."

"And she wouldn't say what it was about?" Saffron asked.

"No."

"Hm." The reporter scratched his head. "Well, whatever it is, that'll keep. Right now I'm close to a deadline and I got a big story by the tail." He consulted his watch. "It's almost midnight, and if Gribov means it, he'll be showing up any minute with Olga." He tossed off the last of his drink, waved a vague good-bye to the Learys and motioned to Holden. "Let's go, Mac."

Amy plucked at Holden's arm as he turned away. "Won't you be back at Henri's for our farewell supper later?"

Holden suffered an acute attack of conscience. He'd almost forgotten that he'd borrowed Henri's car. "Wait for me, I'll be driving you there," he said, and hustled after the retreating Saffron.

On their return trip across the dance floor, he and Saffron had to make a wide detour past a knot of dancers, which forced them to pass close to the circle of Americans. Glancing toward the group, Holden saw the DCM, Bartley Crandell; Cleveland McKelvey, the CIA's Russian expert in Paris; and Cary Wisner. But he didn't pause. He couldn't help noticing that Fay had arisen from a chair near the edge of the dance floor and was looking directly toward him. She was in a filmy green gown and seemed more beautiful and desirable than ever.

Saffron nodded toward her and remarked gruffly, "Hey, Mac, there's yer girl. She wants you."

Holden hesitated. "Lotta people over there."

"Yeah. Whenever the ambassador and his gang are caught in the United Nations like this, they circle the wagons and go into a huddle. But don't mind that." He stood for a moment. "Hey, that babe really wants you, Mac. Lookit!"

Holden darted a quick glance at the American group and thought he saw Fay holding out one hand toward him in what could have been a silent appeal. His heart seemed to turn over slowly, almost as if it had been a leaded weight. But then, all the hurt and disappointment of the past twenty-four hours overcame him and he forced back his very real desire to break away and go to her, regardless of what had happened between them.

Saffron was irritated. He glanced at his watch. "Hey, Mac, we're running out of time. Make up yer mind, willya?"

"Let's go upstairs," Holden responded, his jaw set. He turned away resolutely from Fay's appealing presence there on the edge of the dance floor.

"It's about time," the reporter grumbled. "I got two cameramen waitin' for me and it's my ass if they miss the picture of Olga coming to the UN with Gribov."

Except for the press, the police, and a tall, balding diplomat with a gloomy face, the terrace was quiet when Saffron and Holden reached the top of the red-carpeted marble staircase. But there was a sense of excitement among the crowds behind the police barricades. They shifted about, shoved and pushed, and cheered now and then for no particular reason. In that mysterious fashion through which masses of people communicate with one another, newcomers could be seen streaming from nearby bistros and heading for the barricades.

"They think something's up," Saffron said. "Look at 'em! Buzzing around, shoving the police. Somebody must've started a rumor."

"About what?"

"Could be almost anything." Saffron looked at his watch. "It's almost midnight." He snapped his fingers. "I'll bet I know." He grabbed at Holden's arm. "C'mon, I want you to meet somebody."

They advanced toward the tall, gloomy-looking diplomat who had been staring off in the distance across the traffic in the Place du Trocadero. As he noticed them, he turned in expectation.

"Hey, Mikhailov, what're you doin' here?" Saffron affected a cheery, hearty manner.

"Exactly what you are doing," was the cool reply.

Saffron hustled through the introductions. "Lev Mikhailov, of the Soviet embassy... my friend, Arch Holden." Then, "Heard anything about Olga Varenka tonight?"

The Russian was distant in manner but precise in speech, his English being excellent and almost without accent. "I am informed that Madame Varenka left the Hotel Crillon about fifteen minutes ago with Nikolai Gribov."

"Oh, it's been on the radio?" Holden couldn't help being surprised at the precise information they had been offered.

The Russian gave him a blank stare but didn't say anything. Saffron explained hastily, "Mikhailov has his own sources of information." He continued, turning to the diplomat, "Gonna get her back, Mikhailov?"

The gloomy look on the tall man's face deepened. "That depends entirely on Madame Varenka. Unlike some other countries," and he broke into a thin smile, "we do not abuse the hospitality of the French people."

Saffron wasn't in the least abashed. "Sure, but when there's a defection like this..."

"A kidnapping," Mikhailov amended.

"...a defection," Saffron repeated, going on, "you Russians always insist in having an interview with the defector, don't you?"

Mikhailov nodded. "That has not been possible so far with Madame Varenka, for reasons which you in the CIA are aware."

"So you're going to get to her tonight?"

Again the Russian nodded. "If she will speak to me, I shall ask her if she is satisfied to leave the Soviet Union, considering that she has a very large family in Leningrad."

"And if she says no?" Saffron suggested.

"I do not believe she will refuse," Mikhailov responded,

not raising his voice. "After all, as you of all people must know, she was abducted and forced into hiding by the criminal Gribov." Here his voice rose. "And now he believes he is safe in showing her off. But he is not safe, and I tell you that you Americans have wasted your time and your effort on him and on her."

Saffron warned, "You won't get away with any rough stuff." He motioned about him. "Practically half the Paris police force is out here tonight."

Just then there was a burst of Russian from a walkie-talkie Mikhailov had secreted somewhere on his person. He broke in with a few words in Russian, evidently an acknowledgment. After that, he said to the two Americans, "You must excuse me," and walked slowly across the marble terrace toward the police checkpoint on the Place du Trocadero.

"Guess he means business," Saffron said.

Holden's interest in what was happening to Fay was diverted for the moment. "Can he take Varenka out of here, really?" Considering the strength of the French police and the Paris crowds, it didn't seem likely at that particular time.

"Lev Mikhailov is a powerful guy," Saffron replied. "He may be listed as a low-level secretary at the Soviet embassy, but our people say he's a colonel in the KGB, probably equivalent in rank to our CIA station chief."

"He seems pretty confident of getting Varenka back."

"Mikhailov was just baiting me, trying to find out if we're throwing a special guard around her and Gribov."

"And are we?"

"Not so far as I know." Saffron laughed and made a few penciled notes on a wad of copy paper. "Even if we tried, the French wouldn't let us do it." He put copy paper and pencil back in his pocket. "No, I'd say Mikhailov is just going to try standard Soviet practice if he can get to Varenka, which is intimidation. Did you notice he referred to her large family in Leningrad?"

"That's the threat? Harm to the family?"

"Oh, they never say so, but the defector always knows exactly what they mean and some do weaken. Maybe the Russians already have gotten to Varenka's relatives. Who knows?

Anyway" —and he fairly radiated self-satisfaction— "I think we've got a story tonight."

Holden reacted with curiosity. "Mikhailov seemed to think you are with the CIA. Are you?"

"No. But then, the Russians think all American reporters abroad are working for the CIA, and there's nothing I can do about that." The crowd cheered just then, and there was a noticeable shifting of police lines around the checkpoint. "Hey, what's going on?" The reporter set out at a brisk jog with Holden following him.

A chauffeur-driven Mercedes was inching to the curb as the two Americans arrived at the police checkpoint. Ahead of them they saw Mikhailov towering over the police. Television people with their minicams and portable lighting equipment already were beside the Mercedes, ready for action. The rear door opened. Nikolai Gribov, in evening dress, handed a frightened-looking Olga Varenka to the sidewalk, and the crowd greeted them with applause and cheers.

For a few minutes, the newcomers couldn't move. The TV crews hemmed them in, big lights flashing and minicams grinding away while eager reporters shouted questions at them in a half-dozen languages. It was a scene of utter confusion. Although Gribov seemed to enjoy every moment, there was little doubt that Olga was on the verge of panic. She was exquisitely gowned in a draped gold cloth that slanted from one shoulder and fell in folds about her slender figure. But instead of smiling for the cameras, she hid her face in her hands and Gribov had to coax her to look up. Twice, as he seemed to urge her gently toward the checkpoint, she turned and tried to reenter the Mercedes.

As she passed through the checkpoint, with the police at formal salute and French diplomatic officials bowing, she was still disturbed. Peering past Mikhailov, Holden could see the lines of weariness on her thin, oval face, and he thought he detected tears in her large, dark eyes. He was so disturbed by her obvious distress that he didn't realize at first that Saffron was pulling at his arm. Then he heard Saffron: "Out of the way, Mac. Mikhailov's gotten to Varenka and we better find out what's goin' on."

Holden stepped to one side and let the reporter by into the

confusing mélange of police, diplomats, reporters and television people just inside the checkpoint. The lights flashed on and off, the police shouted directions and the reporters pushed to get into the center of the action.

It was evident that Mikhailov had lost no time in confronting Varenka. In the center of the crowd, she was pinned between Gribov on one side and Mikhailov on the other, and both were shouting at her. She screamed in sheer panic, burrowed into the crowd and emerged on the edge of the terrace of the Palais de Chaillot. Almost at once, the French police formed a protective cordon about her.

Gribov protested. As Mikhailov approached, the two men suddenly fell into a shoving match. But when the television people came running with lights and cameras, they broke off by unspoken mutual agreement. Neither wanted to be projected before the public in such rude circumstances. And yet, there was no doubt among any of the witnesses that Gribov was almost as unnerved as his Russian mistress. Mikhailov alone seemed to have preserved his calm, and now he stood back as if to take stock of his position.

Saffron, with Holden after him, was among the first to get to Gribov and shouted, "What happened? What's Mikhailov trying to do?"

"It is nothing."

"But what did Mikhailov say to Olga?"

"He asks if she will go back to Leningrad, she says no." The singer patted his brow with a large silk handkerchief. "But he does not go away, he asks again, he threatens her family . . ." He broke off, then cried out. "It is terrible what they do to my Olga."

He forced himself through the police cordon and persuaded the dancer to continue toward the ballroom. With a circle of police about them, they proceeded slowly across the terrace toward the staircase. Directly behind them, Mikhailov continued to try to reach Varenka, but couldn't get past the police lines.

Saffron came abreast of the tall Russian at one point and called out, "She won't go with you, Mikhailov!"

Mikhailov didn't change expression. "Not yet. But I have

time." And in this manner the procession reached the head of the staircase.

Now the police formed a phalanx to wall off the unruly group that had followed Gribov and Varenka, permitting the two Russians to descend the red-carpeted stairs between the double line of the Garde Republicaine without interference.

Next, Mikhailov was let through by himself and hurried along behind them. And finally, the horde of reporters, still cameramen and television people pounded down the staircase, with Saffron and Holden caught somewhere in the middle. The soldiers of the Garde moved not a muscle.

While the news detachment was channeled into the ballroom behind the roped-off enclosure facing the receiving line, Gribov and Mikhailov were in another confrontation over Olga at the foot of the staircase. But once again, the police rescued the singer and his mistress. In the receiving line, a glittering Catherine Vaillant stood beside her American general and betrayed not the slightest interest in the proceedings. Yet, as she watched the excited group of reporters and the police shifting about just outside the ballroom entrance, she must have known that Gribov and Olga had arrived.

As the television lights flooded the receiving line, a murmur swept across the ballroom. Even in that sophisticated diplomatic atmosphere, there was a noticeable surge forward. The orchestra faltered. The dancers thinned out. Presently, the music stopped altogether. The murmur of the crowd by that time had increased to a steady undertone, and people had begun to envelop the receiving line in anticipation.

At the head, facing the entrance through which people passed after descending the marble staircase, a protocol officer in evening dress introduced each new arrival. Representing the host of the evening, the United Nations assistant secretary general, an Arab in a flowing white robe and *kaffiyeh* held in place by a gold cord, gave the first greeting—a handshake and a few words of welcome. Then, going down the line, the newcomer received the same gracious attention from each of the dignitaries and their ladies.

The receiving line, however, did not trail off into a void. For at the end, Lev Mikhailov had stationed himself with the appearance of a protective guard, his lanky figure slightly bent, his bald head inclined as if he were brooding over the ills of the world. It was apparent that he would not permit his quarry to pass him without another challenge.

All evening long, the United Nations delegates and their guests had been filing along the receiving line. In normal conditions, little attention would have been paid to what inevitably was regarded as a necessary but not very inspiring procedure. But now, with bright lights on and cameras set, the receiving line was the center of attention.

The protocol officer announced with a flourish, "M'sieu' Nikolai Gribov and Madame Olga Varenka..."

Gribov bobbed in from the draped velvet entrance, his eyes vibrant, his ruddy face glistening with the delight of people who bask in public attention. Directly after him came Varenka, a glamourous figure in her gown of draped gold cloth, even though her lovely oval face was averted from the cameras to conceal her weariness. In a spontaneous gesture, the crowded ballroom exploded in applause. Gribov, who had been shaking hands with the Arab at the head of the receiving line, broke off and waved both arms as if he were a prizefighter. But Varenka, behind him, seemed to shiver just a little. And Mikhailov, at the end of the line, thrust his head forward, glowering at the couple moving toward him.

Holden felt himself being poked in the back. He heard Saffron: "Something's gonna pop right quick. Lemme get in front of you, Mac."

He gave way. "What's the trouble?"

"Varenka looks like she's about to raise hell with somebody."

"Why? Mikhailov?" He nodded toward the waiting Russian.

"Could be, but more likely it's gonna be Catherine Vaillant." Saffron's voice was hoarse. "Just *look* at Vaillant! Gorgeous! And wait till Gribov spots her!"

Still, Gribov seemed very much the star of the proceedings as he moved slowly down the line, shaking hands, smiling, exchanging a few words with anybody who spoke to him. It was something that he did with superb tact and judgment. He was a well-mannered man who thrived on public acclaim.

He remained his attractive, confident self as he reached out to shake the hand of General Ferrender, representing the military presence of the United States. Behind him, half concealed by his bulk, was Catherine Vaillant, but Gribov evidently did not at first notice her. However, Varenka did, and turned aside for a moment in apparent distaste. It was clear that she did not want to be pictured with Vaillant in this televised tableau.

Saffron said to Holden, "Charley Ferrender didn't bargain for this when he took on Vaillant for the evening. When the Americans put one of their big guns into something like this, there's always a reason, but this wasn't it."

Holden saw Vaillant suddenly leave the general's side and step directly in Gribov's path. "Hey, watch Catherine!"

Saffron grunted. "You'd better watch Varenka. She's not going to like this one bit."

Before Gribov had a chance to take evasive action, Catherine had thrown her arms around him and kissed him with a lavish public display of affection. The big Russian singer was taken completely by surprise. He seemed rooted in his tracks, not knowing what to do about the beautiful woman in black who had draped herself around him. Nor was General Ferrender any more alert to what was going on. If it had been his responsibility to make sure that Catherine Vaillant would not be able to disrupt the dramatic surfacing of Olga Varenka, he had failed. As for the Russian KGB man, Mikhailov, he watched the proceedings for just a moment with a fleeting smile, then turned to an assistant and barked commands in Russian.

Holden was close enough now to Gribov and Vaillant to overhead what passed between them. The Frenchwoman, self-possessed and radiant, still encircled the Russian's big head with her arms and, just for good measure, kissed him again. The effect on Varenka, directly behind him, was as violent as an electric shock. She exploded with a burst of outraged Russian expletives, then turned quickly aside to be out of range of the television lights and cameras.

Vaillant retained her viselike hold on Gribov as if she had not noticed her rival. "How wonderful to see you again, Nikolai!" she exclaimed in English. To Holden, it seemed that the choice of language was calculated to impress a potential television audience, not Gribov. And that must have been the singer's understanding, too, for as soon as he could pull himself together and understand what was happening to him, he tried politely to disengage himself and apparently rebuked Vaillant sharply in Russian.

Her face didn't change expression. Nor did she step away from Gribov and resume her place in the receiving line as a proper hostess should have done. General Ferrender, meanwhile, was standing by himself, looking like a lost soul; and the Arab at the head of the receiving line was trying to wave off the television cameramen and the reporters. But the assembled press wasn't to be denied. This was the kind of juicy stuff that the great American public, and the world at large as well, would want to see.

Just outside the range of the cameras, another scene was developing now. Under Mikhailov's direction, a number of stocky Russian operatives in evening dress were converging around Olga Varenka from various parts of the ballroom. "Look at 'em, KGB, every one of 'em," Saffron commented. "And Varenka doesn't know what's happening to her."

All at once, Mikhailov clapped his hands sharply, and barked an order. The group surrounding Varenka began moving in a stolid mass toward an alcove near the orchestra where officials of the Soviet embassy and their wives had gathered. The dancer was so hemmed in that she could not have separated herself from the encircling group even if she had been larger and stronger. She cried out to Gribov in Russian, but he couldn't hear her above the beat of the music and the hubbub in the ballroom. Vaillant had so completely distracted him with her surprise maneuver that he still was tied up in the receiving line. By the time he and the television people realized what was happening to Varenka, the Russian phalanx had succeeded in moving her across the ballroom and smuggling her out a side entrance.

Now it was not Gribov but General Ferrender who approached the victorious Mikhailov. The KGB man had taken up a post near the remaining group of Soviet diplomats and was watching the proceedings with a brooding half-smile. "What have you done with Olga Varenka?" the general demanded. "I've never seen anything like this before. It's absolutely outrageous!"

Mikhailov didn't reply at first, but faced the American with a melancholy smile. "My dear general, we are in France, not

America. You have no right to ask me for explanations about anything at all, and certainly not about the conduct of a citizen of the Soviet Union."

"Come off it, Mikhailov." The American stood his ground. "You just pulled off a kidnapping right here in the middle of the Palais de Chaillot, and that's a crime in France, just as it is in any other civilized country in the world."

"My, my." Mikhailov permitted himself a thin smile. "Did it not occur to you, General, that Miss Varenka had asked for the protection of the Soviet Union against her American captors and that we did not hesitate to give it to her?"

Ferrender was almost apoplectic. "What have you done with her, Mikhailov?"

The bald-headed Russian explained with the indulgence of an adult humoring a spoiled child, "Miss Varenka has asked to be returned to the Soviet Union at once so that she could rejoin the Kirov Ballet and we are going to oblige her."

Abruptly, Mikhailov turned away and left Ferrender fuming at the side of the ballroom floor. The television lights flickered off. The sound people moved their equipment. The minicam operators bustled across the dance floor for pictures of the remaining group of Russians in their alcove, but now Mikhailov turned them away. In response to repeated demands in French and English for Varenka's whereabouts, he merely waved one hand toward the outside of the building. "She is gone, she is gone," he kept repeating. And finally, everybody had to believe him.

With Saffron leading them, the news people now descended on the luckless Gribov, who stood dejectedly near the opposite edge of the dance floor. "What happened, Gribov?" the reporter demanded as soon as he had reached the singer.

Gribov shook his head. "It is terrible . . . terrible."

"Did Olga tell you that she wanted to return to the Soviet Union?"

"No!" For the first time, Gribov showed some animation, but he still seemed confused.

"Do you know that Mikhailov says Olga asked for protection, and that she is being returned to the Kirov Ballet?" Saffron persisted.

"Mikhailov lies." Gribov waved his hands wildly. "The

270

KGB lies. All lies ... lies ..." In sudden outrage, he glanced around him.

"What's the matter, Gribov?" Saffron asked. "If you're looking for Varenka, she's gone. The Russians took her out that exit," and he pointed to the side door behind the alcove where the remainder of the Soviet delegation could still be seen.

"Varenka?" He brandished his fists. "No, I get Varenka back. I look for Catherine Vaillant ..."

"What do you want Vaillant for?" Saffron asked.

"What for? You see what she do?" Gribov's anger overcame him and he began shouting in his frustration over the course of events. "Catherine make my Olga jealous ... Catherine work with KGB ..."

Someone else in the crowd of reporters shouted at him in English, "Can you prove that, Gribov?"

"Proof! Proof!" Gribov yelled, waving his arms. "You see what Catherine did? You need proof?"

Saffron glanced around. "Maybe we'd better ask Catherine about it."

But, as Holden soon reported after a brief search, Catherine Vaillant had vanished. General Ferrender, somewhat discomfited, was standing alone in the receiving line. Now having recovered his professional detachment, he simply refused to answer questions. While the assembled press was thus engaged, Holden saw Bartley Crandell, the DCM, beckoning to him from one side of the ballroom. He quickly responded to the summons.

Crandell wanted a fill-in. He listened gravely to Holden's quick review of events—the apparently accidental placement of Catherine Vaillant in the receiving line, her surprise demonstration of affection for Gribov that so unsettled Olga Varenka and the daring manner in which the KGB had spirited the dancer from the Palais de Chaillot. "And now, Vaillant too is gone," Holden concluded.

Crandell gritted his teeth, then shook his head. "We had a tip that the Russians were going to pull something off tonight, and we were warned about Catherine Vaillant," he said in a subdued manner. "That's why we asked G-two to let us have General Ferrender and assigned Vaillant to him for the night as a translator. We thought she would betray herself." Here he made a gesture of sheer frustration. "But she just outfoxed Ferrender and all the rest of us. And so did Mikhailov."

"And now she's gone?" Holden asked.

"I guess so, but I'd rather you didn't say anything to the reporters about it," Crandell responded. "Last we heard, the agent who was supposed to watch her said she'd gone out with the KGB group that had Olga Varenka, and the whole gang got into a caravan of Soviet cars and headed for the Charles de Gaulle Airport."

"Then that's where I'd better go?" Holden suggested.

Crandell put a restraining hand on his sleeve. "You've been a first-rate contact, Holden, and we don't want to get you into trouble. You'd better keep your distance now. We've complained to the French Foreign Office that the Russians have taken Olga Varenka from our custody, and I expect the French police will try to stop them from flying her out of the country."

"And Vaillant?"

"I should think the French would want to talk to her, too. There's not a doubt in my mind that she is a double agent, but I expect the Russians would keep her in custody, too."

Just then, Saffron made his way across the dance floor. "Hey, you gotta drive Henri's car out to de Gaulle Airport," he called. "The Russians are headed that way with Varenka."

"Don't go," Crandell counseled. "You might get hurt."

"I can't let the guy down," Holden said. "He's depended on me."

"But there's somebody with us who wants very much to see you," Crandell reminded him. "She's over there with Mrs. Crandell."

Holden saw Fay Carroll standing beside an older woman, looking lovelier than ever. "She's marrying Bainbridge and going off to some godawful post where I'll never see her again," Holden told him. "What good will it do me just to go over there and try to be polite about it? I hate it!"

"But you don't hate her," Crandell objected. "And she's been trying to attract your attention. . . . She wants to talk to you."

Once again, Holden gave way to an unreasoning rush of anger. "If she wants Bainbridge, let her have him."

Crandell's manner became soothing as he tried to quiet him.

"You must know that Fay was left all alone at the Ritz when her mother went off to New York. And her stepfather's still there."

Saffron had reached them by this time and was wrenching at Holden's arm. "Hey, let's go. I gotta story to cover."

Crandell frowned at the reporter. "If you please, Mr. Saffron..."

Saffron wouldn't be denied. "On yer horse, Mac. You can talk to this guy anytime, but not when the Russkys are trying to get away with mayhem, assault and battery, kidnapping and almost every other crime in the book." Once more he tugged at Holden's arm.

"Wait!" the diplomat protested. "Don't you see Fay's waiting over there?" And he nodded toward the American diplomatic group.

Holden hesitated, then moved toward Saffron. "What about Bainbridge?" he asked.

"He's on his way to Katmandu now," Crandell said.

By that time, however, Saffron already had a firm grip on Holden's arm and was steering him across the dance floor. "Had to break it up, Mac. You got Henri's car keys, and we have to get moving."

At the edge of the dance floor, Holden managed to halt momentarily and look back at the American diplomatic group. There, he saw Fay still smiling at him. She beckoned to him but he didn't notice. He was trying to sort out what he had just heard from Crandell.

Had he been left to his own devices, Holden would have gone back to Fay for an explanation. But Saffron was pulling at his arm and cursing a blue streak. "C'mon, goddamit, you can't run out on me now, not when I gotta deadline and a big story breaking right over my ass..."

Reluctantly, Holden gave in to him. Together, they ran from the Palais de Chaillot to Henri's car. In the distance, they heard police sirens screaming. The pursuit of the fleeing Russians already had begun.

There are some of a younger generation who complain that the French have become a craven people who are interested only in their own comforts and the value of a franc. These

273

skeptical souls of a new generation accuse the French government, as well as its people, of proceeding with exquisite care for fear of offending the Russians. Or if not the Russians, the British. And if not the British and the Russians, then the Americans.

But those who know the French know such suppositions are untrue. In fighting for their own land, the French are ever courageous. In maintaining a sense of *savoir faire* in their dealings with each other, they are unexcelled. And finally, in their defense of suffering womanhood, they have the valor of lions.

Once the French police had been alerted to the bold Russian attempt to avert Olga Varenka's defection, they mobilized in frantic haste and set out in hot pursuit. At first the Russian cavalcade had an advantage in the race toward the airport. In spite of repeated warnings from French radio that the Aeroflot scheduled flight for Leningrad would be refused permission to leave Charles de Gaulle Airport, the fleeing Russians would not halt. The pursuers gained on them in the outlying sections of Paris through superior knowledge of the narrow roads. Once the Russian cars were within sight, warning shots were fired. Eventually, one car swerved to a side street and halted, while the rest swept on.

When Saffron and Holden arrived with the ragtag array of reporters, they found that Olga Varenka had been delivered to the French police unharmed. The four Russians who had been in the car with her were being interrogated by French officials through a long-winded interpreter in uniform.

The ever-aggressive Saffron charged into the Franco-Russian confrontation, trying to make sense out of what was going on. When he returned, he was grinning. To Holden, he called, "C'mon, get me to a phone, I gotta call the office."

"What happened?"

"Varenka's sorry she created such a fuss. Wants to get back to Nikolai Gribov right away."

"And Catherine Vaillant?"

Saffron chuckled. "Y'know, the French are going to let her get away. She's with the rest of the KGB in the other cars that went on."

"But why don't they grab her when they can?"

"Very simple. She'd just be an embarrassment, a double agent both they and the Americans should have caught a long time ago. And they'd as soon let the Russians have her, because she's just a big load of trouble wherever she goes." He half pushed, half shoved Holden into the driver's seat of Henri's car. "C'mon, Mac. Let's go, gotta make a deadline."

While Saffron was talking to his office from a pay telephone in a nearby village store, the French police motor column swept by with a great honking of horns and wailing of sirens. It was bound toward the center of Paris on its triumphal return trip. And in the lead car, Holden caught just a glimpse of Olga Varenka sitting in the front seat beside the driver. In the wan light of a street lamp, she seemed very pretty and quite content.

Chapter Nine

In the depths of her frugal French soul, Marie had known all along that this night would be a financial disaster for the house of Durand. Now, in the dreary post-midnight hours after the United Nations Ball, she noted with tortuous satisfaction that her fears had been realized.

Everything was costing a great deal more than Henri had expected. But then, she told herself with grim precision, she had warned him that this was the way it would be. Yet, as always, he had not listened to her. He wanted to be the generous host, to salute his friends upon their departure. Very well, then! Marie determined that he would have to face up to the consequences of his foolish hospitality.

At the festive table in the rear of the establishment, the Learys' farewell dinner was winding down. Professor Leary, Baron von Norden and even the youngster, Gareth, were each proposing toasts. Toasts, Marie reminded herself, in gratitude to Henri but drunk with Henri's liquor. As an additional calamity, she saw that the three regulars had left the piano bar without too much coaxing to participate in these costly honors. And where, by the way, was the pianist, Holden? The ungrateful American had been let off by Henri to bring back the Learys for their farewell dinner and hadn't so much as even telephoned to explain why he had not done so.

When the Learys had arrived by cab from the Palais de Chaillot with the Baron, this quixotic Henri, this addlepated husband of hers, had insisted on paying the driver to make up for Holden's failure to do as he was told. She made a mental note that the pianist was, in consequence, to be docked for the night since he had performed no work either at the piano or elsewhere. These Americans! So utterly irresponsible!

To dissuade Henri from another such venture, Marie set down in her handwriting the cost of the free dinners, the free wine, free cordials and free coffee with dismal certitude.

Of the employees in their establishment, Marie was somewhat more resentful of the photographer, Stephanie, than any of the others—with the possible exception of Holden. For there was Stephanie, dining with Gareth Leary and his parents at the festive table—a free dinner for an employee!

It had annoyed Marie that Henri would not discuss his private party with her that evening. This affair, he had insisted, was his way of showing appreciation for friends who had been good and valued customers of their establishment. And he would not give in to Marie's argument that true friends would not accept such costly expressions of gratitude, but would be glad instead to pay for themselves on their last night in Paris.

In addition to playing host, he had been fussing for some time now, with his short-wave receiver, trying to pick up special news announcements. Already, he had heard the BBC bulletins that night which reported Gribov's presence with Olga Varenka at the United Nations Ball, their quarrel and Varenka's sudden departure from the Palais de Chaillot with a Russian escort.

Annoyed by the piteous noises of the short wave, Marie asked her husband, "Must you do that?"

He kept fiddling with the dials. "I am waiting for more news," he said as the receiver emitted ever louder squawks of inner torment.

"These noises are giving me a headache," Marie protested.

Henri eyed her calmly. "You do not understand, my dear. It is important that we should know what the Russians intend to do with Varenka, now that they have her back."

Marie flared back, "Whatever they do or not do, will that add one sou to our income, my Henri? Will it decrease our taxes by one franc? I appeal to you to tell me how this matter will affect us in even a small way."

Henri was unmoved, twirling the knobs of his receiver to produce more strange noises. "Foreign affairs such as this do not immediately affect us, my dear," he admitted.

He raised a cautionary finger. The receiver had stopped

squealing, and settled down to a sober if lamentably unemotional English of a routine BBC reader:

"We interrupt our regular transmission to take you to Paris for a special announcement."

Dead air, a few squeals from the receiver, and another flat, unemotional English voice cut in:

"We are informed that Madame Olga Varenka, the defecting Russian ballet dancer who earlier tonight decided to return to her homeland, has again changed her mind and will accept a French offer of political asylum. Mme. Varenka's latest reversal averted what might have been an ugly clash between her Russian escort and French police outside the Charles de Gaulle Airport. We return you now to our regularly scheduled program."

When Henri had translated this intelligence into French for Marie, she commented without rancor, "This lady may change her mind once again, my Henri." Then after due consideration, she added, "I am reminded that Nikolai Gribov telephoned not long ago while you were at the table with the *famille* Leary and asked if Madame Vaillant were here or if we expected her. When I assured him that I had no knowledge whatever of Madame Vaillant, he seemed greatly relieved and asked us to provide a special table for two with champagne and flowers in an hour's time." She consulted her wristwatch. "It means that he will be here shortly with Madame Varenka. I ask you, my Henri, are these Russians also to be the guests of honor with free champagne, free flowers and no doubt free dinners?"

Henri, trying to restore himself in his wife's eyes as a practical man, said in a businesslike way, "You will note down, please, the cost of M'sieu' Gribov's various requests for food and services tonight, and I shall see that the reckoning is put on his table before he departs."

Watching her husband leave the radio to direct waiters in organizing the Russian's table, Marie murmured to herself, "Ah, my Henri, even the street urchins would take advantage of your generosity if your wife did not protect you."

She noted down the cost of champagne and flowers for the Gribov table, and thoughtfully added a cover charge. In some ways, perhaps, the evening had not become quite the disaster that she had expected. A small recovery such as this was not to be disregarded.

Between Henri's preoccupation with the Gribov table and Marie's usual concentration at the cash register, Holden's tardy appearance at the piano shortly afterward attracted little attention except among the regulars. The hour was late, and they had been on the point of drinking up, but his appearance caused them to delay their departure. Holden seemed unkempt, his clothes were rumpled and he hit a clinker on the piano as he began playing, all symptoms of his inner disturbance.

The regulars were on him at once, considering him fair game. "How many times you make love tonight, Arch?" Marcel Valleau demanded, leering at him over the glossy piano bar.

Holden pretended he hadn't heard. He settled back, and slipped into hs easiest and most familiar routine, some old Gershwin standards, dexterously brought up to date with modern arrangements. Henri and Marie glanced at him momentarily when they heard the piano, and independently decided that they had more important matters to worry about than their wandering pianist.

Amused by Holden's glum silence, Enzo Pastore observed to his colleagues, "Arch is not talking. Maybe he did not get laid."

"But he wants to," Karl Eilers proclaimed solemnly. Seeing a dull flush of mingled impatience and anger spreading from Holden's forehead around his ears and to the back of his neck, the German chortled, "Look! Look! It is like he is in heat, that one."

Holden would not let himself be provoked. He began banging out his Gershwin tunes, a sacrilege even among saloon pianists.

Now the Frenchman took charge of the hazing. Pretending to take Holden's part, he advised his colleagues with mock seriousness, "Let us be more considerate, my friends. Let us remember that Arch is in love." He indicated the pianist with a wave of his hand. *"Regardez, mes amis!* A young man in love, but a young man without a girl!" He smiled sadly. "It is a pity, a regrettable spectacle."

The Italian seemed to ponder these observations, then looked up with a judicious air and raised a question. "But these young Americans," and he transfixed Holden with a reflective look, "they do not know the difference between making love and getting laid. Is it not so?"

Holden still refused to let himself be drawn into the discussion, and continued working away at the Gershwin standards. Eilers took a crack at him. "Who you love, Arch? This Catherine?"

"It is not Catherine," the Italian protested. "Catherine is too old for him, knows too much." He held out both hands in the manner of someone who had made a remarkable discovery. "No, he loves the pretty little American, Fay Carroll." He prodded Holden. "Is it not so, Arch? You want Fay Carroll?"

Holden was grimly silent as he pursued his routine on the piano. Eilers shook his head. "But here we see no Catherine, no Fay. So no love for the poor man. A pity!" Then the German slapped the surface of the piano bar for emphasis. "We must see that our friend should be laid." He pretended to glance around. "I tell you what, Arch," and he lowered his voice confidentially, "tomorrow I will bring you someone *extraordinaire*. You wait."

Holden could stand it no longer. "Lay off, you guys," he growled, not missing a beat.

The Italian, more sensitive than the others, was remorseful at once. "We mean nothing, Arch. We just have a little fun."

"It's not very funny," Holden retorted.

Now Valleau became a little more sympathetic. "What happened, Arch? Has the little American deserted you?"

Eilers prompted, "You have not heard? The little American marries her former husband, Spencer Bainbridge, and goes tomorrow to the end of the earth, Nepal in the Himalayas!"

There was an interruption. "Ah, you guys are nuts. Lay off the kid, willya?" It was Saffron, the reporter, who had come up unnoticed behind them and now was climbing on a bar stool. Holden, too, had been unaware of his entrance, for the regulars were sitting at the piano bar in such a way as to screen off who passed in and out the big front door of Henri's.

Saffron called to a waiter, "Let's have a beer, Louie, and make it fast, I'm thirsty." And he continued to Holden, who

280

now had shifted to something contemporary in a slower beat and lighter tone, "Mac, you shoulda come to the airport with us. Lots o' doin's."

The regulars, to a man, fell silent. Above the *pianissimo* mood of his music, Holden said, "Wouldn't mean a thing to me."

"Yeah?" Saffron hunched over the bar with a crooked smile. "For openers, just before the big Russian Aeroflot plane took off for Leningrad, Mikhailov rushed Catherine Vaillant aboard and the French didn't even try to stop him."

"Poor Arch," Valleau commented. "He liked Vaillant, no?"

"She lay him with style, I betcha," the Italian chimed in.

It took every bit of Holden's self-restraint to ignore their comments and continue his modern mood piece on the piano. In a somewhat strained voice, he asked Saffron, "Are you sure it was Vaillant?"

"Saw Bart Crandell, the DCM at the American embassy, and he also identified her. Want any more proof?"

"Then," Holden concluded gloomily, "she had us all fooled; she was a double agent all along."

Saffron expertly lifted a beer from a passing tray and held it up in anticipation. "Sure, but you won't get the French and Americans to admit it officially. I'd suspect they're glad the Russians pulled her off the job." He lifted the beer glass and made a slight gesture, "Well, cheers," and drank a deep draught.

Henri, sensing the suppressed excitement at the bar, had stopped just behind Holden. The *patron* was interested in the evening's events. He said to Saffron, "The BBC has announced that Varenka did not leave with the Russians . . ."

"Yeah, I know," Saffron interrupted.

". . . and Nikolai Gribov has telephoned me," the *patron* continued suavely, "to say that he is bringing Varenka here to celebrate." He indicated the prominently placed table that had been set for two and decked with flowers. "We are prepared," he said.

"You got a good publicity sense, Henri," Saffron commented somewhat grudgingly. "The office sent me back here for the story as soon as the embassy tipped us to what was going on."

"I will have Stephanie take pictures," Henri offered.

Saffron finished his beer and called for another. "Don't bother Stephanie. We got a photographer coming. And you're going to have so many French newsmen and foreign correspondents in this joint in a few minutes that you won't even have room for these guys," and he indicated the regulars.

Eilers knocked on the bar as a signal to his colleagues. "Reporters, pah!" He motioned to Valleau and Pastore as he slid off his bar stool. "We go!"

While the regulars were settling up with Marie at the cash register, Henri hurried to the front door to warn Shukri, the doorman, of the forthcoming invasion. Then, the *patron* made sure that everybody in the kitchen was alerted.

While this was going on, Holden continued his aimless improvising at the piano; and Saffron, alone now at the piano bar, nursed his fresh beer with both hands encircling the glass. Holden, trying hard to suppress his emotions, desperately wanted to ask the reporter if he had seen Fay Carroll; but the most he would trust himself to do was to ask, "Were many people at the airport with all that going on?"

"Yeah."

"See anybody else you knew?"

"Just Bart Crandell, as I said." Saffron darted a keen glance at the pianist. "Couldn't figure out what he was doing there until I saw an embassy car picking him up, American flags on the front fenders, motorcycle escort—all that kind of thing. And there were a couple of guys in the back." He had caught Holden's attention. He continued: "First thing I knew, the car was waved out on the field, picked up speed and made it to a part of the airport way downwind where a PIA liner was just scheduled to take off."

"PIA?" Holden asked, still maintaining a semblance of background music.

"Pakistan International Airlines," Saffron explained. "Well, the embassy car got there just as the cabin attendants were swinging the door shut and the people on the field were rolling the stairway to one side. Next thing I knew, the pilot was racing the engines. The plane would have moved off, but I guess there must have been radio instructions from the tower, or something. All of a sudden the pilot cut the engines, the airport people put the stairway back in position and the cabin attendants reopened the door. And, do you know? A guy got out of the American embassy car with a coupla bags and made it into the plane. Right after that the pilot took off for good."

"Why are you telling me this?" Holden asked.

"Thought you'd be interested," Saffron said, taking a pull at his beer glass. "I know I was."

"Why?"

"I knew French Customs would stop the embassy car for a routine check as it came off the field, just to be sure no contraband came off the plane, so I was right there with the customs people when the car came through," Saffron said. "Bart Crandell didn't want to talk to me; and the other guy, McKelvey, who's pretty high up in the CIA, never talks to reporters. But," and he laughed, "while they were assuring the Customs people that everything was okay, I asked the French driver about the passenger who got aboard the PIA plane. Can you guess?"

Holden grumbled, "Quit playing games, Saffron."

"Oh well, it was Spence Bainbridge." With a gesture of elaborate unconcern, Saffron drained his beer glass.

"All by himself?" Holden's voice was faint, his heart was pounding in his ears and his hands had slipped from the keyboard. There was a faint spark of hope within him that something might have happened to delay Fay's marriage to Bainbridge and her eventual departure with him.

Saffron nodded and repeated solemnly, "All by himself."

"But why PIA?" Holden asked, afraid to bring the conversation around to Fay Carroll. "Thought he was going to Katmandu in Nepal."

"I asked about that," the reporter replied, with the appearance of giving routine information. "PIA stops at Karachi, and Bainbridge would be getting a plane there for Katmandu."

Holden tried to work at the keyboard, but his heart wasn't in it. Once again, his hands dropped to his lap. "What d'ya suppose happened? I understood Bainbridge was to marry Fay tomorrow, and then they were taking off for Nepal."

"Yeah, that was what I heard, too," Saffron said crisply, "but the signals got switched. Soon as I got to the office, I asked if there was any wire copy about Bainbridge or the Carrolls, and the wire editor gave me this . . ." Without comment, the reporter handed Holden a blurred and half-crumpled carbon of an Associated Press dispatch:

MINEOLA, N. Y. (AP) - THE NASSAU COUNTY GRAND JURY TODAY INDIC TED WACO TEXAS CARROLL, TEXAS OIL MILLIONAIRE, ON CHARGES OF MISAPPROPRIATING FUNDS OF SEVERAL ESTATES OF WHICH HE IS EXECUTOR.

Holden scanned the copy, mystified, and handed it back. "What's it all about?"

"That's what I asked Bart Crandell when I called him at home," the reporter said. "At first he didn't want to talk. Then he talked for background, that is, so he wouldn't be identified. . . ." He took another pull at his beer glass, wiping his mouth with the back of one hand.

"Come on, Saffron," Holden flared in impatience. "Let's have it, willya?"

But Saffron appeared to be enjoying himself by letting his information out in driblets. "Seems that Fay's mother got so alarmed when she found out Carroll was dipping into Fay's estate that she gave their lawyers permission to investigate and act. And this," he held up the AP story, "is the first result."

"I knew Mrs. Carroll had gone to the states . . ." Holden began.

Saffron interrupted. "No mystery there. Crandell told me all about it."

"You must have hit him when he was in a good mood," Holden said. "He didn't do much for me."

"That's the difference between a piano player and a reporter," Saffron quipped. Then he went on, "Y'see, from what Crandell tells me and what I can piece together, this Carroll dipped into Fay's mother's estate but got the old lady so scared she wouldn't peep. She began squawking only when she suspected he was taking from Fay too, and that's when the lawyers for the Deak estate—Fay's father—got busy with their investigation. And you'll notice Fay's mother took off just before this indictment was returned."

"Where's Mrs. Carroll now, d'ya know?" Holden asked.

"Sure, she's put herself where Carroll can't get to her. Out in the Menninger Clinic in Topeka, Kansas."

Now Holden began to understand why Fay had appeared alone that night at the United Nations Ball, and why she had remained with the members of the United States Mission for so much of the evening without once going on the dance floor. In his disgust over his own blindness, he came down heavily on the keyboard in a crashing dissonance that startled everybody in the house and particularly Saffron. "Hey, guy, what in hell's the matter with you?" the reporter demanded.

"I've been such a damn fool," Holden said, almost as if he were talking to himself. "I saw Fay at the dance tonight, making motions as if she wanted to talk to me and I'm so stupid I never even went near her."

Alarmed by the alternate silence and unpleasant noise on the keyboard, Henri came hurrying over to the piano. "Is anything wrong?" he asked Holden.

"No, I'm okay."

"Are you sure? Your music is not—shall we say—very even tonight." The *patron* glanced suspiciously from Saffron to Holden, as if to accuse the reporter of having upset his pianist with some untoward remark.

Saffron was quick to come forward with an explanation. "You know how it is with these musicians, Henri. All temperament! We'll get him back on his regular routine in a coupla minutes, never mind."

Henri was dubious. "Ah yes, temperamental musicians," he repeated, gave Holden a peculiar look.

Holden pulled himself together and tried to concentrate on his nightly routine, but with little success. His mind fairly reeled with questions that he wanted to put to Saffron, and the reporter well understood that. "Take it easy, Mac," he muttered. "You'll find out all about it before long."

"Fay didn't marry Bainbridge before he took off for Nepal, did she?" Holden demanded.

"Hell, no." Saffron leaned across the piano bar and lowered his voice. "You keep this to yourself, Mac, and don't you say who told you, but I know for a fact that the ambassador ordered Bainbridge put on the first plane out of Paris tonight that would get him anywhere near his new assignment. Because once the embassy here knew Carroll was indicted in this financial hanky-panky, a lot of people figured Bainbridge would be dragged into the case sooner or later. And the ambassador didn't want him in Paris when it happened. Way out there in the Himalayas," and Saffron indicated how far off he thought it was with a sweeping gesture of one arm, "maybe the investigators will forget about the guy."

In his embarrassment over his own lack of understanding of Fay's position, Holden was reduced to running through basic chords—not a very brilliant example of the saloon pianist's art. And once again Henri came to him, this time with a sharp rebuke. "What is this with you?" the *patron* demanded. "I pay you to play music. You call this music?"

"Sorry," and Holden swung into some ancient favorites of his employer's, beginning with "Valentina."

To which Saffron appended a comment, "Henri thinks modern music ended with '*La Vie en Rose.*' Give it to him next."

"Good idea," Holden responded, and followed the reporter's suggestion. It gave them both a little more time to go over what had happened to Fay, Bainbridge and the Carrolls. One thing finally became clear to Holden: the pressure on Fay had been removed. And at last, she could do whatever she wished.

"As soon as I get done tonight," Holden said to Saffron, "I'll take a cab to the Ritz and get Fay out of bed."

Saffron shook his head and studied the pianist with a crooked smile. "Bad timing, Mac. She's not there."

"Then where is she?" Holden's voice rose sharply. He skipped a few bars of *"La Vie en Rose,"* to Henri's obvious displeasure.

"Bart Crandell took her home with him," Saffron said coolly. "She'll be staying with him and Mrs. Crandell until things clear up a little. Bart says she's going right on with her studies at the Conservatory, no matter what happens."

Holden sobered. "Well, I s'pose I can't barge in on the DCM at three or four A.M., can I?"

"Not very well." Saffron tried to be encouraging. "Hey, Mac, slow down. Your girl's still where you can get at her, she's not taken off for the moon. Whatever the two of you want to say to each other," here his grin widened, "it'll sound just as good tomorrow or the next day as it does tonight."

"But damn it all, Saffron, you don't understand," Holden objected. "I just haven't handled this very well."

"Cheer up, Mac," Saffron consoled. "None of us have, including the whole goddamn American embassy."

There was an uproar just then outside Henri's and the door to the establishment was suddenly flung open. From the piano bar, Holden and Saffron could see the giant Shukri, in his fancy doorman's uniform, trying to keep out an unseemly mob of shouting, gesticulating men and women. Some of the combatants carried tall stands with battery-powered bright lights; others had television minicams, motion picture cameras and all manner of still cameras. Everybody seemed to be yelling, most of them in different languages, so the end result was chaos.

Without warning, the pressure on Shukri became intolerable. Although he made the greatest effort to stand his ground, the unruly crowd finally shoved him aside as if he had been a mere bit of flotsam and came pounding into Henri's. The *patron* and his wife both gesticulated in alarm, not knowing what to make of this intrusion, until Saffron bolted from the piano bar and reached their side.

The reporter held up both arms and shouted, *"Attendez, attendez...."*

The men and women in the front of the invasion halted abruptly, having recognized him. They turned and began calling to the people behind them to stop shoving. Saffron followed up his advantage by shouting once again, "Lots of room in here, folks. All of you are going to get in, so quit pushing." Those in front, realizing the problem, repeated what he had said in a babel of tongues. On sudden inspiration, Holden decided it might help if he played something to help restore order to the proceedings. He swung into a martial air of World War I vintage, "Madelon." To everybody's astonishment, then gratification, the invaders quieted, formed in orderly lines like schoolchildren and obediently filed into Henri's establishment.

Then, as if in predetermined accord, they parted ranks and permitted Nikolai Gribov to enter in his best operatic manner, leading a much subdued Olga Varenka by the hand. Although Gribov's evening clothes were in disarray and his opera cloak hung rakishly from one shoulder—mementos of his encounter with the mob—he still looked very much the leading baritone

287

of his time. As for Varenka, she was more imposing than ever in her off-the-shoulder gold brocade.

As if on cue, the Learys and their guests arose as they saw Gribov and Olga, and began applauding. Henri and Marie followed. And then, quite remarkably, the throng that had filled the establishment joined with verve and spirit. Holden tapered off his march music and let the piano fade out. And Saffron, acting as self-appointed spokesman for the invaders, explained briefly for Gribov's benefit, "You see before you my colleagues of the international press and also some of our allies of the Parisian press, Nikolai. We mean no harm, and" —this to Henri and his wife— "we will do no harm here if we can only perform our duty."

Gribov flung out both arms, with the palms of his hands thrust upward, and tilted his chin. "Ah, your duty..." He smiled broadly. "You wish more pictures, yes?"

From the rear came a loud voice with a distinct Cockney accent, "Yes, and if the bloody cameras will get out the way, we wish to have an interview with Miss Varenka."

At the mention of her name, the ballerina glanced inquiringly at Gribov, who explained the situation. She nodded, but without much enthusiasm. "Is good, Olga Varenka gives interview," Gribov announced, turning to her with a flourish. "I translate for you."

That seemed to clear the air. The embattled press corps, as with one accord, perched on tables or seated themselves on the floor, while the people with minicams and motion picture and still cameras prepared to photograph the occasion. The floodlights, all strategically placed, tinged the scene with garish unreality.

Between the mob of press people, both electronic and print, and the enormous interest in Gribov and his Olga, all other activity in Henri's halted by common consent. Even the waiters disposed themselves at the edges of the group to view the proceedings. Such notoriety had not come to Henri's since that dim and yet glorious time when the German invaders in 1944 had rushed pell-mell from the bar and the Americans, with a few favored French in the vanguard, had come charging in just in time to finish the abandoned drinks. To Henri, one of the symbolic French combat veterans that day, it was to be remembered thenceforth as a time of alcoholic liberation. And he himself had served the first free drinks to the victors.

With a sweeping gesture, Saffron invited Gribov to stand before the cameras and suggested, "To begin with, Nikolai, let us ask Miss Varenka to tell us what happened to her tonight." The singer and ballerina talked together quietly in Russian, both seeming very grave; then, with a fine show of spirit, she began explaining her situation to him with vigorous motions of hands and arms. To all this, he nodded in apparent sympathy; but then, when he began tugging at her arm to try to bring her before the cameras, she resolutely refused. Instead, she beckoned to him to appear for her.

Assuming the lustrous pose of a Don Giovanni separating himself from his Donna Anna, Gribov gracefully faced the cameras, his shoulders squared, his head thrown back. It was as if he were waiting for an orchestra to play the introductory bars of his sweetest aria. Instead, he told in broken English, made eloquent with many an operatic gesture, of his pursuit of his Olga that night, of the assistance of the valiant French police and of the reluctance with which the Russians freed her.

The Cockney voice challenged from the rear, "But didn't Miss Varenka really want to return to Russia, Mr. Gribov?"

The singer's eyes flashed with anger. "Is not true," he shouted. "They kidnap my Olga, thees Bolsheviki. *Then,*" and he emphasized the word heavily, "they say she wishes to return." He loosed a passionate stream of Russian to explain to the ballerina what was happening; and she nodded, apparently in agreement with what he was saying.

Thus reinforced, he taunted his questioner. "You see? Olga tell me I am correct." He seemed defiant as he invited more questions. "You want more? You think I lie?"

Saffron tried to quiet him. "Nobody thinks you're lying, Nikolai." There was a murmur of approval from the assembled press. "But," the reporter continued, "we just wanted a few more details from you because you were there when Miss Varenka was given her choice by the French police of staying with the Russians or returning to Paris with you."

Gribov raised one hand, palm upward, in silent appeal and let it fall to his side. "What else can I tell? I am happy my Olga stays here with me." He stressed that. "Very happy."

In the flat accents of Midwest America, a woman with thick eyeglasses in the front row asked, "But didn't we see you with a French lady recently—a translator at the American embassy?"

Gribov grew red-faced and confused. But before he could blurt out an answer, Pat Leary, who had been listening to the proceedings, broke into the discussion. "Ladies and gentlemen, I think it is unfair to ask Mr. Gribov to answer that question. I believe it proper to request an explanation from the American embassy of the activities of the translator, Mademoiselle Catherine Vaillant."

"And where is Mademoiselle Vaillant now?" the questioner persisted.

"Look around, she is not here." Gribov, enormously relieved, gestured all about him. He repeated the line Pat Leary had given him. "You ask American embassy, yes?"

There was a savage explosion of Russian from Varenka, still sitting at one side with a group of reporters around her. One of the reporters, a lean little Frenchman, burst out laughing and said something to a colleague in French. The second French reporter, who was old and balding, spoke English with difficulty.

"Madame Varenka say thees woman Vaillant is spy for Russians, has tricked Gribov, has gone," and he motioned eastward with one arm, "on Aeroflot plane." He indicated the lean little Frenchman beside him. "My colleague, Pierre Filer of *Liberation* newspaper, hears Varenka say thees in Russian and tells me."

Saffron turned to Gribov in high good humor. "Well, Nikolai, did Vaillant trick you as the lady says?"

Pat Leary grinned. "You answer at your peril, Nikolai."

Gribov seemed less than enthusiastic about making any response. Varenka, however, seemed to understand that he was being asked to clarify his relations with the Frenchwoman and directed a fluent stream of Russian at him. He shrugged, seemed abashed and turned to the assembled press with the air of a helpless child. "My Olga, she say to tell the truth," he began. Then he stopped, frowning. At length, he flapped his arms in a display of inner torment and replied, "Ah, what can I say? I was fool. But my Olga forgive me." He addressed Olga briefly in Russian, apparently telling her what he had just confessed, and was relieved when he saw her laughing and silently bringing her hands together in a gesture of applause.

At that, everybody laughed; the press conference broke up as if by common consent. Most of the reporters and photographers left, but a few of the more independent ones joined Saffron at the piano bar.

"How'd ya like it, Mac?" Saffron demanded, taking possession once again of his favorite bar stool.

Holden, who had been improvising softly in a minor key, nodded. "I think Gribov got out of that one very nicely."

"Yeah, Varenka seemed satisfied," the reporter agreed. He leaned across the piano bar. "How about you? Want me to call Bart Crandell to see what's going on?"

Holden shook his head. "I'm afraid to ask." He swung into an old Gershwin standard, "I'll Build a Stairway to Paradise," but seemed less than hopeful. It just wasn't his night, or so he thought.

Once Henri's had been restored to an appearance of normality, Gribov hugged Olga and called for champagne all around to celebrate their reunion. "You shall have my best champagne," the *patron* announced. Marie, at the cash register, nodded sage agreement. Six bottles of the best champagne at premium prices, billed to M'sieu Gribov, were well worth the trouble to which the establishment had been put during the past hour.

"So now we have *intermezzo,*" Gribov called out, again embracing the smiling Olga as they sat together at their flower-decked table. He held her hand with every appearance of devotion, and she seemed pleased.

"Hey, Mac," Saffron observed at the piano bar, "Gribov's got it made with the ballerina."

"So I see." But Holden didn't seem particularly interested in the opera singer's display of happiness.

"Play something romantic and Russian," Saffron suggested. "Help 'em along."

Holden slammed his hand on the keyboard. "The hell with it." He slid from the piano seat and stretched. "I'm taking a break."

291

The Learys and their guests, who had been on the way out when Gribov called for champagne all around, now delayed their departure. They were standing near the door while awaiting the champagne and what would almost certainly be an outburst of sentimental farewell toasts. At one side, Amy and her children were posing for Stephanie. It was, as she was reminding them, a souvenir—a last souvenir—of Paris. Looking on, Pat Leary and Baron von Norden had fallen into conversation.

As Holden approached, he couldn't help catching the sense of the exchange, and guessed that the two men were discussing Vivian with pithy realism.

". . . but I could not leave her by herself in Paris," Leary was saying. "She is too young, too immature."

"Young she is, but immature she is not." Von Norden, ever the confident man of affairs, was making a smiling assessment. "She knows exactly what she wants, and I daresay she will get it."

"To marry a millionaire?" Leary suggested with a smile.

"Of course."

"But, Baron, she seems interested in diplomats. Am I right?"

"Interested, yes. Devoted, no." Von Norden made a deprecating gesture. "We diplomats are not such a good investment."

"Dependable, however, my dear Baron."

"Well, if you will trust me, I shall see that she enters a good school here, perhaps the *École Politique*, and spends a pleasant and profitable year."

Leary was regretful but firm. "Another time, perhaps. She is already registered to study for her master's in the United States. But Baron, it is most considerate of you—" He broke off as he noticed Holden was standing nearby. "And I suppose, Arch, that you're staying on?"

"Oh, yes. At least until Charley Fourier gets back from Nashville."

"Then where?"

"Oh, I don't know." Holden tossed in carelessly, "Could be some nightclub dates, could be a combo." He smiled apologetically, as if he were about to say something that was completely ridiculous. "Once I even thought of Carnegie Hall."

"The piano, a passport to heaven," Von Norden said.

"Or hell," Holden amended. "In the music business, you never really know."

"Nor in diplomacy, either," the German agreed.

Now Stephanie was approaching with Vivian and Gareth. "A small moment, messieurs . . . a farewell picture."

Von Norden gathered Vivian in one arm. "A final treat!" Gareth came around on the other side of his father and Stephanie began giving them directions. Holden, seeing that he didn't fit in that company, drifted off and joined Amy, who was sitting at a table beside the door, waiting for her husband.

"Going back, what will you do?" he asked.

She was cheerful as always. "Between Pat and Gareth at Yale, I'll be busy enough. It's a good life."

"Better than ballet?"

She had a faraway look in her eyes. "If it were only possible to dance one's life away . . ." She gave herself a little shake. "But there comes a time when the legs don't respond as easily as they once did, and rapid movement interferes with the breathing. Still, we have our memories, we dancers." She turned to face him. "And you? What about your memories?"

"I'm too young to have very many." He tried to duck a proper reply. "What should I remember about Paris?"

She waved a hand around the establishment in lingering fashion. "Surely you'll not forget Henri's . . . and the United Nations Ball, Gribov and Olga and . . . maybe even the Learys." Here she smiled, broke off and lowered her voice as she resumed, "Then there's Fay Carroll and the Four Arts Ball and all the lovely times you two must have had together."

"Please don't, Amy," he interrupted.

"Why not?" .

"It's over." His voice was flat and he turned away from her in dejection.

But Amy wouldn't let him break away from her. She put out one hand in sympathy. "You give up too easily, Arch."

"Why do you say that?"

She ticked off his advantages. "Bainbridge's gone, so Fay's not being forced into marriage, and that's surely something worth thinking about, isn't it?"

He didn't answer.

She paid no attention to his glum mood, but continued, "Then, you don't have Waco Carroll to worry about. I'm sure you've heard about his indictment back home..."

He nodded, but without expression.

"...and that," she resumed, "is going to keep him from interfering with Fay for quite a while. And she called me tonight..."

At once, he was alert. "You talked to her?"

"Of course I talked to her," Amy replied, but didn't seem in the least disconcerted. "What did you think I'd do when she was nice enough to let me know where she was and what she was doing?"

He had been hopeful that Fay, by some lucky chance, had said something to Amy about him; but evidently it hadn't happened. For Amy calmly picked up her account of Fay's call at the point where he had interrupted her. "...as I was saying, when Fay called and told me about her stepfather's indictment and her mother's treatment at the Menninger Clinic, she said she'd decided to stay on in Paris anyway for a while."

"Good!" The exclamation seemed to have been wrenched from him.

Amy patted his cheek. "I'm glad you approve. I knew it would cheer you up."

"Did..." He hesitated, then rushed on, still hoping Fay might have included him in her conversation with Amy. "Did she say anything else?"

"Oh, yes." The little Englishwoman was matter-of-fact. "As you might expect, she's going on with her singing lessons the Conservatory, and she'll be moving back to her old apartment as soon as she can pull herself together."

Now he was confused. "That wasn't her apartment," he objected. "So I suppose she means to stay at the Ritz."

"No, I don't think so." Amy's eyes glinted with hidden humor and she seemed to be suppressing laughter. "I think she said something about an apartment on the Rue Bonaparte, just off the Place St. Sulpice..."

He broke in. "But that's *my* apartment..." Then, in sudden embarrassment, he stopped.

Amy was openly amused now. "Well?" she asked, as if the very question explained itself.

Holden desperately wanted to believe that Fay was returning to him. As if he had been in a trance, he thought again of how Fay had gazed back at him that night at the United Nations Ball, and how he had turned aside because he couldn't believe that she was trying to bring him to her side.

"I wanted to phone her at the Crandells', but I thought it was too late," he said, still feeling very uncertain and somewhat defensive about the entire matter.

Amy was encouraging. "In some things, Arch, it's never too late . . ."

Stephanie had come between them, and Amy ended the conversation abruptly. The leggy photographer had just finished taking pictures of Pat Leary, Vivian and Gareth and Baron von Norden and now she said impulsively to Amy, "You have a good son, madame."

"We like him," Amy said. Out of delicacy, Holden moved away from them because he judged, from what he had overheard, that the two women wanted to talk alone.

"Madame," the photographer went on, "your Gareth will make some fortunate girl a good husband. Of that I assure you."

"Why, Stephanie, how nice." Amy now was more than merely polite. In warm appreciation, she put one hand and patted the photographer's arm, then resumed, "If it hadn't been for you, Stephanie, I doubt if Gareth would have had a very good time in Paris. You have been most considerate of him . . . and, I may add, of his parents."

Stephanie fumbled at her camera. "You are so kind, madame." In a rush of emotion, she bent over the older woman and murmured, "This is a very fine, a very wonderful young man, madame. I want him to stay, I want him very much. But" —and she seemed very grave— "because you are his mother and love him too, I give him back to you."

Henri appeared just then, bearing a tray of brimming champagne glasses, followed by three waiters with still more champagne. *"Attention, mesdames, messieurs,"* Henri began. "We drink tonight so that you will not forget Paris."

The Learys came together, then Gribov and his Olga, the Baron and Vivian, Gareth and Stephanie, and Saffron and the few remaining reporters left the piano bar to join them. Holden, feeling very awkward and uncertain about everything, stood near the half-open door, his head in a whirl of contradictory impulses. He wanted to run out the door, grab a cab, bang on the Crandells' apartment wherever it was. And yet, he still feared that all would in some manner turn out badly, so he remained rooted where he stood.

Henri, having supervised the distribution of champagne glasses, faced his friends and raised his own glass. In the briefest of toasts, he proposed, "To good times!" The company echoed his words and drank, except for Holden who remained near the door, lost in thought.

As Henri and the waiters passed around refills, the big door swung farther open in a slow arc. Fay's head appeared around the door's outer edge, then she stepped inside. She was still wearing the filmy green gown from the United Nations Ball.

She smiled at Holden. "I'll have some champagne, too," she said.

Breaking into the chorus of welcome for the unexpected guest, Amy Leary called out to Henri, "One more glass, please. And hurry!"

Holden, rallying from the first delightful shock of surprise over Fay's appearance, took over Henri's champagne bottle, secured two glasses and poured one for Fay and himself. They hadn't spoken to each other. There was no need. They both understood that this was, at last, the coming together they had both wanted since their first meeting.

Holden felt a surge of pride and joy, standing beside her. Her head was brushing against his shoulder. One of her hands rested lightly on his arm.

Somehow, he found his voice. "I've waited so long for you."

"Why didn't you come to me at the Palais when I wanted you?" she asked. But there wasn't even an implied reproach in either her tone or her manner.

"I didn't know, I couldn't believe . . ." He fumbled for an explanation.

"It's all right, honey," she murmured. "We're together now, and that's all that matters."

They kissed without self-consciousness, not a bit concerned at the chattering, celebrating group about them. "Seems like a long time since we met on a ladder at the Four Arts Ball," he said.

She looked up at him, smiled and nodded. For both of them, it was enough to remember how they had met. The strains and trials and misunderstandings that followed had melted away.

Pat Leary, having overheard Holden's reminder of the ladder at the Four Arts Ball, promptly proposed, "Let's drink to the ladder." And they did.

"Y'know, that Four Arts Ball made history in other ways, too," the older Leary remarked. "It was the twenty-fifth anniversary of my meeting Amy in Paris."

"Oh, but Daddy," Vivian protested, "you aren't going to go through that business all over again of telling us how you met her when she didn't have any clothes on, are you?"

"She looked pretty good then." Conscious that he was on the verge of a domestic *faux pas,* Leary added hastily, "Still does, even if she *is* dressed."

"But you've never given me a twenty-fifth anniversary gift," Amy objected.

"What'll you have?" he asked.

"Something for all of us," she replied with a smile and a nod toward Holden. "Arch said it best in his pretty song for Fay: 'Wake Me Up in Paris on a Sunny, Springy Day.'"